# Sammy's Hill

# Sammy's Hill

A NOVEL

## Kristin Gore

**talk miramax books**

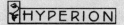

For information address:
Hyperion, 77 West 66th Street,
New York, New York 10023-6298.

ISBN: 1-4013-6029-7
978-1-4013-6029-0

FIRST MASS MARKET EDITION

Designed by Christine Weathersbee

10  9  8  7  6  5  4  3  2  1

*For my family*

# Sammy's Hill

*Early to Rise*

THE PARTY REALLY started to rock when Willie Nelson and Queen Nefertiti began pouring shots. I downed one and felt my stomach immediately replaced by a large liquor bonfire that spread through my chest, its flames licking up the inside of my throat. Willie leaned over and whispered that Winnie the Pooh had the hots for me. No way! I loved that guy! As I watched Winnie get down on the dance floor, throwing smoldering Pooh Bear glances in my direction, I all of a sudden felt myself floating. Flapping my arms, I rose higher and higher. Soon I was at thirty thousand feet, and a bit chilly. I plucked the edge of the cloud nearest me and draped it over my shoulders, fashioning a cumulus-nimbus pashmina. Feeling quite stylish, I surveyed the landscape below. I checked in with the mountain ranges, the vast oceans, the tiny cities, the—

". . . exceptionally long lines at the gas station. Congressman Francis, do you expect some sort of bailout package for Exxon?"

NPR's Morning Edition crackled into my consciousness to remind me that I was not a party-hopping sorceress but rather a Capitol Hill staffer who only had twenty minutes to get to work.

Huh. If I didn't do shots with Willie Nelson and Nefertiti, then why did I feel hungover? A brief glance into the kitchen brought it all back. Right, the bottle of wine from the ninety-nine-cent store. It had seemed like such a good deal at the time.

Okay, twenty minutes. Considering I was supposed to meditate for thirty, I'd have to postpone that until later. I'd also have to delay the fifteen-minute stomach crunch set, the do-it-yourself manicure, and the new dictionary word for the day. I promised myself I'd get to all that, but I knew I was lying. In reality, I would crawl home after working late, feeling too exhausted to do anything but maybe test out some ninety-nine-cent tequila.

But it was way too early in the day for such cynicism. As my dad always said, anything and everything is possible in the morning.

I'd never been a morning person.

I checked the clock. Seventeen minutes and counting. As I fed Shackleton and began scavenging for clean clothes, it occurred to me how difficult these simple tasks would be without my right arm. What would I do if I suddenly lost it in some sort of escalator or escaped hungry lion accident? People laughed, but I lived only a few short miles from the zoo. So I took a moment to do what I always did whenever these neuroses attacked. I reached for a sling from my pile of medical supplies, fashioned it around my right arm, and continued my routine with this new handicap, confident that I would be the one with the last laugh when I was so ludicrously prepared for life without my right arm.

"Amazing," they'd all say, "can you stand how quickly she's adapted? Why, she's just as capable as she was before! Maybe even more so!"

And thanks to my brilliant foresight, it would be true. I'd just nod and smile and continue my life as a well-prepared, one-armed genius.

I snapped myself out of this daydream to concentrate on the extraordinarily difficult task of opening a container of yogurt with just my left hand. And then, as I gathered up my work folders, cleverly using my foot to lift my briefcase up to the table, I caught sight of Shackleton's mossy gills. Oh no. The mossy gill death sentence.

I had managed to inadvertently murder eight Japanese fighting fish over the course of the previous eleven months. I had never meant to kill them. In fact, I did absolutely everything by the book, but they still died. Mr. Lee, the pet store owner, assured me I hadn't done anything wrong. I secretly suspected he was keeping something from me—some critical piece of caretaking instruction or water-purifying product that would keep my fish alive—because whatever it was, by withholding it, he ensured my lucrative repeat business. He played the helpful counselor, however, and, according to him, the Japanese fighting fish sometimes just lost their will to live after a simple change in surroundings and performed a sort of fish-style hari-kari. Three of them wasted away, two of them became grossly bloated, and Jacques, Moby, and Ballard had all developed mossy gill disease.

I looked sadly at my ninth and longest-living fish, the six-month trouper whom I thought had changed my luck. Shackleton, so named for miraculously surviving an unfortunate wintertime power outage that had turned his bowl into an icebound wasteland, stared bravely back. Amazingly, he had lived through being thawed out. I had assumed this proved he was some sort of fish messiah, a powerful spiritual leader of the marine realm. But I should have known that even the mightiest of fish couldn't survive for long in my murderous clutches.

I was beginning to obsess about the implications for my fitness as a future mother if I couldn't even keep a tiny little fish alive for more than a few months when I caught sight of the clock. Twelve minutes. I quickly grabbed some magazines for the commute and rushed out the door, barely remembering to shed my sling along the way.

The good thing about working for a senator I respected was that I felt like I had a chance to make a positive difference in the world every day. The bad thing was that I worked so hard I didn't have time to notice things like the fact that I was wearing two different shoes until I was already on the Red Line, rapidly approaching my stop.

And the pathetic thing was, I probably wouldn't have noticed at all if I hadn't caught the snickering glances of two perfectly groomed Senate pages and looked down to let myself in on the joke.

In my opinion, it's not totally unreasonable to mix up two pairs of shoes of the same style but slightly different colors, like a navy blue and black loafer. Embarrassing, sure, but understandable, particularly if one didn't have a right arm to turn on the closet light while one rooted around with one's healthy limb. But a tan sandal and a bright red sneaker? I was fairly certain the only people capable of that would have to be somewhat mentally handicapped. Apparently, they could also be me.

I decided to act like I knew exactly what I was doing, and shot a pitying glance at the two page-babes—a glance that communicated how sorry I felt for them that though they were immaculately coiffed, they clearly hadn't heard about the newest look to hit the runways. And I, I who read the *Economist* for fun on the way to work because, yes, I was that smart and genuinely interested in what it had to say, also happened to be on the cutting edge of fashion. How sad for them, my demeanor purred. How fabulous to be me.

With that work done, I exited the Metro at Union

Station and made my way down First Street to the Russell Senate Building, holding my head high and silently cursing the fact that I didn't have time to run into a shoestore and buy anything that made me look less like a clueless fool. But, I mused, even if I did have the time, there are some things money just can't buy.

Janet, the ultracompetent, middle-aged personal aide to the senator, glanced up as I entered the office. While talking on her phone headset, stapling a stack of briefs with one hand, and making a scheduling change with the other (difficult multitasking even with two perfectly intact arms), she also managed to smile at me.

"RG'll be here in five. He needs the committee brief right away," she said, in her pleasant but no-bullshit tone.

"It's all ready, no problem." I smiled back, trying to project confidence and professionalism before my first cup of coffee, which was no small feat.

RG was office shorthand for Robert Gary, junior senator from my home state of Ohio. The committee brief was for the Senate's Health Care Committee hearing on prescription drug plans for the elderly, scheduled to begin that morning. And I was responsible for the brief, along with shepherding the constituent slated to testify, because I was a domestic policy adviser to Senator Gary.

The fact that I had managed to become a health care analyst for a United States senator at the age of twenty-six still surprised me, and I lived in fear that someone would realize how ridiculous it was to have given me this sort of authority and fire me on the spot.

Born and raised in Ohio, I owed my passion for government to my mother, a political science professor for whom fostering interest in public service came naturally. From the beginning, I'd been an eager and enthusiastic student. And perhaps most significantly, my mom's only full-time one.

Under her tutelage, I'd learned early that participation was paramount and that change could be just an effort away. Together, we'd drawn up campaign posters for local candidates, passed out voter registration forms, and canvassed neighborhoods for initiatives in which we'd believed. In the mornings before school, she'd helped me read the newspaper and answered my questions. In the evenings, she'd edited my letters to the president for spelling mistakes. It had never occurred to me that all this might make me an enormous dork. I'd loved it.

I'd begun taking up my own causes in grade school. I'd tried to protect the rainforests, adopt litter-free highways, stop animal testing, ship school supplies to impoverished children in Haiti, and generally save the world one bake sale at a time.

In high school, I'd become obsessed with issues of free speech, railing against censorship and challenging the school newspaper to rise above it. I'd written passionate papers about how freedom and rebellion represented the beating heart of democracy. I hadn't been above invoking these themes to denounce the tyranny of dress codes and curfews.

I'd run for class office here and there, but mainly devoted myself to general activism. It hadn't been until college, at the University of Cincinnati, that I'd developed a more specialized interest in health care policy. This interest had grown out of a particularly intriguing freshman seminar on communicable diseases—a seminar which had provoked both a passion for health care reform as well as a terror of the essential vulnerability and filthiness of the human body. From that seminar forward, a sore throat was never just a sore throat—it was much more likely the beginning stages of Ebola, rickets, or wasting disease. Since then, I had dedicated myself to doing the little I could to prepare for the disasters that were sure to befall my relatively defenseless body.

I had also devoted myself to studying the complexity and flaws of the country's health care system. Its inadequacies and inequalities had offended and embarrassed me. I hadn't been able to understand how the government could continue to allow nearly forty-four million Americans, many of them children, to go uninsured. I'd been horrified to discover the price gouging that went on, and the toll that it took on lower- and middle-class families. And as my mother's daughter, I had resolved to do what I could to bring about change.

While slaving away on my thesis, I had landed interviews with Ohio's nineteen members of the House of Representatives and both senators. Senator Robert Gary had impressed me as head and shoulders above the rest with his thorough grasp of health care issues and his long-term vision. As he'd answered my questions and talked about his plans for reform, I'd felt a mixture of awe and inspiration.

I'd sent Gary a copy of my thesis and immediately volunteered for his reelection campaign upon graduation. I'd been flattered and terrified when he'd remembered me, complimented my thesis, and asked me to work with his domestic policy team specifically on health care issues. I'd thrown myself into it, written a couple of noteworthy briefs, and after Gary had won in a landslide, been asked to join his D.C. staff. Which was how I'd suddenly found myself in a position of real influence. Scary, but true.

I barely had time to sync my BlackBerry and scan e-mails before Janet was buzzing my line.

"RG's here. He added a meet-and-greet with the teachers' union, so you only have ten minutes *right now* to get him up to speed for the hearing. Go."

As I rushed to his office, I wondered if I would be able to brief him in only ten minutes if I didn't have a tongue. I could probably come close if I was equipped with markers and flip charts and more advanced charade talents than I currently possessed, but it would be tough. I'd been told I had very expressive eyes though, so as long as I could use those . . . oooh, no tongue and blind, now that would probably stump me. How exactly would I go about—

"Can I help you with something?"

Senator Gary's sarcastic impatience put an end to my planning by alerting me that I must have been standing in his office looking like an entranced idiot for a good ten seconds. After a quick calculation I decided to pass on explaining that I had been musing a blind, tongueless existence and just get straight to the briefing.

"I'm here to prep you for the hearing, sir. Is now an okay time?"

He just looked at me for a moment and then nodded. He was tired, I could tell. He was a good-looking man and I thought the gray flecks in his dark hair made him look distinguished, but the deepening creases in his forehead and the bags under his eyes just made him look ragged. He was a workaholic with one-year-old twins at home, so that accounted for some of it, but I got the sense he was worrying about something else in the deep, portentous way he often had about him.

His blue suit, white shirt, red tie uniform was crisp and pressed as usual, but I noticed he had a yellowish stain on the collar of his shirt. I promised myself I'd gently bring that up after we got through the briefing. He'd be grateful without being embarrassed. I knew just the tone I'd use.

"Okay, sir, your committee today will be hearing testimony from Alfred Jackman, a constituent from your old congressional district. He's eighty-three and suffers from a kidney condition that leaves him in intense pain much of the time. The prescription drugs he needs are unaffordable on his budget of Social Security and pension payments, so he makes regular trips to Canada to obtain the cheaper generic versions that should be available to him here."

"And Medicare in its current incarnation doesn't cover what he needs, correct?"

"It doesn't come close, sir."

"And the price controls in Canada allow him to save what, forty to sixty percent?"

"He shaves fifty-five percent off his drug costs on average, sir."

RG was nodding and I felt lucky all over again that I worked for someone who actually understood the policy issues he was being briefed on. One of the major shocks of my twenty-six years was the discovery that a distressing number of the people holding the reins of our democracy were glad-handing lightweights. Not RG, though. He actually cared.

"That's it? That's all you've got? This will be a disaster if that's all you've got for me."

And the fact that he actually cared was the only thing that made putting up with his bullshit worthwhile.

"Well, no, sir—I have a list of pertinent questions for you to ask and I've also drafted the remarks you should lead off with to frame Mr. Jackman's testimony in the larger issue of the travesty our nation's health care system has become."

"I'd like to avoid the word 'travesty,' Samantha. We can't just point out the problems. People don't like that. Do the remarks include a blueprint for the future?"

I loved that phrase. It always made me feel like an architect, which I had really wanted to be in the third grade. I had even designed several projects to practice, my most elaborate being a shoebox village painstakingly conceived for the squirrels that lived in my yard. With grand expectations, I had perched it in the branches of the oak tree next to my bedroom window, but it had been brutally shunned. I had always believed it was the squirrels' loss—Reebokville had really been a rodent wonderland, resplendent with zipwires and even a fire pole from the spa down to the Acorn Lounge.

"Of course, sir. Your standard speech outlining steps towards a single-payer universal system."

"Good. This needs to go well today. C-SPAN's taking it live."

"You'll be great, sir."

"I'm not the one I'm worried about. This Jackman fellow has been fully vetted?"

I had spent approximately a hundred and thirty-six hours on the phone with Alfred Jackman, his various doctors, Canadian pharmacies, you name it. I knew Jackman's health history better than my own. For instance, I knew he had a double-jointed thumb that throbbed when it was going to rain, but I didn't know whether or not I was still in possession of my adenoids. Were they or were they not removed when I was six? My mom claimed the surgery had just been to extract my tonsils, but then why would I have named the doll I got that year Adenoida? It can't have been a coincidence, as pretty as that name was.

"In my opinion, Mr. Jackman will give tremendous testimony, sir."

"Tremendous? Really? Will it rock everyone's world?"

RG was capable of swinging from impatient irritation to playful ribbing in a heartbeat. This was a good sign, though, because he wouldn't have been teasing me if he weren't happy with the briefing.

"At some point we also need to discuss the reception this evening, because there'll be a couple . . ."

I trailed off as I watched RG return to his e-mails and proceed to completely ignore me. After a few seconds, he looked up.

"You're still here?"

Janet stuck her head in the doorway.

"The teachers have arrived, Senator," she said with a questioning glance in my direction.

"Send them in, but interrupt me in ten minutes with an important call."

"Of course."

It was time for me to go. If I was going to point out the collar stain, it was then or never. There wasn't time to conjure up the perfect tone I'd planned. I contemplated aborting the mission. Maybe the stain on his collar made him look more "of the people"? Maybe I was a giant coward.

"Um, sir?"

RG looked up, annoyed.

"It's just, um, there's something on your shirt, sir. Something yellow. Not white. Like the rest of your shirt."

I motioned helpfully towards his collar. He looked down and spotted it.

"Baby formula. Got it."

There, that wasn't so bad. He was even smiling at me. Strange that it seemed to be his mocking smile, but I'd learned to take what I could get. I started out the door.

"Thanks for the fashion tips, Samantha. I can see I've got a lot to learn from you."

He was looking pointedly at my mismatched shoes. Fantastic.

I mumbled something about a new style, but he was already greeting the teachers who were shoving past me, eager for their ten minutes.

I had five voicemails from the Capitol Hill Police when I returned. A representative sample: "Ms. Joyce, we have an Alfred Jackman down here. He's setting off the metal detector but refusing to take off his jacket or shoes until he talks with you. Please call us back when you get this."

Could it be 9:00 AM already? The clock on my computer informed me it could in fact be 9:15. The phone rang accusingly.

"On my way!" I shouted at it as I raced out the door.

Ralph was on duty when I arrived embarrassingly out of breath from running down the three flights of stairs to the security checkpoint on the ground floor. Ralph always reminded me of what I imagined a basset hound with an eye lift would look like. Lazy and sad but with a perpetual look of unnatural surprise. We had found ourselves on the same Metro train one evening months ago, and he had confided in me that his new job didn't hold a candle to the excitement of his previous stint driving the Oscar Mayer Weinermobile up and down the Mall. But he had felt compelled to bow to his girlfriend's demands and exchange his hot dogging ways for the more staid and respectable work of a Capitol Hill guard.

"Hey, Sammy," he drawled, "your boyfriend's being detained."

He jerked his thumb towards the guard office where, through the wire-latticed Plexiglas, I could see Alfred Jackman staring at the ceiling.

"Did he do something wrong?"

Alfred Jackman was scheduled to testify before the

committee in thirteen minutes. Why were they hassling a harmlessly shriveled eighty-three-year-old man with a kidney problem? I felt my demeanor lurch perilously towards outrage but battled myself back to politeness.

"I can't imagine he poses any serious threat to national security."

I smiled but Ralph looked unconvinced.

"He's been real disrespectful. He a U.S. citizen?"

Oh Lord. Don't go all Ashcroft on me, Ralphie. Not today of all days.

"Of course. Look, this is really all my fault. I was supposed to meet him down here when he arrived. He's just very old, you know?"

Take pity on us, I commanded in my head. For the millionth time I wished I was a Jedi knight and could employ the extremely persuasive mind control skills of the Force. And for the millionth time, crossed fingers would have to substitute.

"He claimed he's here for the committee meeting?" Ralph asked, his skepticism obvious.

I nodded officially.

"Very sad health history. He went through a lot to be here today."

If you looked up "professional, but grave" in the tone dictionary, you'd find my name next to "master of."

Ralph laughed.

"I bet he did."

Fine, be cynical, you tone-deaf Botoxed basset hound. But don't screw with my committee hearing.

"Come on, Ralph, I really need to get him in there. Can't you let him go? He couldn't have been that uncooperative."

Ralph was shaking his head. Was he kidding me? Would the ACLU need to be contacted? Did they have an AARP branch? I glanced at my watch and felt a rising tsunami of panic. I clutched Ralph's arm and made intense eye contact.

"Ralph, the fate of our nation's health care system is in your hands. If you care about poor, uninsured children, if you care about suffering senior citizens, if you care about justice . . . well, then, I think you know what to do."

I could practically hear the faint chords of "The Battle Hymn of the Republic" echoing in the background as I stared pleadingly into Ralph's eyes, silently willing him to do the right thing.

And he answered duty's call with an explosion of hysterical laughter.

"You're too much," he gasped between guffaws, "I love you ones fresh off the bus."

I smiled tightly.

"May I escort Mr. Jackman to the committee room, now?"

Ralph could hardly breathe.

"Poor, uninsured children . . ." He dissolved into unmanly giggles. "Yeah, go ahead and take him," Ralph waved me away. "Good luck with that."

I turned my back on the hilarity and hurried over to

Alfred Jackman. I rushed into the booth, hoping Ralph hadn't alienated our star witness too much.

"I'm so sorry for the misunderstanding, Mr. Jackman. If you'll just come with me—"

I stopped short as I detected a familiar smell in the small office. Good Lord, had the guards been smoking pot in here? Did that explain Ralph's paranoia and uncontrollable giggling? Oh no, was I supposed to report that? I wasn't cut out to be a narc. I quickly decided to pretend I had a cold. Or that I had lost my sense of smell in a chemistry experiment gone tragically awry. It could've happened. It still could. Best practice for that possibility by not smelling anything, certainly not the unmistakable scent of marijuana saturating one of the guard shacks of the Capitol Hill Police.

"So, um, I hope you weren't too inconvenienced . . ." I soldiered on.

Alfred Jackman looked up at me with bloodshot eyes arranged in a loopy stare.

"Looka here, it's the pretty lady," he grinned goofily at me. "Do you ever feel like you could just sit and stare at wallpaper for days and days? It's so beautiful."

Even as I noted the bottle of Visine sticking out of Alfred Jackman's pocket, I clung desperately to denial. But he wouldn't stop talking.

"Are there gonna be any nachos at the hearing? I took a little something to calm the nerves, but now I'm afraid I've got a bad case of the munchies."

Denial cut me loose. The eighty-three-year-old kidney patient I had handpicked to persuade the Senate Health Care Committee to embrace Senator Gary's prescription drug proposal—this tiny, grizzled grandfather of twelve sitting before me—was baked out of his head.

## July's Highs

JUST STAY CALM, I told myself. Address the problem in a levelheaded way.

"I wasn't aware that you smoked," I managed to croak.

"Oh, not cigarettes, I never touch cigarettes. Those things'll kill ya."

Uh-huh.

"I do love the ganja, though!"

There it was.

"Do you like the ganja?" I heard Alfred Jackman ask me as I tried to slow my hyperventilating.

Okay, take control. I could handle this. Or I could run. I caught sight of Ralph still laughing by the metal detector. He gave me a thumbs-up.

"No, Mr. Jackman, I don't like the ganja," I replied in a voice so high-strung it vibrated. Was I being totally honest here?

"Too bad. I've got top-grade quality stuff from Canada. You should try it."

I needed to sit down. For a couple months.

"I thought you went to Canada for your Lipitor and Nexium and the other prescription drugs you need," I flung at him accusingly. "That's what you told me. That's what I signed up for."

He looked a little hurt, in a really stoned way.

"I do," he replied. "But the pot's real cheap, too. And it helps with the pain."

I grasped at any remaining reserves of sympathy deep within me. This old man was in pain most of the time. That was the bottom line. And our country's lack of adequate Medicare drug benefits was making his few remaining years a stressed-out nightmare. If he got a little TLC in a doobie packed with THC, maybe that wasn't such a terrible thing. I tried to look at this crisis with fresh, less-vengeful eyes.

"Cracker Jacks'll be fine if you don't have nachos," he offered.

My BlackBerry was buzzing a hole through my hip and I knew before I even checked my watch that it was past 9:30. The hearing had started. I had to do something. As a press pool approached the checkpoint, I took Cheech Sr. by the elbow and led him firmly toward the committee holding room. When we passed by the double doors of the Russell Caucus Room, I saw the chairman in the midst of his opening remarks to the crowded, camera-filled room. The other senators were fanned out on either side of him, their dark suits and somber expressions forming a homogenous, high-powered arc. Before we could make it past, RG looked straight at me. I registered the concerned expression in his eyes with a bottomless sinking feeling. It took all my strength to muster up a confident smile but he didn't look comforted. Which wasn't that surprising, since according to a vast amount of photographic evidence, my attempts at fake smiles made me look like a drunken stroke victim. Which would have made me only a slightly better candidate for testimony than Alfred Jackman.

We were at the door to the adjacent holding room. I turned to my Stone Age stoner and was overpowered anew by the pungent marijuana smell that seemed to be cascading out of his pores. For the first time, I realized there was no saving the situation. He could not go in there and testify, no matter how compelling his story was. And what should have been a major victory for RG was about to be rendered an utter disaster. Crap, crap, crap.

Instead of leading him into the holding room, I steered Alfred Jackman further down the hall to a private restroom. If he hadn't been so out of it, he might have been confused as to where I was taking him. As it was, he seemed preoccupied with the effects that the cocktail of pot and prescription drugs was unleashing on his system. He shuffled alongside me happily, pointing out the purple dots he claimed were filling up the hall like warm, shiny bubbles.

"And there's one right on your nose, like a big violet mole," he said as he lightly touched my face with his eighty-three-year-old, thoroughly drugged finger.

"Thanks, I'll remember to get that checked out at the dermatologist," I replied as I wrestled with the restroom's large window. It finally gave and opened up enough to allow room for an overmedicated old man and a soon-to-be-fired health care adviser to climb through.

Please let there be a cab, please let there be a cab, I prayed to the Taxi God as I assisted Alfred Jackman with his landing on the sidewalk outside. In moments of stress, I often turned to a stable of very specific gods in the hopes that they might hear my direct and heart-felt appeals. How often did a deity like the Taxi God get prayed to? I counted on him rewarding my attention with a little love.

Like manna from heaven, a cab came to a stop directly in front of us as we completed our window escape. I helped Alfred Jackman into the backseat and watched the cabdriver wrinkle his nose in the rearview mirror.

"He's very old and not feeling well," I officiously explained. "Could you please take him back to his room at the Hyatt Regency at New Jersey and Constitution Aves.?"

The driver responded with an extremely bored shrug. Alfred Jackman turned to me.

"Are we taking a ride to the hearing?" he asked, while batting away some sort of imaginary atmospheric pattern he'd discovered in the cab's interior.

"The hearing's postponed till tomorrow. I'll stop by your hotel this afternoon to go over the new schedule, okay?" I smiled brightly at him.

He patted my hand.

"Sure, sure," he said, "however I can be helpful, sweetheart."

No, really, you've already done too much.

I handed the cabdriver my last ten-dollar bill until I cashed this week's paycheck (which would then provide me with only slightly more than ten dollars, good old government salary) and sent the dynamic duo on their way.

Ralph was screening a tour group and only had time to give me an odd look as I burst through the front door moments later. Even if he'd been unoccupied, I doubted he would have asked me many questions. Despite our Metro ride bonding, I was essentially just one of a legion of young staffers he watched pass through these halls year after year. As long as I didn't set off any alarms, he really couldn't care less why I was reentering the building when I was allegedly currently inside it.

I rushed into the hearing room just as the chairman was saying, "Perhaps we won't be hearing testimony from Mr. Alfred Jackman after all. For the last time, is Mr. Jackman or any of his representatives pres-ent?"

I felt RG's eyes latch onto me like a hawk's, but I couldn't look at him. Taking a big gulp of sweaty committee room air, I approached the microphone on the table facing the panel of senators. Even completely sober, it was terrifyingly surreal to sense a roomful of policy makers and journalists focus all their important attention on me.

"Mr. Jackman's been taken ill," I squeaked in a high-pitched traumatized voice. Huh, not the crisp, drippingly intelligent tone I had always felt sure I'd be able to deliver in such a moment. And on top of it, I was shaking. Fabulous.

"We're sorry to hear that," boomed the chairman.

I dug my nails into my leg to try to stop the quivering before it provoked concern for my well-being.

"Yes," I heard myself continuing, "he was present and prepared to testify, but suddenly experienced unfortunate side effects from the medicine he had taken for his condition."

Okay, so far no lying. I begged the God of Persuasive Explanations to smile upon me.

"As the committee may be aware, Mr. Jackman has to travel to Canada to obtain the drugs he desperately needs to manage his intense pain. He's eighty-three years old and this sort of stress leads easily to exhaustion. Despite that, he was looking forward to sharing his experiences with the committee today in the hopes that he could play a small role in improving the lives of the millions of his fellow senior citizens who are imploring their representatives here in D.C. to provide them with a comprehensive prescription drug benefit plan."

Out of the corner of my eye, I saw some reporters

scribbling rapidly in their pads. Could I really pull this off?

"However, despite his best intentions, Mr. Jackman was in no shape to testify this morning."

That's for sure.

"Given the circumstances, he hoped he might be able to postpone his testimony until tomorrow."

I stopped talking at last and held my breath. Perhaps it would have been a better idea to keep breathing regularly, but I was too nervous. And I had been the reigning champion of the lunch table hold-your-breath contests in fifth grade, so I felt fairly confident I could wait out the response without losing consciousness. The chairman adjusted his reading glasses and cleared his throat. Was I turning blue yet? I was a bit out of practice.

"This committee hopes Mr. Jackman feels better and looks forward to his testimony tomorrow morning," the chairman intoned.

Sweet, sweet breath. *Ech*—stagnant, stagnant air. I'd forgotten about that. But the important and unbelievable thing was that disaster had been narrowly averted. I nodded to the panel and backed away from the microphone, doing a victory dance in my head.

I should probably have held off from the mental celebration, because my lack of total concentration on backwards walking led to me tripping over a camera cable and tumbling sideways onto a row of seated journalists. An extremely plump, middle-aged AP reporter broke most of my fall, and my flailing arm managed to clock a young man from the *Washington Post* sitting next to him in the face.

I heard RG quickly ask the chairman a procedural question and silently thanked him for directing attention away from the crash site.

"Oh God, I'm so sorry," I whispered to my victims as I regained control of my splayed limbs and renegotiated my relationship with gravity.

"No problem, didn't feel a thing," the rotund reporter winked at me.

I believed him. But his neighbor didn't seem so unscathed. He had a nasty scratch on the side of his otherwise handsome face and his glasses were somewhere on the floor beneath his chair. It was clear from his distressed expression and blind-man-feeling-his-way arm movements that he couldn't see a thing without them. I hurried to help him, stepping hard on his foot in the process. And not with the soft, bright red sneaker, but with the unforgiving, sharp-heeled sandal. He yelped in pain and swatted at me, trying to defend himself from this crazed enemy combatant who had come out of nowhere intent on mauling him. I knew that's how I had come off, but I was really trying to redeem myself. I located his black-rimmed glasses and placed them placatingly in his hand.

"I am so, so sorry," I tried again.

He put on his glasses and turned towards me, revealing himself to look remarkably like Clark Kent. I felt my heart race a bit as our eyes met, and I struggled to remind myself that despite the physical similarity, I wasn't really in the presence of a disguised superhero. Was I? The fact that he was a reporter prevented me from finding him *too* attractive. Reporters weren't my type.

"It's okay, don't worry about it," he said unconvincingly.

"Oh no, I've cut you," I replied as I noticed the scratch on his face was beginning to bleed.

I'd actually drawn blood. How horrifying. I glared down at my fingernails accusingly. That was no way to treat Clark Kent.

"I'm fine, I'm fine," he muttered dismissively, flipping through his notebook and finding another pen in his jacket pocket.

He turned his attention back to the committee hearing, leaving me to stare helplessly at his scratched and distracted profile while Senator Rollings's thick southern accent launched into a diatribe about "metty-care" somewhere behind me. As Clark Kent scribbled down some notes, I felt an overwhelming urge to touch the scrape on his face. I had a tissue in my pocket. Could I just blot away the blood? Probably not without asking first.

"Can I at least get you a Band-Aid or something?" I whispered into his ear.

"I really need to hear this," he replied in a distinctly annoyed tone.

Oh God, he hated me.

"Oh, right. Well, sorry again," I stammered at his turned-away shoulder. "See you around."

I felt myself blush a deep scarlet as I fled the room. At least that meant I was matching half my footwear.

I still hadn't recovered at 5:30 that afternoon when it was time to accompany RG to the American Foundation for AIDS Research reception at the Washington Hilton. An afternoon visit to Alfred Jackman's room had discovered him passed out, surrounded by minibar wrappers. I'd managed to convince him to hand over the remainder of his stash until he finished with his testimony by swearing I would be personally responsible for its safekeeping. The brief victory rush had been immediately replaced by paralyzing anxiety when I realized I had voluntarily taken possession of a large Ziploc bag full of grade-A Canadian weed.

I was acutely aware of its presence in the innermost pocket of the bag my trusting grandmother had given me for Christmas as I hurried with RG towards the waiting tinted-window sedan. I swore I heard the rustling of leaves and plastic as I walked—and I imagined everyone nearby could also hear it, as well as instantly discern what it was. I felt like the agitated protagonist in an update of Poe's "The Tell-Tale Heart." In this version, revised for the slacker crowd, my contraband bag of weed would rustle loud enough to drive me mad and reveal my crime. I was feeling queasy as I settled into the car beside RG.

"How's Mr. Jackman feeling?" he asked me with a

raised eyebrow as the car pulled out of the Russell Building parking lot and into traffic. RG knew something was up but he didn't want to know the details. Which, given what they were, was just fine with me.

"He'll be fine tomorrow, sir. There's nothing to worry about. I'm sorry about the delay."

"Good," was the terse reply. No need for further discussion, RG had far more on his plate than the few items that concerned my area of expertise. He demanded intelligence and efficiency, and normally I was up to the task, if just barely. So far today I had come up a little short.

I took out the AMFAR folder.

"I've got the guest list with the people that need some extra attention highlighted. For example, Nick Simon's been feeling neglected. He mentioned something about not putting our money where our mouth was, and I assured him . . ."

RG interrupted me. "Samantha."

I looked up from my piles of briefs.

"Yes, sir?"

"Are you okay?" he asked, a little gruffly.

Oh God, he was pointing to my bag. He knew. Had he recognized the rustling? Had Alfred Jackman squawked? That was it. I was fired.

"Sir, I know this looks bad, but I'd like you to know that I've only smoked pot five times in my life, and the last time was over eight years ago and I never even liked it because I couldn't remember really basic things the next day, like my phone number. And I've never ever done anything else, except for drinking, but only in a fairly responsible way."

RG looked at me with an utterly bewildered expression.

"You've got a nasty bruise."

I looked to where he was pointing at a yellowish mottled mark on my arm, just below the shoulder strap of my bag. I knew where it had come from—Clark Kent's sharp belt buckle had left its mark.

"Oh, that. Yeah, I'm fine. Non-drug-related injury," I offered weakly.

RG stared hard at me for a few seconds, then shook his head and began leafing through the AMFAR briefing memo. I sat gazing out the window, feeling shell-shocked from my all-star performance. I tried to think about how RG spent most of his time contemplating weighty national policy issues, so there was a small chance that my random drug history confession got instantly forgotten in the company of far more important thoughts.

Ugh, I was a moron.

Alarm bells interrupted my descent into a self-hatred spiral, as my BlackBerry's calendar reminder function noisily alerted me that it was the one hundred twenty-first anniversary of the Brooklyn Bridge. I silenced the alarm and mentally registered the holiday as RG kept reading.

In high school I'd become intrigued by *The Big Book*

*of Holidays* that the guidance counselor had kept behind her desk. What had started as an art-house resolution to celebrate the less-popular holidays like Arbor Day and Janitor Appreciation Day had gradually grown into an ongoing fascination with obscure anniversaries. Once I'd embraced the theme, I'd found my calendar quickly filled, and the joyous upshot was that every day became a holiday for something. I celebrated them in different small ways, sometimes just by mentally acknowledging them, sometimes by doing more. For example, to celebrate the fourteenth anniversary of the publication of Deepak Chopra's first book, and the subsequent birth of his self-help empire, I'd treated myself to the new Indian restaurant on Dupont Circle. For the Brooklyn Bridge? Maybe I'd sleep in my "I ♥ NY" onesie.

Through the window I watched the various embassies on Massa-chusetts Avenue blur past before we turned onto Connecticut Avenue and slowed to a stop next to a crowd of cameras, lobbyists, and AIDS activists.

RG put the folder down and closed his eyes. When he reopened them, they were sharp and clear.

"Time to work," he said with a genuine energy that impressed me. The least I could do was rally something similar.

"Absolutely, sir. This is your crowd."

He moved his hand to the door handle and stretched his neck from side to side.

"Good job on the talking points," he added.

I nodded. I knew they were good. I had spent two hours on them.

"And Samantha . . ." he continued.

"Yes, sir?"

He looked directly at me, the corner of his mouth hinting upwards.

"You should really get out more."

And he was gone. A hundred hands to shake, as many promises to make. I took a second to try to compose myself, feeling more and more certain that it was an unattainable goal. Then I collected my BlackBerry, my briefings, and my bag of pot and followed Senator Gary into the crowd.

# Summer Surprise

How Liza convinced me to join her for happy hour at the Irish Times the next day was still a mystery to me. She was my best friend, and she had managed a mildly persuasive argument about celebrating Alfred Jackman's twenty-four hours of sobriety, but 6:30 was way too early to be leaving the office, even on a Friday night. It didn't matter that RG had already left to fly back to Ohio for the weekend or that Janet had gone home early for her son's birthday dinner, I still had to answer to myself and my mountains of unfinished work. And neither of us was easily pushed over.

I compromised by deciding I'd have a couple beers for Liza and Alfred and then head back to my desk for a slightly buzzed wrap-up. Everybody would win.

"So the hearing went great!" Liza squealed supportively as she hugged me beside the bar stools.

"Yeah, amazingly, Mr. Jackman pulled it off." I still couldn't quite believe it.

"You mean *you* pulled it off," she loyally insisted. Liza was the only consistent cheerleader in my life, and didn't seem to mind this thankless and often seemingly pointless role. She also had an odd fascination with documentaries about reformed S&M enthusiasts and was an avid Red Sox fan, so it had occurred to me more than once that maybe she was just a glutton for punishment. She was tall and angular, studiously stylish, and naturally gorgeous. I had met her at a fund-raiser in Cincinnati— RG had needed food to go as he dashed out the door postschmoozing and Liza had been the caterer. After she moved to D.C. months later to handle events for the Mayflower Hotel, we'd become close friends.

Liza was the sort of girl one was alternately jealous of and shocked by. She was genuinely sweet and captivatingly attractive, but insisted on continuously stumbling into poor choices, mainly of the romantic persuasion. Or in many cases, the purely physical one. She went for preppy, jocky, unfaithful men. There were plenty of these to go around in D.C., and go around they did. Her latest had been recovering from a knee injury sustained during a weekend rugby game on the Mall. He had insisted on buckling on a knee brace every time before sex and then had left her for his physical therapist—a petite redhead who'd apparently been handier with the straps. Liza had felt at an occupational disadvantage and was still bruised by the breakup. I, on the other hand, was overjoyed to be rid of him and his penchant for trying to provoke me into debates over the merits of Hooters restaurants and all-male country clubs.

"To Sammy Joyce and Alfred Jackman, today's stars of the Senate." Liza clinked her Bud bottle against mine and took a celebratory swig.

I'd drink to that. Alfred Jackman *had* done a pretty great job. His marijuana-withdrawal–induced grumpiness had been interpreted by everyone else as frustration with the inadequacy of the health care system, and the list of legal drugs he needed for his condition, along with their exorbitant price tags, had made a definite impression on the committee. Senator Gary had made his point and Alfred Jackman was safely out of my jurisdiction, so the beer went down easy. That is, until Liza elbowed me in the side, effecting a sort of mini-Heimlich.

"What?" I sputtered.

She nodded almost imperceptibly towards my right. I swiveled completely perceptibly to check out what she was signaling about, prompting another elbow attack.

"Ouch! Cut that out."

I did see what all the fuss was about, though. The guy ordering a drink one stool over was undeniably hot, and not just D.C. hot, but actual real world hot. He smiled inquisitively when he caught my eye. I immediately swiveled a retreat.

Liza was glaring at me.

"Are you ever going to learn how to check someone out?"

"No," I answered honestly.

Liza sighed. She was the subtle, cool one. I brought something else to the table. A sort of unsubtle anticool, if you will.

"Sorry," I offered. "But he's not your type anyway, is he? I thought goatees had been blacklisted."

Liza had dated three goateed men in a row and her sensitive skin had only recently recovered. She had lately been quite vocal about her new antigoatee platform—one that I'd readily endorsed, as I had always considered facial hair unsanitary. But I had the unsettling feeling that the way our new neighbor pulled his off might induce me to entertain some dirty thoughts.

"Not him," Liza whispered. "*Him.*"

This time her phantom nod more accurately indicated a new bartender who must have just begun his shift. Okay, that made much more sense. He was hot as well, but in a more muscular, less trustworthy way. Right up Liza's alley.

I was just beginning to wonder if our happy hour had devolved into only-a-man-can-make-me-happy hour when Liza refocused her attention on me.

"We'll meet them later. Tell me about the rest of your day," she smiled at me.

And that was another great thing about Liza. She was just the right amount of girly—guy aware but not guy crazy. I had lesser friends who would pretend to be interested in a night of catching up and then morph into giggly backstabbers at the first whiff of Polo Aftershave—women who were lightning fast with the put-down joke or dismissive wave, whatever it took to seem more pretty or witty or larger chested to the nightly swarm of male barflies. But not Liza. She was loyal and genuine, not in an aggressively girl-powerish way, but in a sane and appreciated one.

We spent the next hour talking and laughing, fueled by several more beers and hampered only by my niggling sense of guilt that I wasn't yet back at the office. No problem, I told myself. Wrapping up the workweek was even more fun when I myself was wrapped up in a warm beer glow. After all, a happy employee was a more productive employee. And thankfully, a drunk employee couldn't get fired if her bosses had already gone home for the weekend.

I had just convinced Liza that I really did need to head back but that I really would meet her later when I spotted a man in a wheelchair trying to make his way through the door. A table leg jammed next to the doorway was thwarting his attempts, as his front wheel kept bumping into it no matter what angle he tried. No one seemed to notice his struggle; certainly no one was offering any assistance. Something in his grumpy determination reminded me of a sober Alfred Jackman, and before I knew it I was on my feet and hurrying towards him, while Liza tried to get the hot bartender's attention under the guise of ordering another beer.

I approached the patrons of the offending table—a young buttoned-up couple on what seemed like their first date—and fixed them with a polite smile.

"I just need to shift you guys over for a second, no need to move," I exhaled as I attained a firm grip on their table.

Before they could respond I gave a quick tug, dragging the table clear of the doorway and out of the wheelchair's path, and, in the process, upending the full pitcher of beer they'd just ordered onto the white-silk-blouse-clad chest of the startled woman.

I stood helpless for a moment, trying to calculate these latest entries into my karmic account balance. Did helping a handicapped man make up for assaulting an innocent woman with cheap beer?

"What the hell is wrong with you?" the man in the wheelchair demanded.

Interesting. I had been expecting gratitude from him, anger from the couple. He was completely throwing me off my game.

"I was just trying to help," I explained feebly. "So you could get through the door."

"I can take care of myself. I don't need any help from a klutz," he barked loudly enough for the entire bar to hear.

Right. Okay, so maybe the beer-drenched couple

would also have surprising reactions, but in a good way. I turned my attention hopefully and apologetically towards them. The woman was crying softly as she tried to cover the wet T-shirt effect of the spilt beer with a flimsy cocktail napkin that was nowhere near up to the task. Her companion looked bewildered and concerned.

Hmm. So I'd offended a crippled man and reduced a nicely dressed woman to tears. Karma-wise, I was pretty sure I was down.

My own eyes began to burn ominously as I felt the gazes of the surrounding clientele disapprovingly fixed upon me. The three beers I'd drunk had unfortunately softened up my normally slightly thicker skin, and I knew that in this state, nothing could bring a tipsy meltdown quite like the wrath of strangers.

"I'm really sorry," I whispered to the couple. My voice had apparently been chased away by the surge of acute embarrassment swelling through my chest.

I was about to turn and retreat back to Liza (who was where, by the way? Just watching me suffer?), when I felt a strong hand on my arm.

"Well, thank God someone got this night started," a voice above me drawled.

I looked up to make eye contact for the second time that evening with the very-hot-even-for-the-real-world guy from one bar stool over.

"Hi," I whispered, wondering if my voice planned on a long vacation.

He smiled at me and I felt my neck rash flare up.

I had always had very specialized physical manifestations of anxiety—uncontrollable shaking when self-conscious before authority figures, laughing fits in the presence of scary animals, and, when confronted by extremely attractive men I wanted to like me, a severe neck rash.

It began with a deep flush, which quickly dissolved into tiny red bumps that paraded from my chestbone to my ears. It was relatively rare—the guy had to *really* do something for me—and it was never, ever pretty.

I kept a fashionable scarf my mother had given me in my bag for such emergencies, but my bag was back at the bar stool, leaving me no choice but to wrap my hands around my neck in what could possibly be construed as a whimsical gesture, but much more likely looked like a bizarre self-strangulation pose. Maybe he was into that?

He had averted his gaze and was looking kindly at the shaken couple.

"Why don't you give her your jacket?" he suggested to the man, who quickly complied, covering up his date far more efficiently than the paltry napkin had managed to do.

"And why don't both of you have another round on me?" he continued gallantly. "That is, when the bartender's done hitting on your friend," he smiled back at me.

I turned around to see that the bartender was indeed

talking conspiratorially with Liza, who appeared to be writing down her number on a cardboard coaster. My annoyance towards her dissipated, replaced by extreme gratitude that she had been oblivious to my disaster, because that had allowed me to be much more satisfactorily rescued by—

"My name's Aaron," he offered helpfully, sticking out his hand.

"Sammy."

"Well, it's a pleasure to meet you, Sammy. You were really sweet to try and help that guy. Unfortunately, he's a grouchy drunk, in here every night. You didn't know what you were getting yourself into."

No, I sure didn't.

"Now, can I get *you* a drink?"

Yes, you sure can. He was staring at me, looking more and more handsome by the heartbeats pounding in my ears. Handsome and . . . expectant. Oh right, time to answer him out loud.

"Uh, sure. Sock it to me."

Sock it to me? *Sock it to me?!* Where the hell had that come from? Wasn't that an old catchphrase on *Laugh-In*? What had provoked me to say it? And the tone I'd used hadn't been playful at all, which would have saved it—it had instead come out in a sort of guttural way, which just made me sound crass and demanding. That wasn't me! What sabotaging seventies poltergeist was channeling me from the other side? I decided to get my Ouija board revenge later, there was an image repair emergency to tend to at the moment.

"Uh, let's see . . . do they serve Klutz Martinis here?" I asked in what I prayed was a much more appealing tone. "That's my signature drink."

Aaron laughed.

"Hmm, afraid not. But I think they've got a Good Samaritan shot with a Bad Break chaser," he smiled at me.

"Sounds great."

We made our way back to our stools just as Liza looked up from her huddle with the hunky bartender. She glanced at my neck and quickly and smoothly handed me the scarf from my bag.

"Liza, this is Aaron. Aaron, Liza."

I fashioned the scarf around my neck as they shook hands.

"And this is Ryan." Liza indicated the bartender.

Ryan was certainly a looker, and at the moment he was surreptitiously looking me up and down. Oh, Liza, no. Not another one.

"Ryan's going to show me some of the mixers they have in the back. I've been looking for some better deals for the Mayflower." Liza smiled at me as she disappeared after Ryan through the door behind the bar.

"Well, that worked out. Now I won't be being rude when I only pay attention to you," Aaron said.

Nope, nothing rude about that. And even if that

was a little line-y, it sounded charming coming from him. Where was that accent from? Somewhere southern. Maybe a little south of heaven?

I inwardly wretched at my tumble into cheesiness and was only mildly comforted by the fact that no one would ever know those words had existed in my brain. But I knew. It was time to pull it together. He wasn't *that* great.

"You work for Senator Gary, don't you?" Aaron continued. "I've seen you around."

He had? When? Where? Had I known I was being watched? Had I been doing anything embarrassing? The chances that I had been were distressingly high.

"Yeah, I'm Senator Gary's domestic policy adviser." I smiled brightly at him, trying to blind him with either my freshly whitened teeth or my relatively impressive job title.

"Wow, that's great. I'm impressed!"

Those Crest Whitestrips were a bitch to put on, but they really worked.

"And what about you?" I asked, feeling a little more confident.

It seemed as though he also worked on the Hill. I hoped so. I wanted to be involved with someone who cared about the same things I did. Oh, but what if he did something really low level? That was fine with me, but would he be threatened by my success? I hoped I hadn't emasculated him—that was no way to start the serious relationship we were clearly destined to have.

"I'm the head speechwriter for Senator Bramen," he answered.

John Bramen. Senior senator from New Jersey, ranking member on the most powerful committee in the Senate, early front-runner in the presidential race, all-around major heavyweight. A jerk by most accounts, but an extremely successful one. We were just fifteen fast months away from the election day that very well might make Bramen president. Aaron's ego probably wasn't too bruised.

"Gosh, that must keep you pretty busy."

Could I be any more bland? It was dangerous to dare myself.

"It's challenging, but rewarding. And it only drives me to drink every other night." He smiled modestly.

Would I tell our children that his smile was the first thing I fell in love with? Assuming I could get a word in edgewise as their father smothered me with passionate kisses for the rest of my life.

Aaron was checking his watch. Oh no, bad sign. Say something witty, I yelled at myself. Look alluring, goddammit! I felt my neck rash flare stronger under the mounting pressure.

"Actually, Bramen's on *20/20* tonight and I'm supposed to watch," Aaron said.

There it was. I was getting the Heisman after a mere ten minutes. Sadly, that wasn't even a personal record. But I'd really been digging him. This sucked.

"The thing is—I'd much rather stay here talking to you," he continued.

Really?

"Plus, for the safety of the other patrons' outfits, I really don't think you should be left unsupervised," he continued. "Do you mind excusing me for a second so I can make a quick call?"

I felt myself fall instantly and deeply into infatuation. To mark the occasion, I smiled goofily at him as he moved away to dial his cell phone. Technically, I was supposed to be returning to the office, but what if this guy turned out to be the love of my life? In the big scheme of things, which was more important—killing myself to succeed at work or finding a soul mate? The unnerving thing was that at this stage of my life, it was sort of a close call.

I decided to use the phone call time wisely to come up with good conversation topics and prep some of my go-to stories. I knew I had a foolproof bit about water parks, but how to segue? Should I open with embarrassing cell phone stories? Certainly a natural transition and I definitely had a bevy of them. But sometimes when I mimicked the static crucial to such stories I inadvertently spit a fair amount, and that probably wasn't all that seductive. I clearly just needed to get him drunk pretty quickly.

"I'm afraid I have tragic news."

He was back. It turned out his frown was just as tremendous as his smile. It made him look sexily disgruntled.

"I couldn't get through to someone to tape the show for me, and Tivo's not returning my calls, so I've unfortunately got to head out. I'd ask you along, but I know a lady such as yourself wouldn't let me get to the Barbara Walters stage before we've even had our first real date."

"No, of course not. Babs is well on the way to second base."

"Exactly, I feel we need to build to that sort of intimacy. Maybe warm up with some good old-fashioned *60 Minutes*."

"It's so refreshing to meet a true gentleman."

Laughing, he took my hand and leaned down to kiss it.

"Till later, then." He smiled one last breathtaking time and was gone.

Back at my apartment that night, I endlessly replayed every moment of my interaction with Aaron, mercilessly punishing myself for not coming up with the cleverer responses that seemed so obvious hours later. As I lay there festering, repartee hindsight was 20/20 in more ways than one.

I was also vaguely curious how Senator Bramen had done on the show. Probably very well, he was so polished and professional. One of his glaring faults being that he knew how polished and professional he was— the fact that he'd never run for president before was a miracle given his soaringly high opinion of himself. I didn't have any personal experience with Bramen, but

I'd heard plenty about him through the Hill grapevine since arriving in D.C.

Though Bramen and RG had been elected to Congress the same year, Bramen had apparently devoted considerably more of his time during the ensuing decade to relentless pandering and self-promotion. His undisguised ambition coupled with his aggressive maneuvering had propelled him from the moment he was sworn in towards an inevitable race for the presidency. I'd heard others say that anyone who really knew Bramen didn't mistake his motivations for a genuine desire to improve the lives of his fellow Americans. To the contrary, they understood that he was clearly in the mix for his own betterment.

In my opinion, this made Bramen the polar opposite of RG in terms of integrity and style. And yet the very qualities that I deplored in Bramen were the same ones that had garnered him tremendous clout on the Hill. He held far more sway than RG did, as unfair as that seemed to me.

I wondered how well Aaron knew Bramen. Was he aware of his boss's considerable shortcomings? I hoped that he wasn't, because I sensed I'd have trouble being with someone who willingly worked for such a tainted cause. And there could easily be a respectable reason for Aaron's ignorance, I argued to myself. Perhaps he was too new on staff. He was certainly far too good-looking.

I decided to give Aaron the benefit of the doubt

pending further investigation since there was a perfectly good chance that he just didn't know the truth. Perhaps it was my role to enlighten him! Maybe once Aaron fell madly in love with me, I could persuade him to renounce Bramen, leave his job, and come work for RG, thereby effecting a harmonious merging of my personal and professional lives—a goal I'd been feng shui-ing towards for months. As I gazed up at the glow-in-the-dark constellations adorning my ceiling, I fantasized about all my stars aligning at last and drifted delusionally off to sleep.

Monday morning came much quicker than I was prepared for. I had gone into the office for a few hours on Saturday and then spent most of Sunday Rollerblading with Liza along the Potomac. I wasn't what you would call a strong Rollerblader, and Liza had needed to turn back often to encourage me along. I'd never thought it was a wise plan to have wheels strapped to my feet, but Liza had insisted it was good exercise, and at the very least, it was refreshing to have a better excuse for taking a few tumbles. Plus, the kneepads, elbow pads, and helmet were fun to wear. They made me feel very lethal and important and, when I closed my eyes, I imagined I was participating in something far more adventurous and risky. And given that my eyes were closed, that usually was in fact the case.

I felt distinctly sore as I dragged myself out of bed, which wasn't a sensation I enjoyed. As I waited for the shower to warm up, I started thinking about an article I'd read about people who were born without nerve endings, which resulted in them not being able to feel any pain. I wasn't sure if it was possible to develop this condition, but if it was, I felt pretty certain I was not prepared for it. However, after a brief internal debate, I decided that the condition was too high concept to train for on a Monday morning. I opted instead to spend my shower time reviewing the proper defensive responses to various animal attacks.

When I was younger, I had begun this training by arranging my stuffed animals in various stations around my house to help me practice. The rule I made was that I would go about my day-to-day life, but whenever I made eye contact with any of these stuffed animals, I had to practice my emergency response on the spot. This resulted in various episodes along the lines of me trudging to the bathroom in the middle of the night, stumbling upon my plush alligator, and feeling compelled to continue my journey in a fast-paced, diagonal run (since alligators could only run fast in a straight line, one had to change direction frequently to survive their chase). Or, while clearing the dishes after dinner, spotting my stuffed bear atop the hutch and immediately dropping to the floor in a tight, impenetrable ball. My parents were briefly alarmed at what appeared to them to be erratic, Tourette's-like behavior onsetting at a relatively early age. Once I explained the training regimen, my mom gave me a subscription to *National Geographic* and my dad suggested I get outside more.

I had just finished dressing and was reviewing shark attack survival tips when I made eye contact with Shackleton. He stared at me woefully from his bowl, seemingly too tired to nibble at his fish flakes. His gills had become even mossier over the weekend, though a Saturday afternoon trip to Mr. Lee's pet store had elicited nothing but assurances that I was doing everything right. This had only served to increase my doubts about Mr. Lee's overall veracity. I should have known not to trust him the first day I walked into his shop—how could anyone really believe that a man named Mr. Lee, who played the fifties song "Mr. Lee" on a loop over his store's stereo system, was interested in anything but his own bottom line?

Poor Shackleton. I wondered what the chances were that he had a Japanese fighting fish version of the no-nerve-ending condition and was therefore being spared whatever pain his slow death was causing. I blew him a kiss and arranged my most beautiful Japanese fan behind his bowl in an effort to make him feel more at home. He acknowledged my gesture with a feeble flutter of his tail.

My BlackBerry buzzed with an urgent message from Janet telling me to get to the office as soon as I could. No time for a sit-down breakfast. Luckily it was the eighty-first anniversary of the invention of the Klondike Bar, and I had bought a box of them over the weekend in celebration. I grabbed a bar from the freezer and bolted out the door.

When I hurried into the office, Janet eyed my wet hair with the expression of a public health inspector noting a restaurant that wasn't up to code. She gave me a split second to feel self-conscious (though the wet hairdo special was hardly out of the ordinary for me), before nodding towards RG's office.

"He came in early this morning. Asked to see you," she instructed as she turned back to the ringing phone.

I entered to find RG at his desk, reading and finishing up his breakfast of a half grapefruit and a handful of vitamins—a breakfast so far inferior to my chocolate fudge Klondike Bar, I almost felt sorry for him.

Until I remembered that he was the powerful United States senator and I was the lowly aide who was about to be . . . what? Tested? Reprimanded? Promoted? I was fairly certain we could rule out that last possibility.

"I got a call last night from John Bramen," RG said after ignoring me for a good two minutes while he finished reading a news story.

Really? That was quite a coincidence. Goodness, was word already out that Aaron and I were soon to be an item? It seemed unlikely.

"He was impressed with the way the committee hearing went on Friday and he wants to work with us in a more official capacity," RG continued.

"He wants to cosponsor the bill?" I asked.

"That's correct. So I'm going to need you to bring his staff up to speed on its intricacies."

Wow. We'd been angling for a high-profile cosponsor because we knew that scoring one could give the bill the momentum it needed to pass, but this was a surprise. Bramen had never even been on our list. Yet if he liked the bill and wanted to lend his name, I didn't see anything wrong with using him to get something good done.

"Well, that's great, sir. Isn't it?"

RG peered at me over his reading glasses.

"It's probably good for the bill. We'll see how great it is overall as we go along."

I watched RG shuffle through his papers with a tightened jaw and felt troubled. Though I'd learned early on that senators often had to work in partnerships that weren't perfect fits, I could tell from RG's manner that he and Bramen weren't simply mismatched. I sensed an undercurrent of genuine dislike.

"What do you mean, sir?" I asked, hoping for clarification.

RG sighed.

"Look, I felt compelled to accept Bramen's offer for the sake of the bill, but I wish we didn't have to work with him, because he can't be trusted. And neither can his staff. You'll need to stay on your guard."

Oh dear. So Bramen's cosponsorship wasn't great news. And worse, RG was explicitly warning me about

Bramen staffers two days after I'd become infatuated with one. The feng shui dreams of seamlessly melding my personal and professional lives appeared doomed. But I wasn't quite ready to let go of the fantasy.

"Okay. But do you think that every single member of Bramen's staff is untrustworthy?" I heard myself asking. "Without exception? I mean, couldn't some of them be okay? Like if they had just started maybe, or if they were a fluke or something?"

RG's baffled stare terminated my tangent.

"Never mind, sir," I continued quickly. "I just was, uh . . . I was just collecting my thoughts."

Which I resolved to do in silence from now on. As much as I wanted validation for my hypothetical relationship, I understood that it wasn't worth sounding like an idiot in front of my boss. Or sounding any more like one, at least. RG was looking hard at me.

"Are you up for this, Samantha?" he asked, with the slightest hint of apprehension.

Of course I was. I would do everything in my power to make this bill a success. Which included proving I was much more competent than my recent display indicated.

"Definitely, sir. You have nothing to worry about."

RG gave a satisfied nod.

"Great. Now, don't let Bramen's people bog you down with their interest group bullshit. And keep an eye out especially for any insurance stuff they try to tack on. That's Bramen's trademark—he and the industry go way back, but you've got to keep the bill clean of that crap. Let me know if you run into problems."

With that, he returned to his papers and seemed to forget about my existence—a familiar sign that the meeting was over.

I got more explicit instructions from Janet about setting up a meeting with Bramen's people for that afternoon before returning to my desk to discover that my favorite coffee mug—the one with the magic eye trick picture of Snuffleupagus on it—had been stolen.

I gasped in horror. I loved that mug. I had won it at an Ohio state fair after successfully sinking three Ping-Pong balls into a narrow-necked glass bowl, my college Beer Pong skills finally paying off with a glorious postgrad triumph.

That mug was one of my most prized possessions— I secretly believed it to be a potent good luck charm, which is why I had brought it to work in the first place. It had sat helpfully on my desk for seven months. And now, out of the blue, I'd been robbed of it? Who was the culprit that would commit such a dastardly crime?

I soon had my answer. Mark Herbert, RG's recently hired press secretary, was leaning against the Xerox machine down the hall, chatting with some unseen conspirator and clutching my Snuffleupagus mug in one filthy, stealing claw. He had come to the job highly recommended, but he'd been odd and aloof from the beginning. Now it turned out he was a thief! I knew I shouldn't have felt guilty for instantly disliking him.

The sentiment had been largely based on his elaborate use of hand gestures to illustrate his monologues, but regardless, it was obviously justified. Should I alert RG to the fact that he was willfully employing a criminal?

I moved towards Mark's unsuspecting back, the *Jaws* theme pounding vengefully in my head. Stupid Mark Herbert, coming in here and taking my things—even if he was just "borrowing" it, he was still germing it up. What a jerk.

He was midsentence when I cleared my throat.

"Yeah, listen, Mark, I know you're new here so you don't necessarily know everything that goes on, but that's my special mug you're holding and I'd love it if I could just get it back from you, thanks."

There, I had successfully beaten back the hissy-fit tone that had been welling inside me, and really had managed a very polite timbre, if I did say so myself. I topped it off with a fake (therefore deformed) smile.

He looked surprised.

Didn't think I'd catch you so soon, did ya?

It looked like he hadn't even had time to take a sip.

That's right, sucker, that's how fast I am. Now you know not to mess with me.

"Mark's been making coffee for everyone this morning."

His unseen fellow schemer was now seen, and she turned out to be Mona the scheduler, calmly sipping coffee out of her Pi Phi cup.

"Uh, I was just bringing you yours." Mark had now turned towards me. "You, uh, take it with lots of sugar, right?" He mimed putting in several scoops of sugar.

I was pretty sure he hadn't put enough sugar in there to combat the bitter taste of my deeply inserted foot.

"Thanks," I offered weakly. "Sorry, I didn't mean to suggest you were . . ."

As I trailed off, I wondered why he was the one looking embarrassed. And was I going to finish that last sentence? Probably not—I'd done enough damage; there was no need to fully vocalize my snap suspicions.

"I should get back to my phone. I've got a *Harper's* cover story to negotiate," Mark said quickly, handing over an unscathed Snuffleupagus, and holding his fingers to his head like an imaginary phone before scampering off.

Mona was fixing me with an appraising look.

I tried to deflect her gaze with an oops-oh-well shrug as I backed down the hall whence I came, but I wasn't quite quick enough.

"He has a crush on you, you know."

What?

Mona was nodding calmly as I vigorously shook my head.

"He does," she asserted. "I thought at first he liked me, but then I realized he was only talking to me so he could find out about you."

Mona didn't look as though she'd been overly pleased by that discovery. How could Mark have a crush on me?

Besides some brief interactions that had showcased his affinity for miming and sign language, we'd barely spoken in the three weeks he'd been on staff. Actually, maybe that was precisely how he could have a crush on me. He didn't know any better.

"Oh, I'm sure he doesn't," I tried. "He's probably just wondering how I manage to hang on to my job here."

I laughed self-deprecatingly. Mona looked a little too thoughtful for my comfort.

"Maybe. Anyway, would you be interested in him? He's pretty cute."

Okay, Mark was not cute. But the fact that Mona thought he was made me wish all the more that he would transfer his alleged affections to her. She was a bit brusque and prickly, but she wasn't a bad person. And she spent so much time scheduling RG, I doubted she had much left over for herself. A romance would be good for her. I took a sip of my coffee.

"This is really good."

Mona just looked at me with one raised, slightly bushy eyebrow.

"Um, I've just started seeing someone anyway, so it's not even an issue," I continued, praying for the God of White Lies to pow-wow with the God of Potentially Fantastic Boyfriends and turn this mild fib into a fact as soon as they could manage. It was for a good cause.

Mona looked relieved.

"Oh. Well, I'll break it to him gently," she said. "Is it anyone I know?"

Did she know Aaron? Could she be a valuable source for the necessary background research? I doubted it, and regardless, it was too late to inquire, considering I was supposedly already dating him.

"No, I don't think so. It's going great, but it's still early, so I don't want to jinx it. I'm kind of superstitious, you know."

At least that last part was true. Luckily, my Black-Berry buzzed me into work mode and I smiled good-bye to Mona as I made my way back to my desk.

With Snuffleupagus safely returned to his righteous throne, I reviewed my file cabinet of material on RG's prescription drug proposal, and pulled the pieces I thought would be most necessary and helpful for Senator Bramen's team. The proposal was a good one, but it was bold, and therefore sure to face a contentious battle for passage. Having Bramen on board would signal to everyone that it should be taken seriously. Flaws aside, we needed him for the bill. As things stood, the legislation was on track to gain committee approval in the next month, and then would go on to weather the debate and voting of the full Senate.

I tried not to daydream about what it would mean if the bill actually passed, because there were so many hurdles along the way, but I couldn't help but get energized by the prospect. My brief time in D.C. had made me aware of just how difficult it was to effect positive change, but working for RG had also bolstered my faith in the potential for progress, and I wanted my confidence to be rewarded with a tangible advancement—something I could point to and know was improving people's lives. I firmly believed that a comprehensive prescription drug plan for the millions of Americans struggling to afford their health care would provide just that.

After organizing the pertinent material for the Bramen team to my satisfaction, I mentally reviewed RG's advice about dealing with them. He had mentioned that I should watch out for "interest group bullshit," and referred specifically to Bramen being cozy with the insurance lobby. I had heard other rumors to that effect, but until now had never had any reason to look deeper into them. I knew RG's health care positions inside and out, but I was still learning the ropes when it came to the other ninety-nine senators.

Since RG had been too busy to elaborate, I Googled my way to the relevant information. Evidently, Bramen's father had made the family fortune in medical insurance, and John Bramen Jr. had continued to foster these relationships despite the occasional conflict of interest with providing affordable medical coverage for his constituents in the lower and middle levels of the income brackets. From the articles that I scanned, it seemed that Bramen was a bit of a hypocrite on the issue—championing the need for reasonably priced health care yet perpetually making deals with various insurance companies that consistently drove up premium prices. These very insurance companies in turn provided continual funding and support for his campaigns.

From what I could gather, Bramen hadn't been taken to task for these relationships by many people in his party, mainly because he'd managed to cover himself fairly well.

Ugh. As I digested the ramifications of this distressing information, my stomach began to ache. Only as my discomfort increased did it occur to me to wonder if my pain could also be related to my ice cream bar breakfast.

A quick search of my desk turned up some sample packets of Tums my gynecologist had given me in an effort to up my calcium intake. I decided to give them a shot—perhaps I could stave off osteoporosis and settle my stomach at the very same time. A brilliant double punch!

Just when my mouth had achieved peak tablet capacity, my phone began to ring.

"Hay-woah?" I attempted valiantly.

"Hi, this is Natalie Reynolds from Senator Bramen's office. Is this Samantha Joyce?"

"Mmm-hmmph."

"Pardon me?"

I took a big gulp of coffee.

"Sorry, this is Samantha. How can I help you?"

As Natalie talked about the meeting scheduled for that afternoon, I focused on how her clipped tones made her sound like a perky telemarketer—and no matter what she said it was hard to believe she wasn't reading from a script.

I happened to love telemarketers and looked forward to their calls. I found the concept of telemarketer as human being an infinitely fascinating one. Who were they? Did they enjoy their jobs? How much abuse had they endured that day and were they appreciative that I was welcoming them with open arms?

Since they were calling me and doing everything in their trained power to keep me engaged and interested in what they had to offer, I felt there was no reason I shouldn't ask them lots of questions about themselves. It was always fun to come home and have voicemails from them on my phone, and I would often call them back just to chat. I almost never actually bought anything, but I always enjoyed the conversations.

Over time, I had definitely developed favorites. Zelda from the phone company was one of the stars. I had her personal extension on speed dial and called her up periodically just to check on things. She lived in Daytona, Florida, with her husband and two little boys, and worked the phones sixty hours a week to try and save for their kids' education. She herself had only made it through junior year of high school, though her husband had completed two years of college, but both of them dreamed of better things for their sons.

By the time Natalie "Telemarketer Voice" Reynolds had finished talking, I had agreed to e-mail her the majority of the proposal research and meet her at Senator Bramen's office in the Hart Building at two o'clock. There, I would work my magic to welcome the Bramen team while simultaneously protecting the integrity of the bill. There was no need to tie my stomach into knots. It was all going to be fine, if I had anything to do with it, which I did. I made a mental note to get more Tums.

I planned on taking advantage of the lunch hour ("hour" being a euphemism for twenty minutes) to prettify in the event I ran into Aaron, though I understood that my plans for a future with him might be dashed if it turned out he had knowledge of his boss's crimes. Still, it didn't hurt to look good. What prettifying entailed exactly, only time and the contents of my purse would tell. I could usually count on some ChapStick and a brush being in there at the very least, but I didn't want to get my hopes up. I didn't even have time to at the moment—there was way too much work to get through. I finished off my coffee and hunkered down.

It was twenty minutes to two when I finally made it to the bathroom to assess the appearance situation. It was a dismal sight. First of all, I certainly wasn't dressed for a date, except for one with the Laundromat later that evening. My knee-length skirt was wrinkled, unfortunately not in a stylish way, and my silk tank top was marred by a large soy sauce stain. I now noticed with dismay that the cropped cardigan sweater I'd grabbed from the bottom of my closet to hide the soy sauce stain had a spray of spangles around the neckline. Where had this sweater come from? How had I not noticed the spangles? I was also distressed to discover that I'd left my brush at home and my hair had dried uncooperatively into a lank mini-mullet. And worst of all, I'd sprouted an unsightly pimple on the tip of my nose sometime in the hours since breakfast. I'd felt it coming on all morning, but maintained a state of denial. Unfortunately, the mirror was no enabler. How could a pimple get so big in such a short amount of time? I had neither the tools nor the time to deal with it—I had to get over to Bramen's office.

On my way down the stairs, my cell phone started blasting an orchestral version of Madonna's "Like a Virgin," the tune Liza had somewhat annoyingly programmed to be her special ring. The volume was turned all the way up and several passersby stared at me as I fumbled for the phone. I smiled back at them like I knew exactly what I was doing—a confident attitude I felt was worthy of the Material Girl.

"Hey, I can't talk now. Can I call you in a bit?"

"Oh, too bad, I'm outside your building—I just had a picnic with Ryan on the Capitol grounds."

Ryan the bartender had already asked her out? I was clearly behind schedule. Though I doubted I'd be wowing Aaron into a date with my current look.

"Hang on a second, Liza, are you *right* outside?"

"Yeah, come on out! Take a break!"

"I can't take a break, but I do need a favor. You have three minutes to perform a makeover using whatever you have in your purse. I'll see you in thirty seconds."

I snapped the phone shut with Liza's squeal of delight ringing in my ears. She loved any sort of contest—a trait her older brothers had exploited when they were growing up by getting her to do their share of the chores, whether it was taking out the garbage or walking the dog, just by saying that they'd time her. Though I never consciously intended to take advantage of this weakness of Liza's, I had to admit that it came in handy at times.

Ralph was screening a large group of male Marines as I passed the security checkpoint on my way towards the door. The group struck me as overwhelmingly uniform in their crew-cut masculinity—they even managed to turn their heads on cue to watch me pass. I felt self-conscious and decided to take control by waving hello to Ralph. Though I still hadn't completely forgiven him for his obstructionist mockery during the Alfred Jackman incident, I knew I would need him on my side in the future so I figured it was worth it to declare a truce in my head and resume friendliness. Ralph paused in his duties to return my wave.

"You should pop that," he offered helpfully as he pointed to the tip of his nose.

Truce over. Calling attention to a woman's zit before a squadron of red-blooded young Marines was a human rights violation.

I heard a few of them chuckle as I sped through the door and out into the glaring sunshine.

It was the sort of late July day that wouldn't let you forget that D.C. was built on a swamp—the pungent humidity had turned the air into something viscous and swollen, and my mini-mullet was quickly slicked to my neck with sweat.

"Over here!" Liza called from the minimal shade of a nearby tree.

I checked my watch as I ran down the steps to her. Ten minutes to get to Bramen's office. Granted, the Hart Building was very nearby, but I had to leave time for getting through security and negotiating the halls.

"I've got a meeting I need to look good for. Aaron might be there."

"I'm on it," Liza replied with total seriousness.

She was the best.

Over the next three minutes, she turned our little patch of sidewalk into an emergency salon. She of course had not one, but three different kinds of brushes in her purse, along with various volumizing sprays and gels that she expertly spritzed and dabbed onto my limp locks. She was a whiz with these sorts of products, whereas I found them too mysterious and intimidating to ever know how to even approach them. I would stare at them in the drugstore aisles like a visitor from another planet fresh off the spaceship—curious but very, very confused.

This deficiency made me all the more appreciative of Liza's mastery of all things cosmetic. She finished my hair with a satisfied nod and stepped back to survey my outfit.

"I didn't notice the spangles this morning," I assured her.

"Wear this instead," Liza commanded, handing over

her                                              infinitely
hipper jacket and whipping out her concealer to tackle
the vile uberpimple.

"Hmm . . . I'm a little scared to pop it at this stage,"
she fretted.

"I know. It could lash out unpredictably if provoked."

"Exactly. I'm opting for cover-up only. And I'll do
your neck, too, in case the rash comes back. Stay still."

Liza did what she could and was topping me off
with a little blush when I opened my eyes to see Aaron
standing directly behind her, observing the process
with a cocked head and rakish smile.

"Could I get in on a little of that? My cheekbones
have been dangerously undefined all morning," he said.

He had his shirtsleeves rolled up and his suit jacket
tossed over his shoulder. As I tried to keep my attraction
in check, I noticed that his tie was bringing out the deep
green of his eyes. I felt my stomach sprout wings and
flutter up towards my chest. It had a nauseating effect.

"Hey," I said, with a tone of forced nonchalance.

"Ooh, I gotta run," said Liza, checking her watch in a
convincingly worried way. "Thanks for letting me practice on you, babe. I'll call you later. Good to see you." She
waved at Aaron and hurried off.

"Is she a makeup artist?" Aaron asked.

"Of sorts," I answered, deciding to act like I *had* just
been doing Liza a favor. "So what are you up to?"

He looked around.

"Well, I'm supposed to be heading back to the office, but I could be convinced to make an ice-cream cone detour if it included the right kind of company. Any interest?"

"I really wish I could, but I've actually got to get to your office, as well."

"Oh?"

He had a way of punctuating questions with his eyes. They glinted in a probing way and his brows didn't actually lift, but they managed to suggest that they could if properly aroused.

"Yeah. Senator Gary sent me over to meet with Natalie now that Senator Bramen's agreed to cosponsor the prescription drug benefit bill. And actually," I checked my watch, "I'm two minutes late."

"Uh-oh, get ready to face the wrath of Natalie."

Aaron walked beside me towards the Hart Building.

"Just remember that her bite is much worse than her bark. But you look like you can handle it."

I wasn't quite sure what I looked like—I hadn't had a chance to review Liza's work in a mirror before Aaron had surprised us. I could feel my neck rash flaring and my pimple throbbing evilly on my nose and could only hope the concealer had been up to the challenge. As I walked with Aaron, I tried to identify things about him that I found unattractive. The most I could come up with was that his feet were on the small side, but there was plenty I couldn't see. Maybe he had webbed toes or something. Though now that I thought about it, that would be pretty cool.

He dropped me outside Bramen's office door with a mock salute that would have evoked a stinging memory of Ralph's treachery had I not been so pleasantly focused on keeping my knees in a non-buckling position. He smiled and continued down the hall to a separate entrance.

The receptionist put a call on hold when I entered the office.

"Oh yes, Natalie's been expecting you. One moment."

Been expecting me? I was seven minutes late. That wasn't enough time to have "been" anything for long. I resented the word choice.

Natalie swept in from a back hall, all four feet, eleven inches of her. She had the polished veneer to match her voice—an expensive suit, manicured hands, and highlighted hair twisted into a flawless French braid. Again, did these women really accomplish such feats by themselves, using technology available to anyone? I found it hard to believe. She looked as though she was possibly made of plastic.

She was blinking rapidly at me as she extended her hand. Her touch was cool and lotioned.

"Oh, good, I was worried you might have gotten lost," she said sweetly.

"Nope, not lost, just good old-fashioned late!" I smiled heartily.

She laughed quickly, as if she didn't have time for it.

"Well, why don't we get started. Right this way."

I followed her back down the hall and into a staff room filled with offices delineated by dividers. It was similar to RG's office setup, yet somewhat grander.

"Have a seat." She indicated a chair beside her immaculately organized desk.

She turned to her computer and didn't speak for several long seconds, which had the predictable effect of triggering my babbling reflex. I lived in fear of awkward conversational lulls, even imaginary or necessary ones, and consequently rushed to fill them before they had the slightest chance of growing legs.

"This is a really great space. Lots of light. Can you have real plants in here? I can't over in my pod," I blurted frantically.

"Thanks," she tersely replied, apparently opting to respond to my opening compliment and ignore the rest of my outburst.

She continued scrolling for something before pausing again.

"Oh, and what did you want to know about—the plants?" She looked up from her screen distractedly.

I nodded, feeling idiotic.

"Yes, they're real. Someone else takes care of them."

She returned to her work with a dismissive wave of her hand.

After another ten seconds of silence I tried again, but in what I hoped was a more appropriate vein.

"We're glad to have Senator Bramen on board," I said brightly.

"Mmm," Natalie replied. "Let's just make sure it doesn't blow up in his face, shall we?"

Excuse me?

"It's a fairly good bill overall," she was continuing, "but some of the language is a bit too blunt. We're going to need to put in some wiggle room for people in order to get the necessary support."

No, no, no. This was the bill that was supposed to bring about real change. Not another waffling, half-assed attempt that would get muted into irrelevance by the end of the process. Bramen's people needed to understand that. The rush of annoyance melted the remainder of my insecurity.

"Actually, I believe the bill's boldness is what makes it attractive. It's very clear in its objectives," I declared.

"That's precisely what people won't like. Don't worry, I heard you were pretty green. These are things you learn as you go along."

I stared at her as she clicked her way into some more computer files. She was maybe thirty-two. Thirty-four at the most. Certainly not old enough to be this condescending or cynical, in my opinion. I felt my hackles rising.

"Maybe people will find its clarity refreshing." I tried to keep my tone reasonable, as if I was just thoughtfully contemplating this possibility and tossing it out there.

Natalie snorted. Unlike her weirdly quick laughter, this sounded more indigenous to her nature.

"What, I'm being serious!" I said.

Now I was downright indignant.

Natalie fixed me with a condescending smile.

"Calm down, it's going to be just fine. You've done a really good job with this—it's just a little rough. We've got to polish it up before Bramen can start selling it."

I resisted the urge to turn around to check for the four-year-old she must have just been addressing. Surely, that tone wasn't meant for me?

Good Lord, it was. I was beginning to suspect that Natalie and I were not going to be very good friends. I spent the next few minutes contemplating the possibility that she was really an evil fembot or some other sinister futuristic machine sent to thwart the goodness of humanity. As she busied herself at the computer, I glanced around her office for clues to support this theory.

Besides a few airbrushed and perfectly framed photos, and a brand-new-looking teddy bear wearing a T-shirt that read "Grin and Bear It" (in my head I dropped into a tight, protective ball upon eye contact), Natalie had very few personal effects on display. If she was indeed human, she was clearly the sort of woman who kept her work area clinical and contained—really not the kind of person I could relate to.

I tried to remind myself that she was working for a

senator who was ostensibly on our side, and that so far she was just talking about tweaking the language rather than the substance of the bill, but the mechanical ickiness she oozed even as she just sat there typing made me shudder in spite of myself.

"You're cold already? I guess I'm too late."

Aaron's voice snapped me out of my discomfort. I looked up to find him holding out a chocolate ice-cream cone towards me.

"Don't tell me you haven't been secretly craving one all day. Just give me the honor of being the man to fulfill your desire."

Though I was faced away from the desk and towards Aaron, I could sense the air around Natalie tighten tensely. But from my perspective, he was a welcome distraction.

I smiled and decided not to tell him that in light of my Klondike Bar breakfast, he would've had to have been at my apartment at 7:00 that morning to claim the honor of providing me my first ice cream of the day. Then I blushed as I thought about how it was he might have ended up at my apartment at 7:00 in the morning.

Natalie's exasperated sigh broke my reverie.

"Aaron, we're trying to get something done here."

Aaron winked at me as he turned to Natalie.

"I would've brought you one, too, but they didn't have any fat-free yogurt and I knew you wouldn't even consider eating anything else."

Natalie must have heard him, but she didn't waver from her computer screen–absorbed posture.

"Go get 'em, girls." Aaron waved as he disappeared down the hall.

Natalie seemed pissed off. I had nothing against fat-free yogurt and in fact really wished I enjoyed the taste of it, and I furthermore found it annoying when effortlessly hot guys made mocking comments about women's diets, but this was a tricky case. Aaron might be my intended, and Natalie I just didn't like.

"Um, can I help with something?" I asked as I licked my ice cream.

She seemed to twitch at the sound of my voice.

"You know what, why don't I just work on this and e-mail you a draft later on."

It wasn't a question.

I made my way back to the Russell Senate Building buffeted by conflicting emotions. By the time I'd snubbed Ralph on my way to the elevator, I'd come up with a plan for dealing with Natalie. I'd wait for her to make her changes, and then simply get RG's okay to shoot them down. Problem solved.

Meanwhile, I was much happier about my interaction with Aaron. Even as I warned myself to be cautious, I couldn't stop grinning all afternoon. And then at 6:00 that evening, I received an e-mail from him asking me out.

I hesitated, but not for long. It would be stupid to turn him down just because he worked for Bramen, wouldn't it? Who cared what RG said—I wasn't going to let his paranoia dictate whom I could or couldn't date. I'd make my own decisions—I'd give Aaron a shot. I said yes to Thursday night, thanked my various gods, and began plotting my three-day transformation into a supermodel.

# Eyes on the Prize

I TOOK THE drastic step of waking up an hour early the next morning to fit in some emergency exercise. Since it was the thirtieth anniversary of the filming of *The Exorcist*, I decided to dash over to Prospect and M Street and attempt a workout on the outdoor set of steep stairs that had been famously featured in the movie. I myself had never (and would never) watch *The Exorcist*, because I was an enormous wimp when it came to horror flicks and my sporadic attempts to toughen up always ended disastrously.

When my dormmates had urged me to watch *The Shining* in college, I'd only lasted fifteen minutes and still had to give up my single because I couldn't be alone for the following three months. It didn't occur to me until later to wonder whether that had been exactly their plan.

But I understood the cultural impact of *The Exorcist*

and felt the anniversary of its filming was worth celebrating. Additionally, running up and down the stairs a
few times was hopefully going to make up for weeks of
less than healthy living and whip me instantly into
shape.

Seventy-five stairs was a lot of stairs. For some de-
monic reason, I spent the entire sweaty time reviewing
my previous relationships in my head. This was rarely a
good idea. There hadn't been that many serious ones—
only three that lasted more than a few months. And
though I didn't regret any of them being over, there
were still plenty of unresolved issues to obsess about.

As well as many cringe-worthy moments. I spent the
entirety of my second stair set painfully remembering
my phone-stalking pursuit of Jason Shambers, a good-
looking consultant my mother's friend had set me up
with when I first moved to D.C. We'd had a charming
lunch filled with promising chemistry and agreed to get
together for a movie that weekend. I couldn't believe
my luck—brand new to D.C. and not knowing a soul, I
already had a date with an extremely attractive native.

He said he'd call on Saturday morning. He never did.
By six o'clock that evening, I'd decided the only reasonable course of action was to begin calling him repeatedly
and hanging up when it went to voicemail. When he finally called at 10:00 the next morning, he said he had
sixty-two calls from my number on his caller ID, but no
messages, and was everything all right?

No, it clearly wasn't. I feigned total surprise and spent

an agonizing minute wondering aloud what could possibly account for such a weird thing—maybe a crossed wire glitch was somehow to blame? I said I had rung him once before going out just to check on the movie status, but certainly not more than once. Definitely nowhere close to sixty-two times—gosh, he must have thought I was insane! But now he knew that it was the phone service that was the nutty one and . . . wow, look at the time, I really had to run.

He politely played along and we agreed to reschedule for later. But he left it to me to call him and I was too suffocated by shame to even consider trying to rekindle his interest.

Why hadn't I realized the sudden ubiquity of caller IDs? It was a question I punished myself with during times such as these.

I'd tried hard to erase the whole incident from my mind. Unfortunately, his phone number (which I'd of course memorized during the course of that fateful evening) had the troubling distinction of sharing the first three digits with Liza's home number, so I lived in fear of accidentally calling him and prompting him to reconsider that restraining order.

Revisiting this embarrassing episode, along with the litany of other dating gaffes and romantic missteps I torturously reviewed as I puffed up the stairs, just caused them all to burn even darker and stronger in my memory.

I realized suddenly, as I finally finished the grueling fourth set, that, along with my legs, I'd spent the last half hour exercising my demons. This struck me as particularly counterproductive and homophonically ironic given the location. I made my gasping way home feeling like I might have missed an opportunity.

At the office three coffees later, I'd decided that the past, no matter how unchangeably brutal, was prologue to the dreamlike relationship I was about to embark upon with Aaron. I was tougher and wiser because of my mistakes and would obviously never repeat them. And I was a different person in other ways—more confident, secure, and settled. Not objectively per se, but relatively to when I had first moved to Washington at least.

Partly due to my new attitude, partly due to the excessive level of caffeine coursing through my bloodstream, I had an amazingly productive day. I spent most of it laying the groundwork for the series of open meetings RG was planning to host across Ohio during the Senate's summer recess at the end of August.

Open meetings were large, scheduled gatherings that served as forums for dialogue between RG and his constituents. Anyone could come to ask questions or air concerns, and RG would stand there for hours, ensuring that everyone had their chance at face time.

I loved open meetings, and not only because RG was particularly good at them. I thought of them as festivals of accountability and communication (though granted, they could sometimes be tedious and boring), and given that they encapsulated the basic relationship at the heart of representative democracy—the one between the electee and the electors—it shocked me that more senators didn't initiate them.

RG wanted the August round of open meetings to center mainly on health care concerns, so I was to be his traveling staff on the trip. I obviously wanted everything to go as smoothly as possible, and was deep in planning mode. There were sites to pick, vehicles to rent, awareness to raise, bills to succinctly summarize into plain language, and multiple other tasks to keep me busy.

Wednesday passed in a similarly hectic haze and Thursday arrived before I knew it. I woke up abruptly, thanks to a 5:30 AM phone call from my mom, who wanted to make sure everything was okay, as she had just woken up from a dream that I'd been crushed by a giant paper clip.

My mom wasn't one to put a lot of stock in dreams, so I was a bit surprised by her call. As she described how the paper clip had just fallen out of a predawn sky, I could hear "Yellow Submarine" playing in the background and I wondered if she had the CD on repeat as usual. My mom had been both a political science major and a UK rock groupie at Berkeley in the sixties. She'd welcomed the British Invasion with open and eager arms, and had fallen particularly hard for all things Beatles, Rolling Stones, and the Who, to name a few. In her opinion, the music that had come out of the United Kingdom had been far superior to anything the States had shown for themselves. In her early twenties, she'd organized fan clubs, convinced my dad to grow out his hair, and spoken with a British tinge to her midwestern accent.

After completing graduate school, she had turned down a job at Stanford to live in Ohio with my father, who had committed himself to modernizing the dairy farm that had been in his family for generations. Amidst the hubbub of this transformed and thriving operation, my mother had raised me to pay close attention to the world of public service while she herself had happily taught at the local community college.

And every once in a while, she did things to remind me that in addition to being a political science professor, she was also a recovering Anglophile. Like watching BBC America for hours on end or saying someone was "pissed" to communicate that they were drunk rather than angry. Although occasionally both applied.

When she finished the tale of her disturbing dream, I assured her I was unmooshed, promised I'd call later, and decided to use the unexpected extra hour to make myself as irresistible as possible, since I was fairly sure I'd have to meet Aaron straight from work.

When I closed my eyes in the shower, I, too, had an image of me being crushed by a giant paper clip. Thank you, Mom. I was mildly concerned by the possibility that she'd experienced a legitimate maternal premonition about my imminent doom via oversized office supplies, and resolved to be extra alert that day.

I was disgruntled to discover, upon critical examination in my bathroom mirror, that I had not pulled off the supermodel transformation as scheduled. I told myself I didn't look bad, though. Plus, as every falsely modest model on the planet infuriatingly said, beauty came from within. Luckily there was still time to achieve spiritual peace and wholeness via intense meditation before I had to catch my train to work.

Daily meditation had been one of my Chinese New Year's resolutions, though I'd only managed to honor the "daily" part of it for the first week. I didn't mind sitting still for thirty minutes—quite to the contrary, I was thrilled to have spiritually sanctioned laziness be a regular part of my day—but I did find it very difficult to clear my mind of all thoughts. Even if my only thought was, Come on, it can't be *this* hard to not think about anything, I had failed.

It had been three weeks since my last meditation, I confessed to the little wood-carved Buddha I placed next to me for inspiration. His chubby oaken face gleamed forgivingly. I closed my eyes and began flicking away my thoughts, eager for the serenity of spiritual enlightenment.

An hour and fifteen minutes later I awoke with a start, jolted by the earthquake rumble of the garbage truck lumbering down my street. I wiped the drool from my mouth and looked around, disoriented. The clock grinned devilishly back at me. It had got to be kidding. In what felt like the blink of a mantra, my time surplus had turned into a deficit, and I now had only seven minutes to get to work. So much for inner peace.

I arrived frazzled and sweating and couldn't shake a manic, rushed feeling for most of the morning. I'd taken the elevator up with Mark Herbert, who'd looked panicked to find himself in an enclosed space with me. He'd stared at his feet the whole time, and, feeling too stressed to combat the awkward silence, I'd pretended to be crucially involved with my BlackBerry.

A fresh printout of the Hotline greeted me at my desk. I scanned the compilation of headlines large and small, pausing to absorb any buzzworthy quotes from lawmakers and journalists. Along with The Note, a daily summary of political news available on ABCnews.com, the Hotline was the Page Six of Capitol Hill.

It was difficult not to skip straight to the comedy section that included the best political jokes by Jon Stewart, Conan, Letterman, and Leno from the night before, but I patiently skimmed the entries in order, alternately pleased and outraged by the news it delivered.

Congressman Harris had apparently compared homosexuality to his wife's compulsive shopping disorder—a "terrible disease that must be fought with firm compassion." Brilliant. So glad such intelligent, progressive leaders were shaping national policy.

Laura Harris had bought more than four hundred thousand dollars' worth of designer clothing from various D.C. department stores in the six months they'd lived in the district. After her third credit card was denied, a gossipy salesclerk had called the *Washington Post*.

The ensuing brouhaha didn't sit well in Harris's New Mexico district. It certainly didn't help that New Mexico was one of the poorest states in the Union, and had particularly suffered during the last six years of national recession. Angry constituents and newspaper editors had been demanding an explanation.

At first, the congressman had responded with a joke about how hard it was to rein the little lady in when she always looked so pretty, but to his surprise, this hadn't quieted his critics. He'd subsequently gotten misty-eyed with Diane Sawyer over his wife's "problem," and now, the congressman seemed to be trotting out a "love me, I'm a homophobe" plea to win back the approval of his base.

Since Congressman Harris had been one of the leading fund-raisers for the president's reelect the last time around, I tried to prepare myself for the inevitable statement from President Pile about how he could "look Jeb Harris dead in the eye and tell he was a good man." But could anyone ever really be prepared for such inanity?

As presidents went, Pile had been a disaster. His administration had made a tremendous mess of things over the last seven years, and by practically all accounts, its reign had proved an unmitigated catastrophe. Their economic, social, and environmental policies, or more accurately, lack thereof, had plunged the nation into a brutal recession and set America back a decade or more. The international community had become accustomed to shaking its head at America's troubles and did its best to prevent the Pile administration from spreading its unique brand of arrogant ineptitude beyond American borders.

It was a sad state of affairs. Even Pile's own party had a sense of how bad things had gotten and most of them were falling all over themselves to distance themselves from the administration. The vice president, Dan Linkey, wasn't even attempting a campaign. Tarred by multiple scandals, he was going to be busy enough avoiding indictment.

The only good thing about how terrible the Pile years had been was the fact that the country was desperate for new leadership to clean up the wreckage. With that in mind, I spent a few minutes absorbing the latest stories on the nascent presidential campaign. Fifteen months away, it was already commanding a substantial section in the news summaries.

Besides Bramen, there were six other candidates from his party vying for the nomination. Yet so far, only two of them appeared poised to give him a run for his money. Melanie Spearam was a senator from Illinois and the only woman making the race thus far. She intrigued me with her icy professionalism and dogged ambition, and I wondered if she could go all the way. I'd never interacted with her in person but continued to watch her from an interested distance. According to the Hotline, she was posting strong numbers in New Hampshire and appeared to be receiving a substantial amount of press attention.

Though I was thrilled by the idea of a female nominee, I felt more drawn to Wilson Rexford, the other leading contender in the top three. Rexford was a thirty-seven-year-old congressman from Seattle and the youngest person running. In my opinion, he emanated a brand of passionate exuberance that I hadn't yet identified in any of the other candidates. Rexford was the son of a beloved governor who'd died at a young age, and he seemed to feel like he didn't have any time to lose. Indeed, he conducted himself like a man ready to pull out all the stops to make his mark, including summoning up blistering rhetoric his more staid competitors shied away from. I always enjoyed reading about him and suspected he was capable of big things.

Liza interrupted the campaign update by calling to vent about a coworker who noisily cracked his joints.

"No, you're not being unreasonable, it *is* gross," I commiserated. "Have you said anything to him?"

She hadn't.

"The worst is the thing he does with his neck—he warms up to it by doing all his knuckles in order, followed by his ankles. Then he rolls his head around and unleashes this disgusting finale of crackling pops."

"Okay, stop, you're making me nauseous."

"I know! It's sickening. I can hear these little gurgles, like his veins are being squelched or something, and—"

"Liza, I'm serious."

"Oh, right. Sorry."

It was too late—my limbs had gone weak.

For a health care analyst obsessed with obscure diseases, I had a remarkably low tolerance for any discussion of necks, wrists, or Achilles' heels. It was an odd phobic trifecta I tried to avoid divulging to anyone but close friends. My psych-major college roommate had said it was fairly normal for people to feel skittish about these body parts, because they were a human being's most vulnerable points, but I'd never met anyone who seemed as bothered by them as I was.

Once I'd been forced to think about any of the three in a concentrated way, I pretty much had to take a five-minute time-out to recover. And, if confronted by any visual depiction of harm to these areas, the damage could be much more severe. There were a remarkable number of movies that featured suicides via violence to the wrist area, and more than once I'd had to be helped out of theaters and given paper bags to breathe into.

In short, Liza should have known better.

"Can you move your arms yet?" she asked, guiltily.

"I'll be okay," I whispered bravely.

I was still feeling a bit limp ten minutes later when I had to brief RG on a conference call that afternoon with a group of hospital administrators.

He looked wan and stressed again, though he seemed to be absorbing all the background I was downloading. He fiddled with his watch as I wrapped up.

"Okay, sounds good. Are you setting up the call?" he asked.

"Yes, sir. And I'll just stay on and follow up afterwards."

He nodded, and fought back a yawn. I wondered how much sleep he'd gotten the night before. Perhaps he'd benefit from a little meditation.

RG checked his watch a final time and brightened suddenly.

"Jenny and the boys are stopping by in a few hours on their way back from the museum," he told me, for no apparent reason other than the fact that he seemed excited about it.

That was another thing I liked about RG—he had a very pure, boyish quality about him when he was happy, and his wife and children seemed to make him happier than anything else could. I had always found this refreshing, particularly in an environment where too many people seemed to treat their family members as necessary props to be occasionally trotted out, yet avoided the majority of the time.

"That's great, I'd love to see them. The boys must be getting big."

It felt odd talking to RG about anything besides work, especially in such an informal, friendly way.

Though I was only reciprocating his tone, I worried it was still somehow insubordinate.

But I *was* curious to see the boys. Jack and Jeffrey Gary had been born the same week I'd begun work in RG's D.C. office. Accordingly, there was a part of me that felt that my professional arc was somehow developmentally tied to their progress. We were certainly both associated with the same senator.

I stopped musing about how the twins and I had both been cutting our teeth in different ways over the past few months and tuned back in with the uncomfortable feeling RG had just said something I hadn't registered.

"Pardon me, sir?"

"I asked," he enunciated tersely, "what you're still doing here. Aren't we done?"

Okay, friendly time over.

I scurried back to my desk to begin setting up the conference call, but was delayed by the arrival of an e-mail from Aaron.

TO: SAMANTHA JOYCE [SRJOYCE@GARY.
SENATE.GOV]
From: Aaron Driver
[aidriver@bramen.senate.gov]
Subject: Best Date Ever
Text: Sammy, we still on for tonight? Don't
torture me, say yes. How about meeting at the
Oval Room (bar, not actual, unless you can

arrange entrance in which case let's go crazy)
around eight? I figured we could throw some
beer on some people before grabbing a bite to
eat somewhere. Let me know.

Once again, I hesitated for a moment. It would be so
easy to get out of this. But I knew I didn't want to.

TO: AARON DRIVER [AIDRIVER@BRAMEN.
SENATE.GOV]
From: Samantha Joyce [srjoyce@gary.senate.gov]
Subject: Re: Best Date Ever
Text: I'll see you there at eight. I'll be the lady
needing to be rescued from the angry mob.

I found it slightly more difficult than usual to concentrate on the work at hand, but managed to set up the
conference call without a hitch. A few hours later, I
was passing by RG's office on my way to the hall when
I heard the sound of babies giggling. Apparently Jenny
and the twins had arrived.

"Samantha, come in here and settle this, would you?"
RG called out to me.

Settle what? Did I have to take sides? Choose between my boss and his wife? This seemed like a lose/lose
situation.

"Absolutely, sir," I chimed.

When I walked in the office, Jack and Jeffrey were
crawling around on the couch.

"What do you need, sir?" I asked, professionally hiding the fear in my voice.

"Jenny and I have tie-breaker shots to make, but the twins just woke up. Do you mind watching them for just a second?"

Jenny was holding RG's Nerf basketball in her hand. The hoop hung on the private restroom door behind them. It wasn't normally there; RG only brought it out for special occasions.

Jenny looked reproachfully at RG. She was forty-one and softly pretty, and she carried her gently curvy five-four frame with a directness that hinted at her sharply active mind. I still didn't know her well, but I'd heard bits and pieces about her from other people in the office. Apparently, she and RG had been grad school sweethearts and as her husband had worked his way through Congress, she had worked part-time while desperately trying to conceive. It had taken over a decade and lots of fertility treatments, but she'd finally become pregnant. Since the twins' birth a year ago, she had devoted herself to motherhood, and beneath the fatigue, she glowed like she'd won the lottery. However, at this exact moment, she looked disapproving.

"Robert, you can't ask her to do that," she said.

RG turned back towards me.

"Look, I know it's illegal to ask you to do this in the capacity of being my employee, so will you do it just as a friend? Leave ten minutes early or something to even everything out."

"Of course. Shoot away," I answered.

Jack and Jeffrey were stereotypically adorable—all dimples and huge blue eyes. They peered out eagerly from the cave of couch pillows that had cushioned their nap, taking in as many of the sights and sounds as they could gather. I stared back at them, marveling anew at how completely identical they were. In fact, the only way to tell them apart was their different-colored overalls. Jack was in blue, Jeffrey green. Or was it the other way around?

The one wearing green began to cry. The Garys immediately looked over.

"Everything's okay," I said confidently as I began to bounce him gently on my knee.

"It's all right, Jeffrey," Jenny called soothingly, before returning to their game.

Jeffrey's identity confirmed, I clucked maternally at him as I bounced. Jack stopped his crawling to stare at me—his expression seemed to convey that he hadn't realized I could make such noises. I was accustomed to being underestimated.

Slowly, Jeffrey stopped crying. I varied my clucks with some oinks and moos, to keep Jack's interest. I was all of the sudden reminded of a loathsome article in one of those magazines that focused exclusively on how to keep a man interested in one's bikini-ready body. The article had suggested trying new things in bed, like role-playing. It read, "Even if you're not one for bestiality, pretending to be a barnyard animal can really turn a guy on."

Even if you're not one for bestiality? The phrasing suggested that being for or against bestiality was a casual decision that could go either way. I'd picked up the magazine in the interest of getting rock-hard buns in ten minutes or less and here I'd been confronted with an implicit acceptance of sex with animals. I'd been alarmed at the time and was distressed to recall it now, especially with two one-year-olds watching me intensely. I hoped the memory of that horrid article wasn't projecting out of me and smutting up their auras.

It didn't seem to be. They were both grinning at me happily. They really were amazing. As I gazed maternally back at them, I felt an unfamiliar warm feeling.

It took a moment to realize the source: Jeffrey was joyfully pissing through his diaper onto my suede skirt.

Staying calm was my second instinct. By the time I had determined that was the best course of action, I couldn't retract my first one, which was to shriek in damaged-suede alarm.

The Garys sprinted over and snatched the boys up, asking me worriedly what was wrong with them, what had happened?

I quickly assured them everything was fine, pointed out the urine development, and apologized for overreacting.

"Oh God, suede," Mrs. Gary said sympathetically.

"Is that bad?" RG asked.

I guessed fabric trivia wasn't included in the long list of things RG knew everything about. To be honest, it barely deserved to be on the list of things I knew vaguely about. When my mom had given me the suede skirt for my birthday—a surprisingly hip present from her—she'd mentioned that spilling liquid on it was a bad idea and had made me promise not to wear it in the rain. Her pointed tone suggested that she believed if she didn't say anything, I would rush to change into the skirt at the first sign of a thunderstorm. I had worn it for my date with Aaron because I thought it made me look more stylish than I actually was.

"I'm so sorry, Samantha. We'll pay for it to get dry-cleaned, of course," Jenny Gary was saying to me.

Was there a one-hour dry cleaner nearby that wouldn't mind me waiting on premises in my underwear? If there was, it probably wasn't an establishment that'd be a good idea to frequent.

"Oh no, don't worry about it. No problem at all," I insisted as I made my way towards the door.

I fended off a few more apologies and escaped to the restroom, where I transformed the medium-sized urine stain into a giant-sized water one, before returning to my desk in defeat.

I was supposed to meet Aaron in forty-five minutes, and I still had a long call list to return, plus a briefing on the National Institutes of Health's new study findings to write. On top of it all, I was sick of panicking, at least for the moment. There wasn't time to race home to change and my only other option was the gym clothes I kept optimistically and fruitlessly packed in a bag under my desk.

So, he was either going to go for me stained skirt and all, or it was his loss.

As I made my way to the Oval Room forty minutes later, I pondered whether my newfound calm was the symptom of a recently contracted mind-altering disease. Could I have somehow become infected with meningitis of the brain? Now that I thought about it, my neck was stiff and my head was throbbing a bit. If my fears were founded, there really wasn't much I could do beyond deciding to make one of my last nights alive a memorable one.

This decision led me to my shot of tequila while I waited for Aaron. Just a little waker-upper to get me going, followed immediately by a breath mint to protect my reputation.

Aaron arrived fifteen minutes late, but with a flower Pez dispenser.

Flower and candy in one. Strong move.

I pointed out my skirt stain immediately, to assure him that I was well aware of its presence. He laughed at the story, which made the whole peeing episode seem infinitely worthwhile.

Aaron steered me towards a little table against the wall and ordered some wine. As I sat across from him, I felt hot and tongue-tied as familiar waves of panic flooded my nervous system. Clearly, the newfound calm had fled. At least that meant the meningitis scare was over.

He asked me my impressions of D.C. and how I had enjoyed my time here. He asked about my family and life in Ohio. But he mainly talked, and I gladly listened.

He was fascinating to absorb, all dazzle and eloquence. He was twenty-nine and had grown up in the Florida panhandle, but both his parents were from Alabama, which helped explain the accent. He'd gone to Tulane Law School, but decided not to be a lawyer. If he were someone else, this would have struck me as a waste of time, but with him, it seemed a mark of character. He'd always wanted to be an English teacher, but had sort of fallen into speechwriting through a law review connection. He made his life sound full and inviting and ripe for sharing and he had an intense, burning way about him that made me want to intrigue him.

After our second glass of wine, he took my hand and I felt my heart drop a little nod of acknowledgment.

"How does Chinese sound to you?" he asked intimately.

I longed to answer him in fluent Mandarin, but could only manage an unimpressive nod.

He put his hand on the small of my back as we made our way out of the bar. I felt guided, if not quite safe. And I wanted more of him touching me.

Over mushu pork and kung pao chicken, we talked about our jobs. Not the boring details but the distinctive experiences that periodically reminded us that we were part of a unique world. I decided he needed to be more thoroughly vetted before I could tell him about the Alfred Jackman incident, but I did talk about some other senior citizen constituents who kept me motivated. Ones who hadn't been responsible for my being in possession of a felonious amount of marijuana less than a week ago.

I told him about Flora Henderson, a seventy-six-year-old widowed grandmother who'd called the office the other day to get advice on how to choose between two medications—she needed both but could only afford one and her doctors refused to advise her. She had voted for Senator Gary and thought he was "a very smart man who really cares about people," so she wondered if she could get his advice. I ended up talking to her for forty-five minutes and did my best to help her. After I got off the phone, Flora's voice and dilemma stayed in my head, and I ended up working even later than usual that night to research the bill that would hopefully bring her relief.

Aaron stared at me for a long, neck-rash-flaring moment when I finished my Flora story.

"You're different," he said simply.

Different *good* or different *euphemism for weirdo*? I couldn't tell from his distant, musing expression. What thought was he staring at from the inside of his head? In an instant, he was back, focusing all of his smoldering attention on my face.

"You really mean what you say. And you hold on to what's pure about this business. Most girls around here are jaded or defeated, but you've got a spark," he finished.

I felt flattered and embarrassed.

"Oh, just give me a little time," I said airily.

"No, I'm serious. You literally got pissed on today, and yet you exude this sense of not being able to wait to get back to work. That's different, believe me."

Had I really managed to intrigue him? Thank you, Flora.

I smiled demurely and sipped my wine.

"Well, I don't want to get you too worried that I'd rather be someplace else right now," I smiled at him. "Work's great, but this is almost as good."

Aaron laughed engagingly.

"I'm happy if I'm pulling a close second," he said. "I'll try my best to edge past by the end of the night."

I was just imagining that he wouldn't have too much trouble when I remembered that I'd planned on being sensible. I couldn't get carried away. There was still too much I didn't know about Aaron.

"So how is working for Bramen anyway?" I asked, hoping his answer would either reveal that Aaron was aware that his boss wasn't the best person, or that he'd been working for him for too short a time to really know.

"It's great," Aaron replied.

Hmm . . . not the reply I'd been hoping for.

"He has a reputation for being a bit . . . self-absorbed," I said carefully. "Do you find that to be the case?"

Aaron laughed.

"Do they let you in the Senate if you're not?" he asked with a grin.

Well, yes, actually. I was happy to submit evidence, but Aaron kept talking.

"Look, Bramen's an ambitious guy," he continued. "He does what it takes to get ahead. And I can relate to that. I mean, I'm not devoted to him or anything. I'd leave in a second for a better job. But it doesn't get much better than writing speeches for the future president."

I stared at him for a moment. Which part of his answer should I object to first? I'd intended to stay positive for the sake of the children we might still someday have, but I felt myself growing argumentative.

"Bramen doesn't necessarily have the nomination sealed up," I pointed out. "Any of the others could still get it."

Aaron shook his head.

"Spearam and Rexford might prove a little tough, but the other three aren't going anywhere," he said confidently.

The other three were Ellis Conrad, Hank Candle, and Max Wye. All of whom still had plenty of time to catch fire, in my opinion.

Conrad was a four-term senator from Michigan and the only African-American candidate for the presidency. I found him articulate and persuasive, and I noticed that his colleagues in the Senate always listened closely when he spoke.

Hank Candle was a less compelling orator but a congressman from Rhode Island of unassailable integrity, consistently leading the charge on ethics investigations and championing a legislative commitment to human rights. In photos, he looked to me like the head Keebler elf, though I doubted this was the image he was shooting for.

And Max Wye was the governor of Louisiana and the sole candidate from beyond the Beltway. Though some raved about Wye's intelligence and uncanny ability to connect with people, he had been unable to capture the attention of the national press corps thus far. As a result, I still didn't know all that much about him. But I wouldn't write any of them off this early in the process.

"You really don't think they have a chance?" I challenged.

Aaron shrugged.

"None of them will be able to raise the cash," he said simply.

He seemed so sure of himself and of the world of politics. Had Bramen's self-importance rubbed off on him? Or was he already conceited all on his own? Either way, I suddenly had an urge to rattle him.

"I don't like Bramen," I announced.

I normally didn't announce my dislike for people until I'd at least met them, and then usually not to anyone who worked directly for them, but I was being shocking.

"Yeah, I picked up on that," Aaron replied. "Why not?"

"I think he's arrogant and slimy and much more worried about his own political career than with really helping people."

So there. I hoped Aaron was appropriately shaken. He looked instead like he was trying not to smile.

"What? What's so funny?"

He put his hand over mine.

"You're so fiery and idealistic," he said. "And so new to D.C.—"

"Are you saying I'm naïve?" I interrupted him.

I hated it when people called me naïve.

"No, not naïve," Aaron replied. "Just . . . young. In a good way. And beautiful."

He stared into my eyes. To my annoyance, I momentarily forgot the biting retorts I'd been planning. Dammit! I tried hard to remember them.

"I understand if you don't like Bramen," he said softly. "But can we be adults and agree to disagree? Because I do really like you."

I kept my mouth shut for a few moments. Aaron still had his hand over mine and I could feel my neck rash burning underneath the tight, sleeveless turtleneck I'd worn for cover. Like it or not, I was attracted to him. Maybe I should drop the argument for the moment.

"Okay," I said finally. "To being adults." I raised my glass.

"As long as it's fun," Aaron clarified with a smile.

"As long as it's fun."

We drank some more wine and covered safer topics until we'd made it solidly back to flirtatious ground. Aaron really was very charming. Maybe I'd been too uptight about the whole Bramen thing. Did it really matter that much?

When the check arrived, we cracked open our cookies and read our fortunes aloud. Mine assured me good luck was coming my way. I criticized it as vague and generic, but secretly took it as an excellent sign for the prognosis of our relationship.

Aaron's fortune stated that he was extraordinarily good with his hands. Though I normally hated it when fortune cookies tended towards description rather than prediction, I didn't have as much of a problem with this one.

Aaron held up his hands for my perusal.

"What do you think? Instruments of genius?" he asked.

"Absolutely," I nodded supportively.

"Hmmm," he pondered. "Well, they haven't done anything spectacular yet, but maybe they're just waiting for the right muse," he said suggestively as he smoothed my hair away from my eyes, letting his hand linger on my cheek.

Maybe it was the three drinks I'd consumed, maybe it was the MSG, but I felt like I was falling in love. As we walked out of the restaurant and into the muggy night, he slid his arm around my shoulders.

"Have you ever been to the monuments at night?" he asked.

I hadn't. It hadn't ever occurred to me that it would be a fun or safe thing to do. But all of a sudden it seemed like a fantastic plan.

"Uh-uh. Is it my lucky night?" I asked, sincerely hoping it was.

"Well, there's actually a tower being built down the block from my apartment, and if you squint at it from my balcony, it looks a lot like the Washington Monument," he offered.

"I think I should be the judge of that," I said.

And we were off.

Back at the apartment Aaron shared with his friend Mike, who was thankfully out of town, we opened a bottle of champagne and surveyed the view from his balcony.

"To be honest, I'm getting more of an Eiffel Tower feel," I said with severely squinted eyes.

He answered me by saying something in French, which I couldn't understand but found extremely sexy.

I had a lot of trouble with languages. Even the foreign words that had been completely assimilated into the English language I felt insecure about. For example, I couldn't say "croissant" the way it was supposed to be said and tended to stumble and mumble over the word. Phrases like "joie de vivre" and "pied-à-terre" I avoided wholesale.

"Pardon?" I asked, using the flat American pronunciation.

"I suggested that if you close your eyes completely, you can call it whatever you like."

I obliged, and was coming up with something my champagne-saturated brain considered very witty to say, when I felt his warm lips on mine.

I'd found in my previous experience that it was relatively difficult to have a good first kiss. This was a really good first kiss.

All thoughts flew away, followed quickly by several articles of clothing.

We made our clawing way back inside to his couch, where I spilled the rest of the champagne on my skirt.

"I guess I just wasn't meant to wear this skirt today," I managed breathlessly as Aaron freed me from my bra.

"I couldn't agree more," he answered, his hand moving down my back. "Let's get you out of it right away."

Yes, let's.

## Play As You Go

I WOKE UP in his bed at 6:00 the next morning, my head stuffed with happy haze. He was breathing regularly beside me, and I stared at his tousled head and toned, bare torso as I reviewed the facts in my head.

Yes, I had slept with him, despite my long-standing policy of absolutely never sleeping with anyone on the first date. On the positive side, I had accurately determined that he didn't have any relationship-ending perversions right off the bat. If he had been into anything weird, immediate sex would have brought it out, which meant that in some ways it was a wise vetting tactic. And we'd used protection, of course.

On the negative side, RG had just warned me to be wary of all Bramen staffers. I was now lying naked in bed with one of them, which suggested I'd let my guard down just a tad.

Had I just slept with some sort of enemy? Had James Carville and Mary Matalin felt this way after their first night together? Even if they had, they'd clearly managed to make their relationship work. And Aaron and I had the advantage of working for people who were supposedly on the same side. I decided not to dwell any more on the negatives, because I wanted to stay in my pleasantly glowing good mood. And the night really had been fun.

It was also a stroke of luck (good old accurate fortune cookie) that I had woken up before him, because being awake first was the only foolproof way to ensure that he didn't observe me snoring indelicately. Plus, it granted me a little extra time to plot our morning-after inter-action, as much as I was able to, at least.

Oh Lord, what would happen when he woke up? Would it be weird and awkward in the champagne-less light of day? How much time did I have here? When did he get up for work? Did my breath smell horrible? Could I slip into the bathroom, rustle around for mouthwash, and slip back into bed to pose myself attractively without disturbing him?

I made it two-thirds of the way through my plan before stepping on something sharp on my way back to the bed. I yelped and brought my foot up to rest on my knee as I examined the damage—a mangled paper clip that had been embedded in the carpet had pierced the soft skin on the sole of my left foot.

I extracted the paper clip and was trying to inspect the wound when I lost my balance and tumbled into a small pile of laundry that was neither soft nor aromatic.

Perhaps the yelp had woken him up, perhaps the thud of my still-naked body hitting his floorboards had, but regardless, Aaron was soon standing over me with a sheet wrapped around his waist.

"Are you okay?" he asked.

He looked both puzzled and concerned.

"Totally fine," I said brightly. "Just attacked by a vicious paper clip," I explained as I pointed to the offending slip of metal.

I stifled a gasp as I realized my mother was a psychic genius. Granted, it hadn't been an oversized paper clip, but probably any danger to her only child's well-being loomed larger than life in a mother's subconscious. The important thing was, I had been mauled as predicted. I needed to call and inform her of her miraculous talent at the first opportunity.

"God, I'm sorry," Aaron said. "I should really clean up around here."

He helped me to my feet and as I stood close to him, I wondered if my freshened breath could make him forget that his first post-coital image of me had been my awkwardly splayed body entangled amongst his dirty laundry, and not the planned angelically-sleeping-with-sheet-snaked-seductively-around-me pose.

He was kissing me, so there was hope.

Could we have a leisurely morning and maybe even

commute to work together? I wondered, even though I knew I couldn't possibly wear my battered skirt to the office without attracting unwanted attention. Still, maybe we could lie in bed a while longer and he could play with my hair.

"I'm afraid I've really got to race to the office today," he said ruefully, politely nipping my fantasizing in the bud.

"Oh yeah, me, too," I said definitively.

He helped me gather my clothes and called a cab. He tried to give me money for the fare, but I refused to take it. After a sex-on-the-first-night date, I really wanted to avoid any behavior that made me feel even vaguely whorish. He didn't press me to accept it but he did say he'd call me later and gave me a lingering good-bye kiss.

I walked into my apartment fifteen minutes later, feeling a bit disheveled and hungover, to find Shackleton floating belly up in his fishbowl.

I instantly dissolved into tears. My poor brave fish had died alone, the one night in the course of his time with me that I hadn't slept nearby. Had my overnight absence been too much for him? Had I been unknowingly regenerating his will to live and thoughtlessly shirked my duty? The guilt came streaming in.

Sure, he had overcome tremendous odds and lived much longer than any of his predecessors, but he had still led a tragically short life, and I felt responsible. After leaving a mucous-y and somewhat accusatory message on Mr. Lee's store's answering machine, I went to Shackleton's bowl to fish him out with the net.

As soon as the plastic touched his body, he gave a little start, righted himself, and swam to the bottom of his bowl. I was so shocked I shrieked for the second time that morning. And I was not a shrieker. What the hell was going on?

Shackleton's gills were still mossy and his swimming seemed a bit labored, but he was undeniably alive. I'd never seen him do any sort of belly-up napping maneuver before, and though I was overjoyed at his second resurrection, I had the uncomfortable feeling he had just been trying out his death position in preparation for the inevitable. Like people who plan their funerals to the extent of testing out the feel of different coffins.

I scattered some fish flakes into his bowl and dried my tears. Shackleton would live to swim another day. I felt relieved, though also exhausted and slightly dizzy, thanks to the morning's mood roller-coaster ride.

As I got ready for work, I tried to recapture some of my original morning bliss by thinking about how well Aaron and I seemed to fit together in almost every way. We obviously had some issues to work through in terms of our professional allegiances, but everything else had been perfect.

His arms had been surprisingly strong—surprising only because his suit shirts hadn't hinted at what a fine physique they covered. Those arms would be perfect for loading our bags on top of our sleek yet sensible station wagon when we took our three children on vacation to the gorgeous coastal town where our comfortable but not ostentatious second home would be waiting for us to fill it with joyful laughter.

But I was really getting ahead of myself. There was a wedding to plan.

I felt a momentary pang of betrayal when I realized I was imagining saying "I do" to someone other than Steve Martin, whom I had consistently fantasized about marrying since I was twelve years old and watched *The Jerk*, *Roxanne*, and *The Three Amigos* in steady rotation. Even throughout my various relationships, no one had held a candle to him—he was a genius in my eyes. My ardor had only matured as I became aware of his other work. He'd been the main reason I began sporadically buying the *New Yorker*, and along with a CD of his banjo playing with the Earl Scruggs band, I also owned several copies of his books and the issue of *People* magazine that rightfully named him one of their fifty most beautiful.

Every once in a while, I had entertained the strong possibility that I might never meet Steve Martin, much less marry him. And even if I did manage to meet him, how could I make him fall for me? I had experienced a brief ray of hope when I'd read he'd dated Anne Heche for several years, for that signaled to me that he could be open to less conventionally "stable" women. Maybe I had a shot, after all.

But now I was twenty-six and I'd met Aaron. I refused to compare the two of them, but perhaps it was time to explore another reality. Was I ready?

I reached a satisfactory compromise by imagining a wedding with Aaron that Steve Martin could still be intimately involved in. Not as the groom, but as the minister! Brilliant! If I couldn't get married *to* Steve Martin, at least I could get married *by* him.

And who better to do the job? He was intelligent, funny, reverent when he needed to be—I just knew Aaron would love him. I wasn't sure if Steve Martin was an ordained minister, but these days anyone could use the Internet to get certified to marry people. Aaron and I were going to have the best wedding ever!

That romantic triangle worked out, I turned my attention to the dress, food, and flowers. I was just beginning to mull the pros and cons of arriving at the reception via hot air balloon or Segway scooter, and realizing that the answer was probably neither, when the phone rang. Was it Aaron checking to make sure I got home all right? I didn't remember giving him my home number, but I was definitely listed. Whenever I moved, I immediately made sure I was in the phone book, so that telemarketers could easily find me. I also signed up for lots of things on the Web and included my home number even when they didn't ask for it, towards that same end.

It was my mom.

"Sweetie, is there any chance you can come home for my birthday?" she asked.

My mom's birthday was in three weeks, which did fall during the trip to Ohio with RG, but we were scheduled to be elsewhere in the state that day.

"I really want to, Mom, but I've got to work. I'm sorry," I replied.

"Oh, okay," she said, unable to hide her disappointment. "We'll just celebrate later."

"Well, I'm sure Dad's planning something for you," I replied, in a bid to make her feel better. "He usually does."

"Yeah, usually," she sighed. "But things have been really hectic with the farm this month. And though you know how much I adore your dad, when he gets preoccupied, he couldn't organize a piss-up in a brewery."

It took me a moment to decipher my mom's remark. After applying what I'd learned of British slang in the years living with her, I determined that "piss-up in a brewery" referred to a drinking session in a bar, or other place in which beer was brewed and readily available for consumption. So she was suggesting that my dad could sometimes get too preoccupied to organize even the simplest and most obvious of events. Interesting. Occasionally, talking to my mom was like taking a linguistics class.

"Oh, hey, Mom!" I shouted, happy I could distract her with fantastic news.

"What, honey?" she asked, mildly alarmed at my volume.

"Remember the dream you had that I was injured by a paper clip?"

"You were mooshed, and it was a giant paper clip," she corrected.

I triumphantly regaled her with my real-life paper clip injury adventure, leaving out the crucial details of where I had been and whom I had just slept with.

"Have you made an appointment to get a tetanus shot?" she asked.

Huh?

As might be expected, considering my horror movie positions and squeamishness regarding all things wrist, neck, and ankle, I was not a fan of getting shots. Even the little finger pricks for blood samples really bummed me out. I was used to children being braver than I was at the doctor's office, and I felt no shame consoling myself postshot with the complimentary lollipops normally reserved for them as I trudged dramatically through the waiting room, casting woeful glances about me.

The idea of getting a shot that wasn't absolutely necessary to prevent my death by terrible disease was abhorrent to me. It was a big reason why I'd never been overseas—I wasn't sure I could handle all those inoculations.

"I'm pretty sure I'm up to date on tetanus," I said uncertainly.

"If you're not positive, you should go," she ordered.

Surely I didn't need a shot. I now felt very gloomy about the paper clip incident. I got off the phone and examined my wound. Was it my imagination, or was the skin around the edges of the wound turning slightly greenish? Good Lord, I could practically feel the gangrene spreading through my leg.

The receptionist at my doctor's office said I wasn't due for another shot for two more years, but then why was I starting to lose feeling in my foot?

She assured me I was fine. I hung up feeling anything but. If it wasn't tetanus, what terrible disease *had* I contracted? I slathered antibacterial cream on my foot, bandaged it up, and spent the rest of the morning routine on my spare pair of crutches, preparing for life without my left foot in the event I had treated it too late. I would be the brave opposite of Daniel Day-Lewis's Academy Award-winning character. Whereas he'd had use of his left foot and nothing else, I'd have command of everything except that one extremity. With a little bit of practice, I'd be ready for my role.

At the office hours later, I absentmindedly massaged my crutch-chafed underarms as I scanned the Hotline and The Note online. Clicking on a link to a *Washington Post* article, I vaguely wondered about the reporter I had assaulted at the Alfred Jackman hearing. Had his scratch healed sufficiently? Had there been an infection? Any scarring? I wondered as I read.

After bringing myself up to date on the latest New

Hampshire coffee klatches attended by Bramen, Spearam, Rexford, Conrad, Candle, and Wye (the list of nominees from the party sounded like a law firm with too many partners), I took a moment to pray that one of them would pull it together in time to win. Lord knew we needed a change in direction.

Though the country seemed eager to toss Pile out of office, Pile's party was hoping to avoid the same plight, and they were frantically strategizing to find ways to recast themselves in a more palatable light as the presidential campaign got under way. The unpopularity of the Pile regime limited the size of their party's field; there were only three declared candidates. Leading the charge thus far was Will Frand, the other senator from New Jersey besides Bramen and the current majority leader of the Senate who had served as a trusted partner of the administration. Frand seemed to understand that this association was something he'd have to overcome to win America's support.

Facing an even steeper challenge was Ken Pile, governor of Nebraska and the president's younger brother. Despite the unpopularity of his last name, he seemed hell bent on fulfilling what he firmly believed was his destiny, using whatever means necessary. Indeed, the Pile clan often gave the impression that they found democracy inconvenient. Corporate aristocracy fit their ambitions much more snugly, and they'd done their best to push the country in that direction during their suspiciously long reign.

The only one of the three candidates with any legitimate distance from the administration was Governor Cain Brancy of Georgia. He had butted heads with the Pile posse multiple times and was amassing a grateful following as a result. But should he be the one to take over, would he really provide the desperately needed change in course?

I found myself biting down hard on my lip as I finished the campaign summary. There was so much at stake in the next election and yet it was too far off to justify working myself into a high blood pressure frenzy. I quickly clicked over to the joke section of the Hotline in a bid to relieve my anxiety and prevent further injury.

An e-mail from Aaron that arrived shortly after wooed me further into a good mood.

To: SAMANTHA JOYCE
[SRJOYCE@GARY.SENATE.GOV]
From: Aaron Driver
[aidriver@bramen.senate.gov]
Subject: Re: Best Date Ever
Text: I don't think my subject heading for
yesterday's e-mail turned out to be hyperbole.
You're amazing. As I think about you today, give
me something to ponder: what's the "r" stand for?

p.s. I've taken four aspirin and still feel like I was
run over by a liquor truck

I took a moment to celebrate the fact that I had not
bedded one of those guys who didn't get in touch for
days post-sex. Aaron was attentive. I vowed to ensure
that Steve Martin truly understood the depths of
Aaron's sensitivity, so he could tailor his sermon to
appropriately honor this crucial trait. I felt it would
serve as one of the pillars of our marriage.

My reply:

To: AARON DRIVER
[AIDRIVER@BRAMEN.SENATE.GOV]
From: Samantha Joyce [srjoyce@gary.senate.gov]
Subject: Re: Best Date Ever
Text: The best thing for a hangover is a little
hair o' the dog. I've had two whiskey sours
already and everything's looking sunnier. Thanks
for a great time last night. The "r" stands for
"Riley," my middle name. And the "i"?

I felt pretty good about it. Friendly, but short, commu-
nicating that I had my own life and had no intentions
of being his clingy new girlfriend. And I kept the fact
that "Riley" was the name I had picked out for my first
daughter (obviously his first daughter, as well) to myself, which I felt was strategically a good move. Yet, lest

I seem too distant, I had ended with a question, encouraging ongoing contact.

I could probably teach a course in close readings and literary analysis of e-mail messages. I spent the rest of the morning plowing through my piles of work, and by lunch, I had his reply:

To: SAMANTHA JOYCE
[SRJOYCE@GARY.SENATE.GOV]
From: Aaron Driver
[aidriver@bramen.senate.gov]
Subject: To the Lovely Lady Riley
Text: I dig the name Riley. The "I" stands for "Ice-Fool," my rap name. I'm huge in France.

We went back and forth a few more times throughout the day, and I felt confident enough that I would see him again that night that I turned down an invitation to go to the new Will Smith movie, which was a fairly big deal for me. But relationships were all about sacrifices. I told Liza I'd go to the matinee with her the next day, provided Aaron and I didn't sleep too late.

So imagine my surprise when, at 7:15 that night as I was finishing up some talking points for RG's health care events the following week, I received this:

To: SAMANTHA JOYCE
[SRJOYCE@GARY.SENATE.GOV]

From: Aaron Driver
[aidriver@bramen.senate.gov]
Subject: Re: I think "smurf" should be an entry
in Webster's
Text: Got to head out to an event. My Bberry's
running low on fuel so I need to turn it off until
I can smurf me a charger. Hope you have a great
night. See you soon, Riley.

Come again? So we weren't going to be hanging out? I
moved from surprise to annoyance to insecurity in record
time. Incapable of successfully fighting the feeling that
I'd just been blown off, I called Liza for backup. She was
at the Irish Times again, hanging out with Ryan while
he worked. She urged me to meet her there, but I really
wasn't in the mood. She assured me that Aaron would
much prefer to hang out with me that night, but probably didn't want to come on too strong and scare me off.

It was true that I was a dynamic, independent woman
who didn't want to be pinned down, as far as Aaron
knew, so it seemed a plausible explanation. I felt better
until thirty seconds after I hung up with Liza, when I
started wondering if his "event" was a date with another
woman, which would be technically legal for him, psychologically disastrous for me.

The horror. I didn't want to peer into this dark possibility but I found that I couldn't look away. I needed to
know. I scanned the Capitol Hill newspaper *Roll Call*,

and all of my reception circuit e-mails, to see if there was an obvious event that Aaron would've needed to grace with his presence. Hmmm, it was tough to tell. There was a handgun control dinner and an education event along with a dozen other things Bramen could be attending. Why hadn't I procured a copy of his schedule? I needed to get on that pronto.

I was dialing Bramen's office number and warming up my fake Polish accent to try to wile some information out of the receptionist, when I was suddenly reminded of the Jason Shambers caller ID debacle. I put the phone back down and took a deep breath. I would not be a psycho. Those days were over, those mistakes had been made. I was ready for a mature, secure, grown-up approach to relationships.

Which, it turned out, sometimes involved staying home alone on a Friday night and pouring one's heart out to a telemarketer in Daytona, Florida.

I hoped Zelda might have some insight into Aaron's behavior, being from the same state as him. I hadn't had very good experiences with Florida up until now. I'd gotten severe food poisoning on my trip to Disney World, a third-degree burn on the beach over spring break, and a bad case of lice from a Palm Beach hat store. But I fervently believed that Aaron could change my luck.

In the past, Zelda had given me great advice on everything from my long-distance plan to where to place a tattoo if one wanted to experience the least amount of pain during the process (just out of curiosity), so I felt I could really depend on her. Maybe she could shed some light on how Florida men operated, as well.

Zelda said that Aaron sounded like trouble and warned me to keep my eyes open.

"What do you mean?" I asked. "Why would you say that?"

"Well, you said he works for this Bramen character, and that Bramen's a bad guy," Zelda answered. "So what does that make Aaron? I mean, would *you* ever work for an asshole if you didn't have to? No. Because you care too much. But there are plenty that don't, and believe me, I know the type. Either this guy Aaron's an asshole himself, or he doesn't care that he works for one, which is just as bad."

I winced at Zelda's words. In a few sentences, she'd managed to summarize all my doubts about dating Aaron. The very ones that I'd recently decided not to focus on.

"But I talked to Aaron about all that," I protested. "And yeah, I wish he worked for someone else, but it's not that big a deal. He doesn't love Bramen, but he admires what he's achieved. And being Bramen's speechwriter *is* a prestigious job. So, you know, I can be an adult about it."

And I could be. I'd always be idealistic, but I didn't have to be unrealistically demanding of people. That wasn't any fun.

"What does being an adult have to do with it?" Zelda replied. "If he's not the right guy for you, it doesn't matter how old you are. Just promise me you'll at least take things slow."

It was too late to go slow. I felt myself getting annoyed at Zelda.

"Yeah, fine, I gotta go," I said irritably.

I hung up the phone and got ready for bed, feeling frustrated. I was used to being told what to do in my job, but I wanted to be my own boss when it came to my romantic life. I shouldn't have called Zelda. I was strong enough to figure things out on my own.

Yet as I tried to fall asleep, I couldn't shake the feeling that something was going wrong. If not in my romantic life, then somewhere else.

It was times such as these that I always got very worried about alibis. What if my weird feeling was intuition (which was even more plausible now that I knew about my mother's psychic prowess), and I was sensing that right at that very moment, while I was home alone with no witnesses, someone was framing me for a terrible crime?

Being falsely arrested was one of my greatest fears. Every time I read about new DNA tests freeing an inmate who'd spent nineteen years in prison for a crime he didn't commit, a chill passed through my body. What a horrendous waste. And though the inmate had insisted he was innocent all along, the system had plunked him in a cell. If it could happen to him, I always shuddered, it could happen to me.

My only guard against such a terrifying twist of fate was the Polaroid camera I kept in the corner of my apartment. I had designated this spot the "photo alibi corner," and in addition to the camera, there was also a chair and a clock at head level on the wall behind it.

I headed to the corner to relieve my anxiety, grabbing the *Washington Post* along the way. Only after I had taken a picture of myself with one outstretched arm did I breathe a little easier. I waved the Polaroid around and watched my salvation slowly materialize.

It was a good one. The picture revealed that all the important
elements—the time on the clock carefully positioned over my right shoulder, the date on the newspaper I held at chest level—were clear and visible. Perfect.

All that was left was to send it to myself via certified mail. Then, no matter what someone tried to plant to the contrary, I would have incontrovertible proof that I had been in my apartment on August ninth at 10:22 PM, and not off committing the crime they claimed I had.

Cursing the post office for its lack of late-night service, I calmed myself with the knowledge that I'd done all I could for the time being. Feeling slightly safer, I slipped the Polaroid into a readied envelope and drifted off to sleep.

The next day, as we waited in line for movie tickets, Liza reminded me that she would always provide me with an alibi. It was too much effort to explain all the reasons that might not be possible or preferable, not least of which was the resultant guilt that would gnaw at my soul as I sat rotting in my cell, knowing that Liza was rotting elsewhere, imprisoned for her loyal perjury. But I just nodded and gratefully thanked her. It was the thought that counted.

Things were going well with Ryan, according to her. They'd seen each other four times in the last week, talked every night, and gotten into six fights. In her mind, this qualified as a wildly successful courtship. Fights were like foreplay to Liza, and therefore an essential part of a romantic relationship. If she couldn't incessantly argue with her boyfriend, it just wasn't going to work out.

I congratulated her on the good news, but wondered silently how long it would take before she caught him with someone else. A guy would have to be completely crazy to cheat on Liza, and she had a knack for handpicking the insane ones.

A high-octane action movie preview starring Borden Dent shrieked onto the screen as the lights went down. There were a few chuckles from the audience. Borden Dent was a multimillionaire Hollywood movie star who had recently declared his intentions of running for president. In *Entertainment Weekly*, he had denounced both major parties and explained that he was offering another way, without providing any details as to what that way entailed. The only clear thing one could take away from the interview was evidence that his ego could no longer be contained via regular stroking at premieres and awards ceremonies. Borden Dent needed more and was banking on America falling in love with him all over again in a different role. I shook my head and helped myself to the Milk Duds.

I kept my cell phone and BlackBerry on vibrate during the movie, just in case Aaron wanted to get in touch with me. Tragically, he didn't, but Will Smith managed to cheer me up, as always. Liza and I spent our post-movie coffee time debating whether or not he and Jada were happily married. I maintained that they absolutely were, but Liza had her doubts, which secretly only made me all the more positive my opinion was the correct one.

To feel better about ourselves, we followed it up with a less frivolous conversation about the current developments in the Middle East, but reconsidered the wisdom of this move when we both fell into depressed funks. That was the problem with the news. It was rarely good for one's psychological health.

I was walking up the stairs to my apartment building when Aaron finally BlackBerried. It read:

TO: SAMANTHA JOYCE
[SRJOYCE@GARY.SENATE.GOV]
From: Aaron Driver
[aidriver@bramen.senate.gov]

Subject: Oh wherefore art thou?

Text: Lovely Lady Riley, what are you up to? If you're around, call me on my cell.

I briefly wondered what it would be like to be the kind of person who could receive that message and then calmly continue up the stairs to her apartment and settle in before calling, but I stopped wondering to focus completely on plopping myself down right then and there while extracting my cell phone with one hand as I double-checked Aaron's number with my other.

"Hey there," I said when he answered the phone seven seconds later.

"Wow, that was fast," he replied.

I hadn't thought of that. Curses.

"I'm the quickest draw in D.C. I'm surprised you hadn't heard."

Aaron laughed, thank goodness.

"Hey, I'm not complaining. I like instant gratification as much as the next guy."

Was he calling me a slut? I hoped not. That could put a crimp in our marriage plans.

"Listen, I was wondering what you're up to tonight," he continued.

Yes, yes, yes, he wanted to hang out again.

I tried to sound casual.

"I hadn't decided on any one thing yet. Why? You throwing your hat in the ring?"

There. That was pretty good.

"I've got this bachelor party to go to in your neighborhood, but I kind of want to bail when it gets to the strip club portion of the night, so I was hoping I might come by for a visit."

Huh. Interesting dilemma. Did I agree and basically stay home all night waiting for him? That didn't feel right.

"Okay, great. I really don't know where I'll be, but give me a buzz and if I'm in the vicinity we can organize a rendezvous," I compromised.

"All right, then. Hope to see you later," he said.

As soon as we hung up, I panicked about the conversation. Had I been too distant? Had I been too pliable? Had I basically just given my permission for a booty call? Was that a bad thing?

The only thing I felt good about was the use of the word "rendezvous." Firstly, it was of French origin and I'd pronounced it flawlessly. But mainly I was pleased that it gave me a more clandestine image. I'd never fully grown out of my fourth-grade desire to be a spy. This had blossomed after the failure of Reebokville—Squirrel Resort and Spa, when I'd abandoned my architect designs and gone questing for another vocation.

A pigeon shat on my arm and brought me back into the present. Though I'd been told that getting crapped on in such a fashion was good luck, I'd assumed that this was the belief of people who weren't aware that bird excrement was chock-full of diseases and fungi. Burdened by such distressing information, I knew that my shoulder required a sponge bath with heavy disinfectant.

I stood and continued up to my apartment, where I found Shackleton lying listlessly on the pebbles at the bottom of his bowl. He was still alive, but he looked severely unwell. I found his death pose practicing incredibly unsettling but I felt helpless to respond in any proactive way. It was past six o'clock, which meant Mr. Lee had closed up shop for the night. Besides, as far as Mr. Lee knew, there was no Shackleton anymore, due to my dramatic answering machine message announcement of his demise. He had probably already raised the price on his remaining Japanese fighting fish in anticipation of my inevitable visit. Shackleton needed to live. We had to beat the system.

"Don't let the bastards get you down," I urged supportively.

The glazed look he gave me in response seemed to indicate that he already had.

After sterilizing my shoulder, I meant to take a shower, get dudded up, and head out on the town, but it was nine o'clock before I knew it and I had done none of those things. Maybe the night was meant to be one of healthy self-improvement. I checked the list of things I'd targeted to learn over the summer. It seemed a bit hot for knitting or learning Morse code. As I continued going down the list, arbitrarily eliminating each option, it occurred to me that I was probably irritable from low blood sugar. Luckily, learning to cook was on the list, second from bottom.

My refrigerator seemed to have other plans. It contained a bottle of soy sauce, a liter of root beer, and a jar of pickles. The freezer coughed up a container of Cool Whip and a bottle of vodka.

As I was eating a spoonful of Cool Whip to get a little sugar in me, I started reading the back of the carton. It urged me to call Cool Whip's 1-800 number with any questions and concerns. That sounded good to me.

After listening to some soothing hold music, a woman named Beverly came on the line and asked how she could be of service.

"Nice to meet you, Beverly. I'm Samantha. And I've just been enjoying some of your Cool Whip product," I started.

"Cool Whip is a wonderful product, we're so pleased you've been enjoying it," she rearranged my words in response. "Are you aware of its versatility?" she continued. "It can be used in several very tasty recipes."

"Really? At the moment I'm working with pickles and soy sauce. Is there any potential there?" I asked. I decided to leave out the vodka and root beer. I didn't want to make anything too easy.

Beverly seemed stumped.

"Are you sure you don't have any Jell-O or something?" she asked desperately, after several moments of silence.

Actually, I think I did remember buying some Jell-O last winter during my tuberculosis fright. It had turned out to be a cold and I hadn't had to restrict myself to hospital-type food after all. I checked my cupboard. Sure enough, a little cardboard package of raspberry Jell-O lay covered in dust.

"Got it," I proclaimed triumphantly. "Raspberry flavored."

"Great," Beverly said, sounding relieved.

After she explained how I could make a mouthwatering parfait enhanced with layers of Cool Whip, she asked me how many people I needed to serve. This led to a long discussion about Aaron and my fledgling relationship and the call I had received that afternoon about the bachelor party. I hastily explained that he was a gentleman, so if he did drop by, it would just be for a nice visit to see how I was doing. It wouldn't be like a booty call at all, because neither of us was that kind of person. Perhaps I could offer him a Cool Whip treat as he proved what a loving boyfriend he could be, taking time out from his night with the guys to pay attention to me.

Beverly clucked skeptically.

"I bet you a container of Cool Whip Lite he shows up messy drunk sometime after midnight," she said in a wise and foreboding tone. "If I'm right, you've got to buy the carton; if I'm wrong, I'll send you a complimentary one."

Did she and Zelda know each other? It was unlikely, but they were both so down on Aaron. They weren't even giving him a chance!

"You're on," I said, agreeing to call back the next day to inform her of how she'd completely lost the bet.

"We'll see," she said calmly. "Enjoy the parfait!"

But I didn't feel like cooking anymore when I got off the phone with Beverly. I ate some pickles and retreated to my bed with the Cool Whip and a spoon.

It was 1:15 in the morning and I was just finishing watching *Harold and Maude*, when Aaron BlackBerried me that he was waiting on my doorstep.

Two minutes later he was sprawled on his back on my couch, one stinking drunk leg dangling over the edge of it as he rambled incoherently about his brilliant idea for a drive-through donut shop.

I felt a stomachache coming on. Stupid know-it-all Beverly. The Cool Whip turned over smugly in my belly.

But at least he'd shown up at all, I argued with myself.

"How was the bachelor party?" I tried, as I arranged myself in a chair across from him.

He looked confused, then blinked for a long moment.

"Oh, ish good. Ish good. Shud proby go back soon," he slurred.

Uh-huh.

He was really wasted. I tried to sort out how I felt. I was certainly shocked, despite the Cool Whip lady's warning. I was also bummed he wasn't in kissable form, because even with a certain sweatiness and sodden appearance, he was still looking good. I felt torn—both happy that the impulse to see me had penetrated his drunken haze and bothered that he hadn't felt the need to keep it together a little more in my presence. Maybe he'd feel bad tomorrow?

"Betsu I ken say letter 'A' longer 'n you. Come on, les see . . . Aaaaaaaaaaaaaaaaaaaaaaaaaaaaaaaaaaaaaaaaaaaaa aaaaaaaaaaaaaaaaaaaaaaaaaaaaaaaaaaa . . ."

He was definitely going to feel bad tomorrow.

"Hey, yer not doin' it!" he said, in a profoundly injured tone.

"Yeah, I don't really feel like it," I answered.

"Oh."

He looked a little offended.

"I jes wanned come see ya, cuz yer my girl," he explained.

Actually, that was kind of sweet.

He was on his feet again, if just barely.

"Gotta head back t'party," he said as he lurched towards the door.

As I watched him negotiate the stairs back down to the street, he turned and looked up at me with a messy smile.

"I think I lurvya," he said before turning back around.

I deciphered his declaration just as my drunken David Cassidy unsteadily rounded the corner and disappeared off towards some seedy strip club.

He thought he loved me?! This was hot breaking news. Sure, he was hammered out of his gourd, but what about "in vino veritas," the one Latin phrase I was familiar with? Thank God he'd gotten drunk! It could have taken months for him to reveal his true feelings—I felt a sudden rush of warmth towards whoever had decided to get married and invite Aaron to his bachelor party. I'd thank them at the wedding. This was a brilliant development!

I checked the clock. Two AM on a Sunday morning. I consulted my calendar and noticed with a little gasp that it was almost the twenty-ninth anniversary of the epic series finale of *The Partridge Family*. This couldn't be a coincidence; it had to be some sort of validation that true love had indeed struck. It was too late to call anyone with the good news so I celebrated solo by making vodka Jell-O shots, and then drifted off into a tipsy dream that Aaron and I were romping joyfully through a Cool Whip wonderland.

## Down Low, Too Slow

He called me at three PM the next day.

"I heard my evil doppelganger got loaded and possibly harassed you last night. Let me know if he crossed a line—I will track him down and kick his ass," he said when I answered the phone.

"Oh, I'm sure his hangover is doing that already," I replied. "But thanks for the offer—it was actually kind of exciting to get a late-night drunken visit. He had some entrepreneurial plans involving being able to purchase fresh donuts without leaving one's car."

"Uh-huh, uh-huh. Yeah, I've heard that guy is really going places."

"You know, Krispy Kreme already has that in some areas," I added.

"I didn't know that. I don't think he was aware of that, either. That's fascinating stuff," he said.

I could tell Aaron was embarrassed, which I found

reassuring. His behavior hadn't been that atrocious, and it *had* produced an intoxicated declaration of "lurv," so I was willing to let it slide.

He asked what my week looked like and we made tentative plans to get together for lunch on Tuesday and for something more on Thursday evening, provided our work schedules allowed. RG's committee was scheduled to vote on his prescription drug proposal on Wednesday, so I didn't feel confident that I'd have a social life option for most of the week, but hopefully I'd have something to celebrate by the end of it.

I spent the rest of Sunday catching up on research and thumbing through an enormous book of prescription drug descriptions and prices. I tried to commit as many of the important medications as I could to memory, but didn't feel I'd been overly successful at the task. It left me with the same defeated, overwhelmed feeling I'd always gotten when I'd tried to read the dictionary. I really needed my learning to be in some sort of narrative format. Why couldn't Robert Ludlum write a prescription drug thriller? Perhaps it was sort of an oxymoronic request, but it would really help me out.

Zelda called as I was getting ready for bed to apologize for being so judgmental. She said that she only wanted what was best for me, but was worried that she'd overstepped her bounds. I graciously told her not to worry about it and proposed that we get back to normal. I certainly wasn't going to break up with Aaron per her advice, but I didn't want to break up with her, either. She was my favorite telemarketer. And a good friend.

Monday arrived along with an e-mail from Natalie containing a draft of the bill she felt Bramen could "sell." According to her, he had signed off on it and they were eager to begin circulating the "new, more pragmatic approach." This revealed itself to be the watered-down, sell-out version I had feared. It preemptively backed off a lot of the more progressive measures in anticipation of opposition. Under their revision, the bill would actually *raise* prescription drug premiums by as much as twenty-five percent for traditional Medicare recipients, and it wouldn't even address the issue of importing lower cost prescription drugs from Canada and Europe. This was unacceptable. The bill was supposed to be about changing the system for the better, not compromising to the point of irrelevance.

My pulse was racing by the time I finished reading her revisions. Though my initial plan had been to get RG's permission before shooting down Natalie's changes, I now felt that they required an immediate response and RG was tied up in meetings until late afternoon. I couldn't go to Joe Noon, RG's chief of staff, as he was still on his extended business trip to Russia. So I'd just have to take matters into my own hands.

I stomped furiously towards the Hart Building, glowering at Ralph as I passed. He didn't seem to notice my intimidating stare, which only made me more incensed. By the time I made it out the door, I felt I had some pretty good lines practiced in my head ("cowardly cop-out" and "pragmatic pussyfooting" were two I kept returning to, as I had a soft spot for alliteration), and I was ready to face Natalie's polished armor.

Which was lucky, because as soon as I reached the street I noticed her walking with an older man I didn't recognize. I hadn't planned to launch into my diatribe in front of a third party, but I felt compelled to confront Natalie as soon as we made eye contact.

"Oh, hello," she said unenthusiastically when she saw me.

She turned to the man beside her.

"Daddy, this is someone I work with. Um . . ."

She didn't remember my name, which she didn't seem at all embarrassed about.

"I'm Samantha," I offered my hand to Natalie's father.

"Dr. Reynolds," he responded.

His hand was just as manicured as his daughter's.

"Samantha works with Robert Gary," Natalie continued. "The junior senator from Ohio. Senator Bramen's considering helping him out with the prescription drug benefit package he's been struggling to put together."

Ugh. She was the worst.

"Yes, I read through the revisions you sent, and I have to say, it feels like most of the substantive stuff has been gutted. I really don't think Senator Gary's going to go for it," I said in what I felt was an impressively even tone.

"Really?" Natalie replied. "I thought Gary wanted to get this bill passed. The only way to do that is to be a little less brazen and a bit more practical."

"I think Senator Gary agrees with me that pragmatic pussyfooting does more harm than good to the overall effort," I shot back triumphantly.

Natalie merely blinked at the alliterative assault.

"I'm sorry, Daddy, I didn't expect to get into a side-walk debate during your visit," she said in a gratingly syrupy way to her father. "Samantha, could we discuss this a little later?"

"Don't postpone anything on my account," her father insisted. "I've got to check in with the office anyway," he said, as he took out his cell phone and moved away.

Natalie's dad looked as though he enjoyed a good dispute. Natalie, on the other hand, appeared chagrined to have to address my concerns right then and there. She sighed deeply and fixed me with her mechanical gaze.

"Samantha, I know you don't believe me, but the bill you drafted has no chance of getting passed. President Pile would never sign it—his team would defeat it before it even got to his desk. This new version makes it possible for more bipartisan support, and therefore more difficult for Pile to dismiss. We've got to take a step-by-step approach to this issue, and I promise you it's in your best interest to go along with our line of attack. When Bramen is elected president next fall, you have my word he will make it a priority to enact more comprehensive legislation. Until then, we need to do our best to give Americans a little taste of what's to come."

She stared patiently at me for a moment, like she was waiting for my brain to catch up with hers. I understood her perfectly. She was dangling the prize of distant future help to induce us to drink Bramen's Kool-Aid and happily sign on to his game.

"Now you said you didn't think Gary would go for our version, which suggests you don't know for sure," she continued. "There's a chance he sees the bigger picture more clearly than you do. Why don't you check in with him and we'll talk later today."

She looked very martyrlike as she finished her monologue; as though it had really been a strain to walk me through everything but she didn't mind, because she was doing it for the greater good of Bramen's candidacy. I stared defiantly back at her.

"I'll do that, but I have *no doubt* that Senator Gary is looking at the bigger picture. I can guarantee you that he's considerably more concerned with providing relief for stressed seniors than with how well Bramen's going to do in the Iowa caucuses," I said.

Take that, you cynical witch.

She smiled patronizingly at me.

"Well, perhaps Gary will be able to put aside any personal jealousy to allow us all to move forward on this."

Oh, that was too much. RG was not jealous of Bramen. Was he? Regardless, he shouldn't be. And the suggestion that he was by a Bramen staffer was offensive.

"What do you think Senator Gary might be jealous of?" I heard myself saying. "Bramen's shameless pandering? Or maybe his kickbacks from the health insurance industry? Believe me, I'm thrilled that Senator Gary runs a different kind of operation. And I hope we never, ever become like you."

I hadn't meant to take it that far; it was almost as if some other being composed solely of my defiance and indignation had taken control of my voice.

Natalie's lip curled poisonously.

"Oh, I don't think there's any danger of that," she hissed condescendingly.

I sneezed powerfully and unexpectedly—I didn't even have time to direct it into my hand. Where had that come from? Was my system just now picking up on the fact that I was allergic to Natalie?

She recoiled and turned to rejoin her father, her high heels clicking a rhythmic retreat.

I recovered from my sneeze and took stock of my recent accomplishments.

Eschewed self-control and diplomacy for knee-jerk confrontation.

Check.

Alienated person boss identified as key ally.

Check.

Resorted to ambush, juvenile name-calling, and sneeze attack in lieu of reasoned, mature conversation.

Check, check, check, and check.

Huh. Not the most glowing inventory. But though my style had left something to be desired, I felt I'd been substantively in the right. I'd stood up for the integrity of RG's bill. And for him. That had to count for something.

"Does he have five minutes?" I asked Janet when I returned to the office.

We had a briefing scheduled for that afternoon, but I felt he should know sooner about my showdown with Natalie. Janet looked doubtful.

"I'll call you if he does," she said pessimistically.

I returned to my desk to tackle the itinerary for RG's Cleveland open meeting, but was quickly sidetracked by an e-mail from Aaron.

TO: SAMANTHA JOYCE
[SRJOYCE@GARY.SENATE.GOV]
From: Aaron Driver
[aidriver@bramen.senate.gov]
Subject: roadrunner or wile e coyote
Text: which do you identify with? need to ensure we're compatible.

Under other circumstances, his e-mail could have been well received, but as things stood, it only served to remind me that Aaron worked with the horrid Natalie as part of a team that was trying to corrupt our bill. I drafted an angry response informing him that we couldn't see each other anymore as long as he insisted on working for such terrible people and was about to send it when his "can we be adults" plea rang in my head. I hesitated. Was I overreacting? Was it childish to blame him for Natalie's crimes? I deleted the message and tried a milder response.

> To: AARON DRIVER
> [AIDRIVER@BRAMEN.SENATE.GOV]
> From: Samantha Joyce [srjoyce@gary.senate.gov]
> Subject: Re: roadrunner or wile e coyote
> Text: wile e. all the way. i find the roadrunner
> annoying. wish he'd get eaten. in case you didn't
> know, your coworker natalie is trying to mess
> with our bill and replace it with some typical
> bullshit. you work with awful people. i think she
> is actually an evil fembot and not human at all.
> can you confirm or deny?

I sent it off and turned to my other work. I reserved an auditorium for RG's late-August meeting in Cleveland, and then alerted the local unions that it would be taking place. They always ensured a sizable turnout. I had just finished a conversation with a cantankerous fire chief who wanted to make sure that refreshments would be served at the meeting when my BlackBerry buzzed Aaron's response.

To: SAMANTHA JOYCE
[SRJOYCE@GARY.SENATE.GOV]
From: Aaron Driver
[aidriver@bramen.senate.gov]
Subject: Re: roadrunner or wile e coyote
Text: interesting. a roadrunnercidal streak. very
sexy. i'm really sorry about the bill hijinks. rest
assured that i have nothing to do with it. as for
nat, jury still out. have caught her plugging
herself into the wall to recharge and drinking
diet wd-40, if that's a clue.

Hmm. That was funny and made me feel better, but I still wasn't positive that I could let Aaron completely off the hook. Just then, Janet buzzed my line.

"RG can see you now, but he's got to leave in fifteen minutes, understand?"

I assured her that I did. I entered RG's office to find him highlighting a news article. I waited a moment for him to finish.

"I have to leave soon, you know," he said without looking up.

"Yes, sir, I didn't want to interrupt," I replied.

"Go ahead, Samantha. If it gets too taxing for my brain to highlight a piece of paper and listen to you at the same time, I'll be sure to let you know."

I wished he were in a slightly better mood to receive the news I had for him. Oh, well.

"You probably haven't had a chance to read the revised copy of the bill Bramen's office sent over. I forwarded it to you this morning, but I know you've been too busy to—"

"I read it," RG cut me off.

Really? When had he managed that? Janet had insisted one time that he was a speed-reader, but I had never believed in the existence of speed-readers. Maybe it was time to convert.

"Okay, well, then you know the problem already. They basically gutted it. Bramen's domestic policy person seems to think these revisions improve the bill's chances, but I of course told her that this goes completely against—"

"I'm going to agree to it."

What?

"Excuse me, sir?"

"This version does have a better shot at getting passed," he said matter-of-factly.

Okay, he clearly had not sped-read it thoroughly. He'd probably inadvertently skipped over the part where they'd upheld the ban on importing drugs from Canada and effectively raised the premiums on the cost of drugs for the sickest and oldest Americans. I knew speed-reading wasn't all it was cracked up to be.

"I realize they raised the premiums and abandoned the import proposals, but it's still a big step in the right direction."

Wait a minute, he *had* read those parts?

"But, sir, isn't it worth it to fight for the better bill?" I protested in alarm.

RG put down his highlighter. Uh-oh, I knew I was out of line. What the hell had I been thinking, questioning RG's judgment? Even if I disagreed with him, vocally challenging him was idiotic. I braced myself for the inevitable dressing down.

"I know you're disappointed, Samantha, but this won't be the end of it. We'll get this passed and we'll try for more later," he answered very calmly and not unkindly.

I didn't know what to say. I was relieved that RG hadn't lashed out at my insubordination, but I felt like my ideological rug had been pulled out from under me. RG had told me to be on my guard; to protect the bill against this sort of thing. And now he was just caving?

"I knew that working with Bramen would result in some deal-with-the-devil fallout," he continued. "He has his own petty agendas, and he's using this bill as political leverage for the primaries. But to be honest, I expected his revisions to be much worse. His team has taken some good measures out of the bill, but they haven't added as much crap as I thought they would. So we're going to take the compromise for the sake of making progress, imperfect though it is. It's still going to help a lot of people. Okay?"

"Okay," I managed in a half whisper as I stared dully at my hands.

"I hope you're not too disillusioned to keep working for me," RG said, only half-jokingly.

I hoped so, too. I glanced up to find him looking searchingly at me.

"Of course not, sir. I'm just, uh, surprised," I stammered. "So, um, should I tell Natalie that you've signed off?" I asked, feeling the lump of resistance in my throat swell dangerously large. Perhaps I wouldn't even be physically able to do such a thing.

"I'll just call John directly," RG answered.

At least that was nice of him. I left RG's office and slunk back to my desk burdened by the weight of this unwelcome development. I surfed some news sites to try to get my head back in order. A headline about a new movie called *Rise of the Machines* seemed to have particular resonance as I contemplated the painful victory of the Bramen operation. Natalie had been right after all. Could it be true that her slick calculations made her a more effective domestic policy analyst? Was I destined for a career filled with disappointment and disillusion? I'd never thought RG would back down from a fight for a better way, never thought he'd opt for the softer, more mainstream route without stronger reservations. Had I just been naïve? What was going on?

The movie review suggested that human beings could still triumph in the end, so maybe there was hope. It was actually a glowing article filled with praise for the actor and director's "groundbreaking work," which wasn't surprising given that the "news" site on which it was featured was owned by the same parent company as the movie studio. This disguised advertising tactic, though increasingly popular, never failed to rattle me. And it gave me a creepy feeling when, on this same site, I read a very positive article about a particular politician. Was the politician also owned by the parent company? One never knew.

Ugh, I felt like I needed to take a shower to wash the day's scum off me.

That feeling stayed with me the rest of the week, despite multiple scrubbings. I felt disoriented and unsure of myself in a new, uncomfortable way. And whenever I thought about RG's compromise, I felt disillusioned all over again.

RG's committee voted to pass the revised prescription drug benefit bill on to the consideration of the full Senate. I noted the triumph sullenly, and didn't feel any urge to participate in the wild victory celebration I had previously penciled in for that night in the event things went our way. The glittery top hat bought in anticipation stayed firmly in the bottom drawer of my desk and the Mardi Gras beads remained coldly undistributed. People seemed to sense I was out of sorts and avoided interaction, which only embittered me further.

Aaron was the only person who attempted to cheer me up, and he was roundly punished for his bravery. I canceled our date, refused to see him, and ignored his calls and e-mails for several days. I didn't care if I was being immature. I just couldn't forgive him for working with Natalie and Bramen.

To his credit, he was persistent. He continued to leave voicemails and started e-mailing me every hour on the hour. And all of his messages were incredibly sweet and funny. I was impressed, despite myself.

On Wednesday, he vowed to eat nothing but fortune cookies until I agreed to see him again. His e-mails began to include short updates on the toll this was taking on his body, as well as his latest fortunes and how he was interpreting them as hopeful signs that he'd soon get to be with me again. His latest had been, "You will conquer obstacles to achieve success." He assured me that he wasn't even adding the "in bed" tag line that people usually tacked on to the end of their fortunes to make them more exciting. He wanted me to know that he was a gentleman. A slowly starving gentleman.

I finally relented and agreed to see him Friday evening. And as soon as I was with him again, I felt better. He was charming and entertaining and very attentive. By the end of dinner, I had consented to temporarily forgive him for his association with Bramen as long as he agreed that Bramen was a force for evil.

"But it was Gary who really disappointed you," Aaron pointed out.

I shot him a dark look.

"Never mind. Okay, Bramen is Satan. Absolutely. Shall we drink to it?" Aaron said quickly, holding up his glass with an endearing grin.

I ended up spending the weekend with him.


The following week, the Senate adjourned for its August recess. Though that meant they weren't in session any longer and therefore didn't need to stick around D.C. to be present for votes, lots of senators stayed for a while anyway in order to work in a more focused way on particular proj-ects. Others took family vacations or returned to their home states to campaign and reconnect with constituents. RG tried to do it all. He stuck around for a few days, then took a vacation with Jenny and the boys, and then spent the remaining time canvassing Ohio.

I woke up on RG's last day in the office before his vacation with a sense of relief. Ever since his "betrayal," I had maintained a respectful but mopey distance from him (which seemed to go completely unnoticed), and my melodramatic commitment to shunning contact was beginning to strain. His absence promised to make it much easier.

I had also managed to deal with Natalie entirely via electronic communication—the coward's medium. We were on civil typing terms, and though I knew I'd have to face her sooner or later, I was happy to postpone as long as e-mail would enable me to.

Aaron and I had followed up our weekend reunion with sleepovers every night. He was in my bed now, and I lay still for a while, listening to his alarmingly slow breathing. My doctor had told me that, like an unhurried pulse, this was a sign of a very healthy person. She had refrained from commenting on the fact that it was such a foreign sound to me that I had called her up in a frenzied panic. I appreciated her restraint and felt proud that I was the paramour of such an in-shape stud. She agreed I was to be congratulated.

My own pulse was racing as I attempted to keep my eyes closed and enjoy the peaceful moments before the alarm clock forced the start of the day. Lately, there'd been additional incentive to delay the opening of my eyes—Shackleton had persisted in his death pose practicing and I was convinced I would soon be witness to the real deal.

As usual, the moment I consciously decided to keep my eyes shut, it required a Herculean effort to do so. I irrationally feared that the degree of difficulty of keeping them closed was directly proportional to the odds that Shackleton had at last succumbed, so I struggled valiantly, my face fiercely screwed into a twisted and determined mask. I heard Aaron chuckle softly.

"It's okay, he's still alive," he said as he kissed the end of my scrunched-up nose.

Oh. I relaxed my face and opened my eyes slowly. Aaron was already getting dressed and Shackleton was indeed still among the living, but more specifically among the mossy-gilled, labored swimming living, which was a distinct and doomed subset.

"I gotta run, baby," Aaron said as he moved remarkably lithely towards the door (he *was* in good shape!). "I'll call you later."

He smiled at me and closed the door. I sighed happily to myself, enjoying this new routine. Before I finished dressing, Aaron BlackBerried to remind me that it was the first day of the Metro strike. I had forgotten all about it and consequently hadn't worked out a backup commute plan. He must have anticipated this, because he included the number of a cab company to call, warning that they'd be in high demand that morning. I felt settled and taken care of until I remembered that I didn't have any cash.

I went hopefully to the laundry quarter drawer only to find a single dime staring up at me, lonesome in its out-of-place inadequacy. Wow, I really had *no* money. Though I was fairly messy in some ways, I was not one of those people who'd stumble across forgotten cash in pant or jacket pockets, so I didn't even attempt to forage for surprise stashes. The only bills I ever discovered unexpectedly were misplaced, unpaid ones.

I did some quick calculations. I had twenty minutes to get into the office. That wasn't enough time to walk. That wasn't even enough time to run. I didn't own a scooter or a bike or anything like that. Except, wait a minute, yes I did. I owned Rollerblades.

Fifteen minutes later, I was decked out in kneepads, elbow pads, hand guards, and a helmet as I haltingly weaved my way down Massa-chusetts Ave., my briefcase strapped over my shoulders like a backpack. It was already a muggy ninety-nine degrees and I was quickly drenched in sweat. I concentrated intensely, because I was unskilled to the point that any tiny crack could send me flying. I tried to ignore the yells as I wobbled past a construction site. They didn't sound like the normal catcalls; these sounded more mocking. I had neither the time nor balance to retaliate and so I pressed onward.

I was rolling unsteadily past the Russell Building driveway when a squirrel raced across my path, sprinting for dear life towards a nearby tree. I swerved to avoid it, righting myself just in time to get a close-up of a bike courier taking me out. I went down hard on my side, one of the only places not protected by padding. My hand guards scraped along the concrete as I rolled violently to a crumpled stop in the middle of a sticky puddle formed by a dropped and melting ice-cream cone. Was I dead? I looked up at the little crowd of people who'd quickly assembled. Did I wish I was?

The bike courier had stopped long enough to un-twist his wheel before sprinting off. I had just been one more obstacle to his frenetic efficiency.

"Are you okay?" a woman asked as she checked her pager.

"Yeah, thanks, I think so."

She nodded without looking up and moved off. Just as I felt the ice-cream puddle ooze through the fabric of my shirt, I thought I caught a glimpse of a familiar face on the edge of the now-thinning throng of specta-tors. Was that Clark Kent? It was hard to tell with my hair still flung across my eyes. I could sense that most of the crowd seemed a little disappointed it hadn't been a more serious accident—something they could authoritatively report on around the water cooler. But the man who looked like the Clark Kent reporter I'd attacked at the hearing seemed more bewildered and concerned. Oh God, if that really was him, then he must consider me one of the clumsiest people on the planet. And at this point, a genuine threat to public safety. At any rate, he was now moving off along with the others.

I winced as I gathered myself together. After cleaning up as best I could, I changed into my work shoes and limped inside. Ralph looked alarmed at my roughed-up appearance.

"Were you mugged?" he asked, his hand moving to his holster as he scanned the horizon for perps.

Was he really concerned or just eager for some action?

I was too defeated to investigate, so I just shook my head and trudged through the checkpoint.

"Do you know you look like you were?" Ralph called after me.

I ignored him. When I got to my desk, Mark Herbert was waiting for me with a bottle of aspirin.

"I, uh, saw you outside, when you . . ." he made a tumbling movement with his arms and then slapped his hands together to simulate a spectacular crash. ". . . And, uh, I thought you might need some of this." He wiggled the aspirin bottle and looked down at the floor. "Are you okay?"

"Thanks, Mark, that's really nice. I'm fine."

"Oh good. Well, let me know if I can get you some ice or something," he said shyly as he walked off.

Down the hall, I saw Mona quickly disappear behind her desk in a post-eavesdrop retreat.

Aaron called to check that I'd made it to work okay. I informed him I had Rollerbladed without going into any unnecessary details. He called me adventurous and said he looked forward to massaging any sore muscles later. I willed the swelling in my hip to reduce to a more alluring lump.

RG BlackBerried me late afternoon to ask for copies of preliminary briefings on his open meetings. Apparently he wanted to take them with him on vacation. The problem was, I hadn't prepared any. I'd assumed he wouldn't be working during his vacation, a stupid assumption in retrospect, and had planned on typing them up the week he was away. I fought back the surge of panic and rushed to Janet for advice.

"Well, he's not scheduled to fly out till eleven tomorrow morning, so . . ." she offered skeptically.

"So if I get it done before then I could have it messengered to him?" I finished.

"I guess so. Technically. *If* that's okay with him."

I was pretty sure she wasn't going to ask him for me. I knocked on his door.

"Yep," he said distractedly as I stuck my head in. "Oh, do you have those briefings for me?"

I wished ardently that I did, but that didn't get me far.

"Actually, sir, I've just gotten some updates I wanted to incorporate into them. Could I get them to you first thing in the morning?"

RG looked briefly annoyed, but then nodded his head.

"Fine, fine."

"Great."

I started to turn back around.

"Oh, I almost forgot," he interrupted me. "I have something for you."

He waved me farther into his office as he fished around in his briefcase.

"I came across this at home and thought you might like it. Jenny and I have two copies."

He handed me a record album titled *Blind Blake's Bad*

*Feeling Blues* that featured a photo of a depressed-looking blues singer.

Perhaps my moping hadn't been so unnoticeable after all. RG had a slight smile on his face when I looked back up at him.

"Blind Blake's helped me through some crises of confidence in the past, and I figured you might want to check him out."

It wasn't quite an apology, but RG was certainly acknowledging the distress he'd caused me. His manner was compassionate in a wise, removed way—like he felt my pain, but considered it inevitable and maybe even necessary and instructive.

"Thank you, sir," I managed to say, feeling genuine gratitude. "I'm sorry I've been a little out of it lately."

"Just do your job, Samantha. I hired you because you care about the same things I do. And if you stick with me, you'll have a chance to enact some real change. I'm not going to be the junior senator from Ohio forever, you know. Blind Blake and I have got some other plans. Understand?"

I thought I did. RG had been considered an up-and-comer to watch ever since his arrival in D.C. Certainly not to the extent Bramen had, but still, RG's potential hadn't gone unnoticed. His name had even been bandied about during the Sunday talk shows' discussions of possible presidential candidates last year. Most people assumed that he'd skipped this campaign cycle because the Bramen machine looked so invincible. There was no question that Bramen had begun planning for this run over a decade ago, whereas RG had spent his time striving to do the best he could by his constituents. Was RG jealous that he hadn't laid the same groundwork for greater glory? I hoped not.

"Yes, sir. I'm honored to be working for you, sir."

"Great. See you in Cleveland."

I carried Blind Blake back to my desk with me, feeling considerably lighter. I still didn't agree with RG's compromise on the prescription drug benefit bill, but I did believe in his essential goodness and commitment to service. He was one of the only people I'd come across who could make ambition sound like sacrifice, which for genuine public servants, it truly was. RG wasn't in it primarily for himself, but he *was* in it. And I hoped, for the sake of a lot of the causes I believed in, that he'd go far.

The realization that I had at least seven hours of work ahead of me and it was already the end of the day completed my sense of a restoration of order. Ahh, I sighed contentedly as I guzzled my coffee, all was right with my world once more.

At 8:30, when I was a sixth of the way through the briefings I needed to finish for RG, Aaron BlackBerried.

To: SAMANTHA JOYCE
[SRJOYCE@GARY.SENATE.GOV]

From: Aaron Driver
[aidriver@bramen.senate.gov]
Subject: sexy senorita
Text: finally finished for tonight. am about to
consume ungodly amounts of margaritas and
chips. up for a little south of the border fun?
and before that, would you like to join me for
mexican food?

After blushing deeply and cursing the fact that I couldn't sign on to Aaron's plan, I called to inform him of my sad fate.

"You're gonna be there all night?" he asked incredulously.

"For a large portion of it," I answered regretfully.

"Wow. Okay, then I'll come visit you later. And Sammy?"

"Yes?"

"Natalie told me you had a nasty crash this morning. I guess she witnessed it. You okay?"

Other than hating Natalie with a white-hot passion, I supposed I was fine.

"Oh yeah. Just a couple scrapes and bruises. They make me look tough."

"All right, you sexy beast. See you later."

"See you later" was how we'd been signing off lately. Aaron hadn't repeated his drunken declaration of "lurv" for me since the bachelor party episode, but I felt confident that he'd eventually express it again. Maybe even in the sober light of day.

By ten o'clock, everyone in the office had left. By 11:00, I was jittery from my steady intake of caffeine. At midnight, I listened to some Jon Bon Jovi for motivation. At 1:00, I ate a PowerBar and air-boxed for five minutes. At 2:45, I was twenty minutes from finally finishing when Aaron showed up. He smelled of tequila and was carrying a large package from Sport Authority.

"For me?" I asked.

"For me, actually. But you're involved. You almost done?" he asked in a happy, drunken way.

He seemed very proud of himself. As I finished up, he began unwrapping his parcel. He'd evidently bought himself a pair of Rollerblades sometime during the course of the margarita-fueled night and he appeared to be thrilled with his purchase. I readied the briefings for an early morning delivery and watched him try on his new footwear out of the corner of my eye.

"Do you know how to Rollerblade?" I asked. "Because it's actually quite difficult."

"I was hoping you'd teach me," he answered.

He convinced me to change into my pair with some you've-gotta-get-right-back-on-the-horse logic, and then steered me towards the office door.

"I've gotta get my stuff," I protested.

"No you don't. We're gonna warm up here," he answered.

Did he mean inside the Russell Senate Building? Really?

He really did. We spent the next hour gliding down the long, smooth marble halls that ran the length and width of the building, our wheels making a gentle whirring sound as we flew along. I had walked these halls for over a year, but the quiet darkness of the early Saturday hour transformed them into invitingly mysterious terrain. Devoid of pedestrian traffic and polished to crackless perfection, the floors were slick and inviting. We created our own breeze as we picked up speed and Aaron wiped away the hair that blew into my eyes. I felt speedy and slightly out of control, and wondered how much he was supporting me. He had either done this before, or he was a natural.

We had an unspoken agreement to stay silent as we bladed, in an effort to evade detection from the Capitol Police stationed three floors below. Any noise echoed loudly in the empty halls, and in our silence, we attuned ourselves to the building's sleepy creaks and pipe whispers. I felt I was exploring the place more slyly and intimately as we soared along. It had always seemed a giant, impersonal thing—a power factory unconcerned with my particular place or pace. Yet in that moment, and for the first time, I felt faster than it—like I could chart a course and glimpse its secrets before it heard my buzzing and swatted me down with its imposing inertia. Maybe this place was beatable after all. Maybe I was learning the ropes just by listening.

Aaron and I returned to RG's office and collapsed on the couch in the reception area. I felt an urge to share my exhilarating new sense of direction with him, but before I could sort out how to articulate it, he was on top of me kissing my neck.

"Not here," I whispered as he pawed at my clothing.

"Why not? There aren't any cameras."

"It just feels wrong," I tried to explain.

"Come on, doing it in one of these offices is a huge high. Trust me."

It would have been tough for him to say something that would have made me less inclined to sleep with him in the near future. Why did guys ever, ever think it was a wise or prudent thing to allude to past sexual escapades with other women? Whether it was inadvertent or not, it was certainly idiotic. This was an egregious offense. Almost as bad as when a college boyfriend had attempted to spice up our short-lived romance by suggesting I get some blow job tips from his ex-girlfriend. What was wrong with these people?

I glowered at Aaron in the darkness. Unaware or unfazed, he stuck his tongue in my ear. I pushed him away.

"What? What's wrong?" he asked in innocent confusion.

"I don't want to know the particulars of all the sex you've had before me. And I certainly have no desire to re-create any fondly remembered scenarios, okay?" I hissed dangerously.

"Whoa, whoa, whoa. Calm down, baby. I'm sorry. I didn't realize what I was saying. You're taking it the wrong way."

"And how am I supposed to take it?"

As he sat there insisting on the harmlessness of his intentions, a reel of unwelcome images came cascading into my mind's eye. There was Aaron with another woman. There he was stripping her clothes off. I couldn't seem to stop the tape. And tragically, the female star of my mental torture was achingly gorgeous. I also knew instinctively that she had broken up with Aaron and that he still pined for her. Would she want him back? Did she ever call him? Did she live or work nearby?

These were all questions I had zero desire to entertain, but I seemed to have little say in the matter. Why wouldn't my brain listen to me?

"Okay, it's fine," I cut him off. "Let's just go home."

I gathered my things and we had a decidedly less romantic Rollerblade back to his place. We managed to actually trudge with our skates on, which takes a considerable commitment to a bad mood.

I felt like giving up and continuing to my apartment to spend the night alone, but I was irrationally concerned that such a move might drive Aaron to call that horrible other woman and rekindle their romance, and so I stayed, in all my exhausted, pouty glory. Aaron was acting slightly cowed, which, though appreciated, wasn't that sexy. We exchanged hellos with his roommate, Mike, who was watching *Top Secret* in the living room and building some sort of beer can pyramid, and went quickly to sleep.

I got up early the next morning to ensure the safe delivery of RG's briefings. On my way back to my place after tending to them, Aaron called to tell me he had to leave last minute on an overnight New Hampshire trip with Bramen. I hadn't yet forgiven him for his having dated anyone before me, but I was still distressed at his imminent departure. He said he'd call from the road.

A dozen roses greeted me upon my arrival home. The note read, "Sammy—no one and nothing compares to you. Love, Aaron." This produced two delightful effects. One, Sinead O'Connor's song played on a loop inside my head for the rest of the day, negating the need for headphones and an iPod as I went about my chores. Two, I had further proof that Aaron did in fact love me, whether or not he chose to verbally express his devotion.

Later that night, when Sinead finally petered out, I retrieved a dusty record player from underneath my bed and broke out *Blind Blake's Bad Feeling Blues*. It was some serious music, unlike anything I'd ever heard. Blind Blake's voice dripped with disillusioned heartache; his chords seemed to emanate from abysmal depths. I followed along with my eyes closed and drifted off to sleep feeling like maybe I didn't have it so bad after all.

# Roadshow

THE FOLLOWING WEEK was a blur of trip preparation and continued Aaron immersion. We'd really begun to spend most of our free time together, which was wonderful for the most part, as my infatuation was still in full bloom. However, when he'd complained about my going away with RG and I'd pointed out that *he'd* just gone to New Hampshire with Bramen, Aaron had suggested that Bramen's trips were more important. Needless to say, that hadn't gone over well. Aaron had backtracked and sworn that he didn't really think that and was just sad that I was leaving. We'd made peace, but I'd felt the old tension creeping back into our bliss.

I was grateful that the Senate was out of session, because the less-frenzied atmosphere proved more conducive to ensuring RG was about to have the four best open meetings of his professional career. They were scheduled for Cleveland, Toledo, Columbus, and

Cincinnati, in that order. RG had expressed an interest in traveling by train instead of car for as much of the trip as possible, which I was both excited and nervous about. Though I knew all the statistics about how many more auto accidents occurred in relation to train derailments, I felt more in control when I was either the person behind the wheel or knew the person who was. Perhaps introducing myself to the conductor before each leg would help put my mind at ease.

The night before I was scheduled to meet RG in Cleveland, Liza, Ryan, Aaron, and I went out in Adams Morgan, one of my favorite D.C. neighborhoods. Liza convinced me to vamp up for the occasion in some ligament-spraining stilettos that made it impossible for me to walk comfortably for more than a few feet at a time. I felt like an invalid. She assured me I was a hot invalid. Ryan offered that his favorite porn movie was *Hospital Ward Hoochies*. I wondered how much longer he was going to be on the scene.

Once the dancing started, I was barefoot within thirty seconds and infinitely more comfortable. A veteran of countless solo home dance parties, I was a bit more self-conscious in front of a crowd and tended to restrict the majority of my performance to joke moves. I was particularly skilled at the running man and some of M.C. Hammer's more advanced parachute pants maneuvers. Aaron was more a product of genteel dancing schools and had a little trouble keeping up. Though I appreciated being with a man who could spin and dip me with confident authority, I'd never warmed to the whole dancing school culture. Growing up, its elite prissiness had turned me off, though I knew there was a good chance its products regarded my particular style as vulgar and immature. Aaron didn't seem to mind it and he even laughed appreciatively at my extended tribute to Madonna's "Vogue" video.

Liza and Ryan did the lambada the entire night, regardless of the song. When we finally had to leave at 3:00 AM because the place was closing down, we were sweaty, tired, and energized at the same time. I couldn't bear the thought of reimprisoning my carefree feet, so Aaron gave me a piggyback ride to the cab.

It was as we were pulling up to drop Liza and Ryan off that Ryan put his hand on my leg and suggested we all spend the night together. Liza looked horrified. Aaron seemed amused. I tried to make the proposal less distressing by laughing about how fun a sleepover party would be, but insisting that unfortunately I really had to get a good night's sleep in preparation for my trip. Ryan warned me not to work my butt off because it was "so fine as it is" and climbed out of the car. Liza followed with a glazed, quiet expression and closed the cab door without saying good-bye. Ugh. When we got home, I didn't know if I should call her immediately to make sure she was okay or pretend that nothing had happened. Aaron insisted rather insensitively that Liza was a big girl who could take care of herself. Luckily, he added endearingly that he needed my undivided attention because he couldn't get enough of me. I decided to call Liza in the morning.

I woke up excited for the trip but reluctant to leave. Aaron got dressed as I finished packing. Was he really going to miss me? Was I really going to pack graham crackers and a jar of Marshmallow Fluff? I wanted to have snacks for the road, but maybe I should stick with ones that required less assembly. On the other hand, Fluff was remarkably tasty.

"Don't forget your charger," Aaron said as he tossed it to me. "I always forget mine."

Did he want to make sure I was fully charged so that he knew he'd be able to keep in touch with me? In my previous experience, guys didn't tend to think this way. But maybe he was different.

"So . . . what are you up to for the rest of the week?" I asked in an impressively casual way.

I knew he had a lot of work to do, but I was really referring to what he was going to do at night when he wasn't hanging out with me.

"You know, this and that. I've got a college buddy who might stop through for a couple days."

"Buddy" generally meant male, right? There was no way to fish around without sounding paranoid. Which, of course, I was. Good Lord, had I always been this jealous? I didn't remember myself that way. I found it frustrating that Aaron had this effect on me. Even with his faults, he seemed to possess some quality that made me want to hold on suffocatingly tight to him and I had to spend a lot of energy resisting the impulse for both of our sakes.

He carried my bag to the Metro stop (the strike had mercifully only lasted two days), where he turned me to face him.

"Ohio better not steal you back," he said as he kissed me good-bye. "Or it'll have to answer to me."

I smiled and kissed him long enough to provoke a "Get a room!" cry from a passing skateboarder.

Half an hour later, I browsed the magazines at an overpriced newsstand while I waited for my plane to board at National Airport. For some reason, I hadn't gotten the latest issue of the *Economist* in the mail yet, and the cover advertising an article about Europe's take on the American health care system signaled that it was an issue I needed to check out. I scooped up a copy and also nabbed an *US Weekly* for good measure.

The flight to Cleveland was just over an hour long—certainly not enough time to fully engage in the *Economist* article, but just time enough to update myself on the recent Hollywood rumors. I was sandwiched between two businessmen in dark suits—one was typing furiously on his laptop and the other thumbed importantly through a large financial-looking manuscript. I self-consciously hid *US Weekly* between the folds of the *Economist* in the hopes of appearing more professional.

Before I made it through a single celebrity photo caption, I found myself engaged in a silent elbow war over the armrests. I firmly believed that the occupier of a middle seat, by virtue of the fact that she was clearly the least comfortable, should have first dibs on the two flimsy armrests that defined her inferior space. My rowmates seemed to disagree, and the battle was fierce. I glared out of the corner of my eyes at my opponents. On top of being ungallant, they were no doubt germ-ridden, as well. I cursed them in my head.

I finally attained a strategically strong position towards the front of both armrests, where I could slowly inch backwards, knowing my enemies' elbows had nowhere to go. Satisfied, I turned my attention towards giving the appearance that I was reading very serious political articles while I secretly soaked up the latest celebrity gossip.

An hour and fifteen minutes later, as I made my way through the Cleveland Airport, I noticed a slight commotion at a nearby ticket counter. A little entourage of people was urgently explaining to a hapless airline employee that they really needed to get on that particular plane despite its sold-out status and their lack of tickets.

"I'm supposed to be in Des Moines in two hours. Would you please just ask if anyone is willing to give up their seat?"

As soon as the woman spoke, I recognized her voice and slowed to take a closer look. Sure enough, it was Melanie Spearam, senator from Illinois and current presidential candidate. I stopped completely to observe her, pleased by the unexpected opportunity to do so. Most people considered her the first woman in the country's history to have a viable chance of being elected the leader of the free world. For though Bramen led the pack of candidates, Spearam was close behind and gaining in the polls.

However, at the moment, she had apparently missed her connection and was nearing a meltdown—a rare sight, or at least rare when the cameras were around. They weren't at the moment and she was taking the opportunity to launch into a full-fledged fit.

I wondered why she was even flying commercially, given that her husband was a wildly successful Chicago businessman with his own fleet of planes. It had been nastily rumored that she never would have won her Senate seat without her husband's connections—people had gone so far as to suggest that the insatiable philanderer had essentially bought the Senate seat for her, to more or less permanently get her off his back.

I had always considered this to be ninety-percent sexist smear tactic, but as I listened to the icy insults she was currently hurling at the intimidated airline official, I wondered if maybe there was some truth to it after all.

"Do you understand what's at stake here?" Senator

Spearam coldly inquired for the fifth time. The airline employee was calling for backup.

My own crisis awaited me at the hotel. Zack Globerman, senior RG staffer in charge of the Cleveland office, smiled tightly as I climbed out of the cab. He was ten years older than me and had never warmed to the idea that I had any real authority or skill. He also had an annoyingly sanctimonious way of suggesting that staying in Ohio was the more pure, honorable route for a student of public service. He often called me "DC," which irked me to no end.

"We've got a problem," he said without even a hello. "Ronkin's gotten some folks riled over the Canada thing and they're forming a pretty big protest area."

Oh crap.

Don Ronkin was an abrasive talk radio personality who hated RG and used part of every show to rip him apart. A lot of people listened to him, mainly because he was entertaining in his hostility. The level of vitriol he spewed conjured up images of someone mostly savage, foaming at the mouth and spazzing about in a slanderous rage. Who wouldn't find that interesting? Many found it repulsive, granted, but there was no denying the popularity of the show. I had heard RG explaining to someone once that anything that appealed to people's baser fears and insecurities tended to carve out a permanent niche, like it or not. I hadn't wanted to believe him, but the evidence was beginning to pile up.

Ronkin had lately seized upon RG's prescription drug proposal and particularly his support of the plan to allow Americans to import cheaper medicine from Canada and Europe. Though this had been neutralized in the course of the compromise with Bramen, Ronkin could not forgive RG for ever even entertaining the thought.

I made a regular practice of downloading transcripts of Ronkin's shows (it only played in Ohio so I couldn't listen when I was in D.C.) just to keep abreast of what he was saying. On RG's plan, he had spared no ire.

"Basically, the moronic Robert Gary wants to take jobs away from hardworking Americans and flood the country with cheap, dangerous, foreign drugs. Does that sound like a good idea to you? Of course not. Call in and tell me your thoughts."

Ronkin's strategy sought to hijack people's natural patriotism for his own misleading ends. Unfortunately, it was fairly effective. And now Zack was telling me that the open meeting scheduled for the next day, the big Cleveland kickoff, was in danger of becoming a public relations quagmire.

Mark had done a great job of alerting a lot of the local press to the event, inviting many of them to tape it or run it live so that those who couldn't be there could still be kept apprised. It wasn't just about press for the event, it was about making more people aware of the opportunity to interface with their representative.

The open meetings weren't scripted in any way, and therefore not guaranteed to go well for RG—it really depended on how he handled the questions. On the whole, people were generally respectful, and if they disagreed, did so in a polite way. But I knew better than to expect Ronkin's crowd to adhere to these understood rules of civility. We were going to have trouble on our hands.

Zack looked panicked.

"They've been rehearsing their heckling all day. Who does that? Can heckling be rehearsed?"

"It can when Ronkin's in charge," I answered grimly. "Are they planning on staying outside in their own area, or do you expect them to pepper the crowd?"

"I don't know! I just got wind of this an hour ago. They tried to recruit Kara to their ranks, not knowing who she was, of course."

Kara was a college student who'd been interning in RG's Cleveland office the last two summers. She was smart and dedicated and I always hoped it would be she who'd answer the phone when I called. I got along with her well and she would remind me of myself at her age if she wasn't so outgoing and put together.

"Is Kara around?" I asked.

"Yeah, she's upstairs setting up RG's room."

Great. I much preferred to hear bad news from her

than from Zack, so I planned on pumping her for the details.

"Okay, calm down. We're just going to have to deal with this. Gimme a little bit to think."

"You better come up with something, DC."

I really disliked him. But I knew he was right.

Upstairs, Kara was rigging up a fax and Internet connection in RG's room. She smiled when I came in.

"Thank God you're here. I was just plotting how to slip a Valium into Zack's Diet Orange Crush," she said good-naturedly.

"Is that still the only thing he'll drink?"

"No, he has an occasional papaya juice if it's iced down enough. Stocking the office refrigerator is a nightmare. I've taken to calling him Z-Glo to cheer myself up as I'm slaving away."

I laughed. Though I'd heard J-Lo really got an unfair rap with the whole diva reputation. I didn't claim to know the truth, I just took the debate as further proof that you can't believe everything you read. Which didn't stop me from reading all of it.

"So what was your impression of the Ronkin posse?" I forced my brain away from the J-Lo musing and back on the bigger ass problems at hand.

"They're fired up for sure. Trying to recruit anyone who passes by. They shouted at me that if I loved my grandparents, I should do anything I can to stop Robert Gary from poisoning them."

Hmmm. Compelling argument.

"And do you love your grandparents?" I asked, cutting right to the heart of the issue.

"Nana pesters me about my double pierce, but yeah, they're okay," Kara answered. "I'd be opposed to their poisoning."

So the Ronkin folks had a hook.

"Anyway, I stuck around and talked to them for a while," Kara continued. "I never let on that I wasn't on board. I figured it would be more useful if they thought I was on their side."

Kara was smart. Zack would've exploded in their faces and threatened police action. I probably would've tried to bore them into submission with well-reasoned opposing arguments.

"And what else did you learn?" I asked.

"They're fairly well organized, have a ton of camera-grabbing signs, and are planning some sort of costumed heckler. There was still some debate as to whether it should be a giant weasel or an executioner, and whether it should be wearing a beret or a turban."

"So it's a culturally sensitive crowd," I said dryly.

"Yeah. One of their arguments is that importing cheaper drugs from Canada and Europe would provide a steady cash flow to other governments that could then use American dollars to fund terrorist activities."

Right. Canada was well known for that.

"Okay, well, do you have any suggestions for how to

deal with these geniuses? Would they be responsive to an offer of a sit-down with RG?"

I knew they probably wouldn't be, but I thought it was worth investigating. Sometimes groups that were really interested in press attention appreciated being taken seriously by the individual they claimed to despise, and would slightly tone down their tactics in exchange.

"I don't think I have enough experience to be able to evaluate that," Kara said. "But they didn't strike me as overly reasonable."

I helped Kara finish setting up RG's mobile office as I mulled over the problem. RG arrived shortly thereafter to work on a speech he was giving in the morning before the open meeting. I decided to be upfront with him about the predicament.

After I determined his mood.

"How was the vacation, sir?"

He looked tanned and rested.

"It was good, thanks. What's going on here?"

Vacation small talk ruled out, I dove right in. Once RG was in work mode, there wasn't any distracting him.

"Well, sir, Don Ronkin's gotten a group organized to protest at your open meeting tomorrow. There's not time to move the location, but I am working on some alternate entrance and exit points, so hopefully we can throw some of them off."

RG looked up at me with a clear, questioning gaze.

"My open meetings aren't restricted to supporters, Samantha," he said calmly.

I knew that. Some of RG's most effective moments were when he was engaged with someone who opposed his positions. He explained his reasoning eloquently and invariably won the respect, if not the agreement, of whoever debated him.

"I know, sir, but this crowd seems solely focused on disruption."

RG nodded.

"All right. Do what you can, and I'll handle the rest. Thanks for the heads-up."

I left him to his work and spent the rest of the afternoon scoping out the event site with Kara.

RG had a roundtable with journalists scheduled for 5:00 PM in a conference room at the hotel that he asked me to sit in on. I stayed in the back with a notepad and pen, ready to write down anything that would need to be followed up on. I'd already placed a tape recorder on the table in front of RG to ensure we had our own documentation of everything that was said, as I'd learned in the past that some journalists tended to invent quotes out of thin air.

Around minute twenty-five, I started to get the tiniest bit bored. RG was answering the eighth question about ethanol, and though I knew it was an important issue—especially to Ohioans—it just wasn't my particular passion. I surreptitiously fished the *Economist* out of my bag and was about to open it up to read the scathing

European condemnation of America's health care system, when a reporter mercifully switched the topic away from ethanol.

"Senator Gary, many seniors are confused and aggravated with the current state of Medicare. How would your proposal help make the system less complicated and easier to navigate?" asked a middle-aged man from the *Plain Dealer*, Ohio's largest newspaper.

I always got a kick out of that name. In my opinion, newspapers could do a much better job in the nomenclature department. There were far too many Posts, Gazettes, Times, etc. I enjoyed any name that broke the mold. The New Orleans *Times-Picayune* was another favorite. The "Picayune" more than made up for the boring "Times" intro. The fact that a newspaper would name itself something that meant "of little value or account; petty, carping, or prejudiced" struck me as endlessly amusing and very self-aware.

As RG answered the question, it struck me that some of these questions were very good practice for the open meeting the next day. I took a minute to check how I myself would answer that question, which then led to a fantasy about me being the supreme ruler of the universe (which wasn't even anything I desired, but one thing led to another . . .), and that in turn led to me not having any idea why RG was all of a sudden saying my name.

"Would you mind, Samantha?" he was asking.

Mind what? I'd determined that I would mind being

the supreme ruler (too much responsibility, not enough free time), but I doubted that's what he was referring to.

"Could I just borrow that for a second?" he asked with the tiniest edge to his voice.

Anyone who didn't spend a ton of time with him wouldn't have even been able to hear the twinge of annoyance. What was he talking about? I followed his gaze. Got it. He wanted my copy of the *Economist*. Of course—I thought I'd heard him refer to its health care article during the course of his answer, somewhere around the time I was pondering what planet should house the royal vacation ski condo. Probably somewhere cold like Pluto.

"Absolutely, sir. I've got it right here."

All eyes were on me as I leapt up and delivered the magazine to RG. I wished I had read the piece already and knew what example he was about to reference. Oh well, I'd just make sure I got it back. He would give it back, wouldn't he? It had set me back four bucks.

I listened to RG talking about a particular feature of Sweden's health care system that he admired as I returned to my seat. The *Economist* article evidently had a helpful chart that succinctly summarized it and he wanted to ensure he got the details right as he went forward with his point.

"So bear with me while I just open up to it for a second and . . . hmmm," RG paused.

The room erupted in laughter and I strained my neck to see what had caused the commotion.

Oh dear God.

In attempting to flip to the article, he had flipped to the middle of the *US Weekly* that was still hidden inside it. Specifically, he had flipped to a giant close-up of Lil' Kim's boobs being barely covered by some leopard-print pasties.

I wasn't sure if all the reporters were familiar with the pint-sized rapper's consistently flamboyant style—that it was all part of her image and shouldn't be construed as pointlessly pornographic—but I was pretty sure RG was not. He didn't spend a lot of time reading magazines that had What Was She Thinking? fashion sections.

I felt myself blush a deep crimson. RG cleared his throat.

"Well, I hope everyone's awake now," he said.

The reporters laughed. He removed the *US Weekly* and flipped to the much more staid health care article. I did my best to blend into the wall.

Afterwards, a few of the journalists smiled evilly at me as they filed out of the room. I went to help RG gather his things.

"I'm really sorry about that, sir. I'm not quite sure how that magazine ended up in there," I lied.

RG seemed to know I wasn't being entirely truthful.

"Samantha . . ." he said sternly. "I'd really appreciate it if you could answer me one question."

"Yes, sir?" I replied with tremendous trepidation.

Had I finally pushed him over the edge? He seemed genuinely mad.

"I would like to know . . ." he paused, ". . . just what exactly *was* she thinking?"

It took me a second to realize that he was referring to the fashion section headline of the Lil' Kim display, and that he was joking. Relief cascaded through me. Thank God RG had a sense of humor.

"See you in the morning," he said with a grin.

He handed me both my magazines and was gone.


I had done absolutely everything I could to prepare for the next day's events by eight o'clock that night, and was sitting bored in my room when I realized I hadn't called Liza to check on the fallout from Ryan's foursome proposal.

She was still at work, because the Mayflower was hosting a telemarketers' convention (I had already thoroughly cursed my bad luck for having to be out of town and miss it), but she answered her cell phone right away.

"Hey, how's it going there?" I asked cheerily.

"Oh, fine, fine," she said dismissively.

She clearly did not understand the magical quality of the event she was witnessing.

"Listen," she continued. "Ryan was really, really drunk last night. We did a couple shots of Jäger while you and Aaron were dancing."

Ahhh, the Jägermeister defense. I knew it well.

"Oh yeah, of course," I said benevolently. "We were all pretty loaded. It was fun, though."

"So anyway, sorry if he was sort of an idiot," she finished.

He had been an idiot. But that really wasn't the fault of the shots.

"Hey, don't mention it," I said. "As long as you're okay, that's all I care about."

Hopefully she was realizing Ryan was not her Prince Charming. It usually took about three days between the realization and the start of the complaints, which then meant another two weeks until the breakup. She was fiercely loyal to the idea that all these terrible guys were actually secretly wonderful right up until the moment she could no longer deny their essential dreadfulness, which made that moment incredibly key. Time after time, I did my best to hurry along that flash of realization, but she was stubborn about her pace.

"I'm great," she assured me. "You know, he's amazing in so many ways. I think he's got real potential."

So I was in for at least another month of Ryan. Oh well.

I hung up with Liza after making her promise she would pay closer attention to what the telemarketers were up to and give me a more extensive and satisfying report later on. I left Aaron a voicemail and sent him a BlackBerry but didn't hear immediately back from him.

After rejecting room service based on its exorbitant prices, I snacked on some graham crackers and Fluff and looked up the fastest fire escape route from my room in the hotel information binder. It seemed a little confusing, and I decided to practice it to be safe. On my way back from the successful trial escape, I ran into Kara in the hallway.

"Hey, you wanna go get a drink at the hotel bar?" she asked.

Was it possible she was also bored, even though she lived here? Oh, I hoped so. I needed a partner in crime.

"I'd love to," I answered gratefully.

Over two glasses of wine, Kara revealed that she did in fact have plenty of other places to be, but her boyfriend was working nearby and she was waiting for him before heading back to their neighborhood.

"What does he do?" I asked, hoping that she'd then ask me all about my fancy new boyfriend. I wasn't always the kind of person who just waited to talk—I usually was in fact a fairly good listener—but I felt like letting Kara know that there was something different and wonderful about me this time around, in the event I could still qualify as some sort of role model for her. I knew it was a long shot.

"He's an actor, actually," she answered unexpectedly.

"Really?" I was intrigued. "Has he been in anything I'd know?"

"Probably not. We still have a year of college left, so he's mainly done plays in the Cleveland area, but he's recently landed a couple commercials. He's shooting one tonight actually, for Radio Shack."

I happened to love Radio Shack, mainly for its name. They didn't seem to feel the need to impress anyone, which I appreciated.

"That's great," I said, genuinely enthused.

She seemed quite enamored. She told me all about him, and he did sound funny and cool, but she seemed to be missing the fact that the whole point of this conversation was to get around to me.

At last she asked me about Aaron, allowing me to happily launch into my spiel about his many lovable qualities and the blissful state of our union. I decided to avoid mentioning the tension that existed in our relationship, since that was less easy to brag about. As Kara listened, I imagined for a second that we were sisters. This led to me checking out her foot size to see how productive it would be to raid her closet, which then made me think about the fights we would have when I did so without asking, which then made me imagine the tearful toast she would give at my wedding about how through all the silly arguments and serious life trials, we were the only ones who really understood each other and we'd be there for each other forever. By the time I was done, Kara really was toasting me.

"To the men in our lives—may they realize how damned lucky they are," she said with a smile.

I'd drink to that.

I made my way back to my room after Kara's

boyfriend showed up. As I was testing out the complimentary robe, my BlackBerry buzzed.

> TO: SAMANTHA JOYCE
> [SRJOYCE@GARY.SENATE.GOV]
> From: Aaron Driver
> [aidriver@bramen.senate.gov]
> Subject: Re: thoughts on streaking streets of
> cleveland out of boredom
> Text: hey gorgeous, glad you made it in safely.
> my cell phone's out of juice. call you in the
> morning. good luck tomorrow. miss you.

Okay. High points of his message: 1) the gorgeous ad-
jective—strong opening. Not entirely accurate, but if I
had him fooled, fabulous; 2) wishing me luck on work
stuff—showed he cared about all aspects of my life and
wasn't threatened by my pursuit of a career—crucial;
and 3) he missed me—always important. No indication of the degree of the emotion, but let's assume it's
intense.

Now for the low points: 1) his cell phone's out of
juice? I didn't question that it was, I questioned his distance from all other usable phones. Why was calling on
his cell his only option? Was he out at an event with
Bramen that would run too late to call me when he got
home? Fine, but if so, I'd like to be more thoroughly
informed; 2) continuing the cell phone-out-of-juice

complaints—this didn't speak to a strong sense of responsibility. If he forgets to charge his cell phone, will he also forget to, say, pick up our daughter Riley from preschool? Unacceptable. This tendency would need to be watched and trained out of him; and 3) small point, but he didn't address the subject line or text of my original message to him. Slightly inconsiderate, but could be forgiven via more bouquets of roses.

With that analysis complete, I went over the next day's schedule one last time, requested a wake-up call, wondered if anyone had ever died in the room I was staying in, got up to turn the bathroom light on for protection, and finally drifted off to sleep.

In my dream, Aaron and I were at a rave in Atlantis, shimmying around with strobe-lighted magical creatures and trying to determine whether we had inadvertently taken some sort of drug or if Atlantis was simply teeming with shape-shifting supernatural beings. We never got a definitive answer, though we did do the electric slide with a jive-talking unicorn.

I woke up disoriented, as I always did in hotels. I opened my eyes cautiously, looking with trepidation towards the spot where Shackleton's bowl would be if I had been in my apartment. Instead of him, I saw a cheap knockoff of a Georgia O'Keeffe hanging on an unfamiliar beige wall. My brain worked furiously to make sense of this information. Where could I possibly be? Had I been kidnapped, and if so, by whom and was the ransom sufficiently exorbitant? My brain clicked suddenly into present consciousness and everything became clear. Right. Cleveland. On the road with RG. Open meeting. I did a quick body scan. Yep, all my limbs were intact, vital signs seemed reasonable. I breathed a sigh of relief.

My phone rang stridently, breaking my newfound calm. But I was thrilled to hear Aaron's voice on the other end.

"Hey baby, did you sleep well?" he asked.

I loved that he called me baby. Normally I would have hated it, but with him it felt more adoring than infantilizing.

"Mmm . . . okay I guess. You were in my dream," I replied.

I hadn't said it suggestively, but he took it that way, which, given that he was a guy, wasn't that surprising.

"Give me all the naughty details," he demanded, sounding genuinely interested.

I complied, but had to explain twice that dancing with a unicorn was not a euphemism for anything. He seemed disappointed.

"All right, well, good luck today. I'll call you later, baby."

I got off the phone and realized I hadn't even had a chance to ask him about his night. Kara knocked on my door soon after with a box full of Krispy Kreme donuts and a cup of coffee.

"I'm feeling competitive with the other staff offices. I want Cleveland to be the best stop on the tour, so I'm pulling out the big guns," she explained.

God, I loved Krispy Kremes.

As we sat there devouring the box and running through the day's schedule, I started thinking how fun it would be if Kara came to work in the D.C. office after she graduated. Perhaps I could gently nudge her in that direction—inspire her in some way with my own experience.

"Have you thought about your postgraduate plans? We could really use you back on the Hill," I said in my most gracious and encouraging tone. I was going to be a fabulous mentor.

"You've got chocolate glaze on your ear," Kara pointed.

Yes, I certainly did.

RG's open meeting got under way two hours later in a packed auditorium. Ronkin's protesters had shouted at us upon arrival, and their mascot (they'd gone with the weasel wearing a beret) had danced tauntingly around us, but RG had just smiled and waved and went ahead like a man completely unfazed.

Inside, the room was full and sweaty—uncomfortable proof of a great turnout. Kara and I had put out some boxes of Krispy Kremes and bottles of water at the last minute, which were gigantic hits. I hadn't planned on any refreshments for the open meetings because we didn't have the budget for it, but judging by the happy response to the donuts' presence, I decided it was worth it to spend a little personal money to ensure a successful trip. The curmudgeonly fire chief I had talked to earlier on the phone loudly took credit for the refreshments, explaining to his neighbors that he had "talked some sense into me." I just smiled and thanked him for his support of RG.

RG himself was sweating in the cramped heat, but looking calm and purposeful. He opened up with some general remarks about how great it was to be back in Cleveland, how much he enjoyed the chance to get together and talk, and how eager he was to listen to any and all of their concerns.

An elderly man in overalls stood up and asked about subsidies for farmers. A mother brought up the overcrowding in her children's classrooms. A young policeman asked about the impact of the budget shortfalls. An older lady talked about how annoying it was that her neighbor had put his mulch pile right up against the fence and could RG call him and ask him to move it.

RG listened closely to every question and answered each one fully. He bowed out of the mulch pile call much to the chagrin of the old lady, but everyone else seemed fairly satisfied. He then took some time to explain the prescription drug proposal that was being debated in Congress and described why he thought it would improve the current system if we could get it passed. This prompted a round of questions seeking clarification about the bill's many proposals. Unlike the Capitol Hill discussions of the bill, this one was characterized by simple language devoid of rhetorical flourishes and technical terms. The citizens of Cleveland wanted to know how the bill would help them in very specific, straightforward ways. My job was to follow up with questioners who seemed to need more answers, so I spent my time running around with a notepad and some printout explanations of RG's bill, complete with helpful bullet points.

After two and a half hours, almost everyone had gotten face time with RG and I had followed up with over twenty people, taking down their names and contact information and promising to stay in touch with updates that pertained to their particular issues. I was currently hearing all about Sandra O'Malley's distressing battle with severe halitosis. Sandra wanted to know if Medicare would cover her condition under RG's proposal, and I tried to talk her through it while avoiding breathing through my nose at all costs. Her breath was really, really bad. I felt sorry for her, but I also was feeling increasingly queasy and had a few more people to get to before the crowd completely dispersed.

"So I go through two or three bottles of mouthwash a day, but you can see it just doesn't even make a dent," she breathed threateningly on me.

Yes I could. Ugh. I was starting to wish hard for a

minor earthquake to strike and distract Sandra so I could escape from her breath's clutches, when Kara appeared at my elbow.

"I'm afraid we need you outside for a second," she said very professionally.

I excused myself from Mrs. O'Malley and was about to quietly thank Kara as we walked away, when I realized she hadn't been making up a rescuing story at all. They really did need me outside. The beret-clad weasel had commandeered a bullhorn and was drawing a crowd of cameras.

"We've made our own deck of Ohio's most-wanted public enemies. As you can see, Robert Gary is the ace of spades," the weasel shouted as he flourished a card with an extremely unflattering picture of RG, outfitted with a digitally added beret.

Hmmm, a deck of cards. How original.

Unfortunately, the weasel had positioned himself squarely in front of RG's car. With his successful recruitment of cameras, he had set up a well-documented ambush. RG would have to deal with his heckling head-on and the cameras would be there to catch every exchange. I knew that no matter how well the open meeting had gone, the only coverage that would make it onto the evening news would be conflict footage, since that's what the media seemed to thrive on these days. Zack Globerman was standing near the weasel with his head in his hands. He looked like a sculpture of ineffective despair—a sort of surrendering companion piece to Rodin's *Thinker*.

I turned to Kara.

"We'll have to get him out another way," I said.

Kara nodded.

"I parked my car by the back exit of the hall in case something like this happened," she replied as she handed over the keys. "There's a side exit, as well, but the back's the most secluded. All you have to do is get RG out that way, and then take off for the train station. You can just leave the car there with the keys under the wheel. I'll pick it up later."

She sounded so confident.

"But the hecklers will never let us through," I answered, indicating the riled throng currently blocking the driveway of the town hall. "Unless you have tinted windows, they'll see RG and then the shot will be that he's running away, which we definitely don't want."

Kara shook her head.

"Leave that to me and I'll make sure it's clear. Remember, they think I'm on their side. Just call me when you guys are getting in the car. Okay?"

I nodded uncertainly. I wanted to believe her, but I just couldn't see how she was going to pull it off. I listened to the weasel shouting about RG's Communist credentials and hurried back inside.

RG was talking earnestly to a young man in a navy uniform. He looked up as I walked towards them.

"Samantha, could you take down this man's information and make sure we check on the status of his father's Social Security checks? He hasn't been receiving them and we need to get to the bottom of this."

"Absolutely, sir," I replied as I whipped out my notebook.

The young man gratefully shook RG's hand and told me how to get in touch with him. When we finished, RG was deep in conversation with an elderly man who was very concerned about illegal aliens. He said he saw no reason why their health care should be paid for by taxing the incomes of legitimate residents. I listened as RG patiently explained his commitment to the idea that America was a country of immigrants and we needed to celebrate that fact, and that though he agreed that legal migration was obviously preferable, he couldn't deny basic medical assistance to any person who fell sick or injured in the state of Ohio.

The man did not like what he was hearing and seemed to grow more agitated the more calmly RG spoke.

"But if we welcome them with open arms, what's to prevent them from annihilating the human race?" he responded in a challenging voice.

Huh?

RG looked as confused as I was.

"What makes you think they would do such a thing?" RG asked. "They're human as well."

Had this man really demonized people from other

countries to the extent that he considered them antihuman? This was xenophobia taken to an illogical extreme.

"Oh come on—you've seen all the movies," the old man insisted. "They never want to get along. They abduct people and probe them and destroy all the cities and if we don't put up a fight, we won't have a chance. At the first sign of a spaceship, we gotta blast them to kingdom come."

RG and I simultaneously realized precisely with what we were dealing.

"They're already disguised among us, you know," the man was continuing. "This is a serious issue."

"Thank you so much for your time," I said in a strained but even tone. "I wish we could stay longer, but I'm afraid I've got to get Senator Gary to his next appointment."

The alien hater looked miffed.

"Yeah, okay," he grumbled reluctantly. "Don't forget what I said, though. There's tons more that feel the way I do."

Were there really? RG and I excused ourselves and prepared to leave. I quickly explained the weasel ambush to him and though I could tell RG wanted to confront the situation head-on, I was extremely grateful that he agreed to go along with my plan. I imagined that the illegal alien debate had reminded him that there were some situations that were just best to avoid.

As we slid out the back exit and into Kara's car, I rang her cell phone.

"We're all set," I informed her, praying that her plan would work.

"Okay, perfect timing," she said. "A decoy just rolled by. Hang on a second."

It sounded as though she had put the phone in her pocket. And that she was running.

"Hey, Ronnie," I heard her call in an excited, panting voice. "I just saw that wimp Robert Gary run out the side door and pull off in a van!"

"What? Which way'd they go?"

"That way! We can catch them at the light if we run!"

"Hey, everyone! Follow Kara!"

I heard the weasel take up the cry over the bullhorn.

"Follow Kara! Gary's trying to escape!"

As the sound of a stampeding crowd reverberated through the static, I started the car and pulled gingerly forward. Sure enough, the driveway was clear, and all of the cameras and hecklers were swarming a hapless van stopped at a nearby light. As I turned the car in the opposite direction, I caught sight of Kara next to the weasel at the front of the pack, red-faced and yelling, pounding on the side of the van. Zack was observing her from a short distance away, looking extremely confused. I smiled and sped towards the station, where we caught our train just in time.

# *Oh No*

THE CONDUCTOR HAD been nice enough to come over and shake RG's hand as we boarded. That made him practically a friend, so I felt immediately much more comfortable with our mode of travel. Surely a friend wouldn't derail us. We were going to be all right.

RG spent most of the trip on the phone—first with Jenny, who was going to meet up with us in Cincinnati, and then with some prominent Toledo officials with whom he hadn't touched base in a while. Out of the corner of my eye, I watched him refer to the Toledo briefing I'd prepared for him to check on the names of spouses and children he needed to ask about.

"And how are Lydia and the kids?" he asked one of them.

These details mattered. I'd witnessed countless times how having RG ask specifically about someone's family members made them feel important and appreciated.

And RG did really have an interest in people's families, being such a family guy himself—it's just that there were too many people to keep track of without some sort of refresher.

The two-hour train ride went quickly and we were pulling into the Toledo train station before I had even made a dent in my work. I looked out the window and saw a TV camera set up to film RG's arrival.

"Sir, there's press outside. You'll be on camera getting off the train," I said.

RG ran his fingers through his hair.

"How do I look?" he asked earnestly.

He looked a little tired, but good.

"Great," I said.

"Should I put my tie back on?" he asked.

He'd taken it off along with his jacket during the course of his phone calls as he'd gotten more comfortable in his seat. I thought he looked better without them—more laid-back and approachable.

"I don't think so, sir. I think you look more accessible this way," I said.

RG looked at me quizzically.

"You sure?"

RG never seemed uncertain about anything, except matters of style and appearance. His literal image was not something he seemed to care about paying much attention to. I knew Jenny picked out most of his clothes and I guessed he had gotten used to relying on others' advice in this particular realm, if not in any other one.

I was happy to be looked to for guidance, if a bit un-qualified to be giving it when it came to fashion. Still, I had definite opinions and could be authoritative. Especially if it would help to put RG at ease.

"I am sure. No need for the coat and tie at all, sir."

It looked as though he appreciated my assistance. I felt that this represented a breakthrough of sorts in our relationship. Perhaps if he felt he could depend on my wardrobe and appearance advice, he would consider me trustier overall. Maybe this was just the beginning of me becoming indispensable to his work.

"I don't agree," he said definitively as he donned his tie, rolled his sleeves back down, and reached for his coat.

Or maybe not.

"Senator Gary, how is it to be back in Toledo?" the reporter shouted as the camera focused on RG exiting the train.

"Wonderful, wonderful. I never want to leave," he answered with a smile and a wave.

I quickly spotted our car and steered RG towards it as other passengers and Amtrak employees came over to shake his hand.

An hour later, I was settling into my hotel room and debating whether it was worth it to try and take a twenty-minute nap before I had to accompany RG to a roundtable with employees of Blue Cross Blue Shield when my BlackBerry buzzed with a message from Aaron.

To: SAMANTHA JOYCE
[SRJOYCE@GARY.SENATE.GOV]
From: Aaron Driver
[aidriver@bramen.senate.gov]
Subject: missing you
Text: dear gorgeous, have to head to iowa with
jb for a teamsters event. am investigating all
possible routes to ohio so i can come see you.
how's it going? miss you like the deserts miss
the rain.

Even though it was a blatant rip-off of an Everything But the Girl song, I appreciated Aaron's foray into romantic sentiment. Though I did take issue with the assertion that a desert would in fact miss the rain, since I was fairly sure this was inaccurate. A desert wouldn't be a desert if it got regular rain. Missing the rain was therefore tantamount to desiring a complete identity makeover, which I don't think was what Aaron had been advocating.

The important thing was that he missed me, which almost made up for his poor communication performance since we'd been separated. I tried to remind myself how busy he was, being the head speechwriter of a prominent senator running hard for the presidential nomination, but this only made me remember how irritating it was that he worked for Bramen. In my opinion, he needed to constantly atone for this sin. Still, I couldn't deny that I missed him back.

To: Aaron Driver
[aidriver@bramen.senate.gov]
From: Samantha Joyce [srjoyce@gary.senate.gov]
Subject: re: missing you
Text: in toledo now. narrowly escaped hate-
spewing weasel earlier—will give full report
later. besides the weasel, who was pretty sexy in
a satanic rodent kind of way, not too much
competition for your affections. miss you too.
Like desserts miss whipped cream. i don't know
what that means.

My phone rang as I was pressing send. It was RG.

"Where is my briefing for the Blue Cross Blue Shield
meeting?" he barked accusingly.

Wherever he had put it, because it had certainly
been included in his pile.

"It should be in your binder, sir."

"Well, it's not," he snapped. "I have ten minutes before I've got to be there and I have no idea what I'm
supposed to be talking about. For crying out loud,
where the hell did you hide it?"

"Uh . . . it should be . . ." I trailed off uncertainly.

I'd already told him where I thought it was, and that
hadn't gone so well. He sighed in acute exasperation.
RG was generally great to work with, but intense stress
occasionally made him unreasonable. I quickly debated
my course of action. Should I apologize quickly and
race to the business center to print out another copy, or

was I supposed to endure more yelling? RG cleared his throat as he angrily shuffled some papers. It was looking more like the yelling option.

"Oh, here it is. Never mind," he said suddenly.

He didn't sound quite as contrite as I believed he should, but I was mainly just grateful that the crisis had been mitigated.

The roundtable went fine, followed by a well-attended open meeting in which RG shone once again. I spent my time following up with a couple who needed help getting their son a leave of absence from his military service overseas so that he could visit his dying sister, a principal who wanted to start a Head Start program in her school, and a cantankerous man who wanted a government loan to fix the rear alignment of his pickup truck. I had found that my job often consisted of juggling the truly meaningful and the sublimely absurd. The combination kept me on my toes and made me both exasperated and proud by the end of every long, long day.

After the open meeting finally closed, we made our way back to the hotel.

"Good night, Samantha," RG said gruffly. "Good job with everything," he added.

"Good night, sir," I replied smoothly.

If any other person in my life demonstrated the hot-and-cold, distant manner that RG displayed with me, I would have cut them loose long ago. But the high standards, volatile moods, and mildly emotionally abusive reprimands were worth being a part of his team. That's what I had to keep telling myself.

The next day was my mother's birthday and it dawned gray and rainy, which was odd weather for the end of August. Maybe fall was sending a little preview of things to come. After a breakfast meeting with Toledo firefighters, RG and I boarded the train for Columbus. I waited until he was deep in the middle of reading a policy brief before I called my mom.

"Happy birthday!" I whispered when she answered the phone. "I'm on the train so I'll call you in a couple hours but I just wanted to wish you a happy birthday."

"Aren't you going to sing?" she asked.

I glanced at RG out of the corner of my eye. I stood to move down the aisle, but passengers unable to find seats blocked my path on either side. A lot of people had recognized RG as we'd boarded, so I imagined some of these lingering standbys were interested in overhearing whatever he had to say.

"Um, it's not the best time at the moment," I told my mom, smiling at the people who had started eyeing my seat the moment I stood up.

I sat back down.

"Come on, honey. Ever since you were two years old, you've always sung to me first thing on my birthday. I don't need any presents—I just want to hear your sweet little voice."

There were a couple lies in that statement. First of all, she certainly did need presents. She always said she didn't, or would just tell people to "make me something," but if the day arrived without a pile of gifts—at least two-thirds of them fairly fancy—there was going to be big trouble. Secondly, though I might have a "sweet little" talking voice, my singing voice was anything but. When I was nine, my church choir director had asked me to just mouth the words. Shrieking orangutans sounded more melodious than I did. Either my mother was tone deaf in her maternal love, or she enjoyed silently laughing every year first thing on her birthday.

"Mom, I really can't . . ." I said as I checked on RG. He was sitting beside me in the window seat and appeared to still be absorbed in his reading material, but I was perched right next to him. Ideally, we would have taken over two whole rows across the aisle from each other so as to give him plenty of space, but this train was unusually packed.

"Please!" my mom begged. "It's not like I have any other children to sing to me. If I don't get to see you on my birthday, I'd at least like the song."

Oh, good Lord. All right, fine. I turned my back completely to RG and inched to the farthest possible edge of my seat. I angled my head down towards the floor, cupped my hand around the phone, and began singing a muffled and horribly discordant rendition of "Happy Birthday."

Though I was singing as softly and quickly as possible, it seemed to go on for a painfully long time. A few of the standing passengers edged away from me, or was it my imagination? I was racing through the "dear mo-om" finale when I felt a tap on my shoulder. I sped through the final line and turned to face RG, who was holding his hand out.

"Yes, sir?" I asked apologetically.

"Could I borrow the phone for a moment?" he asked.

Before even telling my mom I had to go or clicking "end," I passed the phone to RG. To my surprise, he put it directly to his ear.

"Hi, Mrs. Joyce? This is Robert Gary. I just wanted to wish you a happy birthday and tell you your daughter is doing a terrific job."

Wow. Now that was a good present for my mom. Far better than the mini-Zen garden I had purchased in a rush at the Borders in Toledo. I could practically hear my mom's pride and excitement crackling from the receiver still pressed against RG's ear. She was certainly saying something—RG's face had reverted to its listening mask.

"Well, I'm not really the best judge of things like that, Mrs. Joyce, but I think she looks very healthy," RG replied into the phone.

Oh my God, what was my mom saying? I made a move to snatch the phone back before I caught myself. RG had a half smile on his face.

"I'll do that, Mrs. Joyce. Looking forward to seeing you, too. Bye-bye now."

RG clicked the phone shut and handed it back to me.

"Thank you, sir," I said. "That was incredibly kind of you. I'm sure it made my mom's day."

"No trouble at all," he answered as he returned to his reading material.

What in the world had she asked him? I had a feeling I was going to miss not knowing, but I plowed ahead anyway.

"Um, sir? Just out of curiosity, did my mom ask you something embarrassing and inappropriate?"

RG smiled at me.

"It depends on your definition. She asked me whether your skin was clear or broken out. She said it rarely breaks out, but when it does, it's usually because you haven't drunk enough water."

I blinked in pain.

"Got it. Thanks for telling me. Sorry to subject you to that, sir," I managed to reply.

"Like I said, no problem."

I sunk deep into my seat and wished I could disappear. I wondered if my genius mom knew that blemishes were also often caused by stress. In which case, she should feel directly responsible for any that popped up in the near future.

Our Columbus events passed by in a blur, and before I knew it, it was the following morning and we were arriving at the health care symposium at my alma mater, the University of Cincinnati. Jenny and the boys met us in the holding room. My own parents had left that morning on a surprise birthday trip to a romantic bed-and-breakfast, otherwise they doubtless would have attended as well.

I loved having Jenny and the boys around during work events, because RG never snapped at me when they were there, and generally seemed to enjoy a more lighthearted approach to everything. This invariably improved his performances as well, because he always did better when he was relaxed. I wished his family could be with him all the time.

As RG kicked off the symposium with some eloquent remarks about the need to move towards a single-payer universal health care system, a belief I ardently shared but couldn't express nearly as articulately, I looked around nostalgically. The conference was being held in the same room I had taken my senior exams in, and I found myself inadvertently checking the clock, worried that we would run out of time before I could get all the answers. This feeling of intellectual urgency haunted me generally, which I supposed wasn't a bad thing, since it kept me in a constant state of feeling like I needed to learn more. The only downside was an occasionally nervous stomach, often mistaken for appendicitis.

Sometime after RG's opening remarks, as a long-winded presenter was droning incessantly on about

something tangentially related to the topic at hand, a
message from Aaron buzzed through the boredom.

To: SAMANTHA JOYCE
[SRJOYCE@GARY.SENATE.GOV]
From: Aaron Driver
[aidriver@bramen.senate.gov]
Subject: Whipped Cream
Text: back in dc. teamsters went well. are you
still coming home? sorry i haven't been able to
be more in touch—the schedule with Bramen's
been completely crazy. i miss you more than i
can say and hope the trip's gone great. can't wait
to see you. it's been way, way too long. have you
forgotten what I look like? i'm glad you're the
one who brought up whipped cream. let's discuss
further when you get back. be good, AD.

Interesting. I had made up my mind that it was justifi-
able to be mad at him for keeping in such poor touch
over the past week just in time for him to send a sweet
and uncharacteristically mushy message. Maybe this necessitated a shift from prickly and self-righteous to flirty
and seductive. Before I had time to draft a reply along
this new line of attack, I received another message.

To: AD LIST
From: Aaron Driver
[aidriver@bramen.senate.gov]

Subject: FW: Senate to Install Extra Cameras
Attachment: Press Release.doc (50 kb)
Text: Uh-oh. Big Brother likes to watch!—AD

The attachment was a short news story about how the Senate buildings were beefing up security and installing cameras in the foyers of all the Senate offices. Some people were complaining about an invasion of privacy, but the installation was proceeding forward.

I was just proofreading the part of my reply that suggested a "naked whipped cream summit" when Jenny appeared at my shoulder. I clicked out of the message quickly, blushing and guilty.

"I hate to ask you this, but can you hold Jack while I go change Jeffrey?" she whispered apologetically.

"Of course," I nodded, sliding my BlackBerry back into my bag and accepting the sleeping bundle of baby she was holding out to me.

While she was gone, I developed an itch on my nose and my BlackBerry buzzed with more messages, but I could tend to neither as my hands were full of Jack. He was cutely drooling on my shirt as his eyelids twitched with some baby dream. Wow, my arms were starting to ache. How did Jenny do this all day? Feel the burn, I told myself. Pretend this was an exercise class. That actually didn't help that much, because if it was indeed an exercise class I would have scheduled it on my calendar but never shown up. Or shown up but faked a debilitating cramp at the first sign of a tough task. The undeniable presence of muscle work in my current predicament made it therefore impossible to imagine it was an exercise class.

I was just beginning to much more realistically imagine I was being tortured for heresy on some sort of medieval device when Jenny returned.

"Thanks so much," she breathed as she effortlessly gathered Jack on one arm while perching Jeffrey on her hip.

Steroid use was the only logical explanation for her superhuman strength. I tried to check for a telltale mustache, but Jenny had already turned away and was headed back to their seats at the front of the hall.

I listened as RG spoke for a bit about the need to prevent Medicare from being privatized and took a few notes. Soon, someone else was describing his unhappy journey through illness under managed care. The long-winded presenter interrupted to ask some long-winded questions. I pulled my BlackBerry back out to continue drafting my scintillating reply to Aaron.

I had several new messages. The first was from Aaron himself. Wow, three messages in a row, unprompted by a response. Maybe he really was missing me. I clicked on it happily.

TO: SAMANTHA JOYCE
[SRJOYCE@GARY.SENATE.GOV]
From: Aaron Driver
[aidriver@bramen.senate.gov]

Subject: re: FW: Senate to Install Extra Cameras
Text: you pushed "reply all" on your response.
thought you should hear it from me first. i'll call
you later.

What was he talking about? I hadn't sent my message
yet. I clicked over to my Sent Messages folder to investigate.

Holy crap.

To: AD List
From: Samantha Joyce [srjoyce@gary.senate.gov]
Subject: re: FW: Senate to Install Extra Cameras
Text: hey sexy, thanks for the heads up. speaking
of which, i can't wait to see you too. i'll be back
sunday—given the senate's new camera
installation, perhaps our naked whipped cream
summit should accordingly best be held in one
of our apartments where we have some control
over the videotape. i'll set it up. xxx, sammy

Holy, holy crap.

How had that happened? I rapidly rewound my
memory. It must have occurred when I'd hurriedly
clicked out of the message upon Jenny's surprise appearance by my side. I hadn't clicked out at all. I had
clicked into a world of pain. Good Lord, who was on
"AD List"? I sent Aaron a panicked message asking
just this question before checking the other messages

that had come in with a sinking sense of irreversible
dread.

Oh Christ.

To: AD LIST
From: John Bramen
[jfbramen@bramen.senate.gov]
Subject: re: FW: Senate to Install Extra Cameras
Text: Please remove me from whatever list this
is. Thank you.

To: AD List
From: Clare Yardley
[clare.yardley@nbcnews.com]
Subject: re: FW: Senate to Install Extra Cameras
Text: What the hell is this? AD, have you finally
been fired and started operating some sort of
soft porn site?

There were several more. And Aaron didn't even try to
assure me that this wasn't a completely humiliating
turn of events. He replied that there were over two
hundred people on "AD List," which was a lethal mixture of friends and high-powered political and media
elite, many of whom he also considered "friends," as
unbelievable as that seemed to me. And I had e-mailed
them all.

I slowed my hyperventilating to check in on RG,

who was making his closing remarks. There wasn't anything more I could do at the moment—I had to steer the Garys off campus and to the next event. If, somewhere along the way, I stumbled across a time-traveling contraption that could take me back to before I had orchestrated my own ignominious downfall, then I would do just about anything in return. Was the God of Rewinding Time listening? I doubted it. She never had been before.

I spent the rest of the morning in a palpitated haze of searing regret and frenetic distraction. RG had a busy schedule to stick to, and my damage control efforts were forced to take a backseat to my professional duties. As I accompanied the Garys to their many events, I vainly searched for an upside to the whole mess. None presented itself.

Had I gotten Aaron in trouble? It was tough to see how I couldn't have. Oh God, he must hate me now. I couldn't even bear to look at the impact on my career. And at the moment, I didn't even have time to. We still had to get to a lunch with the Cincinnati chapter of the nurses' union, a campus rally for a living wage for the service workers, an open meeting/town hall, and a district schools reception.

Hours later, the hotel room's clock radio informed me it was nearly 11:00 PM when I finally flopped down on the bed in exhaustion. For once this trip, Aaron answered his cell phone.

"I hope this doesn't mean you're rethinking the naked whipped cream summit, because I found that very intriguing," he said in a lighthearted way that indicated maybe he wasn't about to dump me for being a technology-impaired moron.

"You don't hate me?" I asked, surprised.

"Of course I don't hate you. I'm beginning to think people should have to get a license to operate a Black-Berry, but I don't hate you," he replied.

So he hated me a little. Okay, I could work with that.

"Listen, I am so, so sorry. I feel like a complete fool. Do all your friends think I'm an idiot?"

Please don't let all his friends think I'm an idiot.

"I heard 'sex fiend' more than 'idiot,'" he said.

"Well, the two aren't necessarily mutually exclusive," I replied.

He laughed.

"Look, it's really embarrassing," he offered sagely, "there's just no getting around that. But I don't think it's a deal breaker or anything."

A deal breaker? Was he referring to our relationship? I normally would have found this a gross turn of phrase, possibly warranting annoyance, but I didn't feel I had much of a leg to stand on at the moment. I was operating from a down position.

"Oh. Okay. Well, good," was all I could manage.

"It might be a little uncomfortable for a while, but it'll blow over. There are tons more important things going on in the world for everyone to care much more about than the mistake of a random staffer for a semi-obscure senator," he said.

If he was trying to make me feel better, he definitely wasn't succeeding.

"I mean, if someone who worked for Bramen did this, it would be a different story," he continued. "But as it is, people will forget it quickly."

Oh please.

"But I'm *dating* someone who works for Bramen," I said. "Doesn't that pose some sort of danger?"

Aaron didn't pick up on my mocking tone.

"Yeah, that's true," he replied. "But I still think it will be fine. Stop worrying about it, baby."

"Uh-huh," I replied.

If I hadn't been the one who'd just so royally screwed up, I would have picked a fight with him. But as things stood, I just needed any help I could get.

"Listen, is there any way to convince people that the whole thing was a joke?" I asked.

"You can try," he answered, "but D.C. doesn't usually get jokes."

I knew he was right. Even in my brief time in Washington, I had witnessed countless examples of what appeared to be a shocking lack of a collective sense of humor. Only the corniest of one-liners were recognized as jokes. Anyone attempting something more complex was generally doomed to be misunderstood.

"All right," I said in a defeated tone. "I guess I'll just have to ride it out. Do you think I need to tell Senator Gary about this whole thing?"

Please say no, please say no, please say no.

"Absolutely. There's no question you need to tell him."

Hmmm. Not much wiggle room there.

"Yeah, okay," I sighed.

"It's going to be fine, Sammy," he continued. "I'm still really looking forward to seeing you."

How charitable of him. I sensed I should get off the phone before too much more was said, in the interest of maintaining my humble and apologetic tone.

"Me, too," I kept it brief.

I hung up the phone, hung up on a new kind of un-settled feeling. On top of the basic humiliation I felt about the whole incident, there was an additional sense that something more had gone wrong between Aaron and me. His handling of the whole episode hadn't quite been up to par with the sensitive, loving, and supportive image I had heretofore projected onto him. But maybe he was just strung out from working too hard. For his awful, arrogant boss. I felt myself getting angry, which I didn't have the energy for at the moment.

I thumbed through the many BlackBerry responses I had received throughout the course of the day. The replies from important and possibly offended strangers included two more from high-level broadcast journalists, two from Senate chairmen's chiefs of staff, one from a

Supreme Court clerk, and one from a leading political consultant. His was perhaps the most entertaining.

> To: AD List
> From: Bob Espin [bespin@kstreetgroup.com]
> Subject: re: FW: Senate to Install Extra Cameras
> Text: recommend digital for the recording. whipped cream tends to come out blurry and indistinct on 8mm.

I saved his message in the hopes that it would make me laugh sometime in the far distant future when I could bear to revisit this horror.

# Brand News

AFTER THE BREAKFAST meeting the next day, I screwed up my courage to broach the topic of my latest mishap with RG. I was truly dreading it. We were riding the elevator back up to his room where I was to review the remainder of his schedule with him while Jenny packed up the boys. I hoped against hope that their proximity might keep him in a good mood.

"Uh, sir?" I asked nervously.

"What?" He looked up from his briefing book.

"There's been a bit of a development in my personal life that I feel you should know about in the event it impacts the image of your office in any untoward way," I started.

"Yes?" he asked.

I could hear the slight edge of fear in his voice. He knew I was capable of spectacularly terrible things. I took a deep breath.

"I BlackBerried a sort of risqué joke message to this friend of mine—it was totally a joke—but, um, I accidentally sent it to two hundred strangers. Most of whom are important people on the Hill. One of them is John Bramen. I should mention that this friend works for Bramen, which is really unfortunate and I'm trying to convince him to go somewhere else, but anyway, he does. I'm a total idiot and I understand if you want my resignation."

I averted my eyes and held my breath while I waited for RG's response.

"How risqué was it?" he asked after a thoughtful pause.

"Um, there was mention of dessert products and video equipment," I answered quietly.

"Interesting. It was a joke?"

"Yes, sir."

It basically had been. Me trying to be seductive was inherently a joke.

I looked up in time to see him nod.

"Okay, well, I don't see how this is really any of my business, but thanks for telling me."

The conversation seemed to be over, to my surprised relief. After all my agonizing, RG was being amazingly cool about the whole thing. Even about the Bramen angle.

"Have you sent a follow-up to everyone involved explaining that it was a joke?" he asked.

Why in the world hadn't I done that?

"No, sir, that's an excellent idea. I'll get on that right away."

He nodded again as the doors opened. And we continued down the hall and into the rest of our day as if nothing had changed.

Hours later, as I waited for my flight back to D.C., I composed and sent the follow-up message.

TO: AD LIST
From: Samantha Joyce [srjoyce@gary.senate.gov]
Subject: Luddites Unite
Text: Dear all, yesterday you received a message that was a) a joke, and b) intended for only one person but accidentally sent to a huge list. I want to apologize for the mistake and assure you that after this message I will keep a safe distance between my BlackBerry and me until I learn basic technological skills. Sorry again and have a nice day.
Sincerely,
Samantha Joyce

When I returned to my apartment, I noticed Shackleton immediately. He was swimming perkily around his bowl, all trace of mossiness gone. I had asked Liza to use her spare key to look after him while I was away, and had assumed she was just waiting until I was done with my trip to upset me with the news of his demise, so his metamorphosis shocked me. I called Liza to divine her fish revival secret. She claimed not to possess one.

"I swear I just did what you told me," she protested after intense interrogation.

Fine. I'd just get one of those nannycams and set her up next time I went out of town. I'd get to the bottom of this. She couldn't outfox me.

I spent the next fifteen minutes filling her in on the e-mail debacle (her gasps and groans were not reassuring), and then listened as she caught me up on her week, which had included passing out my card at the telemarketers' convention as requested. She really was a great friend.

As I was hopping in the shower to prepare for the Aaron reunion, my phone rang. I grabbed a towel and snagged the receiver just before the call went to voicemail.

"Yello," I said, slightly out of breath.

"Is this Samantha Joyce?" an unfamiliar male voice asked.

Ah, a new telemarketer! Fantastic. I tightened my towel and settled down happily on the edge of my bed.

"Yes it is," I answered brightly.

"This is Charlie Lawton with the Washington Post," he said.

I already had a subscription. Maybe he was just

calling to check on the service? Or maybe there was some sort of fun promotional deal.

"Uh-huh. I'm a subscriber," I encouraged.

"You work for Senator Robert Gary, correct?"

How had he gotten that information? Oh right, he must have been one of the people Liza had given my card to at the convention.

"Yes, that's correct."

"I wanted to ask you about the e-mail you sent out yesterday. I'm working on a story about e-mail faux pas on the Hill, and yours got forwarded to me by a bunch of different people."

"Oh," I responded, completely deflated.

This wasn't going to be an enjoyable conversation after all.

"Are you free right now to chat?" he asked amiably.

With a non-telemarketer wanting to dive into a very painful topic of conversation? I didn't think so.

"I'm actually just running out the door," I said.

"To the whipped cream summit?" he asked.

What a wise-ass. I didn't have to take this.

"No," I said tightly. "And you know what? I don't think I'm going to be able to help you."

"I'm sorry, I shouldn't have joked like that. Look, it's just a little article. It'll give you a chance to tell your side of the story."

He had a point there. If he was willing to help rehabilitate my reputation and make this whole thing less of a nightmare, maybe cooperation wasn't such a terrible option. On the other hand, publicizing the story only made more people aware of it. I'd like to restrict it to the cozy two hundred strangers presently in the know if I could.

"The story's going to be done anyway," he said, as if reading my mind. "I'd love to talk to you about it so I have complete information before it goes to press. Just one or two statements. I promise to make it painless."

I was fairly certain that painlessness was an impossibility at this point. But if he was going to do the story with or without my cooperation . . .

"Yeah, okay, I'll talk to you," I said with a sigh.

"Great, are you free later this evening?"

Not if everything went well.

"No, I'm afraid not," I said.

"Well, they really want to run this tomorrow. Can you squeeze me in for just fifteen minutes or so?"

I had plans to meet Aaron for dinner in an hour and a half at a restaurant in Dupont Circle. I agreed to meet Charlie at a cafe nearby in an hour. He said we could just talk over the phone, but I wanted to meet in person so he could visualize the depths of my pain and consequently be more likely to take pity in his depiction of the incident.

After a brief wardrobe debate (I wanted to look hot for Aaron, demure and compassion provoking for the reporter), I settled on a medium-ground look of jeans, sandals, and a form-fitting T-shirt beneath a more respectable jacket that I planned to shed for the Aaron portion of the evening. I spritzed on some perfume Liza had given me and headed over to Afterwords Bookstore and Cafe, off Dupont. We had agreed to meet in the Humor section. There was no one else around when I arrived there, so I dove straight into a Gary Larson book to pass the time. I began to hope Charlie would be really late, as I'd also picked out a Calvin and Hobbes collection and a Doonesbury book to skim through, but I reminded myself that I could always come back.

I was laughing over a particularly amusing page when I sensed someone approaching.

"Samantha?" that now slightly more familiar male voice asked.

I looked up into the bespectacled blue eyes of Clark Kent.

"It's you," I gasped in surprise.

It was the reporter I had maimed at the Alfred Jackman hearing. The one who might also have possibly witnessed my Rollerblade tumble. I knew him instantly. He looked momentarily confused, but then placed me in a swift flood of recognition. He glanced quickly at my shoes. No, I was not still wearing two entirely different ones. Nor was I wearing anything with wheels. Though my current pair could probably prove just as lethal, given a chance.

"Well, we haven't actually formally met," he said, offering his hand with a smile.

Was that a scared smile? So much for provoking compassion. In his eyes, I was already a crazed enemy combatant. Oh well. I shook his hand.

"Samantha Joyce."

"Charlie Lawton."

"I'm sorry I attacked you last month, Charlie. I really didn't mean to," I said.

"You've got a mean right hook," he smiled ruefully.

"Well, you know, you bruised me," I said, pointing accusingly towards his belt buckle. "That thing really leaves a mark."

A mother picking out books with her two sons gave me a scandalized look and led her children quickly away. What? What had I done? Charlie looked embarrassed, as well. Oh crikey.

"I was pointing to your belt buckle," I said, blushing deeply. "That's what bruised me. Not your . . ."

I decided it was best to just trail off.

"Right. Well, should we get a table to talk?" Charlie offered, moving right along.

Why not? I needed to sit down.

We settled in at a table in the corner. The waitress asked us if we wanted anything to drink. Charlie looked surprised when I ordered a margarita. I would have ordered something stiffer if I could've gotten away with it. He ordered herbal tea.

"I'm on deadline," he explained, though there was

no explanation needed, given that his was a much more normal order for a late Sunday afternoon.

Though I realized it would be an uphill battle, I felt there was still a small chance I could charm him. I smiled as sweetly as I could and batted my eyes ever so slightly.

"Do you have something in your eye?" he asked helpfully.

No, I did not.

"So what's it like working for the Post?" I asked, interested.

"Oh, it's fine. I'm still pretty new there, paying my dues. Now, how long after you sent the e-mail did you realize it had gone to a list of over two hundred people?"

All right, I guessed we were done with the small talk.

"Uh, pretty quickly. My boyfr—my friend e-mailed back right away," I said.

"Aaron Driver's your boyfriend?" Charlie looked up quickly from his notepad.

"Well, uh, I suppose," I said, flustered. "I mean, we've been dating for over a month now. How many dates does it take until someone's your boyfriend?"

Charlie was scribbling away. Oh God, did Aaron consider himself my boyfriend? We hadn't really agreed to any terms.

"I mean, maybe it's still casual or something. I

guess I should just call him a good friend," I suggested in vain.

"So since Aaron's your boyfriend, it really wasn't that much of a joke message," Charlie said. "It was more of a, er, 'romantic' message that fell into the wrong hands."

I was not at all ready to abandon the joke defense.

"No, it was still a joke," I said firmly. "Don't you joke around with your girlfriend?"

Charlie ignored me.

"Or boyfriend, or whatever?" I tried.

He didn't look up from his pad. I sensed this wasn't going in my favor.

"And how did you feel when you realized your love note had been sent to so many strangers?" he asked.

"It wasn't a love note!" I said shrilly.

"Uh-huh. And what sort of responses to the sex message did you receive from the people to whom it was accidentally sent?"

I tried to calm down. This was my shot at clearing my name. Senator Bramen and anchorwoman Clare Yardley and the Supreme Court clerk and all the others could read this article and see that I really was an endearing jokester victimized by an innocent slip of the finger. This was an opportunity. I needed to regain control of it. I supposed that suggested I had ever been in control of it in the first place, which wasn't accurate, but never mind.

"Look, it was a joke that went awry. I pressed the wrong button on my BlackBerry. It was completely my fault. I encourage all other BlackBerriers out there to take the time to double-check things before they send them off, no matter how frenzied they are with work or whatever. It's definitely worth it to avoid gaffes like this one."

"So this wouldn't have happened if you hadn't sent it when you were in the middle of a busy work day?" he asked.

Finally, I seemed to be getting through to him.

"Exactly," I affirmed. "I was on a trip with Senator Gary and we were in the midst of an extremely hectic schedule. I was just working too hard to pay close attention to sending an e-mail," I explained.

Charlie was nodding.

"Uh-huh. Okay, I think that's all I need. Would you like to say anything else?" he asked.

Yeah, of course. Anything that could complete the task of winning him over to my side. What that might be remained elusive.

"Um, I guess just that I'm really embarrassed and obviously wished it had never happened. And, uh, it was nice to meet you."

Charlie smiled at me.

"Do people ever tell you that you look like Clark Kent?" I asked.

He adjusted his glasses as he put his notebook away.

"No, not really," he answered.

I found that hard to believe.

"Oh, one last question," he continued. "How has your boyfriend reacted to all of this?"

How honest was I obliged to be? I decided the most political thing to do would be to duck the question.

"Oh, I'd rather not drag him any more into this than he already is. Clearly, I'm not really sure if he even is my boyfriend," I laughed.

"Uh-huh. Well, keep me posted," he replied.

What did that mean? Keep him posted on how Aaron was treating me or keep him posted on whether I was taken or single? Instead of clarifying, Charlie shook my hand, dropped some bills on the table, and left. I watched him exit the door and turn the corner, leaving me unsure of how the interview had gone and his true opinion of me. I guessed I'd find out in the morning. I swallowed the rest of my margarita to clear my head.

Aaron was fifteen minutes late as usual, but this time there was no Pez dispenser in sight. As soon as I saw him enter the restaurant, his sly smile directed straight at me, my neck rash flared up, reminding me just how much he did it for me. In fact, the attraction seemed even stronger, despite the tension between us. Or perhaps because of it. He kissed me hello but seemed a bit reserved, as if my recent behavior necessitated a little distance. This slightly aloof posture made him all the more desirable, as I felt a driving need to win him over once more. A part of me objected to the unfairness of this new dynamic, arguing that he should be showing more sensitivity and support, out of kindness and chivalry if not deep affection for me, foibles and all. I gave this voice a Jack and Coke to shut her up, and set about charming him all over again.

Midway through Operation Win Back, the waitress delivered a whipped cream sundae to our table, informing us it was from a secret admirer. Aaron looked around the place and spotted someone he knew at the far end of the bar. He gave him a mock salute.

"Who is that?" I asked.

"Jordan Blake, spokesman for Secretary Smithton," he replied.

"The Secretary of Defense?" I asked, surprised.

"Yeah, Jordan and I went to school together, but I haven't seen him in years."

Did everyone know about my e-mail? I had only sent it the day before, and it was still the weekend. Curse the Internet and its powers of mass distribution.

"Good sundae," I said brightly.

Aaron smiled wryly.

The rest of the evening went something like that. Aaron seemed happy to see me, but slightly embarrassed to be seen with me. This was solved when we returned to his place and turned off the lights.

The next morning I woke up wishing I didn't have to race back to my apartment and then off to work. This feeling was happily trumped by my joy at waking up in Aaron's arms again. More specifically, on Aaron's arms, which I'd somehow managed to pin beneath me during the course of the night, causing both of them to fall asleep. He shook them around like limp rubber chickens to try to restimulate his circulation. I tried to help as best I could.

On my way out, I deemed it in my best interest to steal Aaron's copy of the Washington Post, because I wanted to review the article in preparation for his reaction to it. With any luck, it would be a glorious vindication that would confirm his decision to continue relations.

A headline on the front page informed me that Bramen had just received the endorsement of six different governors. He was looking more and more unstoppable every day.

I flipped to the Style section, ignoring articles about Kevin Costner's latest western (from a quick glance, it appeared he restored order and civilization via gutsy banjo playing), to a not-short-enough article smack in the middle.

### Rx for Trouble: Health Care Aide
### Spreads Dirty Mass E-mail

BY CHARLES LAWTON

Over the weekend, two hundred members of Washington's political and media elite were treated to a titillating message from Samantha Joyce, domestic policy adviser to Senator Robert Gary of Ohio. The e-mail, intended for her boyfriend Aaron Driver, a speechwriter for presidential hopeful John Bramen, read as follows:

To: AD List
From: Samantha Joyce [srjoyce@gary.senate.gov]
Subject: re: FW: Senate to Install Extra Cameras
Text: hey sexy, thanks for the heads up. speaking of which, i can't wait to see you too. i'll be back sunday—given the senate's new camera installation, perhaps our naked whipped cream summit should accordingly best be held in one of our apartments where we have some control over the videotape. i'll set it up. xxx, sammy

Ms. Joyce believed she was replying directly to Mr. Driver, when in fact she was unwittingly re-plying to a long list of Mr. Driver's friends and acquaintances. Ms. Joyce expressed deep remorse over the mistake and explained that it never would have happened had she not been so distracted by work. When pressed, Senator Gary's office confirmed that it pays the BlackBerry and cell phone bills of its staff members, which means Ms. Joyce's X-rated mistake was funded by taxpayer money. Perhaps in the future, she'll refrain from using work devices for personal sex notes and devote her full attention to the needs of the hardworking Americans who elected her boss to his position. Or perhaps not.

I sat down on the curb outside Aaron's apartment, pushed down by an uncombatable sinking feeling. If only I had permanently maimed Charlie Lawton during the Alfred Jackman debacle in some way that rendered him incapable of ever writing such libelous tripe. He was a treacherous little worm, undeserving of his physical similarity to Superman's alter ego. I sat there steaming vengeance until I finally forced myself up. I started down the block on the return trip to my place, but turned around and tromped back to Aaron's door with a stoic and undoubtedly temporary resolve.

"Did you forget something?" he asked in surprise when he opened the door.

He looked so good when he was freshly showered and wearing his suit. I handed the newspaper article to him.

"Charlie Lawton needs to be hurt," I declared.

Aaron furrowed his handsome brow and quickly read through the piece.

"You told him you were working when you sent the e-mail?" Aaron asked with a judgmental frown. "And you identified me as your boyfriend?"

My eyes were already hot with indignation. One blast of a cool response triggered immediate condensation. Precipitation followed quickly.

"Oh come on, don't cry," Aaron said with alarm.

It was too late. I wasn't just crying—that implied some sort of delicate or ladylike behavior—I was full-on sobbing, complete with heaves and hiccups. Through the salty blur of tears and mucous, I glimpsed Aaron's look of bewildered helplessness. He seemed both shocked that I was capable of such a Niagara Falls performance and confused as to how to make it stop. He put his arm around me, subtly directing my face away from the jacket of his suit. I buried my head in it in protest, forcing him to literally absorb some of my pain. He resigned himself to the role of comforter, patting my back and smoothing my hair, less awkwardly as he went along.

"There, there," he said generically. "It's really not that bad."

"Yef it if!" I howled belligerently from my muffled suit cave.

He stayed quiet and continued stroking my hair until

I calmed down, finally tuckered out by my vigorous out-burst. Did that count as a workout?

"Sorry about that," I mumbled as I dried my eyes on his tie. "I think I was already exhausted from the trip."

"Hey, it's okay," he said. "Do you want me to take you home?"

I shook my head. It was best to end this episode as quickly as possible. I splashed some water on my blotchy face and made my way to the door once more.

"Hey, gorgeous," he lied.

I turned to face him. I could feel my under-eyes puff-ing dangerously.

"Yeah?" I asked in a small, defeated voice.

He took my shoulders in his hands and tilted my chin up towards his face. His green eyes bore into mine.

"Do you know how lucky I am?" he asked. "How many guys get e-mails like that from a hot babe like you? Everyone who reads this article is secretly jealous of me. And you know what? They should be."

He kissed me just a little too long.

"Now I've got to change suits," he said in my ear as his hand made its way to my breast. "You wanna stay and help me pick out a new one?"

Forty-five minutes later, I made my way back to my apartment in an entirely different frame of mind. Yes, Charlie Lawton needed to be punished, but my life would go on, made infinitely more enjoyable by my sizzling romance. I had survived worse than this—I would persevere. The *Rocky* theme song echoed in my head as I took the stairs two by two.

Upon exiting the Red Line at Union Station, my BlackBerry buzzed with a message from RG.

To: SAMANTHA JOYCE
[SRJOYCE@GARY.    SENATE.GOV]
From: Robert Gary [rgary@gary.senate.gov]
Subject: WP
Text: Samantha, don't worry about article. See you in the office.

I walked towards the Russell Senate Building feeling like I had some good people on my side. Which helped me immeasurably when I had to deal with Ralph at the security checkpoint.

His look of perpetual surprise was even more pronounced when his face lit up upon seeing me. He thrust the Style section article in front of me while brandishing a pen.

"Can I get an autograph?" he asked.

"Very funny, Ralph. I'm in a hurry," I said with a grimace.

"I didn't know you were so dirty," he continued.

Did this count as sexual harassment? I was in the mood to sue.

I scowled at him as he waved me through.

"Can I e-mail you for free or is it like a paid nine-hundred number?" he cackled to my turned back.

The gapes I received at the elevator made me decide to take the stairs instead. On the second landing, "Like a Virgin" began blaring from my bag. It seemed more ironic than usual. I scrambled to answer it.

"Are you okay?" Liza asked me when I clicked on the phone.

"Yeah, I guess so," I sighed. "It really sucks, though."

"Do you have this Charlie Asshead's number? I'd like to give him a piece of my mind."

I wished I did, because I knew Liza really would.

"We'll have to track him down sometime," I answered.

"Oh yes, we certainly will," Liza said ominously.

We made plans to meet for lunch and hung up just as I entered the office. Janet looked up from manning the phones and smiled obliquely at me.

"We've gotten lots of press calls you need to check in with Mark about. Also, RG wants to plan a strategy meeting for the bill for today or tomorrow. He asked that you set up a good time with Bramen's people, okay?"

She didn't wait for an answer but went right back to juggling the incoming calls. After checking in with my desk, I sought out Mark. He was lingering by Mona's cubicle. They both looked up as I approached.

"Hi there," Mona said heartily.

Mark averted his gaze. I smiled bravely back.

"So I guess you guys saw the *Post* article," I said.

"Sure did," said Mona. "Aaron Driver's the boyfriend you were telling me about?"

Mark carefully inspected something on top of his shoe.

"Yep."

"Huh," she replied thoughtfully.

This piqued my curiosity. Was she a source of Aaron background information after all?

"Why, do you know him?" I asked nonchalantly.

"Not really. Just a little through a friend."

I got the sense there was more information there to be ferreted out, but Mark was nervously clearing his throat.

"So, um, I've gotten some calls about the article," he said quickly, speed-miming answering a phone. "And I'm sticking with a firm 'no comment' from the office."

He accented this by making decisive slicing motions and shaking his head no. I realized that a "no comment" was the best policy, but couldn't they be more officially supportive?

"Yeah, okay," I said, choosing not to voice my distress.

"It should blow over soon," he added. "Are you and Aaron still together?"

He tried to pass this question off as a legitimate information-gathering tactic of an on-the-ball press secretary, but couldn't quite succeed. I blushed slightly as Mona snapped her head up sharply and Mark reexamined his shoes.

"Yeah, we are."

It would have been worse to point out the inappropriateness of the question. Everyone steamrolled forward.

"Good, good," Mark said unconvincingly. "Uh,

there've also been some calls about the trip. It's gotten really great press in Ohio," he soldiered on. "And a positive mention in the *Times*, as well."

That at least made me feel good. I'd worked hard on the trip and though I knew the open meetings and other events had gone well, I was pleased to have more formal corroboration of the success. Certainly the majority of the credit went to RG, since he was the one who made everything happen, but I had played an important role and I felt proud.

"Well, that's good news at least," I responded.

Neither Mona nor Mark said anything in response. Mona still looked angry about Mark's relationship status inquiry, and I decided it was time to retreat to my desk.

Back there, I had a voicemail from Charlie Lawton asking me to call him at the office. Fat chance. I dove into my work to try to take my mind off the article.

Though I was excited to strategize about the upcoming battle to pass the bill in the Senate, I dreaded resuming contact with Natalie, particularly in light of my recent hijinks. But it couldn't be helped. She answered the phone on the first ring with her smooth, mechanical voice.

"Oh, hello, Samantha. How can I help you this time?"

Ugh, why hadn't I just e-mailed? I explained the purpose of my call as dispassionately and succinctly as possible.

"I'll have to check Senator Bramen's schedule," she replied noncommittally. "He's extremely busy, as I'm sure you can imagine. He's got a bit more on his plate than Gary does! But let's try to coordinate."

God, I hated her. The entire Bramen staff suffered from a severe superiority complex.

"Great," I managed in a slightly strangled voice.

"How about I just e-mail you later?" she continued. "Are you comfortable with that?"

Was she implying I was no longer comfortable with e-mail? Probably. And even though that was true, I resented the insinuation coming from her.

"Terrific!" I shouted brightly.

After hanging up, I carefully read through some e-mails, hyperaware of every button I pushed. Would I ever be able to feel comfortable with my devices again?

I spent the remainder of the morning following up with the people RG had interacted with back in Ohio. I e-mailed Kara to double-check the contact information for the young man whose father hadn't been receiving his Social Security checks. She called me back to verify.

"How's it going there?" she asked in an indecipherable tone.

Did she know about the *Post* article? Did she really get a subscription to it out in Cleveland? Knowing her and her uncanny ability to be on top of everything, she probably did.

"Oh, okay, I guess," I said warily.

I didn't mind being honest with Kara, but I still hoped to be someone she'd consider looking up to. It was a dream that just wouldn't die, despite taking multiple hits.

"The weasel's become a fixture on Ronkin's show out here," Kara said. "It even has its own Web site."

"Can we hack it?" I asked, half-jokingly.

"I'm working on it," she replied.

I believed it.

"Let's just not create any sort of Weaselgate," I cautioned.

"Oh, don't worry," she assured me, "I'm much too good."

I also believed that.

"Listen, I saw the *Post* thing and I just wanted to tell you I thought your e-mail was hilarious. Anyone who doesn't see it as a joke is a moron. Too bad about sending it to all those people, but hey, it makes life more exciting, doesn't it?"

She had a point there. What with all the attention and humiliation, there certainly wasn't any doubt that I was alive. This wasn't a month I would glide through anonymously, making a negligible impact on the larger world. Didn't that count for something? I was here. I was on this earth. It was going to be forced to deal with me, like it or not.

"In a weird way, that does make me feel better," I replied.

"Good, I'm glad," she said. "I've got to head back to school next week, but please call me if I can help out on specific trips or anything during the year."

I was going to miss talking to her on a regular basis. We hung up and I made some calls to the Social Security Administration to investigate the backup on the checks. After being transferred seven times, I lucked out and got sent to someone who was actually from Ohio and an RG supporter. Finally, this allowed me to make some real progress. An hour later, I was able to call the young man to tell him his father's backlogged checks would be arriving the following day via FedEx. His surprised and grateful response made me feel like a fairy godmother, sprinkling RG's magic dust to make people's problems disappear. It was a pretty fun feeling, so I clung to it, happily typing up a report of the events to update RG. I knew he'd be pleased.

I checked my home messages after lunch. To my surprise, I had one from Beverly, the Cool Whip lady. She said she'd looked up my number from the record of our conversation after reading an Internet story about my whipped cream e-mail and realizing that she had talked to the very Sammy Joyce featured in the scandal. She sounded hurt and wanted to know why I hadn't suggested a "Cool Whip summit" instead. Wow. The news really *had* gotten around. In addition to feeling depressed at this evidence of its tremendous scope, I also couldn't help but feel a little guilty. Whipped cream had just sounded better. I did enjoy the Cool Whip product and would have been more than happy to give them some free publicity, but this hadn't really been an incident I'd been able to foresee. I'd call Beverly later and try to explain.

Natalie e-mailed soon after I returned to my desk, informing me that Senator Bramen had consented to squeeze RG in for lunch the next day. I stuck my tongue out at her message before forwarding it on to Mona for addition to the schedule. Then I turned on C-SPAN to watch coverage of a bill signing at the White House.

President Pile was doing his best to look grave and historically relevant. Neither came easily to him. As a group of lawmakers stood around him, Congressman Harris right at his elbow, he said a few words about the importance of maintaining the sanctity of marriage between a man and a woman, and of protecting our children from the corrosive effects of "too much diversity." The cluster of all-white legislators surrounding him nodded solemnly in agreement. What all this had to do with the bill Pile was signing to relax logging restrictions in old-growth forests remained a mystery.

Even after seven years of watching him, President Pile never ceased to amaze me. He always sported a blank, deer-caught-in-the-headlights expression that inspired neither confidence nor all that much respect. He'd made a career out of failing upwards, but his disastrous reign as the leader of the free world had used up what had once appeared to be a bizarrely limitless amount of luck. I watched him stumble over a few more sentence fragments before jutting out his jaw and signing the bill with a flourish. At least that was some proof he was literate. I didn't mean to be so callous, but having a shitty president was something I took personally.

The rest of my day was spent continuing to follow up with the groups and constituents RG had interacted with at his open meetings, updating a chart of congressional members' positions on prescription drugs, and fielding calls about the *Post* article. By eight o'clock, I was exhausted. Near the coffee machine, I came across Mark Herbert. He looked away quickly upon eye contact, but steeled his shoulders a bit and made himself look shyly back. That was unexpected progress.

"Uh, listen . . ." he said, looking very uncomfortable. "I apologize for asking about your boyfriend earlier. That was inappropriate." He paused and took a breath. "I just hope you're happy, and, uh, it's nice to get to work with you," he finished.

For someone who communicated with the press for a living, he seemed to find it remarkably difficult to talk to me. He'd even been too nervous to mime along with his hands. His shoulders sagged a bit and he sighed deeply in recovery.

"Thanks, Mark, and don't worry about it," I replied. "We should be friends and then there won't be anything inappropriate about knowing what's going on with one another."

He looked so happy I wondered if I could quantify the impact of my statement and deduct it on my tax return as a charitable contribution.

"So I'm dating Aaron," I reiterated. "Are you seeing anyone?"

I knew the answer, but figured it was polite to ask if we were going to begin a friendship. Plus I had plans to take this line of questioning somewhere specific. I had a seed to plant.

"Uh, no. I, uh . . . no. I guess the short answer is no."

"I'd be happy to hear the long answer," I said encouragingly.

"Uh, actually, the long answer's 'no' too. I haven't dated anyone in a while."

He did sound definitive about this, and also a little embarrassed.

"Well, as long as you've got some good friends to hang out with, who needs a relationship?" I said cheerily.

I knew I was lying as much as he did.

"Do you like working here?" I plowed ahead.

I knew he was good at his job, but I couldn't tell how much he enjoyed it.

"Yeah, I do. Senator Gary's very inspiring to work for," he replied.

That was certainly true. I was glad he recognized that and wasn't just here to pad his résumé. We needed people we could trust.

"We've got a pretty good group," I began. "Mona's really terrific."

I kept my voice very casual. I really did. I was quite proud of myself.

"Yeah, she's pretty funny," Mark said.

She was? I'd never experienced that. But it was great that he thought she was.

"Oh, yeah, I love her," I continued. "I mean, I don't know her as well as I'd like. Of all the people in the office, she's the one I really want to get to know more. She seems like she's just got so much to offer."

Mark looked thoughtful. Perfecto. Or had I lain it on too thick? Did I just think "perfecto"? That was odd.

"Well, anyway, I better get back and finish up," I said.

"See you later," he said with a grin.

I made my way back to my desk with a full coffee cup and a good feeling about making a new friend. I should do that more often. Better still, I had begun my fledgling matchmaking career with subtlety and precision. I was going to get such a heartfelt toast at Mark and Mona's wedding, I got teary-eyed just thinking about it. I took a brief moment to practice looking humble and angelic—two important guises to have down when the entire wedding reception turned appreciatively in my direction. The gratitude I'd get from their families and friends! It was almost overwhelming. Really, I hadn't done that much. Could I say that convincingly? They were going to love me.

Bramen was slated to give a big policy speech in two days, which meant Aaron was slated to be tied up writing it for the next forty-eight hours. RG actually wrote most of his own speeches—certainly all the really important ones—but Bramen generally just supervised the construction of his, which translated to a ton of work for Aaron. When I called him, he anticipated a postmidnight departure from the office. I found this annoying, but managed to bite my tongue before I asked him if he thought the late hours were worth it when his boss was such a horrible person.

I called Liza to see if she was free, but she and Ryan had already made plans. She invited me to go along with them, but that didn't strike me as a wise plan of action. I didn't really feel the need to have an activity anyway—I was exhausted from my day and still worn out from the trip. I traveled home, got some Chinese takeout, watched the first part of a new show called *Who Wants to Marry My Dentist?*, which I decided never to watch again without copious amounts of novocaine, and was asleep by 10:00.

## Faulty Fuse

Now that Labor Day had come and gone, everyone seemed ready to get down to business. The presidential candidates began officially announcing their campaigns and crisscrossing the country in variously themed tours. Bramen was headlining a Back to the Basics bus tour, Spearam had launched her Conversations Caravan, Rexford was riding high astride his Momentum Motorcycles, and Wye had unleashed his Cajun Express. As I read about them all, I daydreamed about a giant drag race that could decide the nomination. It would have to take place somewhere open and flat, where people could really get down and dirty. Maybe Kansas. And even though Conrad and Candle weren't doing as well, they could participate in the vehicles of their choosing, because we were a democracy after all. The drag race would definitely speed up the primary season and inject a little more excitement into it. And maybe it could woo the NASCAR dads back into the party fold.

Those pesky dads were currently enamored with the other side, where Brancy was continuing to pick up steam and far outpoll the president's brother and the Senate majority leader. Not to be outdone by any of his potential rivals for the general election, Brancy had just taken off on a Freedom Fly-Around. I wondered if his route took him over Kansas. He could fly right over the drag race. Would he trail a taunting banner from his plane? Or engage in some skywriting smack talk? My daydreaming did a lot to spice up the morning news summaries.

On the Hill, people were ready to get back down to business as well. Over the summer recess, plenty of constituents had made it clear that they were fed up with Congress's sluggish pace and were prepared to express their frustrations via the ballot box. In response, chastised lawmakers returned to D.C. hell-bent on getting things done. This palpable enthusiasm for productivity bode well for the prescription drug benefit bill—I hoped the legislation could ride the wave before it broke on any ideological sandbars and dispersed into stagnant partisan tide-pools. Timing would be everything.

A companion piece of legislation was making its way through the House of Representatives. If the House succeeded in passing their version the same week the Senate approved our bill, the two could go immediately into a conference committee that would iron out their differences. Then, of course, the agreed-upon identical bill would have to pass both the House and Senate before it could be delivered to the Oval Office, where President Pile was already actively rooting against it.

Though Pile had stopped short of vowing a veto, since even he could sense that such a move would be politically unwise, his administration was working furiously behind the scenes to guarantee that their congressional henchmen killed the bill off quickly. We were working just as furiously to ensure the final bill could be made into law before Congress adjourned for the year, which gave us a little over two months. I felt energized by the challenge. Though the bill fell short of my initial hopes for the legislation, I'd come around to the belief that it still represented positive steps in the right direction. And it was great to feel forward momentum.

However, working with the Bramen crew continued to test my patience. They were consistently arrogant and bossy and I'd grown to dread our joint strategy meetings. Aaron wasn't involved in these, but I still held him accountable for being associated with such a terrible group of people. And in my opinion, Aaron had let slip enough comments to prove that he shared their basic condescension. He swore that I'd misinterpreted these, but I knew that I hadn't. Aaron had listened to my charges, reiterated how much he respected the work I did, and started making me breakfast most mornings as atonement for being part of the Bramen staff. Lucky for him, I'd forgive almost anything for a steady supply of pancakes, though I warned him that he would have to change jobs soon if we were to progress as a couple. He'd nodded and added chocolate chips to the batter that morning.

At work, I fell easily into the new routine of lobbying and strategizing. Every day, we updated a large chart that indicated how the relevant lawmakers were most inclined to vote on the bill based on whatever new information we had managed to gather. The second week of September, we got an unexpected publicity boost with the release of two separate studies from well-respected institutions that claimed that a government-funded health care system, like the one currently in place in Canada, would save the United States two hundred billion dollars a year, which was more than enough money to cover the costs of the nearly forty-four million Americans currently without health insurance. The articles about the studies invariably cited the prescription drug benefit proposal as America's attempt to move closer to such a progressive system.

As I sifted through this beneficial coverage, I was briefly distracted by a distressingly fawning story about Borden Dent, actor turned presidential aspirant. Dent had been parading around in his Prada cowboy boots from one press conference to the next, signing autographs and flashing his trademark smile. He'd portrayed a president twice in the movies and often pointed to these parts as great preparation for the job he sought. He'd also played a psychotic alien, giant ape, and a retarded man with a bad southern accent, but I had yet to hear him touting the learning experiences of these roles. There was still time.

I was clicking out of the Borden Dent article and back into the bill work when a breaking news alert informed me that a rolling blackout had just left Cleveland and Toledo powerless. I turned on the TV and watched the footage. There were hordes of disrupted commuters wandering on foot in a sort of aimless weave down the middle of streets rendered disorderly by defunct traffic lights. Where did our rules go without electricity? Apparently they got absorbed into some sort of primitive hive mind that emerged to fill the void left by the abrupt disappearance of the manufactured power we'd come to rely so heavily upon. Anchormen warned that looting might begin at nightfall. Until then, the city seemed ruled by a steaming sense of purposelessness.

A quick-thinking power grid monitor had apparently acted in time to prevent the blackout from spreading to the eastern seaboard, sparing millions the stress and frustration currently befalling the residents of Ohio. The preliminary reports indicated that the blackout hadn't been caused by any individual com-

pany's negligence, but was more a casualty of the
grossly outdated power grid that RG had been warning about for some time. I'd learned early on that RG
was better than most at seeing the bigger picture and
was occasionally ridiculed for it by those who made
their careers out of capitalizing on smaller, safer political issues. RG wasn't a doomsayer—he always had a
proactive plan for combating the problems he pointed
to—but his detractors wrote him off as a pessimistic
exaggerator. The fact that he'd been proven right time
and time again they refused to address or accept.

RG immediately called for more hearings on the
topic before getting on a plane to Ohio to tour the
hospitals, water plants, and community centers and
offer whatever support and assistance he could provide. I spent the rest of the day updating the position
chart and helping answer the hundreds of calls
swamping the office lines. By dinnertime, I was short
of breath from talking to so many people worried
about loved ones they hadn't yet heard from. I also felt
dizzy and light-headed, the beginning signs of a panic
attack. Some people got sympathy pains. I got sympathy disorders.

Thankfully, power returned to northern Ohio sometime during the night, before too much damage had
been done. RG completed his tour and rejoined us on
the Hill, where the rest of the week blazed by in a caf-
feinated blur of blackout recovery and bill lobbying.
The surprise crisis had served to double our normal

workload, but I'd learned to expect the unexpected in this job and simply adjust my schedule accordingly.

As I headed into the office that Saturday to make my way through a stack of paperwork, I noted that it was the sixty-fifth anniversary of Seabiscuit's win over War Admiral at Pimlico. To celebrate, I ducked into a corner store and bought some scratch tickets adorned with horses, which ended up winning me a free Slurpie. I chose the cherry-flavored kind and arrived at work a little hyper from all the sugar. Mark was also in the office, looking a bit stressed.

"Hey, what are you doing here?" I asked.

"RG may be doing Russert tomorrow," he answered, making talking signs with his hands.

Interesting. That was great, if a little surprising. Bramen had been sucking up most of the press oxygen around the bill, relegating RG to a lower-profile but very crucial lobbying role. As I watched Mark walk quickly away, I realized that I hadn't seen much of him in the last few weeks, which was abnormal since our office was not that large. He used to come up with any excuse to shyly wander past my desk, but now it was almost as though he'd been purposely avoiding me.

Two hours later, he appeared beside my desk.

"Listen, Sammy . . ." he began. "There's something I've been meaning to ask you for a little while now."

"Sure, Mark, go for it," I replied.

"Well, you know when you have something you

need to say, but you're pretty sure the other person isn't going to want to hear it? That's sort of what I've been struggling with," he continued laboriously.

Oh God, what was this? I noticed his hands had remained uncharacteristically motionless throughout his speech.

"Uh-huh," I said cautiously.

"Well, I think I already know the answer to this, but, um, are you and Aaron exclusive? There's a reason I'm asking."

Oh no. I already knew the reason, but did we really have to talk about it? Weren't we past this? I couldn't deal with a vocalized crush from Mark. His feelings for me had been obvious all along. Well, at least since Mona had pointed them out to me. Didn't he know there wasn't any chance of us getting together? Having been on the other end of painfully unrequited crushes more times than I liked to count, I had no desire to be the person stringing someone else along. I liked Mark and was annoyed that he seemed determined to make things permanently uncomfortable between us. I took a deep breath. I needed to put an end to this as definitively as I could while still being kind.

"Yeah, we are, Mark. Look, I really like working with you and think you're a cool person, but you've got to move on. There are plenty of other women who'd be tremendously lucky to date you, possibly one or two of them right here in this very office. But not me. I'm with

Aaron. And I don't think we should talk any more about it, okay?"

I had involuntarily closed my eyes somewhere in the middle of my spiel, as though I didn't want to watch it unfold. It was certainly easier to get through when I didn't have to look at Mark's face. Now that I had opened my eyes, I saw that his skin had turned a deep pink color and he looked supremely embarrassed. Oooh, I should've kept them closed.

"That's not what I—what I was gonna—never mind," he stammered. "Just forget I was going to say anything. It was a bad idea," he said as he hurried off.

All right, that was agonizing but necessary. Mark had needed to be disavowed of any lingering romantic illusions. I hoped we could be friends, but even if we couldn't, at least there wouldn't be any misunderstanding between us. I returned to my work with a resigned resolve.

I made it back home by four o'clock, which helped me feel like I hadn't really put in a full day of work on the weekend. Anytime before 7:00 didn't count as a full day. When I walked in the front door, Shackleton was suspended diagonally facing downwards in his fishbowl. His gills were beating sluggishly, indicating some slivers of remaining life, but I had just about had enough. I used my special crime corner camera to snap a Polaroid of his latest death pose and marched the evidence down to Mr. Lee's pet store.

"You didn't flush him yet?" Mr. Lee asked in horror as I presented the photo.

Oh right. The last Mr. Lee had heard, Shackleton had perished months ago. No, I wasn't keeping him around Norman Bates style. I wrinkled my nose at the thought of the smell.

"No, he's still alive, but just barely," I clarified. "I know I said he was dead on that message, but it turned out he wasn't. He just *pretends* to be dead. All the time. It's very disconcerting. I need something to make him better."

Mr. Lee looked thoughtful and concerned for a few moments.

"Oh, stop presses, I have just thought something!" he cried, his face lighting up. "Come look, come look!"

I followed him back to the fish tank section, where I glanced bitterly at a slew of hale and hearty-looking Japanese fighting fish. Shackleton had once looked similarly sneakily healthy. Mr. Lee pointed to a corner of their tank, specifically at some bright purple seaweed.

"Just in!" he exclaimed. "You must try. It make all the difference!"

"How much is it?" I asked suspiciously.

"For you? Preferred customer? A special deal," he answered.

Back at home and twenty bucks lighter, I cleaned Shackleton's bowl and refilled it with the seaweed remedy. But when I returned him to his hangout, he went straight to the bottom to lie down on the rocks, completely ignoring the new addition. Maybe he just needed a little while to notice it. I wasn't ready to give up hope just yet.

I had plans to meet Aaron later that evening, once he finished drafting a speech Bramen was scheduled to give at the AFL-CIO convention. He'd been working at Bramen's Georgetown town house since early morning, but expected to be released in time for dinner, as the senator and his wife had symphony plans.

Even though I'd also had to work on a Saturday, I felt resentful that Aaron's irksome job continued to cut into our together time. I wouldn't have minded as much were he working for a cause I deemed worthy, but that wasn't the case. And he'd been traveling so much lately, our relationship had begun to resemble a commuter one. The only upshot of this tense arrangement was that it made me really value the nights we set aside to be alone together. I'd read somewhere that successful marriages often depended on such "date night" strategies, so perhaps this was all good practice for the future. I took a hot shower and a long time getting ready, in happy anticipation of the evening. He finally BlackBerried around 8:00.

To: Samantha Joyce [srjoyce@gary.senate.gov]
From: Aaron Driver
[aidriver@bramen.senate.gov]

Subject: why aren't you with me right now?
Text: lovely lady riley, we're at the tombs. up
for it?

The Tombs was a Georgetown bar in Georgetown. In other words, a very collegy bar. But it was fun when it wasn't too crowded, and it served kick-ass jalapeño poppers that I'd developed a mild addiction to my first few months in D.C. I was a little confused as to who the "we" was and why the we was at a bar when I'd been killing time uncontacted for the last few hours, but I decided to just put on some lipstick and head over. I'd find out soon enough.

I should have known when I got thrown up on before I even made it into the bar that it wasn't going to be a good evening. It happened just as I reached the steep flight of steps that led down into The Tombs. Two young guys were propping up a third cohort between them as they made their staggering way to the street. I caught a glimpse of their load's greenish face just as his tortured eyes met mine and he blanketed my upper torso in a sloppy coat of vomit. It was less gross than it could have been, since my projectile barfer had apparently only consumed massive amounts of alcohol in the last several hours, translating into a purely liquid attack. Still, it wasn't that fun.

I stood there dripping for a moment as my assailant beamed an apology from his miserable eyes before stumbling off towards his dorm. My cabdriver, who'd been counting his tips after letting me off, quickly swerved off down the street, lest I try to get back in for a trip home for fresh clothes. Apparently my puke-covered money was no longer good enough for him.

I examined my options. To hail another cab, get home, change, and return could take up to an hour with Saturday night traffic and wardrobe indecision. Taking the subway was not an option as the city planners had annoyingly neglected to put a train stop in Georgetown. It hadn't been an oversight—they'd allegedly bowed to pressure from the wealthy upper crust residents who wanted to insulate their territory from too much contact with the hoi polloi. The most elite parts of democracy's capital city were the most difficult to access. At the moment, I found this irony incredibly inconvenient.

I called Liza for a consultation.

"You have to go home. That's disgusting, Sammy."

"But it already took me a while to get here, and I really just want to—"

"Sammy."

Liza didn't use her stern tone that often. She reserved it for when serious etiquette crimes were about to be committed.

"All right, fine. I'll call you later."

I hung up, resigned to trudge down to M Street to try and hail a cab. But it had already been forty-five minutes since I'd gotten Aaron's message to come meet him, so I at least wanted to pop in and inform him of what was going on with me. Surely he cared.

On the other hand, as Liza had emphasized, I was covered in gross vomit and not looking so hot. Perhaps I'd just BlackBerry.

> To: Aaron Driver [aidriver@bramen.senate.gov]
> From: Samantha Joyce [srjoyce@gary.senate.gov]
> Subject: re: why aren't you with me right now?
> Text: currently right outside the tombs but have had an accident, not of my own doing. i swear. must return home to change. want to come with?—sammy

I sat down on the steps to wait for his response, which I felt confident would entail his momentary appearance by my side. After ten minutes and three different people asking their friends "whaddya think happened to her?" I still hadn't heard from him. What the hell was he doing? Hadn't he gotten my message? Who or what was more important than responding immediately? I stormed down the stairs, stopping in the bathroom to clean myself up a little bit before making my way angrily to the bar.

I found him there doing tequila shots with a group of people, several of whom I recognized as Bramen staffers. The fact that Aaron worked with them was irritating enough; must he willingly socialize with them, too? I felt myself scowling.

"Sammy!" he shouted, after I tugged on his elbow. "We need one more shot," he shouted at the bartender.

"No thanks," I said through gritted teeth.

I'd been doused with enough drinks for one night. Didn't he notice I needed some non-alcoholic assistance?

"Did you get my BlackBerry?" I inquired, completely ignoring the people around us. I didn't like them anyway.

"Huh?" he asked, straining to hear, but not too hard. He was definitely drunk.

The place was pretty packed, which was certainly not the way I liked it. I'd enjoyed the sweaty frantic feel of college bars when I'd been in college, but now it just made me tense.

"Hey, what happened to you?" he asked, when he finally really noticed me.

"Some guy threw up on me," I answered.

"That's gross." He paused to let this sink in. "But what I meant was where've you been? We've been here since three-thirty," he clarified, if it was possible to clarify while slurring one's words.

Three-thirty? That afternoon? I'd still been at the office then. I'd assumed he'd still been working, also. Okay, deep breath. Maintain calm.

"You didn't get in touch with me until eight o'clock.

So I haven't been here, because I didn't know you were here," I said, trying to keep my voice as unshrill as possible.

"Huh? Oh . . . sorry, thought I berried you earlier. It must not've gone through."

Uh-huh.

He looked unfocused. Still hot, in a hazy way, but definitely out of it. I was jealous of the people he'd been hanging out with, and annoyed that Aaron hadn't called me sooner. Why didn't he want to hang out with me? Wasn't I fun? What wasn't fun about me? All right, maybe there were some unfun things about me at this exact moment, but they could be explained away.

"Well, I'm glad you guys have been having such a party," I said in a tone that indicated I wasn't at all pleased by that fact. "I hate to break it up, but I've got to go home. Are you coming with me?"

Even as I said it, I knew it was a bad, bad move. If I was out partying with my friends, would I want to stop the good times to appease a spew-covered harpy who'd done nothing but yell at me since arriving on the scene? Probably not. But, I argued in my head, what if that spew-covered harpy was a significant other whom I cared for very much? Possibly even loved? Didn't that change the equation? I decided not to dwell on the question of why I'd be dating a spew-covered harpy in the first place.

I was still working through my feelings on the subject when Aaron batted at my arm.

"C'mon, don' be mad. Stay and haf sum fun with us." He grinned beseechingly at me. "I'll find you some new clothes. Hey, you!" He shouted at a guy wearing a Hoyas T-shirt and balancing two pitchers of beer on a stack of cups as he passed by.

"I'll give ya twenty bucks for yer T-shirt," Aaron said as he took out his wallet.

"I'm leaving, Aaron," I said pointedly.

"Wait, baby, I'm getting this for you so you don't hafta go home n' change," he explained as he tugged on the stranger's sleeve.

"Dude, get off me," the Hoyas guy yelled, flinging out his elbow and pushing Aaron into a table.

"Wass yer probbem?" Aaron shouted after him.

Then he looked at me and started laughing.

"Sorry, baby. Hold on, I'll ass summon else," he promised.

I grabbed his arm as he made a beeline for a large man wearing a sweaty underwear tank top. I didn't view that as a big improvement over my current outfit. And it certainly wasn't an item of clothing worth twenty dollars. Or a beating.

"Stop, Aaron," I urged. "Forget it. I don't want someone else's shirt."

He looked at me, perplexed. I realized that he was nowhere close to sober enough to understand me at the moment. I might as well save my wrath for when it could have a greater impact.

"If you're having such a fantastic time here, why don't you just stay," I suggested bitterly.

"Okay, sounz good. 'Bye, baby," Aaron agreed much, much too quickly.

Stunned, I watched him return to the Bramen posse at the bar. A few of them looked over their shoulders in my direction, but I ignored them, held my chin up high, and made my sodden way through the hordes of drunken college students towards the stairway and up to the street.

I passed the Exorcist House on my journey to a cab and mused the coincidence of being covered in vomit so close to that landmark of cinematic puke. Had my attacker been possessed by Satan? I hadn't noticed any visible head spinning, but who knew what was happening back at his dorm.

I had just made it to M Street and into an even greater rage over Aaron's behavior when I heard someone call my name. When I turned around, I found myself face-to-face with Charlie Lawton, evil enemy. I flinched backwards, a look of repulsion etched on my face. Combined with my stinky, sopping outfit, I imagined this made for an outstandingly atrocious look. He did appear concerned.

"Hold on a second," he yelled to a man across the street.

He'd apparently just run over to flag me down.

"Hey, are you okay?" he asked.

Did he really need to ask? I clearly wasn't. And there was no way that I was going to be any better after running into him. His fake concern sickened me.

"As if you care," I spat at him. "Are we 'off the record' or should I just lie and tell you I'm fantastic?"

Hmmm. Strategically, I should have waited to hear his answer about being off the record before providing him the sarcastic alternative. If we were in fact on the record, I'd just given up some information. I made a note to myself for future hostile interactions with journalists. He looked a bit taken aback.

"Look, I'm sure you're upset about the article. I wanted to talk to you to—"

"To what, get a follow-up on whether I'd been fired or not?" I began furiously hailing a cab. "I'm still employed, no thanks to you. You're a real jerk, you know."

I couldn't decipher his expression, mainly because my hair had fallen uncooperatively into my face. Even though I couldn't see him, I hoped he looked hurt and chastened.

"Can I help you get a cab?" he asked soberly.

"No! I don't want a cab!" I shouted with my hand still outstretched in a hailing-a-cab gesture. "Go to hell!"

I put my hand down and stomped determinedly off. In the reflection of an opening restaurant door, I saw him impassively staring at me as I stalked away. Good riddance.

My feet were sore and I was thoroughly chilled by the time I made it an appropriate distance away to be able to hail a cab. The ride was fast and bumpy and the tears had started flowing before I made it to my front door. I turned on my light and blearily took in Shackleton wrapped up in the seaweed. He wasn't moving in his nooselike cocoon, but I was too upset to go in for a closer examination. I opted instead to take a bath while I continued sobbing.

I replayed the night's events in my head over and over. In retrospect, it felt like I'd never stopped getting puked on. I really didn't want to be the sort of woman who got shrewish and possessive and yelled at her potential fiancé when he was just out blowing off steam. I imagined that when one worked for an enormous jerk, blowing off steam was important. But Aaron had also blown off our plans—plans I'd been looking forward to; plans I'd spent an hour getting ready for. He'd treated me badly. Hadn't he? Or was I overreacting? I wasn't sure. And I felt exhausted by all the second-guessing.

As for Charlie Lawton, I only wished I hadn't looked quite so haggard or smelled quite so offensive when I'd told him off. He unquestionably deserved my venomous scorn and I felt no remorse having flung it at him. If he felt even a little bad about himself, it had been worth it.

I'd investigate Shackleton's status in the morning. I left a message for Zelda, but refrained from calling Liza, whom I knew was now with Ryan at some sort of horrible fraternity reunion of his. I decided to meditate to further relax and was subsequently dead asleep in a matter of minutes, unaware of exactly where I stood on my journey towards enlightenment.

# Hey Buster

DEBATE BEGAN ON the final version of the bill in both the House and the Senate on Monday afternoon. Though the separate versions had passed quickly and easily, it soon became evident that the political tides had changed. Now that we were a year away from the actual election and the latest polls showed Bramen leading all other candidates from either party, an effort had emerged to deprive him of noteworthy legislative victories that could make him even stronger. Accordingly, several senators loyal to Majority Leader Frand were suddenly threatening a filibuster. Timing was certainly no longer on our side.

The spirit of bipartisanship quickly evaporated, replaced by a contentious mood that hovered in the early winter air. And though the senators continued to address each other in debate as "my esteemed colleague" and "the senior senator from" per the etiquette rules, the phrases seemed increasingly flimsy covers for reservoirs of explosive scorn and combativeness lurking just underneath. I feared for the bill.

I was also still recovering from Aaron's dismal Georgetown bar performance. He'd called me the next afternoon and invited me to hear some music with him as if nothing had happened. I'd readied myself for a grave conversation about communication and respect, but when I'd brought it up he'd just kissed me on the forehead and asked that we save the "relationship talk" for some other time.

"I just want to have fun with my girl tonight," he'd drawled.

"Well, if you ever act the way you did last night again, you can find yourself another girl," I'd replied.

He'd looked surprised, then chastised. And he'd taken my hand and addressed me seriously, which was all I'd asked for to begin with.

"I'm sorry, Sammy, I'm afraid I don't even remember much of last night, which is really embarrassing. Bramen's been running me ragged and I guess I just needed to let loose a little, but I didn't mean to get quite that loose. I'm ashamed. I hope you can forgive me."

I'd seen real remorse in his deep green eyes and felt myself melt a little.

"I don't mean to be a bummer," I'd clarified, "it's just—"

"You're not," he'd interrupted me. "You're wonderful. And I behaved badly. I promise I'll never do it again."

He'd squeezed my hand for emphasis. "I don't want to lose you."

I'd nodded, thinking about how he was about to leave on yet another work trip. I hadn't wanted him to leave. Maybe Aaron had seen that in my eyes and realized he was out of danger. Whatever the reason, he'd slipped back into a lighthearted mode.

"You're really whipping me into shape, you know," he'd teased. "But I'm a willing soldier."

He'd kissed my hand, saluted me, and requested permission to make everything up to me in bed. And we'd returned to our version of normal. I'd felt happy, because physically being with him made me happy, but I'd also become aware that the up-and-down rhythm of our relationship was threatening to lose its charm.

I listened to Bramen speak Aaron's words on the Senate floor during the second day of debate over the bill. They were powerful words, urging the members of Congress to rise above their differences and respond to the critical need for the prescription drug benefit legislation, and though I found it difficult to watch Bramen, I felt proud of Aaron's craftsmanship. Unfortunately, this very craftsmanship fired up the opposition even more. Senators lined up to give long-winded speeches pointing out the terrible flaws of the bill. I tried not to take it too personally.

By Thursday, though the debate had been fierce and not altogether polite, there were still enough committed votes to ensure the passage of the bill. The House narrowly approved it that morning, providing an additional surge of adrenaline. By late afternoon, it looked like Frand was going to be forced to call a vote and the bill might be passed at last. Which is when Senator Rollings launched his filibuster.

Senator Rollings was the eighty-three-year-old senior senator from Mississippi. He spoke about "mettycare" from the position of someone fully eligible for it. From this vantage point, he complained about the federalization of health care, and of the dangers of creeping socialism. He spoke as if on a crusade. He wanted none of this meddling in the prescription drug industry. He wanted government to just leave people alone. He was sick and tired of all these efforts to make things more complicated for folks. And he felt very strongly.

Four hours into his explanation of his feelings, he brought out a stack of telephone books. I watched on C-SPAN as he stared straight at me. Apparently he liked government just barely enough to be involved in it to the point of knowing where all the cameras were.

"This bill would be jest day'sastrus for so many folks," he thundered.

He opened up the first phone book.

"Why, it would be day'sastrus for Mr. Chester J. Abbington," he said, using his thumb to keep his place in the phone book. "And jest as turrible for Mrs. Alfred A. Abson," he continued.

And so on.

By ten o'clock that evening, he and his impossibly drawn-out way of talking had only made it through the Ds. I watched from my desk, unable to go home while the bill I'd poured myself into lay dying a slow death by drawled enunciation. Outside, snowflakes began falling. It was early November and D.C. had only just begun cooling off from the summer heat, but I'd learned to expect anything from the increasingly erratic seasons.

When I was younger, the first snowfall of the year had always elicited a wild, limb-flailing dance to the God of Ongoing Blizzards. My performance was a heartfelt spiritual plea for continued school-closing weather throughout the winter months. My goal was to dance hard enough to please the deity into granting my wish and creating a winter vacation to match the summer one. Though my dream was never fully realized, there had been a glorious three-week stretch of no school due to an enormous blizzard the year I was in third grade. The dance I'd done on its opening night had differed from its predecessors in one important regard—it had featured a round-off into a split for the first time ever, as I'd just perfected the move that month. Given the pleasure it had plainly induced, that feat obviously needed to be incorporated into every snow dance to the God of Ongoing Blizzards from that year forward. It was one of the only things that kept me limber.

But I didn't feel like doing my snow dance when I

noticed the flakes sticking to the large office window. Though I couldn't ignore the rush of pure joy that the sight of snow reflexively evoked in me, it was an ephemeral sensation, rapidly replaced by dark and grumpy feelings that gurgled around in my gut as I watched the flakes fall quicker and thicker. It better just be a light dusting, I found myself thinking, because anything more would create further hassles as we tried to get this bill passed. For the first time in my life, I viewed the snowfall as an inconvenience. Good Lord, was I getting old at long last?

I stayed at the office that night, listening to Senator Rollings drone on and on (how many other eighty-three-year-olds were up pulling all-nighters for work?) and racking my brain for ways around a filibuster. I knew I should have gone home to sleep and returned early the next day, but I told myself I'd race back to my apartment at 6:00 or 7:00 in the morning, shower, change, and get back in time to rely on insane amounts of coffee to get me through the day.

This plan was foiled when I awoke at 6:00 AM from what was supposed to have been a quick nap and looked out onto a world transformed by an ongoing blizzard. Someone else must have performed one hell of a snow dance. The streets were thicketed in enormous drifts that vaguely suggested the shapes of buried cars and fire hydrants and lampposts. All at once, everything felt marooned, including myself.

I glanced down at my attire. I was pitifully ill-prepared for the weather. My knee-length skirt provided zero warmth and my shoes would be a joke in the snow. Why oh why hadn't I stored one of the two snowsuits hanging in my home closet at the office for emergencies? I kept my gym bag here in the event of a fitness crisis that had yet to occur—why hadn't I applied the same planning rationale to severe weather garb?

There was no use beating myself up. I decided to order up a rescue and dialed Aaron's number, despite the early hour. It was almost his wake-up time. He'd be happy to hear from me.

I tried four times but he didn't answer. Maybe the phone lines were down. His cell phone was off. I sent a BlackBerry but wasn't sure it went through. All of a sudden, rescue didn't seem as inevitable.

Fine. I was resourceful. I could handle this. I reviewed my options and decided to go back to sleep. When I awoke a second time a half hour later, the snow was still cascading past the window in thick matrices of white. I often arrived at the office during the early morning hours, and there was always a fair amount of activity in the building by at least 7:00 AM. But when I stuck my head out of the office door, the hall was dark and empty. Had the snow stymied even Janet? This was unheard of.

I returned to my desk and clicked on the TV. There was Senator Rollings, drawling away. He'd almost made his way through an entire phone book, but others waited in a nearby stack. Surely he couldn't keep going on his own—was there some sort of tag team strategy in the works? Was there a relief filibusterer waiting in the wings?

The sight of Rollings hard at work murdering my bill chased away any thoughts of leaving the office. I had work to do here. If others braved the weather and waded in, great. If not, I'd soldier on myself, rumpled from my long night but ready for action. I made two pots of coffee, corrupting the decaf pot to my own purposes, and scavenged in the mini-fridge for a stale cinnamon bun I'd stashed there the week before. Somewhat fortified, I sat down to brainstorm.

Filibusters were nearly impossible to defeat when wielded by experienced and determined foes. But there had to be a way. Rollings and his loyal band of Frand-ites could not succeed in obstructing a valuable piece of legislation. Some Machiavellian strategizing was in order. Unfortunately, I wasn't very good at being devious.

"This bill would also represent a cay-lam'tee for Sanford B. Zines," Senator Rollings was asserting from his soapbox.

I'd always enjoyed the name Sanford. Certainly from the show *Sanford and Son*, but also because of Mr. Sanford the school crossing guard. He was a grizzled, stumpy man who drew little faces on acorns and passed them out to the kids. During my elementary school years, I'd collected four hundred twenty-seven acorn people from Mr. Sanford. Several of them had gone to decorating the ill-fated squirrel village I'd constructed, and the remainder filled a desk drawer in my room at home. My mom had tried more than once to throw them away, complaining that they gave off a rotting smell, but I'd conducted my own evaluation, detected no such offensive scent, and mandated that they remain untouched.

Mr. Sanford had passed away the year before from old age and two failed kidneys, and I had plans to visit his grave with a couple of fresh acorns sometime in the coming year. With any luck, he'd eventually rest forever under the shade of an oak tree, kept company by a self-generating supply of the hard little seeds he'd anthropomorphized to the delight of scores of schoolchildren.

My memories of Mr. Sanford exploded a lightbulb-shattering idea in my head. It started by me wondering if the Sanford mentioned by Senator Rollings bore any relation to my Mr. Sanford. Though one was a first name and the other a last one, perhaps there was a connection somewhere along the line. For example, my middle name Riley was the maiden name of my maternal grandmother, a name that otherwise would have been lost as she didn't have any brothers to carry it on. However, it lived on as my middle name and would enjoy a further life as the first name of Aaron's and my unborn daughter. Perhaps Sanford had experienced a similar trajectory.

This line of reasoning, though extremely far-fetched

in several regards, led me to thinking about how Mr. Sanford would have agreed with me over Senator Rollings about the prescription drug benefit bill—certainly out of hometown loyalty, but also because his own situation could have been improved by the legislation we were struggling to pass.

This, in turn, made me wonder if the Sanford B. Zines mentioned by Rollings would also be in support of the bill, regardless of whether or not he was one of Mr. Sanford's long-lost relatives. If he would be in support of it, I imagined he might be offended by Senator Rollings's presumptuous use of his name as part of his filibuster.

I glanced quickly back at the screen at the stack of phone books next to Rollings. He had been reading one from Jackson, Mississippi. I needed to get a copy of that exact one.

Two hours later, I was deep in the midst of my own phone book reading. My process involved cold-calling all of the people whose names Senator Rollings had read aloud and determining if any of them were sufficiently angry about how they were being used. It was not an easy task. Dozens of people mistook me for a telemarketer, to my personal joy but professional frustration, as this led many of them to immediately and rudely hang up on me.

Of those who stayed on the line long enough to hear my mission out, ninety-five percent had no idea there was a prescription drug benefit bill currently being debated by the Senate. I initially spent exhausting minutes explaining the bare bones of the issue to every caller who would listen, but soon realized I had to simplify the process to preserve both my sanity and the hope of making any sort of progress. For those in Mississippi, I just asked them if they liked Rollings. If they were supporters of his, I got off the phone quickly. If they weren't, I went into greater depth. By noon, I had ten people willing to go on the record that Senator Rollings had misrepresented their views and spoken for them without their permission.

By that time, the office had filled with people who'd battled the blizzard to get to work, but I barely noticed their presence. I was a woman with a plan from which I could not be distracted.

Sure enough, Senator Rollings finished up his thirty-one-hour speech by giving up the floor to his close friend and colleague Senator Lajane, who continued the filibuster. Others were waiting in the wings to take their turn when Lajane tired.

By early evening, I'd completed the first phone book Senator Rollings had read and took my plan to RG. He listened carefully, his eyes lighting up as I went along.

"You've talked to all these people?" he asked deliberately.

The list I'd given him had grown to almost two hundred. I'd gotten into a zone.

"Yes, sir," I replied. "If we put more people on this, I'm confident we could get hundreds more."

He was nodding.

"All right, get Mark in here. We need a press contact we can trust. Are any of these people willing to travel?"

He followed my gaze as I looked out the window. The snow was still coming down pretty hard.

"Right, that won't work anyway," he said before I could answer. "Fine. We'll just go to them."

It wasn't snowing in Mississippi. Furthermore, many of the news outlets in the state were itching for a prominent role in a national story. To my giddy delight, Mr. Sanford B. Zines was one of the first Jackson residents patched through to Tom Brokaw via satellite. For sentimental reasons, I had ignored rules of alphabetization and moved him to the top of the list I'd given RG.

"Mr. Zines, you're saying Senator Rollings had no right to use your name as part of his filibuster? What if Senator Rollings genuinely thought the bill he's attempting to defeat would in fact negatively impact your life?"

I watched Mr. Zines jiggle his earpiece uncomfortably and stare confusedly into the camera. Come on, Sanford, you can do it. He cleared his throat.

"Ernest Rollings should know better than anyone that people don't 'preciate the gov'ment meddlin' in they bizness. As I figger it, that bill's gunna give me some help. Rollings can go suck a hog's ear."

Strong finish. We'd discussed on the phone all the ways the bill would help Sanford B. Zines and his recurring arthritis, but we hadn't gone over obscure animal body part epithets. I was very pleased with his mastery of them. I watched the corner of Tom Brokaw's mouth tug slightly upwards.

"Thanks for your time, Mr. Zines."

The others were equally unscripted. By the end of the news cycle, there were several colorful indictments of Senator Rollings's phone book tactic on the record. Bramen called a press conference to urge those behind the filibuster to cease their "cynical thwarting of the will of the people." C-SPAN carried it live.

"Their claims have been disproved. Americans are sick and tired of being used as pawns for political gain. Let's end this nonsense and get back to doing our job for the people who entrusted us with their well-being. Stop the filibuster. Let's have a vote."

Thankfully, the media kept on the story. Rollings and Lajane and the others leading the opposition to the bill couldn't get ahead of the spin of the coverage. People whose names had been read aloud began contacting our offices instead of the other way around. By midday Saturday, the filibuster was ended and a vote was called.

Though the snow had finally stopped falling, the city

lay paralyzed in its copious clutches. Senators arrived at the Capitol slowly, after frustrating journeys over the laborious terrain. I still hadn't made it back to my apartment since leaving Thursday morning. Aaron had responded to my pleas for help once his phones were up and running again, and had brought me some clothes that were clean but terribly matched. Did someone else pick out his outfits for him? Because he never looked as bad as his taste suggested he should. Luckily, I didn't have too much time to worry about my appearance, what with the excitement of the filibuster buster. I was vibrating with exhilaration and caffeine as I watched the roll call on the monitor.

All of the senators were present for the vote. And the bill passed fifty-three to forty-seven.

When he returned to the office after giving a few interviews in the hallway, RG awkwardly threw his arm around my shoulders in a friendly and unfamiliar hug.

"Really good job, Samantha," he said as Janet and Mark looked on.

I smiled and blushed. I wanted to savor any moment when people weren't wondering how I managed to hang on to my job. I was used to being proud of RG and his efforts. The reverse was a much more foreign sensation.

"Congratulations on the bill, sir. It's going to help a lot of people."

RG grinned.

"So where's the celebration?" he asked unexpectedly.

Wow. Where was it?

"Let me find out, sir," I answered quickly.

"I've got some champagne in my mini-fridge," Janet offered.

She did?

"Break it out," RG said happily.

I rushed back to my desk and called Aaron.

"Hey, babe, are you still at the office?" he asked.

"Yeah, and I need help. RG wants to celebrate. Where should I take him? Quick, quick, he never wants to hang out!"

"Okay, calm down. Hold on a second."

I heard the sound of muffled voices in the background. Was that Natalie? Blech. Aaron came back on the line.

"This crew is headed over to the Capitol Lounge. Bramen's stopping by for a drink with a couple reporters in tow. Do you guys want to meet us there?"

Not really, but was that the best option? I tried to be mature. We *had* worked with the Bramen staff on the bill, so I supposed we could hang out with them in the spirit of celebration. Otherwise, we'd be having competing parties, which was a little weird. This way I could ensure that theirs wasn't a better one. And at least I wouldn't have to face them alone. I'd be armed with my own gang. Ooh, maybe we could rumble. The *West Side Story* theme played through my head as I leaned back in my chair to glance down the hallway at Mark, Janet, and RG drinking their glasses of champagne. They'd better not drink all of it.

"Yeah, we'll meet you there," I answered into the phone.

"Great. Can't wait to see you. And, hey, Sammy . . ." he continued.

"Yeah?"

"Congratulations."

I smiled deeply enough for my cheeks to start hurting. My man was proud of me, too. This was a fun day.

"See you soon," I said as sexily as I could.

I hung up the phone and sprinted down the hall. Mona had joined the little crew, but there was still some champagne left. It went down smoothly and made a warm little Jacuzzi in my stomach.

"To our team," RG said warmly as he held up his glass in a toast. "I couldn't do this without you guys."

My glass was already empty. I glanced surreptitiously at the others. Hmm . . . they all still had some left. I crept my hand from the stem up to the main body of my glass in a bid to cover up the vacancy. There, that was good. From anyone else's perspective, there could still be several respectable swallows hidden beneath my hand.

"Here, here," Janet said.

We all clinked glasses and smiled affectionately at one another. The whole staff wasn't there—it was really just a little group of us, which made it feel more intimate. As I pretended to drink along with the rest of them, gulping down champagne-scented air, I felt lucky and fulfilled.

"Drinking too much air might give you gas," RG said beside me.

And embarrassed. Everything was in order.

## Stand With Custer

A HALF HOUR later, our merry band tramped joyfully through the snow to the Capitol Lounge. It was a little bit of a trek, and negotiating the wintry terrain made me feel like an intrepid explorer. It took me a few minutes to get my snow legs back. Luckily, Aaron had included my winter boots as part of the outfit from hell he'd delivered, so I at least felt satisfactorily shod as I traipsed along.

While the others chatted happily, I hung back a bit to appreciate the effects of the too-early snowfall. The city felt unnaturally hushed and I imagined the ground was in shock beneath the layers of frost and flakes. I closed my eyes for a moment as I walked, listening to the stillness of the icy air. When I opened them again, I was struck anew by how everything glistened a premature silvery blue.

Inside the Capitol Lounge, which glowed cozily with recently assembled holiday lights, Bramen's people had reserved a sectioned-off area for our celebration. I ordered eggnog immediately, partially because of the weather, but mainly because it was the three hundred ninety-sixth anniversary of the first reported eggnog drinking in America (at the Jamestown settlement, as described by Captain John Smith, according to my research). I sipped the dessert drink and wondered if Pocahontas had enjoyed it as much as I did while I watched RG talking to Mark in the corner. It was nice to see him out with the staff. He normally made a beeline for home as soon as he tore himself away from work, restricting the socializing with his employees to scheduled retreats and the annual holiday party.

As I finished my eggnog and ordered another, Aaron strode in with a group from his office. I recognized some of them from The Tombs debacle and felt a surge of anger that I struggled to extinguish, because tonight was a night I wanted to be happy. Aaron smiled at me as he walked over and slid his arm behind my back. His cheeks were ruddy from the cold and some rogue snowflakes were caught in his hair. I felt my neck rash burn beneath my scarf.

"How's my girl?" he asked.

I tilted my head and kissed him.

"Whoa, babe, maybe we should save that for later," he said as he looked around.

Though I thought about mentioning that he should be happy I was kissing him at all, I knew he was right. We were surrounded by work and PDA wasn't the most professional mode of behavior. I had gotten carried away by the moment. And possibly the rum.

"Sorry, I'm just glad to see you," I explained.

"Me too, me too," he assured me. "And I'll be right back, I've just got to make a quick call. Have you met Matthew?" he asked as he turned me towards one of his colleagues and excused himself.

I had met Matthew, but it had been very briefly at a fund-raiser. I was about to remind him of it when he started shaking his head.

"No, I don't believe I've had the pleasure," Matthew said.

All right, fine. I determined not to let that bother me, even though it always irked me when people didn't remember that we'd met. I hated feeling inconsequential, though I'd grown used to Bramen staffers treating me like I was. Matthew was smiling expectantly at me, without a trace of recognition in his busy eyes.

"Good to meet you," I said graciously.

The arrival of Bramen and his posse of reporters interrupted our small talk. They set up court at one end of the bar. As I went for a drink refill nearby, I got a closer look at them and was dismayed to recognize Charlie Lawton among the group. I didn't want that treacherous little worm around during a night I was trying to celebrate. He had yet to be punished for his awful article. I glowered at him and wondered where Aaron was. My honor needed to be defended.

Before it could be properly avenged, Bramen started making a show of calling RG over.

"And this guy's a real soldier," Bramen said heartily.

I turned to watch RG smile at the group, and I noticed that the little line between his right eye and ear had gone hard, which meant he was annoyed. You couldn't tell from any other part of his demeanor, but I had a lot of experience crossing that little line.

I understood the irritation. On top of all the other ways he was a jerk, Bramen was also infamous within his own party for pursuing positive press through any means necessary, which often meant selling out members of his own party to make himself look better. Typically, he'd powwow with one of his hometown journalists and feed them a story that served his purposes, making sure they never hinted that he was the direct and only source.

What surprised me about Bramen's antics was how desperate he was to constantly build himself up, even in regards to the most trivial things. He didn't hesitate to tear into his closest allies in this relentless quest. Over the years, Bramen had successfully reaped dozens of good stories and the intense dislike of many of his colleagues in the Senate.

I watched as RG deflected Bramen's false praise and extricated himself from the clutch of reporters as soon as he could. Something in Bramen's expression as RG walked away made me lean in closer as he turned back to the reporters. I pretended I was retrieving a bar napkin and strained to hear.

"He didn't do crap for the bill, but still, it's always good to make the little guys feel appreciated," Bramen said in a dropped voice that only the listening journalists and I could overhear. "Even if you're the one who did all the work."

He shrugged and clapped Charlie on the back.

"That's off the record, of course. Now, who wants another round?"

Horrified and struggling not to launch myself, fists flying, at Bramen's head, I picked up a bar napkin and retreated to the far corner. Feeling like I might explode, I downed my eggnog and contemplated revenge. Should I tell RG? Where the hell was Aaron? I found RG first.

He didn't seem fazed by my report. He just sighed and nodded his head.

"Yep, that sounds like John."

"But can't we do something? Shouldn't you go set the record straight?" I sputtered.

RG smiled wearily at me.

"Just be happy about the bill, Samantha, and don't worry about the rest. Focusing on that bullshit only perpetuates it, and we have more important things to do."

I nodded slowly. And as I watched a passing group swarm RG with congratulations, I felt myself grow calmer. He was right. We were above Bramen's jackass games. And though I hoped that sooner or later they would catch up with him, I'd try not to waste any more energy on the topic.

A little later, as I was congratulating myself on my new attitude, I spotted Aaron talking and laughing with Bramen, Natalie, and the clutch of reporters. I felt angry all over again, but unable to do anything except furiously glare at the little group. None of them seemed to notice until, as the other journalists scribbled, Charlie looked over and met my gaze. He stared steadily at me for a long moment, which was very unsettling. Aaron finally noticed Charlie's lack of attention and turned around to identify the distraction. Seeing me, he excused himself and walked over.

"Having fun?" I asked icily.

"Come on, let's not fight tonight, babe," Aaron replied.

"Do you know what Bramen just did?" I demanded.

"Sammy . . ." Aaron said in a half-pleading, half-exasperated tone.

"He took complete credit for the bill. I heard him. And you know what that makes him? A liar. A horrible liar. I can't believe you work for him. *And* I can't believe you were just talking to those reporters. Do you know that's Charlie Lawton sitting over there? He trashed me! Why are you associating with all these awful, awful people?"

Aaron looked thoughtful.

"So that's who that is," he mused.

I felt like I might scream. Aaron seemed to sense I was on the verge. He snapped back into appeasement mode.

"Baby, I'm sorry. I didn't know that was Charlie whatever his name is. And I didn't know Bramen did that. Do you want me to go beat them both up?"

Would he? It was tempting, but I knew violence was never the answer.

"Because I'd do just about anything for you," he continued. "I love how fiery you are. I love how much you care. And you know what, you're the real hero of the day," he said sweetly as he took my hand. "You've done incredible work and we need to celebrate. So let's just focus on that. Okay?"

RG's words echoed in my head in the pause that followed. Both he and Aaron had good points. I sighed deeply and tried to release my anger so I could rededicate myself to having a good time. I *had* done good work. And the bill had passed!

"Okay," I nodded, to Aaron's evident relief.

"Perfect. Now you sit down here and relax while I go get you another drink."

To my distress, Charlie Lawton walked up while he was gone.

"Samantha, I was wondering if I could talk to you for a second," he said as he put away his pen and notebook.

I was shaking my head before I even got the words out.

"No. No, you can't," I said firmly.

Before Charlie could say anything more, Aaron returned.

"Can I help you with something?" Aaron asked pointedly.

Would there be a rumble after all? That seemed a little cheesy.

"No, I'm all set," Charlie replied evenly.

And he left. Aaron sat down next to me.

"Are you all right, gorgeous?" he asked.

I nodded. I was. Aaron handed me my drink and took my hand.

Three hours later, long after RG and Bramen and most of the crowd had left, Aaron and I lingered at the bar and flirted tipsily with each other. Though I despised his boss, I couldn't seem to get enough of him, and I was feeling good about the day's extremely successful work. Who cared if Bramen was an idiot? The end result was that the bill had passed. As Aaron twirled a piece of my hair around his finger, I glanced over my shoulder and was delighted to see Mona and Mark camped out together, deep in what appeared to be a very intimate conversation. They were both giggling, and Mona was gingerly touching Mark's arm as she leaned in close. I tugged Aaron over to them.

"Do you guys want to grab a bite to eat with us?" I asked warmly.

A double date would be the perfect way to celebrate the success of my matchmaking endeavor. Mona and Mark glanced at each other.

"Uh, actually, Mona and I were going to go, uh, watch a movie," Mark said as he mimed an old-fashioned movie projector.

I doubted they were going to watch it on one of those.

"Oh, great." I smiled happily.

What did it matter, as long as they were finally getting together? That was the important thing.

"What movie?" I asked amiably.

"Uh, we don't know yet," Mona said quickly.

Through the pleasant haze of my seven eggnogs, it was dawning on me that perhaps I should have just left Mark and Mona alone.

"Enjoy the movie," Aaron intervened. "See y'all around."

Mark and Mona smilingly waved us away. I looked back over my shoulder to see them leaning in and speaking conspiratorially to each other. Was it about Aaron and me? I stumbled over an uneven floorboard before I could fully investigate.

"Let's head home," Aaron laughed as he steadied me.

Okay, that sounded fun.

I woke up the next morning with the pleasant feeling that something very good had occurred. As my brain slid into present consciousness, I remembered the bill passage in an instant and smiled gratefully that the pleasant feeling was reality rather than dream-based. I jumped out of bed to read the coverage on the Internet while Aaron stayed wrapped up in the blanket he had monopolized for most of the chilly night. As I relived the events of the last two days, I skipped with giddy glee over to the door, before freezing with my hand on the doorknob.

I turned slowly and deliberately back towards the room. Without taking a breath, I rapidly retraced my steps, stopping next to Shackleton's bowl. He was floating upside down entangled in the miracle seaweed Mr. Lee had conned me into buying. I'd seen him in this death pose before, but this time something was different. There was a new stillness about his bowl, as though the water molecules had transformed into a slightly different element in response to a silent but momentous development.

I knew even before I used the fishnet to fruitlessly prod his vacated body that this time he was truly dead. I sank down to the floor to process the news. I was a little surprised to discover that despite a certain hardening I'd developed towards Shackleton in response to his penchant for crying "dead," I still felt soft and despairing when confronted with the confirmed permanent loss of him. I had cried for Shackleton so many times that my tears now felt familiar, as if they already knew their favorite ways down my face. I sat on the floor trying to stop crying for what after all was just a fish, but found myself unable to pull it together.

"Are you okay?" Aaron mumbled from the bed.

"I'm fine," I sobbed unconvincingly. "Shackleton's dead," I clarified after a moment.

"Babe, he's always dead," Aaron responded. "Why don't you come back to bed?"

I glared at the foot of the bed from my seated position.

"No, he's *really* dead this time. He went through with it."

"No way. For real?"

This was enough to get Aaron to sit up. He came over and examined the bowl. He even did his own prodding, which felt like a violation. I snatched the net from him.

"Wow, he really is this time," Aaron agreed.

He turned towards me and folded me into his arms.

"I'm sorry, babe, you want me to flush him?"

Perhaps he thought this was a chivalrous move. I disagreed. I wriggled away from him.

"No, I don't," I said bitterly.

All at once I blamed him for Shackleton's death. Maybe I was just lashing out, or maybe I was channeling my anger over other things for which I felt I'd let Aaron off the hook too easily. Or maybe he was rightfully to blame. He'd been the last one to have contact with Shackleton after all—I'd asked him to tend to him when he'd stopped by my apartment to fetch my change of clothes.

"Did you feed him the other day like I asked?" I flung the question accusingly.

Aaron looked bewildered.

"Who? Shackleton?" he asked, as if to buy some time. "Of course I did, baby. Look, I know you're upset. I'm really sorry," he finished.

Did he sound guilty or was it my imagination? I bet he hadn't fed him, thereby depriving Shackleton of crucial sustenance needed to fuel his perpetual battle against the end of his life. I bet Aaron had forgotten, just like he always forgot to charge his cell phone, just like he was going to forget to pick up our daughter Riley from preschool. Well, I wouldn't stand for it.

"I think I just need to be alone for a little while," I said irrationally as I wiped the corners of my eyes.

Aaron looked very surprised.

"Oh, okay, sure," he responded. "Just give me a second to get dressed."

As soon as he left I was seized with regret. Had I really just orchestrated his departure? Hopefully he didn't think it was any sort of permanent arrangement. What had I done? Now a long, blizzardy, hungover Sunday stretched before me, with nothing to do but stare at my dead fish all alone while my boyfriend wandered off to other adventures. This was an entirely self-inflicted, terrible turn of events. And on top of it all, my stomach hurt from all the eggnogs I'd drunk, providing further evidence that I might be developing lactose intolerance.

I ended up having a short, simple toilet-flushing ceremony for Shackleton complete with a reverent playing of the Beatles' "Octopus's Garden." As I watched Shackleton spiral out of my life forever, I spoke a heartfelt prayer and mused about fish heaven. Whatever it entailed, I hoped my sturdy little explorer would enjoy his new expedition.

I finally got on my computer and Googled the news articles about the defeat of the filibuster and the passage of the bill. Despite my real sadness over Shackleton's passing, I felt able to recapture a buoyant sense of pride in the developments of the last few days and I was eager to soak up the coverage. But my satisfaction quickly soured as I read. In practically all of the accounts, the credit went entirely to Bramen. Apparently his "off the record" comments had produced the intended effect. He'd successfully duped the journalists into believing he'd been the main force behind the effort.

Worse, most of the articles included an infuriating quote from an unnamed Bramen staffer that described how throughout the battle to pass the bill "RG and his staff were dead weight that Bramen had to carry on his back. They're amateurs, and we had to spend a lot of time cleaning up their little messes."

Treachery! I knew we should have made more of an effort to set the record straight. Bramen avoided direct quotes, but his staffers clearly didn't. And that quote smacked of Natalie. How dare she?! This was a new low, even for an evil fembot. Aaron was lucky that he'd left, for I surely would have taken out my freshly fueled rage on him. I'd asked him a million times, but *how* could he work with such exquisitely awful people? That quote was just pointlessly destructive and mean, not to mention inaccurate. We'd worked together and the bill had passed; why did Natalie have to poison the victory by maligning us in such a nasty way? Was that really how the game had to be played? If so, I opted for a rules change. And some retribution, please.

The only article that didn't give all the credit to Bramen or include that detestable quote was Charlie Lawton's in the *Washington Post*. I was surprised. I already associated him with unfairly negative spin so I'd assumed he'd be among the culprits. Perhaps he was turning over a new leaf. Though I appreciated that he'd written a far more truthful article than the others, it didn't make up for his past crimes. I still hated him. Goodness, I hated so many people these days. That couldn't be a healthy thing. I glanced at Shackleton's empty bowl and felt an overwhelming sense of loss.

Liza insisted I flee the premises. I agreed once she suggested a field trip to the National Museum of Natural History. It was a selfless suggestion—she knew how much I loved that museum. I decided to return the favor and distract myself from my own troubles by focusing on her during our visit.

"How's Ryan, by the way?" I asked as Liza cocked her head to stare at the African elephant in the main rotunda of the museum.

I liked the elephant, but I was really looking forward to the Dinosaur Hall, where I could check out all the different, obscure species names. The Albertosaurus was a personal favorite.

"To be honest, I'm beginning to have some doubts about him," she answered.

Really? This was good news. Was this the long-awaited revelation?

"Oh?" I asked casually. "How come?"

She scrunched her face up uncertainly.

"I'm just getting a little tired of feeling uncomfortable around him. I mean, he's a natural flirt so I shouldn't take things too seriously, but he kind of hits on other women even when I'm around," she said vulnerably. "I mean, not really," she rushed to clarify. "If they really knew him they'd know he wasn't being serious, but they don't so they sort of look at me weirdly. I don't know, maybe I'm just being paranoid."

I was pretty certain she wasn't.

"You shouldn't have to live your life that way," I offered.

"Yeah, I know," she sighed. "Does Aaron do anything like that?"

"No," I replied gently. "But all guys have their faults. Aaron's certainly not perfect."

"That's for sure," Liza snorted.

"What do you mean?" I asked in surprise.

I had always assumed Liza liked Aaron.

"Oh, nothing, nothing," she said quickly.

I didn't believe her. Sure enough, she took a deep breath and cleared her throat to elaborate.

"It's just, uh . . . maybe he's not the exact right one for you," she exhaled. "Maybe he is," she added quickly. "But maybe not."

She wouldn't look directly at me, and I knew that she felt conflicted about sharing her opinion. The evidence of her struggle helped me keep my anger in check. She was my best friend, and though I was surprised at how quickly the conversation had turned from questioning her romantic choice to questioning mine, I couldn't shake the feeling that maybe she was on to something.

I'd recently found myself avoiding thinking too hard about Aaron's and my future, because when I did, it seemed hazy and indistinct. Did this mean that I was with the wrong person? Or just that I needed to stay in the moment and embrace being young and having fun? I'd prefer to go with the latter explanation. I knew that Aaron wasn't perfect, but nobody was. And didn't it make sense that romance on the Hill, like everything else, involved some concessions? In a place haunted by compromise, I wasn't all that surprised that its spirit had crept into our relationship.

"Yeah, maybe, maybe not," I answered finally. "It's too soon to tell. But what are you going to do about Ryan?"

Liza shrugged and shook her head.

"I guess just take a fresh look at him."

That seemed like the best that either of us could do at the moment. As we approached the Braille display in the Discovery Room, Liza finally met my gaze again. There was a tortured tint to her eyes.

"Do I always pick terrible guys?" she asked plaintively.

Though I was glad we were back to talking about her, her obvious distress was painful to witness.

"Of course not," I lied. "It's just hard to pick a guy who really deserves to be with you."

That last part was true. Liza had a knack for picking insufferable boyfriends but this proclivity did not make her deserving of them. I didn't know how to help beyond praying that an amazing person be flung in her path before she became too attached to one of her bozos.

"Thanks," she said gratefully.

Monday morning arrived swiftly, and returning to work after the bill victory felt like a happy chore. I could sense a positive shift in the way people viewed me at the office. Even Janet seemed to take me a bit more seriously. I tried not to let myself get carried away and fantasize that I was the new office rock star, but it was hard. I'd always wanted to be a rock star. They got away with calling themselves things like Slash and The Edge with completely straight faces.

The Senate passed the final appropriations bill and adjourned until the new year, which completely changed the frenetic atmosphere that had permeated the Hill since the beginning of September. Though the work continued, there was a more relaxed, festive spirit to the place. And before I knew it, Thanksgiving was twenty-four hours away.

Aaron and I were back on good terms. After getting kicked out of my apartment, he'd bought me flowers and made a small donation to the Cousteau Society in Shackleton's name. And most importantly, he'd called to express his outrage over Natalie's quote.

"I'm going to give Natalie a piece of my mind. And talk to Bramen. I know you don't like him, but he can be reasoned with. And this sort of thing just absolutely can't go unpunished. On top of being completely false, what Natalie said reflects poorly on all of us. And most unforgivably, it hurts you. She can't get away with it. I won't let her."

He'd sounded genuinely indignant. And I'd felt adequately supported and defended. Later, he'd described the fight he'd gotten into with Natalie, and how Bramen had agreed to bring up the issue at their staff meeting. Though I could look after myself, I appreciated Aaron standing up for me. Back in his arms, it felt good to be cared for. I snuggled up against him and wished I didn't have to leave.

"Are you going to miss me?" I inquired.

"Of course I am. This place isn't the same without you," he answered as he helped me gather some of the clothes I had managed to strew all over his room.

It was on the way to the airport that he said it. We were two stops away and I'd been resting my head on his shoulder in a sleepy subway-induced haze. Aaron was nuzzling my hair.

"Hey, darling? Are you awake?" he asked.

I sat up straight despite myself. Had he just called me "darling"? He'd never called me anything except my name or some version of "baby." What did the introduction of a new term of endearment signify? Did we need to discuss this?

"What did you just call me?" I asked incredulously.

He looked uncertain. I realized too late that it wasn't cool to make a big deal of this.

"Nothing," he said lamely.

Oh great, now I'd embarrassed him. Why hadn't I just gone along with it?

"I think you called me 'darling,' which I'm fine with," I said in a less pointed and much more encouraging tone.

He looked relieved. I hadn't meant to make a production of the whole thing, but the "darling" had taken me off guard. It had seemed so un-Aaron that I'd just wanted to be certain it was what he'd really said. He kissed me tenderly and assured me that it was.

Too soon, we were at the transfer stop. I reluctantly left Aaron and battled the crowds on my way back to Cincinnati, vaguely happy that I was somebody's darling.

## Faded Luster

BOTH OF MY parents picked me up at the airport, which made me feel like they were really getting old. In my experience, only elderly couples who were winding down and away from the myriad distractions of daily life had the time or patience to make joint airport trips. Thus, though I was happy to see both of them, their presence also mildly depressed me.

As we pulled away from the airport and onto the freeway that would lead us fifty miles outside of Cincinnati to our farm, I settled back into the seat and into my role as their only child. My mom turned around to more efficiently focus all of her attention on me.

"Have you ever had a turducken?" she asked me excitedly.

"A what?" I asked cautiously.

"A turducken," my mom answered patiently. "It's a

chicken stuffed into a duck stuffed into a turkey. Turducken."

For a second I imagined my mom was participating in some sort of spelling bee. Her pronunciation had been quite professional.

"I don't think I've ever heard of that," I answered her.

In fact, I was positive that I hadn't. A turducken. Interesting. It sounded like something that a PETA member would dream up in one of their worst paranoid nightmares.

"Your mother's decided to cook it tomorrow instead of a regular old, boring turkey," my dad explained as he smiled at me in the rearview mirror.

"Interesting," I replied. "But, Mom, weren't you going to be a vegetarian?"

She had mentioned it a few weeks previously. I had chalked it up to Paul McCartney's lingering influence. He'd certainly been in the press a lot lately.

"Yeah, I tried it out," my mom answered. "I was a vegetarian for a few days actually. But then I saw on the History Channel that Hitler was a vegetarian and it started seeming like a dark path."

I nodded as my mom continued.

"So get ready for turducken," she said. "It takes a little longer to cook."

Yeah, I imagined it would. I felt a little grossed out thinking about the mechanics, and hoped that my parents would do most of the handling. I'd compensate by making myself useful in the mashed potatoes and dressing department.

Later, upon unpacking in my room, I discovered that I'd forgotten to bring my BlackBerry charger. Given that my parents' farm was too remote for even my cell phone to pick up a workable signal, my frustration over the missing charger was probably overblown. Luckily, I still remembered how to send out e-mails from a regular computer. Unluckily, my parents had discontinued the Internet connection I'd bought for them for their anniversary because they'd considered it too expensive.

"But I was paying for it," I protested.

"We know, dear," my mom said. "And we appreciate it, but we just didn't use it enough to justify the expense. It's not like you've got a lot of money to throw around."

That was true and difficult to argue with, but my gift had been largely selfish, as it had ensured that I'd always have Internet access when I returned home. Apparently, that wasn't to be.

I fought down a brief surge of panic over how electronically tuned out I suddenly was. I wasn't trapped, I told myself. This was relaxing, dammit.

"Do we at least still have a phone?" I asked with forced calm.

Or had they reverted to a cheaper carrier pigeon system?

"Of course, honey," my mom said. "Who are you calling these days, anyway?"

I hesitated. Did I feel like telling them about Aaron?

Would the news of the romance make them happy or overly protective? There was never any way to be sure exactly how it would balance out. My parents had always been wildly successful at making my boyfriends uncomfortable, though they employed different methods towards this common end. My mom would be overly solicitous, like some sort of saleslady for my charms, and my dad would be silently judgmental and aloof. No wonder men had often accused me of sending mixed signals. I'd been raised on them. They'd seeped into my blood.

On the other hand, I was twenty-six years old and if Aaron renounced his boss and changed a few other things, he just might end up my parents' son-in-law. Perhaps it was time to inform them of his existence.

"Well, I have been seeing this guy," I began.

"Ooh, really," my mom squealed.

"Is he some kind of D.C. yahoo?" my dad asked a bit harshly.

And there it was.

"His name is Aaron and he's not from D.C., but he has worked there for four years. He's the head speechwriter for Senator Bramen," I stated calmly, fighting back the gag reflex when I got to Bramen's name.

I felt a bit like I was giving a school presentation. Except that I was reciting facts about my boyfriend and not about the Beatles. Thanks to my mother's devotion to British rock, it had been the first and only music to which I'd been exposed as a child. I'd liked all of it, but had taken an immediate shine to the Beatles in particular, which turned into a bit of an obsession during my elementary school years. In fact, all of my school reports up until the seventh grade had been about the Beatles. My teachers had sent home notes requesting that my parents discuss a diversification of my interests with me to no avail. I'd listened calmly and then meticulously planned my next oral report about the Fab Four, utterly unfazed.

Before I'd become aware of Steve Martin, my fantasy world had revolved around John Lennon, George Harrison, Ringo Starr, and Paul McCartney. I could still sing along to every song that they'd ever recorded without missing a single word or air guitar stroke, but I had also managed to develop other interests over the years, probably to the relief of my parents and teachers.

"I don't like Bramen," my dad said grumpily. "There's something icky about him."

I agreed completely, but I wondered how much of my dad's distaste was based on the fact that Aaron worked for him.

"And he looks like he spends a lot of time brushing his hair," my dad continued. Bramen did sport a bit of a bouffant.

"He's got a bigger problem than his hair," my mom rejoined. "He's always talking down to people. He's really a bit of a twit."

No kidding. I agreed with all my parents' criticisms, but I hoped to prevent them from associating any negative feelings towards Bramen with my potential husband. It was something I had to keep working extremely hard to do myself.

"Yeah, Bramen's really awful, but Aaron's not so bad," I said mildly.

"Oh, I'm sure he's wonderful, dear," my mom replied. "Tell me all about him!"

My dad returned to his crossword puzzle, but I could tell he was listening.

"Okay, let's see. He's handsome and smart and sweet and—"

"How handsome?" my mom interrupted. "Does he trigger your neck acne problem?"

"It's a *rash*, Mother," I answered testily. "And yes, he does."

My mom was nodding.

"Did you ever ask your dermatologist about that?" she asked. "I mean, there's got to be a cream or something."

I glared at her.

"What?" she asked innocently. "Oh, I'm sorry, go ahead. So he's really handsome . . ."

"Yes. And he's ambitious and fun and—"

"How old is he?" my dad asked, proving that he wasn't as absorbed with his crossword as his posture had previously suggested.

"He's twenty-nine," I answered.

"Then he's old enough to know better than to work for someone like Bramen."

Interesting point. Perhaps we were done talking about Aaron.

"Yeah, that's an issue in our relationship, but relationships are all about compromise, right? Anyway, maybe you guys will meet him sometime and judge for yourselves."

My dad appeared disapproving, my mom, jubilant. I'd vaguely hoped that since my feelings for Aaron were different than those I'd had for past boyfriends, the conversation about him might veer from our standard script. No such luck. Evidently, going home still entailed full-scale regression to the parts we'd always played in our never-ending family play. Clearly, my parents didn't think that Aaron was special enough to warrant a rewrite—that he might be someone whom my dad didn't have to get irritable and negative about; someone that my mom didn't have to embarrass me over. Did I believe Aaron warranted such a revision? I hoped so. I planned on finding out in time for my family's still-evolving second act.

As I dialed Aaron's number later that evening, I listened for the telltale sound of my mother trying not to breathe too loud. She didn't eavesdrop often, but every once in a while her curiosity got the better of her. I imagined that the afternoon's revelations about a new boyfriend might have contributed to just such a situation, and so I listened carefully. She was never very good at it. As one might imagine, given my mom's feelings on Internet access, she wasn't up on the latest technological tools. She didn't use the mute button to eavesdrop, she just tried to pick up the extension and listen very quietly. Then, in focusing on staying silent, she would become too conscious and breathe all the louder, until she'd panic and muffle the receiver with a pillow or blanket. My trained ear could register this whole progression, even while I carried on a conversation with whomever I was talking to.

I didn't hear her immediately, and it didn't matter because Aaron wasn't answering his cell phone. I really hated it when I couldn't get in touch with him. It sent me into a sort of spiraling panicked mode that was both exhausting and inappropriate. But I couldn't seem to help it. I needed to know where he was and why he wasn't answering. And the only way to divine that information was for him to answer and tell me. I found the whole thing infuriating.

I also wasn't a fan of the missed call function on cell phones. Having been burned so horribly by the caller ID incident early on in my Washington career, I was painfully aware of all the ways technology could document my mania. Every time Aaron's phone rang through to voicemail, I knew it was also logging another missed call from my parents' number. This was pretty much the only thing that kept me from calling more than six times.

However, on that allowable sixth call, his number went straight to voicemail instead of ringing through. This meant he had either turned off his phone or someone else was calling him at the exact same time I was. Either way, I wasn't happy. If he had turned off his phone, then he would have seen the missed calls and known I was trying to get in touch with him. Surely he would have reached out to me. I'd left a voicemail authorizing him to call me back at my parents'. If someone else was calling him at the same time, then who was it and had they gotten through to him? I decided I could break the limit and call a seventh time to settle these issues.

It went straight to voicemail. Hmm, I supposed someone could still be calling him at the exact same time. An eighth call also went the immediate voicemail route. Okay, chances were that he'd turned off his cell then. After twenty torturous minutes, I forced myself to end my speculation about why he would have done such a thing without listening to my message and calling me back. I decided to call it a night and get to the bottom of the mystery tomorrow.

When I entered my room, Kitty was lounging territorially on my bed. Kitty was our seventeen-year-old cat, definitively not named by me. Though I had always loved animals, cats baffled me. Even when I'd spent hours at the zoo as a young girl, plotting the rescue of all the incarcerated creatures, I'd never settled on a firm escape route for the lions, tigers, and panthers. They'd unnerved me more than anything else had.

And Kitty must have sensed this inability to relate to all things feline, because she'd treated me from the beginning with what appeared to be a mixture of pity and disdain. She had always tolerated my existence, but otherwise had wanted little to do with me. Many times I'd caught her eyeing me evilly, as if she'd been plotting how to best rid herself of what amounted to a troublesome obstacle to undistracted feedings and affection from my parents. Indeed, Kitty was the closest thing to sibling rivalry I'd ever experienced.

She glanced disdainfully at me through half-mast lids as I surveyed the scene. Though she was an old cat by now, she still managed to give off a sort of punk vibe. Her posture was vaguely challenging. I thought I could take her.

"That's right, I'm back," I said in my tough tone.

She appeared unfazed.

"I know you don't want to sleep in the same room as me, so you're going to have to leave eventually," I continued.

She blinked once and yawned broadly.

"Okay, seriously, I'm getting into bed now," I warned her.

I went over and gingerly turned down the covers. As I slid beneath the sheets, Kitty swiped at me with her left claw, taking a long, shallow scratch of my skin with her as she leapt to the floor. Ouch. I examined my wound as I tried to remember the symptoms of cat scratch fever. There were tiny little blood bubbles dotting the scratch line. Okay, I recalled the most major symptom was swollen lymph nodes in the armpit, neck, or groin. I'd probably have to wait a few hours to check on that, though my neck did feel sore already.

*The Book of Maladies and Diseases* on my bedside table informed me that the other symptoms I needed to watch out for were a low-grade fever, loss of appetite, general tiredness, and headaches. Did I need to inform my parents of my condition? What if I lost consciousness in the middle of the night and slipped into some sort of cat scratch fever-induced coma? No one but Kitty would know what had happened to me, and she certainly couldn't be trusted.

I glanced at the clock. I knew my parents would be asleep already and I wasn't convinced that waking them up with my distressing health news was my best course of action. But what about that coma threat? I decided to write a note. After I completed a draft that gently but clearly explained to my parents what exactly had transpired and who precisely to blame, I put some Neosporin on my wound and settled back into bed. As a last responsible measure, I set the alarm for the middle of the night. If I woke up to it, that meant I wasn't in a coma, which would definitely be a welcome relief.

The next thing I knew I was jolted awake at 3:00 AM to the disconcerting sounds of a Hanson song. Slowly, my circumstances came trickling back into my consciousness. I was at home, Kitty was my sworn enemy, and I was not in a coma as far as I could tell. I checked for swollen lymph nodes but found their presence or absence difficult to gauge as my hand had fallen asleep. I closed my eyes and soon joined it.

The next day was filled with turducken negotiation. It ended up being very tasty, though eating it did feel a bit like conducting a science experiment. After our meal, we played a few rounds of Asshole, the drinking game I'd taught my parents during a particularly long and lonely winter break in my junior year of college. It wasn't really a game for three people, nor was it exactly a game one would choose to play with one's parents, but having grown up an only child I was well used to tailoring group games down to a smaller scale and to accepting that my mom and dad were often my only social options. Luckily, my parents were open-minded people who were surprisingly fun to hang out with. They'd taken a liking to Asshole immediately, accepting the offensive name as part of its rough charm. My dad still hesitated when the game called for him to address either my mom or me as Asshole, but my mom had never felt any need to hold back. She always leapt right into the competitive spirit, and tended to become a bit aggressive when she'd earned the top-ranked "president" slot.

"Drink, Asshole!" she barked at me.

I took a swig of my Corona accordingly, too accustomed to playing this game with her to find it odd anymore that my mother was ordering me to binge drink.

"And you, Vice Asshole, go cut us some more limes," my mom yelled at my dad.

His glance in my direction as he put down his cards and made his way to the kitchen communicated a common goal. We really needed to beat her in the next round. It didn't matter which of us ascended. My nod told him I was on board.

It actually took us three more rounds, but my mom was finally demoted to Asshole. This just happened to coincide with her getting bored of the game. Instead of arguing, we moved on to an hour of Pictionary, a brief touch football game in the backyard, and a pumpkin pie–eating contest. By nightfall, I was exhausted and full to the point of regretful discomfort.

Back in my room as my parents readied for bed, I flipped through my yearbook and thought about Rick Hagen, my high school boyfriend. We'd dated throughout my junior and senior year and I probably would have blissfully stayed with him for far too long had he not dumped me the week after graduation for a sophomore cheerleader. In retrospect, our breakup had unquestionably been for the best, though it certainly hadn't felt like it at the time. Rick had tracked me down in the middle of my junior year of college to express regret, along with the hope that we could be friends. In a charitable moment, I'd agreed. Ever since, we'd seen each other sporadically, always back at home. I didn't have any interest in either dating him again or exacting revenge—it was just nice to connect. I closed the yearbook and dialed his number.

We caught up over some drinks at the Dark Stallion, a neighborhood bar that had been around since I was little. I'd always been drawn to the rearing, cardboard horse above the door and had often begged my parents to take me there. My mom had only let me peek in once when I was twelve and it felt funny now to be legally a part of the shadowy, aged interior.

Rick was as handsome as I remembered. We'd asked a few more friends to meet us, and as we waited at a corner table for them to show up, we passed the time laughing and reminiscing about the things we chose to remember from high school. After a few drinks, I was even able to feign a mature attitude about our breakup.

"So, do you still keep in touch with Misty?" I asked casually.

Misty was the cheerleader's name. She'd been perky and flexible and nothing like me.

"No," Rick shook his head.

I was happy to hear that. Though I claimed to bear her no ill will, I secretly hoped that Misty was a bored failure living someplace very unglamorous. I knew this was immature and uncharitable of me. That's why it was a secret.

"I heard that she's a model in Italy," Rick added.

Hmm. Well, maybe she was a bored, failing model living in a particularly run-down part of Italy. One could always hope. I steered the conversation away from Misty and asked Rick about his father, who'd become paralyzed by a stroke the previous year. Rick had recently moved back to take care of his parents and the farm. He didn't seem bitter about his circumstances, and in a way, I had always assumed he'd end up here. In my memory, he belonged in the places I had lived when I was younger, so it made sense to me that he haunted this region still.

By 11:30, it seemed clear that our other friends weren't going to show up. The beer and intimate conversation had turned me warm and nostalgic. When I returned from the restroom soon after the bartender had made his "last call" announcement, Rick looked up at me, hands resting lazily on his knees. I'd always particularly enjoyed his knees.

"Hey," he grinned at me.

"What's up?" I smiled back.

It was fun to be near him again. The residual excitement still hung in the air between us, but in more of a sweet, musty way.

"It's really great to see you again, Sammy. You seem really good. Really pretty."

Rick had never been a man of too many words and I took his compliments seriously.

"Thanks," I said gratefully.

I looked into his eyes and realized I should be getting home. He didn't agree.

"Could we hang out a little longer?" he asked, as he took my hand. "Maybe I could show you the house. You haven't been back there in years."

That was true. I loved his house. It was a house of firsts, and now the man whom I'd first fallen in love with was welcoming me back. I considered saying yes, partially for old time's sake, partially because the last nine years had definitely agreed with him, but I knew it wasn't an option.

"Oh no, I can't," I answered, with a trace of real sadness in my voice. "You know, I've got a boyfriend, actually."

Rick nodded.

"I figured you would," he said with downcast eyes.

He didn't let go of my hand, which relieved me. I felt even better when he met my gaze again.

"I hope he makes you happy, Sammy. I hope he treats you well and never makes the mistake I did."

It was a sweet thing to say, but long after Rick had driven me home and we'd kissed good-bye on the cheek, promising to stay in touch, his words jostled themselves around in my head, forming new questions upon which I didn't much want to reflect. *Did* Aaron make me happy? *Was* he treating me well? Aaron had certainly made mistakes—was all my compromising worth it? I dialed Aaron's number, hoping to find some reassurance at the other end of the line.

Instead, I found that his cell phone was turned off

once again. I left a message and sat on my bed stewing in a mixture of alcohol and annoyance. Doubts crowded my brain. I halfheartedly battled them back.

I shook my head, took a deep breath, and tried to review the facts to the best of my current abilities. Sure, there had been several times that Aaron hadn't been available by phone or BlackBerry and we'd spent plenty of nights apart. However, his busy and important job could easily account for all of that. Being a part of the same scene, albeit at a lower voltage, I was well aware of just how thoroughly a Capitol Hill job could hijack one's personal life.

Plus, I had spent enough time with him to determine that he genuinely cared for me, whether or not actual declarations of love had been soberly exchanged. And I could tell that he took pride in being a stand-up person, so I imagined he held himself to fairly high standards of conduct. Except he did get too drunk a lot of the time. That was an undeniable fact, and one that conflicted with the whole high-standards premise. Along with the fact that he worked for Bramen. Hmm. Was he capable of betraying me? Even if he hadn't yet, did he exhibit the potential to do so in the future? I couldn't shake the basic insecurity I felt about our relationship. Whether that came from my own personality or from the way Aaron made me feel, I had yet to determine. But it certainly didn't put me at ease.

A burning desire to investigate this train of thought quickly gripped me as I sat there confused. I needed more evidence to build a case for either side. I couldn't just remain paralyzed by uncertainty, rattled by uncomfortable possibilities. But how to collect the necessary evidence? How to take any steps toward knowing just a little bit more?

A glance down at my useless cell phone clicked an idea into my head. Even though I couldn't get a signal on the farm to use my cell phone, I could still call it from a landline and access my messages. The shortcut route I'd discovered for doing this (rather than having to remember the separate number of the voicemail service) was to dial my own number and then press the star button when it went to voicemail. This brought about the prompt to enter my password, which I would do, press pound, and have instant access to my messages. I imagined I could do the same thing to Aaron's phone. All I needed was his password.

I doubted I would have embarked on this midnight sleuthing experiment if I hadn't been a little bit drunk, but once I started, my competitive juices kicked in. I needed to figure out that code, dammit. I refused to be defeated by that annoying recorded voice telling me I had dialed an incorrect one. I tried Aaron's number over and over again. When it went immediately to voicemail, I'd press star and then my password guess. And over and over again I was rejected. I tried everything I could remember about Aaron. I punched in the name of his first pet (Stinky the hamster, making Aaron's porn star name Stinky Funker, which I had found par-

ticularly amusing), Derek Jeter's jersey number combined with Aaron's hometown area code, Aaron's birth-
date (he was a Cancer, the astrological significance of
which I had yet to determine), as well as random number sequences I guessed might appeal to him. But nothing worked. I gave up after an hour, feeling acutely
frustrated and ashamed.

I woke up the next morning determined to never
exhibit such atrocious behavior again. Who or what
was I turning into? I could never tell anyone what I'd
attempted the night before. Maybe I could tell Liza.
But only under very special circumstances involving
martinis.

Aaron finally called midday.

"Where have you been?" I asked immediately.

I didn't want to sound like a smothering girlfriend,
but honestly, we hadn't spoken in days.

"With my family. I figured you were just as busy with
yours, so I didn't want to bother you," he answered.

He sounded surprised at my attitude. And innocent
in general. Was I possibly overreacting?

"I called your cell phone a bunch of times," I said, trying to keep my tone even. "I really wanted to talk to you."

"Oh God, I'm sorry," he answered. "I lost my charger
and haven't had time to get a new one with everyone
in town."

Oh. Okay. Sort of.

"You should have called," I said simply.

"I'm sorry, baby," he replied. "My family's just been all over me. But I miss you like hell," he continued. "How was Thanksgiving?"

He sounded so normal and reasonable that I decided to reciprocate. Perhaps I had been being a bit clingy. Cool, secure girlfriends probably didn't spaz the first second they couldn't get a hold of their boyfriends. I could pretend to be one of those.

"Um, it was good. We had turducken," I said, coaxing my tone back into a casual one.

"Really? I've heard of those. That's a lot of bird," Aaron replied.

"Yeah, I'm still a little unclear about the mechanics of the whole thing. Is the turducken concept something that's employed with other animals?"

"You mean like a cowpigish?"

A fish inside a pig inside a cow, I deciphered.

"Exactly, is that a delicacy I don't know about? Because I'd never heard of turducken. I'm beginning to think I might be culinarily ill-informed," I concluded.

"Hmm, yeah, we'll have to work on that. I'm not an expert myself, but we might be on to something here. We could create whole new dishes just by stuffing different animals into one another."

This was a potentially funny topic of conversation, but I was beginning to feel slightly queasy. I decided to change the subject.

"Did you have fun with your family?" I asked.

"Yeah, it was great seeing them. I managed to catch up with a few friends as well, which was cool. What about you? Have you seen anyone besides your parents?"

I told him an abbreviated version of my night, glossing over the Rick interaction and stopping well short of the voicemail code-assault session.

"That sounds fun. Did you ever date Rick?" he asked nonchalantly.

"Well, actually, yeah, we dated in high school, but we've just been friends for almost ten years," I answered.

"Uh-huh, uh-huh," he responded a little too quickly. "Did he hit on you?"

Ooh, dilemma. Should I be honest with him? I tried to conduct a mental speed-debate of the pros and cons. Ultimately, I'd want him to be honest with me, so I went with the do unto others approach, albeit gingerly.

"It's funny you should ask—he did, a little. But it was no big deal. It certainly wasn't successful."

"What did he say?" Aaron asked. "Did he ask you to go home with him?"

All of a sudden he sounded like the lawyer he was trained to be. Did this mean he was jealous? Oh, I hoped so. It felt so lonely being the only insecure one.

"Yeah, he did. I said no and he dropped it."

"Okay. Do you think you'll see him again while you're there?" Aaron asked.

He *was* jealous.

"No, I don't. Hey, I really miss you," I tried.

"I miss you, too. Sorry for the grilling. I just don't like old boyfriends hitting on you," he said apologetically.

"Yeah, me neither," I lied. "So what are you up to tonight?"

"I don't know. I'm sure I'll find something to do," he replied vaguely.

"Uh-huh. Listen, do you have a lucky number or anything?" I asked, immediately wishing I'd better disguised the non sequitur.

"Pardon?"

"Oh, I was just talking with my parents about lucky numbers and colors. I know you don't like orange. My mom's favorite number is three. Anyway, do you have one?"

I sounded like a four-year-old on Ritalin. Hopefully he thought that was cute.

"Uh . . ." He sounded confused. "I guess I like the number fifty-seven," he said uncertainly.

"Like Heinz 57 sauce?" I asked.

"No, just as in fifty-seven. Do I have to have a lucky number?"

"It might help," I said matter-of-factly.

"Okay. Well, I guess I'd go with fifty-seven then. Or nine."

This was all valuable raw material to work with. Except, wait a minute, I'd pledged never to try to guess his password again. Still, it was good to know more about him.

"Are you still coming home tomorrow?" he asked.

"Yep, as scheduled. Are you up for hanging out?"

"I can't wait," he said sincerely.

I was looking forward to seeing him.

"And tell Rick to stay away from you," he added a bit threateningly.

Wow. All of a sudden he was making me seem well adjusted. It was cute that he was acting protective, though. I got off the phone feeling a bit triumphant.

My parents were washing the dishes in the kitchen when I walked in.

"How's Aaron doing?" my mom asked, as if they were old friends.

She had answered the phone when he called, introduced herself, and asked about the weather in D.C. before relinquishing the phone to me.

"He's fine," I answered noncommittally.

"Is he as slick as Bramen?" my dad asked gruffly.

"I don't know, Dad," I answered with a sigh. "I don't think so."

"Mmm-hmm," my dad mumbled disapprovingly.

All of a sudden I felt exhausted by the family dynamics. On cue, Kitty stalked into the room and deposited a dead mouse on my foot. Yep, it was definitely time to leave.

Both of my parents rode with me to the airport the following afternoon. As I was hugging them good-bye next to the curb, my dad slipped me an envelope.

"Just a little something to celebrate how well you're

doing at your job," he winked at me. "Go out and get yourself something nice. We're real proud of you, Sammy."

And that erased the bad feelings immediately. It wasn't the money that did it—I hopefully wasn't that shallow; it was the way the gesture reminded me of how caring and supportive my parents had always been of me. Sure, they drove me a little batty, but my entire life I had never doubted that I was tremendously loved. As I got older, I became increasingly aware of the rarity of such a feeling, which made me all the more grateful for it. And I knew that no matter what lay in store for me, I had the advantage of a small, tight-knit home team.

"Have a safe trip, Asshole!" my mom called out to me as I disappeared through the sliding doors.

# *You Don't Say*

DECEMBER CAME IN a hurry. All of a sudden the city transformed into a wind tunnel, aggressively blowing in a whole new wintry resolve. I still couldn't rule out the possibility of a random hot streak, given the weather's consistently roller-coastery performance, but there was a new, more permanent smell of cold and early darkness that made me pretty certain that I wouldn't feel warm weather for a long while.

The office atmosphere changed as well. Everything seemed to have taken on a new significance after the success of RG's bill. Pile had felt forced to sign it, which he'd done without fanfare, and no doubt with a dark scowl on his pouting face. Senior groups and health care advocates across the country countered this with smiles and cheers for the new law. The media had devoted a fair amount of ink to the development, and despite Bramen's best efforts (and some more damaging quotes from "unnamed sources"), interest in RG seemed heightened, which contributed to the charged and happy environment the office had become. Though RG was spending most of his time in Ohio since Congress had adjourned for the year, the work carried on.

Aaron's schedule had grown even crazier, as Bramen was taking advantage of the recess to campaign at a frantic pace. As a result, Aaron traveled incessantly, returning to D.C. for only a few days of the week. Though this strained our relationship, it also injected it with an even headier passion, for when we only had a few nights to spend with one another, any festering annoyances were subsumed by a greater sexual tension. If relationships were all about compromise, lately ours was all about compromising positions. I wasn't complaining. And though we didn't feel all that steady or balanced to me, we certainly felt thrilling, which was enough to keep me hooked.

Meanwhile, the flu started making the rounds of Capitol Hill with a vengeance during the second week of December. I upped my vitamin C intake and wondered if it would be too freaky for everyone if I whipped out my surgical mask. I decided for the time being that it might be.

That Thursday, Mona and I accompanied RG to New York City, where he was to be the replacement headliner at the AARP convention. Senator Bramen had pulled out at the last minute to attend a very important party barbecue in Des Moines, and RG had agreed to fill in. He'd asked Mona and me to come along to staff the event. As we pulled into Penn Station, I braced myself for the crush of humanity that characterized New York City for me. I found the place invigorating but overwhelming. I needed practice with this metropolis, and I was happy to have it.

At the AARP convention site, we waded into a crowd of politically active senior citizens who gave RG a hero's welcome. He delivered a rousing speech and spent an hour working the room before returning to the hotel by 8:00. Mona had scheduled a fund-raising breakfast and a roundtable with city public health officials to justify an overnight stay, and she and I drank a little wine to unwind as we prepared RG's briefing books for the following day.

"So, things seem to be going well with you and Mark," I said cheerfully as we sipped our drinks and sorted through the papers.

They weren't public about their new romance, but it was obvious to anyone who paid attention. They ate lunch together every day and left cute little coded Post-it notes on each other's computers. I couldn't tell if they credited me for their love or not, but I was content with the satisfaction of a job well done.

"Yeah, they are. He's really great," she said with a smile.

Mona didn't exhibit any insecurity about her relationship. Given that she'd been aware of Mark's earlier crush on me, I'd been worried that she harbored some sort of animosity towards me now that she was dating him. This didn't seem to be the case, which I found relieving, if a bit surprising. I doubted I'd be as mature were I in her shoes.

"Are you and Aaron still together?" Mona asked after a pause.

"Uh-huh," I nodded. "He's traveling a lot now," I sighed.

"With Bramen?" Mona asked.

Was there a judgmental tinge to her tone? Or was I being hypersensitive?

"Yeah. I hate that he works for him, but you know, it's a good job," I answered.

Mona nodded. She looked like she wanted to say more, but she kept whatever it was to herself and took another sip of wine. Feeling self-conscious, I gulped mine and started babbling about the sacrifices one makes for a relationship. Luckily, by the time we finished the briefings, the conversation had become much smoother. And by the time we had each finished our second glass of wine, Mona had invited me out to an event she was attending later that night with her friend Jane.

"Jane's dad is Trey Gandon, the PR guy, and he's throwing a big party for *CW* magazine," she explained.

*CW* magazine was a new political and cultural monthly that had just been launched. I hadn't been aware of Mona's connections to the New York City party scene.

"Jane and I grew up together in Chicago," she explained. "Trey Gandon is an old friend of my parents. His wife, who passed away a while ago, was my mom's best friend in high school. So we go way back."

I'd forgotten about Mona's Chicago roots. I had always assumed that everyone in RG's office had been born and raised in Ohio like me, but there were a few exceptions. Mona had gone to college at Case Western Reserve in Cleveland and moved to D.C. shortly after.

We headed downtown to the party and met Jane at the door. Inside, flashbulbs lit up the rooms filled with glamorous and important people.

"Is there any chance that Steve Martin will be here?" I asked Jane hopefully.

"I looked over the guest list and I don't think I saw his name," she answered.

That was all right. I wasn't looking that great anyway. Unaware of the possibility of attending such a swanky party, I hadn't packed anything too stunning. My loose blouse suddenly seemed more shapeless than flowing as it hung listlessly over my black pants, and my shoes weren't as elegant as they could have been. Yep, I was feeling distinctly dowdy. My only solace was that Mona was beside me wearing a reindeer sweater and she'd *known* what was in store.

"There's my dad." Jane indicated a handsome man in his fifties. "Let me go grab him—I know he'll want to say hi," she said as she rushed off.

As I reached for a glass of champagne, I saw Senator

Spearam enter the party, decked out in a stylish pantsuit. I wondered if this was something RG would have liked to attend. Had Mona asked him?

"He turned it down," Mona informed me when I inquired.

That made sense. He was probably much happier in his hotel room, catching up on his reading. Jane returned with her dad, who gave Mona a big hug.

"I'm so happy you could make it," he said warmly. "I was just talking to your dad this afternoon."

I liked Trey Gandon immediately. He chatted with us for a few minutes, but got pulled away fairly quickly. Soon after, he was calling Jane over to say hello to Senator Spearam. Turning back to Mona, I noticed that her eyes had narrowed, making her eyebrows even more pronounced than usual.

"What's wrong?" I asked.

Mona looked at me and blinked. She finished her champagne.

"Can you keep a secret?" she asked.

Yes, I certainly could. I hoped it was a good one.

"Of course," I said in my most trustworthy tone.

"All right." Mona breathed softly as she checked to make sure no one was close enough to overhear. "Trey's never remarried, but you know who he's been seeing? Melanie Spearam."

My jaw dropped. He was having an affair with Senator Spearam? Senator Spearam was married! Granted, it was to a notorious ladies' man, but still. I couldn't believe she would do such a thing when she was running for president. After preparing herself so painstakingly for so many years. Why on earth would she take such a risk?

"You're kidding me. Really?"

Mona nodded.

"They've been together for about six months. Trey feels really guilty about it, but you know all about Jeff Spearam," Mona said. "It's not as though Trey's breaking up a real marriage."

"Is Spearam going to leave her husband for him?" I asked.

Mona shrugged.

"I don't know. I'm not even supposed to know about any of this. Trey told my dad and Jane confides in me, but *no one* knows. They've really been amazingly discreet."

"And Trey—er, Mr. Gandon—he really likes Spearam?" I asked incredulously.

"Yeah, he's really taken with her. Although, I guess there are some issues. She's apparently jealous like you wouldn't believe," Mona said.

Really. Wow. And who knew Mona was a font of such radioactive gossip? "That's shocking," I concluded.

We watched Senator Spearam move away from Mr. Gandon and Jane and onto another clutch of partygoers. Besides a backwards glance towards Mr. Gandon, she didn't exhibit any sign of a deeper intimacy. From my perspective, they were pretty good at hiding what was going on.

"I'm going to get a glass of water. Do you want one?" Mona asked.

No, I wanted more champagne. But I nodded yes to the water and pretended to check my BlackBerry as Mona left so that I didn't look entirely lost and friendless. A few seconds into my charade, I sensed someone watching me. I looked up quickly to see Senator Spearam staring at me from across the room. Did she sense that we'd been talking about her? Surely not. I turned around to see who she was really looking at, but no one was there. When I turned back, she had shifted her gaze, leaving me to question whether my imagination had just been playing tricks on me.

I watched Spearam a little longer, wondering what it felt like to be her. Even before I'd heard the salacious tales of her personal life, I'd found her professional one fascinating. She'd spent her life grooming herself to be the first female president of the United States. And now she was within reach of her goal.

Bramen was still leading in the polls, but Spearam was directly behind him, just waiting for him to stumble. For months, the three front-runners had been Bramen, Spearam, and Rexford. By most accounts, Spearam had just been waiting for Rexford to run out of money, with an eye to picking up his supporters and bypassing Bramen in time to grab the nomination. There was no guarantee that she'd be able to pull off such a feat, but as I watched her she appeared cool and confident. She was working the crowd like the professional that she was.

A woman who looked like she must be a model sidled up next to me. She had long, wavy hair and was wearing a short red dress.

"Are you close with the Gandons?" she asked pleasantly.

I didn't realize immediately that she was talking to me.

"Am I? Oh no, I just met them tonight. How about you?" I replied.

"No, I'm here on business."

She looked me in the eyes.

"So, there's nothing going on between you and Trey Gandon?" she asked.

What? This was bizarre.

"Not that I know of," I answered slowly. "I'm sorry, what was your name?"

"I'm Christy," she said with a smile as she moved away. "See you later."

And with that, she poured herself between two people and back into the crowd, leaving me very confused. I wondered what the hell she'd been talking about. And I also wondered why all models with whom I had any connection were named some variation of "isty." Between her and Misty, I was beginning to suspect a conspiracy.

I took a lap around the room to recover from the odd interaction and ended up trapped in a conversation with an elderly woman who kept asking me to identify the various celebrities scattered about, as well as the different appetizers parading by on trays. It was hard to tell whether she was more excited about Meryl Streep or the shrimp kebobs. After twenty minutes, I finally managed to extricate myself from the conversation by telling her I needed to find the facilities, which by that point was actually the truth.

I hated it when hipster places had cleverly hidden bathrooms. Accordingly, I had worked myself into a foul mood when I finally negotiated the oversized plant labyrinth disguising a fake wooden wall that the waiter had assured me swung open into a ladies' room when pressed in the right place. I entered shaking my head in disgust. Not surprisingly, it was deserted. I doubted anyone else would be able to find it without a detailed map.

The first sign that someone else actually had was the stifled sob I heard as I washed my hands. All the doors to the heavy oaken stalls were ajar, but someone was evidently occupying the one at the far end.

"Hello?" I called. "Are you okay?"

Christy peered around the side of the door.

"Oh, it's you," she said weakly, before bursting into sobs.

I looked around for help, but there wasn't any. What was I supposed to do? Should I leave her alone? It didn't seem right to leave a bereft model on the floor of an impossibly located ladies' room that no one might find for years. What if she became incapacitated with grief? She could starve here. It looked like she might already be starving.

"Don't cry," I said helplessly.

"I never should have agreed to this job," she said as she blew her nose. "It makes me feel like a whore. I'm not a whore, I'm a model/actress," she said pointedly.

It was good to maintain that distinction.

"Okay," I said in a validating tone. "That's great."

"It's not great when the only job you can get hired for is to be bait," she said bitterly, before breaking down again.

What was she talking about? I decided to keep my mouth shut and look sympathetic and just let her elaborate at her own pace.

"So I just made a fool of myself for five hundred bucks," she said in strangled gasps. "Throwing myself at this perfectly nice man, with his *daughter* right there—all because this woman is convinced that he's cheating. I feel like such an idiot. This isn't me. This is humiliating. God, the way he looked at me," she said with a shudder.

"Are you talking about Trey Gandon?" I asked in surprise.

After all, Trey Gandon had been the one she'd quizzed me about.

"Yeah." Christy sobbed. "And I'm sorry I bothered you, but figuring out if anyone else was involved with him was part of my fee. That woman is crazy," she said.

"You mean Melanie Spearam?" I asked quickly.

I couldn't believe the story I was putting together in my head. Was Spearam that jealous? Christy looked momentarily hesitant. A doubtful look clouded her wet and vacant eyes.

"No, I don't know her name," she said unconvincingly.

I could tell she was lying. Being a particularly bad liar myself, I could spot a similar ineptitude in others. All of a sudden I wanted to know the truth.

"Of course it's Spearam. I know all about this," I said authoritatively. "God, I'm sorry you had to deal with her," I added compassionately.

This last little touch worked. Christy's eyes welled up again.

"She seemed so nice at first," she said simply. "She told me Trey was her sister's husband and she wanted hard evidence that he was being unfaithful. I needed the money and it seemed like an easy job, but I didn't think about how it would make me feel," Christy continued forlornly. "It's not even that he didn't want me . . . it's the whole . . ."

She leaned over and threw up into the toilet. My heart went out to her. She certainly wasn't the hardened vixen she'd felt compelled to play. She was literally made sick by her actions. Melanie Spearam hadn't chosen her bait very well.

"It's okay," I said as I gingerly rubbed her back.

"I want to go apologize to Mr. Gandon," she said softly. "I don't care about the money anymore. She didn't even believe me when I told her he turned me down. She said maybe I was just saying that because I'd gotten a crush on him."

Wow, Spearam *was* paranoid.

"But he did turn me down. He looked . . . so horrified," she said with a catch in her throat. "Do you think I should explain things to him? So he'll know I'm not like that?" she asked me.

She seemed lost and helpless—and she was really looking to me for guidance, which was a bit frightening. Should she tell Trey Gandon? It was hard to predict what his reaction might be in terms of his relationship with Melanie Spearam, but I liked him and thought it was only fair that he knew the nature of the woman with whom he was involved. I actually felt bad for everyone caught up in this situation. Even Spearam, who was acting so rashly and unreasonably, seemed deserving of sympathy. Years of being married to a lothario in a relationship that had by most accounts substituted power for love had evidently taken its toll. She refused to trust anymore. Still, considering her political aspirations, her recklessness was stunning. Christy was sniffling.

"I think you should explain," I said impulsively. "If you can prevent someone out there from having the wrong impression of you, why not do it? It might make you feel less bad about all of this."

"Really? You think so?" she asked eagerly.

Ten minutes later, I found Mona sipping her water and looking sleepy.

"Come watch this and I'll explain later," I said as I tugged her around a large column.

We observed Mr. Gandon and Jane talking to a couple across the room. As they finished and turned towards us, Christy strode purposefully towards them. Jane put her arm on her dad's protectively. Christy made a gesture of appeasement.

We couldn't hear anything that she said, but over the next few minutes we watched Mr. Gandon's and Jane's faces shift from apprehension to disbelief to horror. Mr. Gandon put his arm around Christy's shoulder in a comforting gesture as he looked quickly around the room. I wondered if he believed Christy's story or if he just considered her unhinged. I followed his gaze to where Melanie Spearam stood chatting with a photographer and celebrity reporter. At the same moment, she looked over at him. I watched her stop talking midsentence. The reporter and photographer turned to find the source of the distraction.

"What's going on?" Mona asked.

She didn't sound sleepy anymore.

"That woman in the red dress was hired by Spearam to lure Mr. Gandon into doing something that would prove he wasn't being faithful to their affair," I whispered quickly.

"What?" Mona asked incredulously.

I agreed it sounded far-fetched. But so had the news of the affair in the first place.

"And now that woman is telling Mr. Gandon about the whole thing. Her name's Christy, by the way. She's a sweet girl. Not all that bright, but a nice person. She feels really terrible about the whole thing."

Mona stared at me.

"Are you making this up?" she asked.

"No, I swear. There was a ladies' room confession. Oh my God, what the hell is Spearam doing?"

Spearam was marching over to where the Gandons and Christy were still standing. The photographer followed her, no doubt sniffing some drama. Even from a distance, we could see that Spearam's normally composed features had worked themselves into a terrible sneer.

"She is famous for her temper," Mona said softly beside me.

Sure, but she was also famous for being incredibly intelligent and thoroughly political. Surely she wouldn't cause a scene here that could expose her affair. This place was crawling with journalists—two of them hot on her tail.

"I knew you were just like Jeff!" Spearam shrieked loud enough for us to hear.

Or maybe she *would* cause a scene.

The train wreck that unfolded before our eyes was impossible to look away from, much as I wanted to at times. All I could do was stare and cringe, amazed that someone who had spent so much time carefully constructing a path to the top could self-destruct so completely in a moment of passionate neurosis. Melanie Spearam had never threatened her political ambitions with outbursts over her husband's much-whispered-about liaisons; what made her act so rashly in regards to her lover's imagined ones?

"So is that what you want? A little whore? You said you loved me!" she was shrieking as the photographers quickly began documenting this unlikely scene.

Trey Gandon was trying to calm her and control the situation as best he could, but Spearam had orbited off into another realm. She would not be mollified. Mona and I had unconsciously moved closer.

"I told you he turned me down," Christy was protesting.

Spearam glared at her before whipping back around to Gandon.

"How many others are there?" she spat.

"Melanie, calm down," Gandon said forcefully.

"*You* calm the hell down," she yelled as she slapped him across the face.

Something in her follow-through made me suspect this was not the first time she had employed that cliché move. Everyone watched her stalk off, her three staffers looking utterly traumatized in the lights of the flashing cameras.

Trey Gandon was immediately besieged.

"Have you and Senator Spearam been having an affair?"

"How long has this affair gone on?"

"Who's the girl?"

"How do you think this affects her presidential campaign?"

"Are you angling to be first man?"

The high-profile party had turned on its creator.

Members of the press and curious guests swarmed in for the kill. I watched Gandon hold up his hand in the gesture of a man determined to maintain control whether he was allowed to or not.

"Thank you all for coming. There's nothing more to be said here. It's my understanding Senator Spearam isn't feeling well. I sincerely hope it wasn't the food. Good night."

And he directed Jane and Christy towards a private hold, ignoring the questions that were still being yelled at him. We watched them disappear into the room and stood speechless for another thirty seconds. Had all that really happened? It seemed impossible. I turned to Mona, still slack-jawed.

"Wow," I said weakly.

"Let's get another drink," Mona said definitively.

That had been enough to get anyone off water. After another drink and several assurances that what we thought we'd seen really had taken place, Mona and I made our way back to the hotel.

"Should we see if RG's awake?" I asked.

Mona looked uncertain.

"I guess we could Berry him," she said.

I sent a message informing him we had news he'd be interested in, but nothing that couldn't wait until the next day. He wrote back that he was still awake reading and wanted to know what was up. Mona and I went up to his suite. Which led to my first ever gossip session with RG.

"You're kidding me," RG said as we finished our tale. "She really lost it like that?"

We confirmed that she had.

"Poor Melanie. We've never gotten along, but it sounds like she's going through a rough time. She must be mortified," he said, shaking his head sadly.

I'd heard RG privately compare Spearam to Bramen in the way that she was fiercely competitive and tended to either use people or feel threatened by them. RG's compassion for her therefore surprised me, though I supposed it shouldn't have. I admired this generosity of spirit, but doubted I could approximate it. Schadenfreude was too tempting an emotion.

"Do you think her campaign is over?" I asked RG.

"I would imagine so," he replied. "Though I don't know, because she's certainly a fighter. We'll have to see how she handles it in the next couple of days."

He shook his head in disbelief. "She's normally so professional about everything. Although if she was ever going to crack I guess it would be now, with the intensity of the campaign. The pressure she's been under has crushed plenty of candidates in the past. She must have just snapped. And this guy must have really gotten to her."

The irony was that Trey Gandon had been completely faithful to Melanie Spearam, according to Mona, who added that Spearam was crazy not to realize how wonderful he was.

"Well, she's a toxic person," RG concluded.

It seemed as though she had finally poisoned herself. The media frenzy over the next few days suggested there was no available antidote to the situation. Spearam issued a statement about a "misunderstanding" and reaffirmed her devotion to her husband, calling suggestions of an affair "scurrilous lies." But the photos of her screaming at Gandon and the testimony of the scandalized onlookers, combined with the development that Gandon's housekeeper opened up to the press about just how frequently Senator Spearam had been a guest at the home, quickly drowned out Spearam's claims.

Gandon was refusing to comment on the crisis, except to call himself a "supporter" of Senator Spearam's who wished her nothing but the best. Other than that, he was responding to every question with a beleaguered "no comment." He had a reputation for being a top PR guy, but he seemed unprepared to properly handle this most personal of projects.

Christy had been very honest about her role in the drama. I wanted to believe this was to fully cleanse herself of her crime, rather than a cynical act of self-promotion, but either way, it was certainly keeping her in hot demand.

Aaron couldn't believe that I'd actually witnessed the whole event firsthand and listened, utterly rapt, as I regaled him with in-depth, personal commentary on the scandalous developments. Feeling like an embedded reporter who'd returned from the front, I happily soaked up his attention. My contentment was marred only by his excited predictions that Spearam's bad break would translate into a windfall for Bramen. When I'd reminded Aaron that I would consider that a terrible development, he'd stopped openly crowing about it, but not quite soon enough.

Though I didn't like Spearam very much, I was a bit saddened by her downfall. Her strong showing in the primary polls had made me proud that the country had finally seemed ready for a female chief executive—something that a lot of people I knew claimed was an impossibility for at least another generation. So I felt dismayed that this important experiment seemed to be over for the time being, as well as irked by the fact that she'd been undone by a sex scandal, of all things. I was really getting sick of those.

Meanwhile, Mona and I had become bonded through our shared witnessing of the unbelievable episode. We now talked regularly throughout the days and she kept me updated on Jane's condition, which was shell-shocked but okay. Mona was just relaying their most recent conversation when CNN broke the news of Spearam's official withdrawal from the presidential race.

"Hold on a second," I said as I turned up the volume.

"Senator Spearam's announcement comes just hours after her husband made a stray comment that got picked up by a boom mike at a business convention he was addressing," the newscaster intoned.

What's this now?

CNN cut to footage of Jeff Spearam talking with another man. His posture indicated he assumed it was a private conversation. The angle of the camera revealed it was shooting from a distance. Jeff and the man were laughing. The audio was crackly, but distinct.

"What's the girl's name—Cindy or something? She's everywhere now," the man said.

"Oh, I've been watching her," Jeff Spearam answered. "Hell, I wish Melanie hadn't wasted her on Trey—I would've screwed that bait."

His companion guffawed.

"Jeff Spearam was apparently unaware that his comments had been overheard," the newscaster continued.

I imagined he was pretty aware of it now.

# Searching the Hay

THE MIDDLE OF December brought a spate of holiday parties. RG held his annual staff party in a small bowling alley we took over for the occasion. I brought Aaron, stuffed myself with chicken wings and beer, and bowled three strikes and eight gutter balls. Consistency had never been a hallmark of my game. The Garys were in good form and fun to hang out with, though certainly distracted by their twins, who were busily exploring anything that had been left unattended at floor level. This turned out to include a lot of purses. Jenny Gary and I were in midconversation when we noticed Jeffrey painting himself black with a mascara wand. This caused me to start humming the Rolling Stones song "Paint It Black," while Jenny rushed over to tend to the situation.

"Oh Lord. Thank goodness that's my mascara," she

exclaimed as she tried to wrestle her makeup kit away from her son.

I joined the clean-up effort and found myself impressed with what Jeffrey had managed to accomplish in such a short period of time. His stomach area designs struck me as particularly inspired. I complimented Jenny on his artistic prowess.

"You sound just like Robert," she replied with a laugh.

"Who does?" I heard RG say from above us.

He and Aaron had apparently just walked over.

"Sammy thinks Jeffrey might be an artistic genius," Jenny informed him.

RG beamed.

"Oh, she's just sucking up," Aaron teased.

I glared at him, but RG just chuckled.

"You must not know Sammy too well yet," he said to Aaron.

"No, sir, I was only kidding," Aaron replied.

I was surprised to see what looked like a hardening of the little line between RG's right eye and ear—the telltale sign of annoyance. Oh no, was he not liking Aaron? I'd initially been nervous for the two of them to meet, particularly considering Aaron's loathsome job, but I'd reminded myself that RG had a kind and encouraging way of giving people the benefit of the doubt. So if RG was irritated, chances were that it was because he just didn't like Aaron as a person. But maybe I was imagining it. Or maybe RG was annoyed because Jack had just pulled down his diaper and peed into a bowling ball.

"Jackson Wade Gary, what do you think you're doing?" he bellowed.

Jack glanced up, looking like he knew he'd done something very wrong. RG took him over to the corner for a private talk. Jenny turned back towards us with a shrug.

"It's always something," she said cheerfully. "Now, how long have you two been together?" she asked.

I turned to Aaron, interested in his response, as well as vaguely worried about the bowling ball that had been left unattended, full of toddler piss. Aaron smiled at me.

"Not long enough," he replied.

That would do for an answer. Jenny seemed to think so, too.

"Well, that's very sweet," she said. "Oops, Jeffrey's throwing up candy cane. Excuse me."

"That *was* very sweet," I remarked after Jenny had hurried off.

"Well, it's true," Aaron said, as he leaned down to give me a respectable kiss.

He smelled like beer-flavored shaving cream.


The next night was Bramen's staff party, held at his well-appointed Georgetown town house. I'd reluctantly agreed to accompany Aaron, after being assured that I'd be shielded from Natalie and we wouldn't have to stay long. He seemed to understand that my attendance was an enormously charitable concession on my part, and was appropriately appreciative.

When we walked in, the first thing I noticed was the ridiculously oversized tree. Either it had been professionally decorated, or the Bramen family was scarily precise. Near the tree was a large menorah. Near the menorah was a kinara decorated with the colors of Kwanzaa. And near the kinara, to top off the politically correct display, there was a large "Happy Eid" centerpiece to make any Muslims feel at ease.

"As a half Hindu, half Buddhist, I find this home exclusionary," I said to Aaron as we walked through the grand hallway.

"Easy," he pleaded.

"All right, I'm just kidding. I suppose it's nice of them to make such an effort," I said as I took his hand and resolved to make my own effort to be nice and supportive. Though I despised Bramen and practically everyone who worked for him, I could be polite for Aaron's sake. Hopefully, it wouldn't be too much of a strain.

"It *is* nice," Aaron replied. "It's not greasy chicken wings and screaming toddlers, but it'll do."

Excuse me?! I dropped Aaron's hand. Did he honestly think that being snobby about RG's party was a wise move? He could go ahead and kiss "nice and supportive" good-bye. I was about to launch into a list of all the ways RG's party had been more fun and comfortable than the stuffy nightmare we were walking into, but Aaron had started talking to a colleague who'd come in behind us. Fine, he'd be set straight later. He could run, but he couldn't hide. I glared at him, took a scone from a passing tray, and surveyed the scene in front of me.

Bramen and his wife were working the room, which was tastefully decorated with expensive-looking furniture. I sensed Aaron gearing up to include me in his conversation so I ducked down quickly to pet a passing cocker spaniel whose ears were impossibly long and silky. I wondered if it was difficult to hear with them flopped over that way. And were those cataracts? This poor dog might be deaf *and* blind. I patted her sympathetically and turned over her tag to read her name. It was Andromeda.

"That's a very fancy name you've got," I whispered.

Andromeda responded by wolfing down the scone I was holding in my hand before I had a chance to stop her. For a disabled pooch, she was quick on the gobble.

"Oh, goodness, please don't feed the dog, dear," I heard a voice above me order.

I looked up at the scolding, curled eyelashes of Pamela Bramen. Laden with mascara, they overwhelmed her flinty eyes.

"Sorry, I didn't plan on feeding her. She took it right out of my hand," I explained as I stood up.

Mrs. Bramen smiled like she didn't believe me.

"Andromeda has a bit of a weight problem. We just can't have guests feeding her," she said crisply.

"But I wasn't—"

She had already moved on to give some instructions to a passing caterer. I walked to the window and stared out at the yard, pretending to admire the lights that were strung through the trees in the Bramens' yard. Please don't make me have to talk to anyone else, please let us go soon, I silently begged the God of Painful Holiday Parties. I wondered if I could just slip away unnoticed. I heard Pamela Bramen's voice ring out.

"Aaron, sweetheart, how are you?" she gushed.

"Hello, Mrs. Bramen, you look lovely," he replied.

I glanced over to see Aaron, Mrs. Bramen, and the evil Natalie chatting nearby. Ugh. How could he stand talking to them? Just the sight of Natalie irritated me. Several other "unnamed source" quotes had popped up since the passage of the bill. They'd all been critical of RG and his staff while exaggerating the role of Bramen and his. But having initially taken Natalie to task for her vile behavior, Aaron was evidently back on civil terms with her. I certainly didn't approve. He caught my eye just as Mrs. Bramen was admiring Natalie's dress, and made a convincing "help me, I'm trapped" expression. I didn't smile.

"Now, is there any chance of you two getting back together?" Mrs. Bramen asked Natalie in a loud and encouraging tone. "You two were just the cutest couple," she continued, resting her hand on Aaron's shoulder.

He was still looking at me. I couldn't be sure what my face was doing, but I watched a flash of panic cross over his. He turned to look at Mrs. Bramen.

"I'd really like you to meet my girlfriend, Mrs. Bramen," he said a bit forcefully.

"Oh, I'm sorry, I didn't realize she was coming. John said—"

"She's right over here," Aaron said, cutting her off a bit recklessly.

Mrs. Bramen looked taken aback as she was turned to face me.

"Oh, hello," she said, extending her hand with a surprised look. "We haven't properly met."

No, we hadn't. But I didn't feel that was my fault. As I was shaking Mrs. Bramen's hand, Senator Bramen joined us.

"Senator and Mrs. Bramen, this is Samantha Joyce. Sammy, this is Senator and Mrs. Bramen," Aaron said with the slightest frantic edge to his voice.

Another time, I would have paid much closer attention to these introductions. But I was distracted. Aaron and Natalie had *dated*? For how long? And how long ago? Why hadn't this been disclosed?

"Your name sounds very familiar," Senator Bramen was saying to me.

Right, from the soft porn e-mail I sent you a few months ago, I replied in my head. Why did Aaron have to say my last name? Why did he have to have dated Natalie? She was one of the worst people I'd ever met.

"I work for Senator Gary," I answered. "I did a lot of work on the prescription drug benefit bill."

The one you corrupted and then stole all the credit for, I added silently.

"Oh, splendid," Bramen rejoined, in a tone that indicated that wasn't at all where he remembered knowing me from. "Well, I hope you're enjoying our little get-together."

"Thanks for having me," I replied in a somewhat strangled voice.

Natalie wisely excused herself as soon as the Bramens moved on. Aaron turned towards me, looking apologetic.

"I'm sorry she had to bring that up. It was a long time ago. And it's not an issue at all," he assured me. "Are you okay?"

I took a deep breath. We were in public, I reminded myself. Which was no place to cause a scene. Spearam had convinced me of that.

"Yeah, I'm okay," I said carefully. "I'm not sure why you neglected to tell me that you'd dated one of my arch-enemies, but let's just forget about it for now."

"Okay, great," Aaron said, relieved.

"I mean, why didn't you tell me?" I asked immediately. "Don't you think that's something I should have been told? You dated *Natalie*, of all people? I can't believe it. Did you sleep with her?" I asked.

"Come on, Sammy . . ."

So that was a yes. Oh God, she was probably the office conquest we'd fought about months ago. I felt sick.

"How long did that whole thing last?" I asked tightly.

"It was just like four or five months. It was nothing," he answered.

"You and I have been dating for five months, Aaron."

"Right," he said, scrambling. "And what we have is something. Something really different and special. I've never felt about anyone the way I feel about you," he continued, as he took my hand. "Wow, your hand is cold."

"You and Natalie must have made quite a couple. Pamela Bramen was clearly disappointed by your break-up," I noted, withdrawing my hand from his grasp.

"Yeah, well, I wasn't. And I'm the one who counts. You're dating me. You're not dating Pamela Bramen," he replied.

"That's just because John Bramen got to her first," I said.

I hadn't really been in the mood to make a joke. It had just slipped out. Aaron laughed. But my expression warned him not to assume that things were completely fine. In my opinion, he'd really screwed up by not letting me know about his history with Natalie. He should have filled me in, if only to avoid the sort of awkward situation that had just transpired. But I understood that guys often took a different view of such issues, and I really didn't want to waste time being jealous and mad when we were out at a party together. Even if it was a miserable party. It was important to keep up appearances, and I was determined to come off as secure and confident, even if that required a bit of acting.

In the cab ride home, Aaron laced his fingers through mine.

"I need you to know that my old relationships mean nothing to me. I never should have dated Natalie—the whole experience was a disaster. And we certainly don't get along now. I wish I'd met you sooner, but I guess I had to make some mistakes before I hit the jackpot. I'm sorry if I made you feel bad. I never want to do that, believe me," he said.

I breathed in deeply before answering.

"Okay. But can you do me a favor and just tell me things like that from now on? It's hard enough that you work for Bramen. I'd like to avoid any more unpleasant surprises. Don't you trust me?"

"Completely," he answered.

He sounded sincere. As we drifted off to sleep that night in his bed, he rolled me over to face him.

"Sammy, I've got to tell you something," he whispered.

Now whom had he dated? Satan?

"Yeah?" I asked apprehensively.

"It's something I've been meaning to tell you for a while. I just didn't really know how to go about it," he continued.

"What is it? What's wrong?"

He'd done some terrible thing. Possibly committed

some sort of crime. I just knew it. I shouldn't have been ignoring my intuition all this time. My mom had been proven a psychic genius with her paper clip prediction. Surely, some of that power flowed through my veins.

"I'm falling in love with you," he said.

That was not a terrible thing. Huh. Finally, the words I'd been wanting to hear from him, and he wasn't even that drunk. He'd really just said it. He couldn't un-say it. Could he? I breathed in slowly.

"It's been happening for a while, and I've wanted to tell you before now, but it just never felt like the right time. I think you're amazing. I love you."

Three and a half months off schedule, but there it was. As he gazed adoringly at me, I felt little channels of joy chase the sleep out of my body. I was fully awake.

"I love you, too," I responded reflexively.

"You don't have to say that," he answered.

But I did. Didn't I? I'd only definitely loved someone once before, though I'd had a fair amount of love-approximating infatuations. This didn't feel like any of those, but it didn't feel like that prior love, either. So maybe it was a new kind of grown-up love? Or a more mature infatuation? I wasn't sure. And now he was kissing me before I could fully sort it out.

"You're addicted to him," Liza said to me on the phone the next day after I had recounted the exciting events.

"Excuse me?"

"You're addicted. It's an addiction. He's like a drug to you," she emphasized.

"I don't know what you're talking about," I replied.

But as soon as I let myself really process her assertion, I agreed with it. I was addicted to him. That was the feeling I'd found so difficult to pinpoint.

"I know you've never been addicted to anything before," Liza was saying. "So it's not something you can understand immediately—"

"What about the jalapeño poppers?" I interrupted. "And that Professor Longhair song?"

I don't know why all of a sudden I was determined to prove I had been addicted to things in the past. The song had been a particularly tough one to beat. So catchy.

"It's just something you might want to think about," Liza said simply.

I already was thinking about it.

"Yeah, I guess I agree with you," I said.

"That was fast," she replied in surprise.

"Well, it sort of makes sense to me. He makes me act in crazy ways sometimes where I'm kind of watching myself from above, not really believing that I'm doing a particular thing but unable to stop myself," I said, thinking of the voicemail password incident.

"Like what?" Liza asked.

I hesitated.

"Are you drinking a martini right now?"

I had anticipated telling Liza about my Thanksgiving

low point, but I had also envisioned martinis being involved when it happened.

"I could be. It's almost lunchtime," she answered.

Twenty minutes later, I was sitting across from her at the Bottom Line, martinis in tow, with a taco plate on the way. She looked a little tired, but ready to help as always.

"So, are addictions always bad for you? I mean, is it bad that I'm addicted to Aaron?" I asked her.

There did seem to be an inescapable negative connotation surrounding the concept of addiction. But what if someone was addicted to doing good deeds? That couldn't be a bad thing, could it?

"Addictions are generally bad for you, yeah," Liza answered.

Drats.

"I mean, if you want to be in control of yourself," she continued. "But forget about the addiction angle for a second. The real issue is, is Aaron bad for you?"

She waited expectantly for me to answer. I tried to organize my thoughts.

"I don't think so," I said uncertainly. "I mean, there are things about him that piss me off—things I'd definitely love to change. I obviously hate that he works for Bramen, which causes a ton of tension. So that's a problem that doesn't seem to be going away. But he's wonderful in other ways. I'm crazily attracted to him. And he's smart and considerate and—"

"He's considerate?" Liza interrupted skeptically.

"Well, he loves me. That's pretty considerate."

I wasn't entirely comfortable with this new trend of Liza asking tough questions about *my* boyfriends, but she'd finally broken up with Ryan, so I couldn't redirect the conversation.

"I don't mean to argue with you," Liza continued. "I just want to make sure you're happy."

"I know. And it's true that Aaron has some serious flaws, but you know what? I do, too. If he can deal with mine, I should be able to deal with his. That's the definition of compromise, right? And when it comes down to it, he makes my life feel more exciting. So I guess I can't really imagine giving him up," I said.

Liza looked at me a moment and nodded.

"So for now, you're comfortable being addicted to him. But you did say that you're not sure you're in love with him," she reminded me.

True. And I wasn't sure. Why wasn't I sure?

"Maybe I'm still falling in love with him?"

"Are you asking me?" Liza replied.

"No, that must be it. I must be still falling in love with him. Mean-while, I'm completely addicted to him."

Liza pointed to her empty martini glass.

"I'm ready to be scandalized by your behavior," she said.

Oh, right. I finished my own drink and told her an abridged version of the trying-to-guess-the-password night. She nodded throughout.

"Perfectly acceptable behavior," she said when I finished.

That was one of the things I loved about Liza. She could be incredibly validating when I most needed it.

"You don't think I'm becoming psycho?" I asked.

She shook her head vehemently.

"No. He made you suspicious. He *inconsiderately* didn't act like a loving boyfriend when you all were apart. Therefore, he must face the consequences."

She sounded like she was handing down a verdict. I felt definitively supported and strong enough to return to the rest of my day, even if I was still uncertain about my exact feelings for Aaron. I thanked Liza and promised to call her later.

Back at the office soon after, I was getting off the phone with a woman in Akron who wanted to know if her pets qualified for the new Medicare discounts when I happened to glance at the date. Not only was it the twenty-year anniversary of the day my parents bought me my Cabbage Patch doll (Annabeth Sue, my first adopted possession), but it was also four days until I flew home for Christmas. Which meant I had less than four days to get all my presents. The shock registered in a rush.

After every panicked, manic Christmas, I always vowed to start collecting my presents slowly over the course of the year, so as to avoid ever experiencing such pain again. And I never, ever followed through. It was usually about a week before Christmas that I started trying to quickly learn a hobby that I could parlay into original gifts. Last year, it had been wood burning. The year before, crochet. Predictably, I was never able to attain the level of mastery needed to be able to produce gifts worth giving, but that didn't stop the attempts. As I sat there staring at the calendar, I wondered how difficult it would be to find a pottery workshop that I could attend in the next few days.

After a few mildly harassing phone calls to various local art stores, I abandoned the pottery workshop plan. But I did manage to make some passably tasty gingerbread people that night at home, which I considered a massive accomplishment. I gave them out to friends and colleagues on my last day in the office. I even gave one to Ralph, in the spirit of holiday forgiveness. He seemed very touched and ate the whole thing in one bite.

Just before I flew home, I remembered that I was about to willingly enter an information vortex, without access to my BlackBerry, cell phone, or most distressingly, the Internet. What was I going to miss? I spent an hour reading The Note and the Hotline to saturate myself with campaign updates while I still had the luxury of doing so.

Spearam's spectacular self-destruction had considerably shaken up the dynamics of the field, and the repercussions seemed to still be sorting themselves out. Upon her withdrawal from the race, all of her fellow candidates had issued statements of praise and support, while immediately engaging in a mad scramble for her senior staff and core followers. Her campaign manager had signed on with the Bramen team, her communications director had joined the Rexford ranks, and her hot-shot political consultant had hooked up with Wye. However, Spearam's major fund-raisers, along with her volunteer staff and broad network of supporters, seemed to be playing coy for the moment, at least according to the update. I imagined that rather than intentionally playing coy, they were more likely still in shock from the recent events.

Were more surprises around the corner? The first caucuses and primaries were just a month away. I resolved to check CNN on a regular basis while I was home to keep up as best I could. For a moment I envied Aaron, whose family was coming to D.C. to visit him, and only for three days. How did other people manage such arrangements? I needed some tutorials. As soon as these thoughts passed through my mind, I felt guilty about them. I was excited to see my parents and it made me happy that they always insisted I come home, even when it wasn't convenient. I enjoyed feeling wanted.

As a special Christmas treat, Aaron rode with me all the way to the airport.

"I promise to keep in better touch this time," he said as we lingered by the security post. "I bought a back-up charger to be sure. You know I have to head up to New Hampshire between Christmas and New Year's, right?"

Yes, I did. I'd started getting copies of Bramen's

schedules to better prepare for Aaron's absences. I nodded.

"Good luck," I said sweetly. "To you, not to Bramen. I hope Bramen has terrible luck."

Aaron took my hostility in stride.

"Feisty as ever," he smiled. "I'll see you on New Year's, babe," he said before kissing me one last time.

I kissed him back, thinking about how he'd never called me "darling" again after that one time I'd made such a huge deal over it. From then on, he'd stuck firmly to "baby" or "babe." Oh well, we'd made strides in other areas.

"I love you, Sammy," he said with his face very close to mine.

"I'm addicted to you," I answered.

I could tell by his expression that he thought this was a very romantic and good thing to say, so it all worked out. I didn't have to lie. He didn't have to feel bad. And as soon as we parted and I found myself alone at the gate, I felt the tug of that addiction. Had I ever missed anyone so quickly? I needed to distract myself.

While browsing the table of contents of the *New Yorker*'s Winter Fiction issue at a newsstand, I spotted the name of a man I'd had classes with in college. I remembered that he had been a literature major, come to think of it. His story was titled "Paper Bag Ladies," and it looked to be his debut piece. I was intrigued, and though I'd cleaned out my wallet in the pursuit of presents for my parents, I was pretty sure I had a couple of bills left.

At the cash register, I was seventy-five cents short.

"Gosh, I'm sorry, I don't seem to have it," I told the scowling woman, after scrounging through my bag in the hopes of discovering loose change.

I could feel the impatience of the line that had formed behind me. I really didn't want to turn to face them. But I also thought that I could possibly have the change in the little secret pocket whose existence I had just remembered.

"Ooh, wait a minute, one more pocket," I smiled at her. "They put these little camouflaged ones in here sometimes, you know. Once I thought I lost my key, and I found it eight months later in the secret pocket of my bag. It was another bag, not this one—"

"I've got a plane to catch," a woman said bitterly from the back of the line.

"Yeah, I don't have it," I concluded sheepishly.

"Here's seventy-five cents," I heard a familiar voice say as its rescuing hand deposited the change into the cashier's palm.

"Thank God," the woman behind me said.

I moved out of the line's wrath and turned to face Charlie Lawton, who stood unsmilingly, but not unkindly, before me.

"Happy holidays," he said. "That's a good issue."

With that, he started to walk away.

"Hey," I said, not sure of what I was going to follow it up with.

He turned around.

"Thanks," I continued.

Maybe it was the holiday spirit, maybe it was feeling flustered over the great change search, but I didn't feel the requisite surge of disgust towards him. Had I learned to forgive? My Sunday school teacher would be so proud.

Charlie started to say something.

"Final boarding call for United flight two-seventy-three to Boston," a manicured voice interrupted him over the loudspeaker.

"That's me," he said. "I've gotta run. See you."

"See you," I replied as he walked quickly away.

As I waited for the plane to pull back from the gate and wished I wasn't sitting in a middle seat, I pondered my new reaction to Charlie Lawton. If I really thought about it, I still hated him, but somehow that hatred seemed like a distant, remembered feeling. Maybe I'd just seen so many worse things happen to people in the interceding months, or maybe I felt content enough with my life that his treachery didn't damage me as much. Or maybe it just took a *New Yorker* Winter Fiction issue to buy my forgiveness. I wasn't sure. Before I could puzzle further through the mystery, my BlackBerry buzzed with a message. I checked it surreptitiously, as I was supposed to have already turned off all my electronic devices.

To: Samantha Joyce [srjoyce@gary.senate.gov]
From: Aaron Driver
[aidriver@bramen.senate.gov]
Subject: re: Best Date Ever
Text: was with you, coming up on a half year
ago. just made it back to my place and found a
strand of your hair on my pillow.
i miss you and love you and i hope you have a
safe and fun flight. yours, a.

I started typing a reply to this unexpectedly sappy and satisfying message, but the flight attendant caught me.

"Please put that away, ma'am," she scolded.

I had a brief flashback to Pamela Bramen.

"Oh, sorry. Gosh, does it really interfere with the air traffic control signals?" I asked with a contrite smile.

"Yes," she said sharply.

Well, all right then. I'd just have to reply to Aaron later on. I settled in to read some winter fiction. It had been bought at a dear price—restored civility towards Charlie Lawton. I hoped it was worth it.

My old classmate Steve Hipistead had written a compelling story. I didn't entirely understand it, which only strengthened my hunch that it was impressive literature. I spent the rest of the flight wondering if I could have inadvertently inspired any of his writing, if not this particular piece, then perhaps other samples of his work, perhaps something he had yet to write. Though we hadn't been close, maybe I'd done some little thing that had stuck with him—something that provided grist for his creative process. Come to think of it, I had often carried my lunch in a brown paper bag to lectures. Could I have been the original "Paper Bag Lady"? I was intrigued by the notion that I might be so anonymously famous.

I skimmed through the rest of the issue and ordered a ginger ale from the flight attendant who'd scolded me. She only filled my cup halfway, perhaps as further punishment. I had a direct comparison, because the person in the window seat also ordered ginger ale and her cup was delivered positively brimming with soda. I thought about saying something, but realized that anything confrontational in light of our earlier interaction could possibly be misinterpreted as abusive, which could in turn bring about air rage charges. The risks were too great. So I decided instead to view my cup as half-full and drank the ginger ale in a too-quick gulp that sent a painful air pocket protesting through my esophagus.

The following days played themselves out in a lazy, warm way. There was a lot of hanging out, a little bit of Asshole playing, a fair amount of Kitty battling—these were the predictable routines that shaped my winter vacation.

I talked to Aaron briefly on Christmas morning, but he was wrapped up in family engagements, which wasn't that surprising. He promised to call me later after whispering how much he loved me. I told him that I couldn't hear him, but assured him I was kidding when that seemed to stress him out.

Three days later, I called his cell phone after my parents had gone to bed. Before I punched in his digits, I pressed the star button, followed by 67. Dialing 67 blocked the outgoing number so it would only show up as "unknown" on another person's caller ID. Liza had turned me on to this trick after I'd confessed to the Thanksgiving debacle, and I'd vowed to use it whenever there was the possibility that I'd need to make multiple obsessive calls to the same number. It was exciting to use technological tools to protect my reputation, though so far Aaron had been fairly good about staying in touch and leaving his cell phone on.

"Merry Christmas!" A young woman's voice I didn't recognize answered the phone.

It was very jarring. Aaron's family had left and he was on a trip with Bramen, so I knew it wasn't his mother or sister. And no one but Aaron had ever answered his phone before. But I knew the kind of people that did answer other people's cell phones. It was probably some overeager New Hampshire staffer. Aaron usually kept his phone on his person, but he'd been known to leave it on a desk in the past.

"Oh, hi," I said, trying not to sound too startled. "Is Aaron there?"

"He's in the shower. This is Darlene—is this Jillian?! I've been looking forward to meeting you!" she said with an enthusiastic giggle.

I felt my heart go cold. It hadn't ever done that before. I'd always assumed that was a figure of speech with no biological basis, but now I knew better. My heart really did feel frigid in my chest, as though my blood had instantly iced.

Jillian was the name of Aaron's sister, whom I'd heard a lot about but had never met. And Darlene? Well, she was someone who was looking forward to meeting Aaron's family and who was answering Aaron's phone (something I'd never presumed to do) while he was apparently showering nearby.

"This isn't Jillian," I managed to say, even though I was having a little trouble breathing normally.

"Oh . . ." Darlene sounded confused. "Well, can I take a message? We won't be going to sleep for another hour or two, so I'm sure he can call you back."

I felt like someone had punched me in the stomach, which validated the authenticity of another clichéd expression I'd doubted. I managed to mumble something and hang up the phone. And then I sat on the edge of the bed, attempting to process the information I'd just received.

I tried for a millisecond to imagine a scenario in which the things this strange woman had just told me could fit into a completely harmless reality. Maybe she was a colleague he'd been forced to share a hotel room with to save the campaign money? Who just happened to be young and female and giggly? Nope, I couldn't come up with a viable justification. What the hell was going on?

All at once, a memory reared up to painfully rede-clare itself. Aaron and I were riding in a subway car. He was nuzzling my hair.

"Hey, darling? Are you awake?" he was asking dis-tractedly.

I'd been confused, because it had been such an odd and unexpectedly tender thing for him to say.

"What did you just call me?" I had asked incredu-lously.

He'd looked uncertain. I remembered that.

"Nothing," he'd said lamely.

And I'd rushed to stop him from being embarrassed, to assure him that it was fine and great for him to call me "darling" in that cute drawl of his. Except I realized now that he hadn't been calling me darling at all. He'd mis-takenly said "Darlene," and been thrilled that I'd covered his tracks for him.

Anger accompanied the horror and disbelief that coursed through me. Who was Darlene? For that matter, who was Aaron? Obviously not the loving boyfriend I'd thought he was. He'd been cheating on me?! How dare he treat me like this? What did I do now?

I picked up the phone to call Aaron back and demand

some of these answers, but I stopped myself. I didn't have a plan and I didn't feel like just being hysterical. I wanted to deal with this, not just scream about it. I needed more information.

I took some deep breaths. Who could Darlene possibly be? She had to be someone up in New Hampshire—it would have been virtually impossible for Aaron to have two girlfriends in D.C. Did I trust any of his friends to give me the goods? I thought about his roommate Mike. Beyond some late-night discussions of his beer can sculptures and love of pausing movies at alarming moments to create stills that he considered a form of artwork, our relationship hadn't progressed very far. Besides, Aaron had mentioned that Mike was out of town visiting the energy vortexes in Sedona.

Thinking about their empty apartment made me wish I could search it. Was there any way to remotely access it? Like a message directly from the God of Discovering Adultery himself, a little voice in my head reminded me of the fact that Aaron had his own home phone line. At first, I didn't understand the significance. The voice waited patiently for me to realize. Of course. I knew what to do. I dialed the number.

When it went to voicemail, I pressed the star button, and sure enough, a recorded voice asked me for the password. I tried 5757 per our previous discussion of Aaron's lucky numbers. To my utter amazement and gratitude for the deity, it worked.

"You have . . . seven . . . saved messages," the recorded voice told me in its stilted two-tone manner. "To listen to your messages, press one."

I pressed one.

"Received on . . . September twenty-ninth at . . . ten-thirty PM," the recording informed me.

"Hey, sweetie, it's me," I heard what I now knew to be Darlene's voice saying. "Just calling to say good night. I've been thinking about you all day. Have you been thinking about me? I can't wait to touch you again next week. Sleep well, sweetie. 'Bye."

"If you wish to save this message, press two now. To delete it, press three now. To listen to other options, press four now."

I pressed two automatically, clutching my stomach, which had just cramped up painfully. September twenty-ninth? That was three months ago.

"Next message, received on . . . October fourth at . . . seven-oh-five PM."

"Hey, baby, it's me. Thanks for the flowers. I just wanted to let you know how much I'm craving you."

The others were all along the same lines. All from Darlene, all recorded in the last three months, all saved by Aaron for what were apparently sentimental reasons. It was clear from the messages that they had an intense physical relationship and managed to see each other fairly often. The sixth recorded message provided a key to her identity.

"Received on . . . December twelfth at . . . eleven AM."

"Hey, honey, you should be getting home around now. We're fueling up the plane and then headed back to Trenton, but I'll see you in a few days. Thanks for fueling *me* up, by the way. I love you, baby."

December twelfth was right around when I'd been in New York—the same time Aaron had been at the Iowa barbecue. I got out my copy of Bramen's schedule. Sure enough, on December twelfth it listed "Return from Des Moines. RON DC."

I checked the other dates that had been mentioned in Darlene's voicemails. They all corresponded to times right after trips Aaron had taken with Bramen. Many of them had been to New Hampshire, but not all of them. However, all of them had been on a chartered plane. Could Darlene be one of the pilots? I had lots of photos of Bramen deplaning that I'd cut out from newspapers when they'd also contained Aaron in the backgrou6nd. I'd often blacked out Bramen's face or added devil horns. Now I realized I should have been doing the same to Aaron. I took out my clippings folder.

There was Bramen walking next to Aaron down the stairs in Iowa. I could see one of the pilots in the cockpit, but he was definitely a man.

Okay, there they were again in another shot—Aaron was farther back this time. I couldn't see the pilot, but Aaron was clearly talking to someone still in the cabin.

And there they were from a longer shot. There was a flight attendant behind Aaron on the stairs.

There she was again.

And again.

And again.

I looked at her closely. She looked about my age, maybe younger. She wore a short blue miniskirt and fitted jacket. She looked put together and made-up, and in seven of the fifteen newspaper photos I had clipped out she was standing very near to Aaron. I wanted to kill them both.

I hadn't even noticed her before. Why should I have? All planes came with pilots and flight attendants—there wasn't any reason for her to stand out. I'd never seen her in person. I'd never contemplated her existence. And she had been sleeping with my boyfriend for at least three months, most likely longer.

I tormented myself by envisioning what was going on in Aaron's hotel room at that very moment. Would Darlene have even mentioned the phone call before they passionately lunged at each other the second he came out of the bathroom all freshly showered and ready for action? And if she had, what had she said about it? I'd managed to spit out an "I'll try him in the office next week" before hanging up the phone. I didn't know why I'd said it—the words had just come out of me in a dead, detached monotone. They hadn't been a calculated part of a clever master plan, but I wondered if I could incorporate them into one now.

I tried to think strategically for a moment. Aaron didn't know I had called. If Darlene had told him, she would no doubt have characterized it as some unknown from work, citing the evidence of my parting statement. If Aaron had checked his cell phone's call log, which I imagined he would have done, he would have found that the call had come from a blocked number, thanks to my star 67 trick. Therefore, he'd have reason to hope that it hadn't been me to whom Darlene had spoken, though he'd undoubtedly recognize the scary possibility that such an interaction could have occurred. I imagined he'd redouble his precautionary efforts from now on.

I didn't have a fully formed plan in my head, but it occurred to me that I should buy some time so that I could confront Aaron and exact my revenge in the most satisfying way. The best way to do this would be to call back and act completely fine, and as if it was my first and only call of the evening. Could I pull that off? It would take serious effort.

After a few minutes of deep breathing I felt calm and resolved. I redialed his number, this time without the star 67 safeguard, but it didn't even matter because the call went straight to voicemail. Of course he'd turned off his phone. I took another deep breath, gave myself a quick pep talk, and waited for the beep.

"Hey Aaron, it's Sammy here. Just calling to say good night. I hope New Hampshire's going well. Can't wait to see you in a few days. I love you. 'Bye."

My voice had sounded almost normal. I exhaled in relief. The message would assure him that everything between us was fine—that there was no need to have any vague worries that the call Darlene had answered could possibly have been me. I wanted him feeling secure. And then I wanted him to suffer. That part I still needed to plan.

Sleep seemed like a laughable option, even though I could sense the tiredness in my body. I made the concession of lying in bed with the lights off, but my mind raced as if it was housed in a fully illuminated, upright posture. Did Darlene assume she and Aaron were enjoying an exclusive relationship? There was a good chance that she did, since I certainly had for myself. I wondered what she would think if she discovered he'd been two-timing her with me. What kind of person was she? Would she care?

I decided to do some investigating. I sat up, turned the light back on, and reexamined the photo clippings. The name on the chartered plane read "Share-Air." I resolved to call them in the morning.

Somewhat calmed by the simple existence of a plan,

I turned off the light again, closed my eyes, and let my emotions come crashing in. I couldn't be sure at what point the sobbing ended and the unconsciousness began—I felt racked and rocked throughout the dismal night.

# Hell to Pay

"SHARE-AIR INCORPORATED, may I help you?" the chirpy voice greeted me the next morning when I called.

"Yes, hello, I'm with Senator Bramen's office and he requested I call about a flight manifest list for his trip back from Manchester tomorrow," I said very professionally.

"All right, ma'am, hold one moment."

My heart beat recklessly as I waited for their next move.

"Ma'am? The computer says that was faxed over yesterday. Do you need me to refax?"

No, that wouldn't help me. I couldn't give them an Ohio number to fax it to without a really good explanation that I didn't have available to me at the moment. Plus, I couldn't be sure my parents even owned a fax.

"Goodness, someone must have misplaced it. You

know what, don't worry about it. It's the regular crew, right?"

"Yes, ma'am, it is," the voice answered.

Share-Air didn't sound suspicious at all. Perfect.

"Great. With Darlene Smith attending?" I asked and held my breath.

There was a pause.

"Darlene Templeton is the flight attendant, ma'am."

"Oh, right. I always do that. I went to high school with a Darlene Smith. Templeton, of course," I said, a little too maniacally. "Well, great, thanks a lot."

"My pleasure, ma'am. And to whom am I speaking?"

I hung up quickly. Luckily, I'd star 67ed the call in the event that they had caller ID, but hopefully that last bit of suspicion would be easily shrugged off by my Share-Air friend.

Darlene Templeton. I longed for Google. But until I could be reunited with fast Internet connections in a few days, I'd have to rely on good old-fashioned sleuthing. Where would I live if I was Darlene Templeton? I gave a little shudder immediately after posing this query to myself. I didn't want to identify with Darlene Templeton in any way—we already had one thing entirely too disturbingly in common. I decided to rephrase the question to "where did that tramp Darlene Templeton most likely live?" and set about making a list of options. First up was Trenton, New Jersey—Bramen's hometown and frequent flight destination.

Information didn't have a listing for her in Trenton. They did have a listing for nine other Templetons, and it occurred to me that she could still live with her parents or other relatives, but I decided not to give up on the notion of a solo listing until I'd tried a few more options.

I'd reached Share-Air at a Newark, New Jersey, number, so I tried Newark information next. Again, a lot of Templetons, but no Darlene. One D. Templeton turned out to be a cranky man named David who didn't appreciate being bothered when he was bleaching his dentures. I could understand that. My experience with Crest Whitestrips had taught me that such activities required one's concentration. I said as much in my apology, but he didn't soften.

I lucked out with the Manhattan directory. There were sixteen D. Templetons and three actual Darlene Templetons. Surely one of them had to be her. I wrote down the numbers and thanked the directory assistance lady, who was surprisingly pleasant. Maybe I'd call her back some other time.

The first Darlene was very chatty, but definitely not the one I was looking for. She explained that she had been Daniel Templeton until her sex change operation the previous week and that I was the first person to call since she'd revised the listing. She hadn't liked the name Danielle, but had wanted to stay in the D family.

"After all, I'm a D-cup now!" she'd gushed.

I could imagine her excitement, but didn't really have time to talk to her. Which was too bad, because she seemed capable of saying fascinating things.

The second Darlene had recently moved to San Francisco and Gilbert, the new tenant, was annoyed to still be receiving calls for her. I dialed the third Darlene's number, wondering if Manhattan was going to turn out to be a complete wash. It went to voicemail after six rings. Please don't let it be an automated voicemail recording, I begged the God of Investigating Adultery Once It's Discovered. This was no time for a machine to tell me I'd reached "two, one, two . . ." etc. Once again, I was smiled upon.

"Hi, you've reached Darlene. I'm not home right now, but I can't wait to call you back!"

The voice was sparkly and unmistakable. I had my woman.

According to Bramen's schedule, the plane was slated to return him and Aaron to D.C. that afternoon. I imagined Darlene would be returning home shortly thereafter, because I was scheduled to fly back to D.C. on the thirty-first and we'd never overlapped in the past, as far as I could tell. How had Aaron gotten out of spending New Year's Eve with Darlene? Maybe she had other obligations, just as I'd had over Christmas. Ugh, he was a dirtbag.

Aaron called to check in midday, but I asked my dad to tell him I was taking a nap. My dad gave me a quick look before complying.

"Of course," he answered gently.

We didn't discuss it any further, though I could tell he knew something was wrong. The next morning, I screwed up my courage to call Darlene again. This time, she answered her phone.

"Hello?" she said in her bubbly way.

"Hi, Darlene, my name is Sammy Joyce. I'm a friend of Aaron's," I began deliberately.

I didn't want to start off identifying myself as his girlfriend and giving her too much of a shock. I needed to work with her a little bit.

"Oh, he's not here right now. He's back in D.C. for work," she answered.

Not here right now? I knew he wasn't, but that phrase suggested he often was there.

"You should try him on his home phone. Do you have that number? He has a cell, but he only uses that for work calls."

She was remarkably cheerful and helpful and not in the least bit suspicious of or threatened by a random girl calling for her boyfriend. She didn't seem very much like me at all. I took a calming breath.

"I'm not actually calling *for* Aaron, I'm calling *about* Aaron. You see, he and I have been dating for five months," I said slowly.

"Excuse me?"

Darlene sounded slightly less bubbly. I felt bad, but I needed to cut to the chase.

"Yes. And I've just discovered that you've apparently

been dating him for I'm not even sure how long, and I thought maybe the fact that we're both dating him but don't know about the other one might be something we want to discuss."

There was a brief pause.

"Is this some sort of joke?" she asked.

"No, I'm afraid not," I answered wearily.

"Aaron and I have been together since June. We're not just dating. We're in a serious relationship. I think you've got to be mistaken," she said evenly, though I could hear the doubt in her voice.

June, huh? That wasn't good. She had over two months on me. Although, at least he'd strayed from her to start up with me. Did that count for something? Possibly in some pathetic way I shouldn't dwell on.

"Well, he and I have been together since August. And I also had considered it a serious, exclusive relationship for the past few months. I'm afraid he's deceived both of us."

"I don't understand," Darlene said.

I sympathized. It wasn't a fun thing to understand. I thought about sending her the *Post* article about the whipped cream incident to prove my claims. I remembered how Aaron had been upset that I'd identified him as my boyfriend. Darlene must not read the *Post*.

"How often do you guys see each other?" she asked softly.

Maybe she was beginning to let herself comprehend.

"Well, we live in the same city, so——"

"You live in D.C.?" she interrupted.

"Yeah, so unless he's traveling with Senator Bramen, he's pretty much with me," I answered.

There was a long pause.

"Basically the only time he's not with me is when he's in D.C.," Darlene finally responded.

We figured out that it had broken down to about fifty-fifty over the most recent, busiest months. Darlene said that she constantly traveled for her job and she knew how hard Aaron worked, so the jagged pattern of their actual physical time together had just seemed like a sacrifice worth making.

"We're apart a lot, but when we're together, it's so intense," she was saying.

Her words javelined into me. Time with Aaron *was* intense. That was one of its draws.

"Are you in love with him?" I asked her.

"Of course," she answered.

I heard her stifle a little sob.

"Are you?" she asked, almost too softly to hear.

Did I feel like going into the whole love-versus-addiction explanation with her? Not really.

"Not at the moment," I answered truthfully.

"How could he do this?" she asked in an anguished tone.

"I don't know. He's a lying rat bastard," I concluded.

I had trouble believing it myself. But that was the

only conclusion I could draw. The man I had fantasized about spending the rest of my days with, the man to whom I'd developed my life's only full-fledged addiction, was a cheating assface. Forgive me, Steve Martin, I never should have strayed.

"I'm going to hang up and call him," Darlene said.

"No, no, wait," I urged.

What was it that I wanted instead? I wasn't quite sure.

"I just don't think he should be able to get away with this," I continued.

"Me, neither. That's why I'm going to call him. He's got a lot of explaining to do," Darlene agreed.

"Right, but if he's been this good at keeping up the charade so far, he's not going to give up easily. He's very smart. I bet he'll try to pit us against one another. I don't know, tell you I'm demented or something," I said.

"Are you?" Darlene asked, in a suspiciously hopeful tone.

"No, I'm not," I assured her.

At least not in a clinical sense.

"Well, then what should we do?" Darlene asked.

It was a good question. I had a half-formed plan. I just needed to sell her on it.

"I think he should have to face us together, so that we can hear what he says to both of us," I said simply.

"What do you mean?" she asked.

"Well, I'm flying back to D.C. tomorrow. Aaron's

picking me up at my place and we're going to a New Year's Eve party—"

Darlene had started sobbing a little again.

"I'm sorry," I said. "It sucks for me to think about him with you, too."

"He told me he had to spend New Year's Eve with his friend who's going through a divorce," she said. "We're meeting up again next week, so I didn't even think twice about it."

That was pretty evil. Using an excuse that also made him seem like a caring and considerate friend. Despicable.

"Do you have plans for New Year's?" I asked her.

"Just going to a bar with some girlfriends. Nothing major," she replied.

"Okay. Well, then, why don't you come down to D.C. instead? Come to the New Year's Eve party. We'll confront him together."

"I don't know," Darlene said uncertainly.

"Would you rather spend the night away, knowing he was with me?" I asked a bit cruelly.

And a bit disingenuously. I doubted any time Aaron and I spent together would be romantic from here on out. But it worked.

"I'll be there," she said decisively.

We exchanged cell phone numbers and agreed that neither one of us would talk to Aaron until we saw him the following night. I hoped I could trust her.

"Do you mind my asking what you do in D.C.?" she asked as we were getting off the phone.

"I work for another senator," I said. "I specialize in health care issues."

There was a little pause, during which I reflected on the significance of my words. I did do important work, and I liked my job. That was the identity I needed to get back to. I had to forget about Aaron, if I could.

"I guess that explains why you're so smart. Aaron must really like that," Darlene said wistfully.

Oh God, I didn't want her getting herself down any more than she already was. Plus, I didn't really want to dwell on the point she was making out of her own insecurity, which was, essentially, that Aaron liked me for my brains. So what, he liked her for her body? Her sexual prowess? This was an unhealthy train of thought.

"He's a jerk, remember that," I responded. "He's not the guy we thought he was, so who cares what he likes?"

"Yeah, I guess," she said weakly.

I needed a conspirator with a little more backbone.

"It's just that he said he loved me," she continued plaintively.

I was instantly reminded of the Melanie Spearam debacle. She had screamed something similar just before slapping Trey Gandon upside the head. Many times, I had shaken my head in disbelief over that crazy scene. And yet maybe Melanie Spearam had gotten it right. If

I had hired "bait" a long time ago, I could have saved myself a lot of this pain.

"Yeah, well, he says he loves me, too," I said with a certain degree of selfish satisfaction.

After all, it had been a recent triumph.

"I'll kill him," Darlene responded.

There was the backbone I'd been looking for. She was murderous. Perfect. I got off the phone, preoccupied with my own thoughts of revenge. I knew in the back of my head that I'd feel other more despairing emotions once the anger wore off, so I held on to it tightly, like a rage security blanket.

"Are you sure nothing's wrong, honey?" my mom asked me in the car on the way to the airport the next day.

I'd tried my best to act normally during the last few vacation moments with my parents, but it had been a lost cause.

"Oh, I'm okay," I replied. "My boyfriend's been sleeping with someone else since before he even met me, but it's no big deal. I'm just flying back to ambush him tonight with the other woman. Other than that, everything's great."

In a rare moment, my mother didn't seem to know what to say. My dad stared straight ahead at the road.

"Yeah, her name's Darlene. It's funny, because he's called me her name before by accident and I assumed he was saying 'darling.' Isn't that hilariously tragic?"

I just kept talking. Finally my mom interjected.

"I have some Valium if you want it," she said simply.

I wasn't sure it would be wise to add Valium to the dangerous emotional cocktail I had going on inside me. I thanked her but turned her down.

As I hugged them good-bye at the curbside, my dad let his hand linger on my shoulder.

"Don't get too sad about this, Sammy," he said. "You deserve a lot better and you're gonna get it."

It was a very sweet sentiment from someone who'd been anti-Aaron from the beginning. I'd considered his disapproval irrational, but maybe it had been father's intuition all along.

"Thanks, Dad," I said gratefully.

My mom tried to press some pills into my hand.

"No, really, I'm okay," I said.

"It's just a little aspirin," she said with an exaggerated wink.

She seemed to think that I might just be trying to keep up appearances. I was past that. But instead of arguing with her, I pocketed the offering and kissed her good-bye.

I scrolled through the backlogged e-mails on my signal-restored BlackBerry while I waited at my gate. Thankfully, the weather was clear and all the planes were on time. Aaron and I had planned to reunite at 6:00 PM at my place to exchange presents and go out to dinner before heading over to the party, but I knew I wouldn't be able to act that convincingly for that long of a time. I clicked compose on my BlackBerry.

> To: Aaron Driver [aidriver@bramen.senate.gov]
> From: Samantha Joyce [srjoyce@gary.senate.gov]
> Subject: homecoming
> Text: hey there—sorry i've missed you the past two days, i came down with a post-christmas virus and basically slept for forty-eight hours. healthy now, and looking forward to seeing you. but i've had some flight changes and am not getting in till later—why don't I just meet you at the party? i can be there by nine. —s.

I read it over before sending it. It wasn't that warm, certainly not funny, but it got the job done. I didn't feel capable of exhibiting more enthusiasm. Hopefully, he wouldn't notice. He did.

> To: Samantha Joyce [srjoyce@gary.senate.gov]
> From: Aaron Driver
> [aidriver@bramen.senate.gov]
> Subject: re: homecoming
> Text: are you okay? you don't sound like yourself. i'm sorry you were sick. i can't wait to see you— i've been thinking about you non-stop. what time are you getting in? i want to see you sooner. love, a.

I decided to borrow one of his tactics and claim that I hadn't received this last message when I saw him later. I felt idiotic having believed his tales of malfunctioning BlackBerries and misplaced cell phone chargers. All of it had been part of his greater deceit. I had foolishly chalked it up to general irresponsibility, but the truth was far more sinister and it left me cold and disillusioned.

Returning to my apartment, I felt the sting of Shackleton's absence more sharply. The stale darkness of my briefly abandoned space struck me as achingly lonely. And after tonight, I feared I would be spending even more time by myself in it. I sensed myself succumbing to numbness.

Luckily, Liza was in town and came over immediately. Telling her the tale from the beginning made my wrath hot and fresh once more. By the time she had decided to accompany me to the party, I felt ready for a showdown.

Liza was of course shocked by Aaron's behavior, but not that shocked, which was subsequently shocking to me. She tried to explain that there was something just fundamentally untrustworthy about him. That he was charismatic and charming, but didn't give off a solid, honest vibe.

"Why didn't you tell me this a long time ago?" I asked, somewhat accusingly.

"I tried to!" she replied.

That was true. And I hadn't listened. I hadn't listened to Zelda, either. Or heeded RG's initial warning to be wary of any Bramen staffer. Had I simply taken that to heart, I could have avoided this entire mess. I wondered who else had harbored serious doubts about Aaron.

As Liza spent the next hour trying to make me look stunning for the ambush, Aaron called seven times. I was pleased that he was frantically trying to hunt me down and satisfied that I was thwarting his attempts with my screening tactics. I had never screened him before in the course of our entire relationship. I'd even answered the phone at wildly inappropriate times just so I wouldn't miss his call. Ignoring him for the first time felt strangely freeing.

After a pep talk from Liza, I rang Darlene. She was on the train, still an hour away. I gave her the directions to the party and asked her to call me when she was outside, so we could coordinate the attack. She agreed and assured me that she hadn't had any contact with Aaron. I was glad to hear a new hardened edge to her otherwise bubbly voice. After a shaky start, she was proving to be a worthy comrade.

I almost felt like changing into camouflage and paint, but Liza insisted that my slinky black party dress was a more stealth way to go. We poured ourselves some drinks, ate some pizza, and prepared to move out.

"I promise I'm still very interested in your life and want to talk all about it," I said before we left.

I felt guilty and self-conscious that we were focusing all of our attention on me. Liza waved this away.

"Plenty of time for that. This is about you and Operation Liberation," she said firmly.

I thought we could come up with a snazzier name than that, but decided not to be critical. I was a bit of a stickler when it came to "operation" monikers. It constantly amazed me how often the authorities in charge managed to inappropriately name military expeditions. One of my favorites from recent history was "Operation Just Cause." Whenever I'd heard it, I had acted out a little dialogue in my head.

"Why are we invading this country?" one voice would say.

"Just 'cause," the other would reply, with an implied shrug.

Clearly they could have done a better naming job. As could Liza have done, but at least she'd captured the militaristic nature of our mission.

"Ready?" she asked me sweetly.

"Ready," I replied.

It didn't take us long to get to the party, even with the increased New Year's Eve traffic. A group of Aaron's friends had rented out a rooftop bar in Adams Morgan, and as our cab rolled up, the street was hopping with energized revelers. After a steep five-flight climb we exited onto the deck, where we were greeted by a storybook party scene. Happy guests created a steady roar of small talk, ringed by latticed walls that were strung with lights and confetti. A forest of tall heat lamps kept everything warm and glowing.

I resisted the urge to scan the crowd and instead made my way over to the bar, with Liza right behind me. She'd done a better surveillance job, which didn't surprise me.

"He's here, he hasn't seen you yet. Don't turn around," she instructed.

This of course led me to start immediately turning around, but Liza had anticipated that and poked me hard in the back to stop me. It occurred to me that she might make a good animal trainer.

"That's better. Now, let's get a drink," she said.

Praise reinforced by treats. She was a natural.

We ordered expensive glasses of champagne and charged them to Aaron's tab.

"Okay, now he's spotted you," Liza said softly. "Here he comes."

I braced myself, but stayed staring straight ahead.

"Here you are!" Aaron said as he planted a kiss on the back of my neck. "I've been calling you."

"Oh yeah?" I said as I turned towards him and half-heartedly returned his hug.

"Hey, Liza, how ya doing?" he said over my shoulder. "I didn't mean to be rude, but I just had to get my hands on my girl."

"I bet," Liza said curtly.

My cell phone rang.

"So, it *is* working," Aaron said with a quizzical glance.

"Just turned it on," I replied as I looked down at the number. It was Darlene. "Excuse me, I've gotta take this. I'll be right back."

I ducked out the door to the stairway. I assumed Liza would keep him occupied for a second.

"Hello?" I said into the phone, wishing Darlene and I had agreed on code names earlier.

They weren't necessary; they just would have been more fun.

"Hi. I'm here," Darlene replied.

She sounded tired and resigned.

"Okay, when we hang up, wait five minutes and then come up the stairs. When you come out onto the deck, make a left. We'll be right in front of the bar. I'll make sure his back is to you."

I returned to Aaron and Liza, who excused herself immediately to go to the ladies' room. Aaron and I were left alone.

"Is everything all right?" he asked.

"Yeah, sorry about that," I smiled at him. "Just a call from a friend."

"From that guy Rick or whatever? Your old boyfriend who hits on you every time you go home?"

I almost burst out laughing at how jealous Aaron sounded.

"No, not from him," I said. "Let's go over here, I want to talk to you."

I led him to the bar and angled his back towards the door.

"Did you see that guy over Christmas?" Aaron asked.

"No, I didn't," I answered honestly. "Did *you* see anyone I should be jealous of?" I asked.

"Of course not, don't be silly," Aaron said very convincingly. "There's only you, babe, you know that. You're the one I'm worried about."

Uh-huh.

"So, did you miss me?" I asked.

I managed to make my voice a little flirtatious. I even rested my hand on his arm. As I smiled disingenuously up at him, I watched Darlene enter and approach us out of the corner of my eye. She was beautiful. The grainy newspaper clippings hadn't done her justice. I couldn't tell whether that made me happy to be in such good company or even more miserable about the situation. I focused solely on the task at hand. I'd sort out my emotions later.

"Are you kidding?" Aaron said as Darlene came to a stop behind him. "I was going crazy without you. It was terrible. We may even have to skip out of this party early so I can get you all to myself as soon as possible."

As he leaned down to kiss me, I turned my head away at the same time Darlene quietly cleared her throat.

"What's wrong, baby?" he asked, concerned.

I looked him in the eye.

"Well, out of respect for Darlene, I'm not sure we should see each other anymore," I said evenly.

"Huh? Who's Darlene? What the hell are you talking about?" he replied.

I could tell he was rapidly forming a strategy, but it was too late.

"I'm Darlene," Darlene said as she stepped up beside us. "Remember me?"

Aaron looked stunned.

"What are you doing here?" he asked lamely.

"Hi, Darlene, I'm Sammy," I said as I stuck out my hand. "It's good to finally meet you. I'm sorry it's under these circumstances."

Darlene shook my hand without taking her eyes off Aaron, who looked like he needed some more time to draft his words.

"I hate you," Darlene said softly.

Aaron looked stung.

"Don't say that, baby," he pleaded, before remembering that I was right there.

"Is that how you kept from slipping up most of the time? By calling us both 'baby'? That's a really clever strategy," I offered.

My sarcasm didn't convey the deep hurt I'd felt at hearing him address those words to somebody else. But I pushed that hurt aside. I didn't want to be weak now. Aaron turned towards me.

"No, Sammy, wait. Listen, I can explain," he tried. "Just give me a minute with Darlene and then I can explain everything to you," he said sincerely.

"No," Darlene and I said simultaneously.

"I'm afraid any explaining you attempt will have to be to both of us. But we're interested in what you have to say," I continued, as I moved to stand closer to Darlene. "So go for it."

She was considerably shorter and smaller than me, which made me feel a bit towering. Statuesque, perhaps? Or Lurch-like? I tried not to think about it. She smelled like jasmine, which I only knew because my mom had tried to grow a jasmine trellis three years in a row when I was younger. She'd spent hours out in the garden, which I'd resented because they were often hours I had wanted to spend with her doing something that more directly focused on me. Despite her hard work, the jasmine trellises had never fully panned out. But I remembered the smell, and appropriately associated it with something that competed for time and attention that I desired and deserved.

Aaron looked from one of us to the other.

"I think there's been a misunderstanding," he finally said.

Darlene just stared at him with disbelief in her wide-set green eyes.

"I think you're right," I responded. "I misunderstood you when you claimed you loved me and were dating me exclusively. I didn't realize that you really meant that you were a lying, cheating asshole. Maybe in the future you can avoid this sort of misunderstanding by just going and fucking yourself."

Aaron looked injured. He took my hand in a panicked movement.

"Sammy, you have to believe me. Darlene is an old girlfriend, she means nothing to me now," he began.

Dropping his voice, he continued, "She's a little psycho, okay? She's done this before."

Even though he had lowered his voice, Darlene had fully overheard Aaron malign her mental health.

"You're a liar," she said in a voice suddenly choked up. "I never want to see you again."

She ran towards the door. Aaron watched her go, with the pained expression of a man forced to make a difficult choice. He turned back towards me.

"She's not the smartest girl," he confided. "And she has this weird thing about me, but I swear there hasn't been anything between us since before I met you."

He sounded sincere, but it didn't occur to me to entertain the notion that he might be telling the truth. I also took no satisfaction in the fact that he had chosen me over Darlene in the heat of the confrontation, or that she'd been the recipient of the "psychologically unstable" charge I had predicted for myself. I could only focus on his appearance post-unmasking. He was no longer handsome and charming to me—I now saw an ugliness that had heretofore been disguised by my projections. It made me want to turn away.

"I don't believe you," I said calmly to him. "I'll never believe you again. Good-bye."

"Sammy, wait—" he protested as he put his hand on my arm.

I wished there'd been a mirror behind Aaron that would have allowed me to catch a glimpse of the look I lashed at him. I don't think that it was a look that I'd ever used before, because I had never felt this specialized strain of intense loathing in the past. But judging from his reaction, the look was lethal.

He dropped my arm as actual fear intruded into his always supremely confident eyes. And he appeared speechless, which was a similarly unfamiliar state for him.

"Don't touch me," I said with a sense of finality.

And then I left. I felt hot and light-headed as I made my way to the top of the stairs. Liza was waiting for me there. She took my arm as we descended.

"He looked devastated as you walked away," she reported. "How are you?"

It was a good question. I felt empowered for sure, and a bit liberated, but I sensed that these could be shell feelings for a deep hurt and confusion that was going sour somewhere inside.

"I'm okay," I answered optimistically.

Liza squeezed my hand as we continued out the

door to the street. Darlene was at the corner, trying to hail a cab. Her face was shiny with streaked tears. I forgot myself for a moment and just felt sorry for her. Where was she going now? Was she heading back up to New York? Didn't she need someone to talk to immediately?

"Darlene," I got her attention. "This is my friend Liza. Why don't you come with us for a little while?"

I felt this was an unprecedented and extraordinarily gracious offer. Darlene looked uncertain, then thankful, in a traumatized way. She just nodded.

"Are you hungry?" I asked.

She nodded again.

The three of us waded through the rowdy crowd on the street to a nearby diner. Over coffee and pie, we autopsied our relationships with Aaron. Though Darlene had similarly strong feelings for him, it became clear during the course of our conversation that that was pretty much the only thing she and I had in common. It's hard to have a girl power night if you can't relate to the girl. It wasn't that she was a bad person, it was just that she was so unlike me in every way. And this realization led quickly and quietly to a subtle dislike of her as an individual, which was probably inevitable, given the circumstances of our interaction. I didn't blame her for everything the way I blamed Aaron; but I didn't feel a tremendous amount of warmth for her, either. And as I listened to her bemoan the fact that now she wouldn't have a ring on her finger by her twenty-second birthday as she'd planned in her goals diary, I found myself resisting the urge to stomp Liza's foot under the table. I knew this wasn't necessary—I felt certain Liza was in just as much pain as I was.

"I really thought he was the one," Darlene concluded after two messy hours.

I knew the feeling.

"And I was so looking forward to quitting my job and just making him food and rubbing his feet and loving him, you know?" she continued.

Okay, I didn't know that feeling. Yep, we were definitely different. It's not that I couldn't relate to someone five years younger than me—I was ready to adopt Kara into my family immediately. It was just that Darlene and I didn't click. How could Aaron have been with both of us when we were so unlike each other? Maybe that had been the point. I checked my watch.

"Well, the good news is, it's literally both a new day and a new year."

Soon after, we said our overdue good-byes and Darlene made her way to the train station and back up to a new life devoid of Aaron. Back at my place, I made my own adjustments. I threw away some photographs and the Pez dispenser and a green glowing ring he'd won for me at an arcade, and moved my bed across the room to a spot underneath the window, straining my back in the process. I took some Motrin and hoped that the new perspective would help shake loose the memories of countless nights spent with Aaron beside me.

From this fresh perch, I surveyed the year ahead. So things were going to be different. No more boyfriend, but at least I still had a job to throw myself into with redirected energy. I also had countless maladies to prepare for and defend against, along with scores of self-improvement projects. I typically reserved any resolutions for the Chinese New Year, but I took a moment to remind myself of my blessings. There were men in my life who weren't stupid, cheating rats. RG was a solid family man, as was my father. Anecdotal evidence pointed to at least a few others.

Aaron had seduced, betrayed, and deceived me. I'd been naïve when I met him; I was numb now. I hoped to divine a lesson from this horrendous experience at some point in the future. But at the moment, I was tired. I had compromised myself into exhaustion. And I felt thoroughly, completely drained.

I sighed deeply and glanced at the street below me. There wasn't any snow on the ground, but the frosty air glowed in a whitish way. I glommed my mouth up against the windowpane and made a face at the night. In the resulting hot breath oval, I used my ring finger to draw a smiley face. My sketch looked sheepish, as if it was aware of its inadequacy. I smiled ruefully at it. So I wasn't somebody's darling after all. That was surmountable. The important thing was that I was nobody's Darlene. I laid my head on my pillow and willed myself to sleep, hoping to feel better in the morning.

## *To Bear, Too Bare*

THE NEXT WEEK brought a return to work as the Senate came back from winter recess to convene a new year. I sat numbly at my desk, trying to lose myself in my many tasks while pretending I was completely fine. And though I was as capable as I'd ever been of keeping up with the hectic work pace, I now felt like I was encased in a dark gray haze. All my fury had faded after my rage-fueled New Year's confrontation, replaced by a listless melancholy. It didn't help that it was winter, which meant short, frigid, overcast days for the most part. But even when I was inside warm and cheerful places, the colors seemed dimmer to me than I knew in the back of my head that they should.

It also didn't help that all of this felt very melodramatic, even though the pain was real. I was dealing with a breakup, a betrayal, but didn't those happen every day? And often to people who had weathered relationships longer than a few months? I couldn't shake the sense that I was being a bit silly, which is why I kept everything to myself and acted as though all was fine. I reasoned that as long as I went through the motions of my routine, no one could have proof that I was as weak and sad as I felt.

I was a little surprised that the rhythms of life were continuing around me precisely as they always had, utterly unfazed by my misery. Everything just kept humming along in the political world and beyond. The first official voting of the presidential race took place in just three weeks, in Iowa and then New Hampshire, and I could sense the mounting anticipation on the Hill. Congressman Candle had dropped out over the holidays due to insufficient funds and a new *Time*/CNN poll showed Bramen's leads in both states had decreased slightly as Rexford and Wye had picked up steam. These developments generated a considerable amount of chatter, with everyone in town offering their opinion on how things would play out. I distracted myself from my hollowness by tuning in and trying to care.

On the evening of a candidates' debate, I was unexpectedly summoned to RG's office, where I found him watching the screen intently.

"For crying out loud, John, give a straight answer on that," he said in frustration as Senator Bramen replied to a moderator-asked question.

I noticed the line between RG's right eye and ear was actually throbbing.

"Doesn't he sound like he overthinks everything?"

RG turned to me. "But then he gets rattled so easily. He's spent his whole life preparing for this race, you'd think he'd be a little bolder."

RG shook his head in exasperation. I watched as Bramen delivered a scripted zinger that I knew had been written by Aaron and felt a surge of anger. I was speaking before I even realized it.

"It's a crime that Bramen's still the front-runner," I spat. "I can't stand him or the people who work for him. They're all a bunch of lying bastards."

RG looked surprised by my outburst, which made two of us.

"Well, I'm not sure I'd go *that* far," he replied with a raised eyebrow, "but they could certainly be running a better campaign."

I nodded with my mouth shut to thwart further eruptions. Though I regretted my vitriol, it was oddly comforting to feel something other than dull dejection. And luckily RG didn't seem all that fazed.

"It's a fundamentally pompous campaign," he continued in a more peeved tone. "John acts like he deserves to just be handed the nomination. It's insulting. Meanwhile, Max Wye sounds like he'd cut off his own leg if it would help the American people in some way."

I agreed. And I desperately wanted Wye or Rexford or Conrad to orchestrate a surge and steal the nomination. Anyone besides Bramen.

"Do you like Wye?" I asked. "Do you want him to win?"

RG didn't take his eyes from the screen.

"Liking someone doesn't qualify him or her to be a good president," he answered.

Yeah, okay, that was a valid point. You could like a moron, but that didn't make him competent.

"But I think Wye would do a better job," RG continued. "Not because I like him more than Bramen, but because he doesn't seem to be in it entirely for his own aggrandizement. He honestly seems to care. I could be wrong about that—I certainly haven't spent enough time with him to know, but I have spent enough time with Bramen to know that he's not to be trusted. He makes cowardly decisions that are often based primarily on making himself look good. I don't think that's a good way to run this country," RG concluded. "As for the others, Rexford's too inexperienced and Conrad's just not catching on. So I suppose Wye is the best of the field."

I wondered whether RG had regrets about not throwing his hat into the ring this time around. He certainly would have had a good shot at the nomination. I believed this even more firmly after having watched the current candidates strive and stumble in the past few months. Did RG doubt his decision? Did he wish he'd taken Bramen on? Did I have the courage to ask him?

I cleared my throat. Nope, I wasn't brave enough. I wanted to assume he didn't have regrets, just because I liked believing in the relative infallibility of his instincts.

RG turned away from the TV and back to some papers on his desk. Were we done watching the debate?

It seemed that I'd been summoned to his office solely for that purpose, which was flattering. And while talking with RG, my gray haze had felt thinner. I didn't want to return to my desk where it bunched in a thick cloud. I racked my brain for something interesting to say to prolong my stay.

"I like the way Wye leans forward when he's making a point," I blurted. "He looks like he might spill right out of the television, which makes him seem more accessible. And a little kooky, which I also like. Good kooky, not bad kooky," I clarified.

RG blinked impassively at me before resuming reading whatever was on his desk. Yep, I'd murdered the moment. Now I had to go serve my time back in my cubicle where I had much more trouble feeling important or consulted. I could feel myself slipping quickly back into the glum funk I'd vainly attempted to escape.

"Oh, Samantha," RG stopped me as I trudged out the door. "I almost forgot why I asked you in here."

Of course he hadn't invited me just to hang out. I was an idiot.

"I want to host some dinner seminars on the efforts to find cures for Alzheimer's and Parkinson's and others within that family of disease," RG said as he referred to the papers on his desk. "I was reviewing the current funding, and it strikes me as wildly inadequate. I'd like substantive discussions, nothing just for show," he said.

"Yes, sir," I replied.

"Could you get me an outline for the series first thing

in the morning?" he asked, turning back to the TV to illustrate that this wasn't really a question.

I nodded to his profile and headed for the coffee machine. It was already 9:00 PM. I was going to need the caffeine.

Mona passed by on her way out for the night.

"Late night?" she asked, eyeing the two cups I'd just poured for myself.

I nodded. Though Mona and I had enjoyed a newfound closeness after our New York trip, I had withdrawn from her along with everyone else in the past week.

"Listen, I heard about you and Aaron," she continued. "And I know you probably don't want to talk about it, but I just thought you should know that it's definitely for the best. He's no good."

Again, this seemed to suggest that she had some historical knowledge of Aaron. She was much too businesslike to make pronouncements on someone else's character based on anything less substantial than hard evidence.

"Thanks, but just out of curiosity, why do you say he's no good?" I inquired. "I mean, do you have any other reason to believe that?"

Mona looked at the ground. Oh, she definitely had something.

"Well, uh, yeah, I guess I do."

She sounded distinctly ashamed. My curiosity was piqued.

"Yes?" I encouraged.

Mona hesitated for a moment longer before unleashing a rush of words.

"I knew about Aaron's cheating. He was with my college roommate's younger sister when he met Darlene, and he dated both of them at the same time and who knows who else before my friend's sister figured it out. And then, Mark saw Aaron with Darlene in New York a few months back, when you were supposed to be dating him pretty seriously. They were making out at a bar. I think Mark tried to tell you, but you thought he was hitting on you instead," she finished, never taking her eyes from the floor.

What?! Oh, good God. That was what Mark had been getting at when he was acting all weird around me and asking if Aaron and I were exclusive? Couldn't he have been a little more straightforward? Although I guessed I had embarrassed him fairly quickly by pre-emptively announcing that he didn't have a chance with me. Why didn't I shut up sometimes and let people get to their point?

"Oh," was all I managed to say at first.

"I'm really sorry," Mona continued. "I should have said something."

"Yeah, why didn't you?" I asked.

She'd had plenty of opportunities. I would have told her had the situation been reversed. It was unkind of her to have kept it from me.

"I didn't want Mark going after you again," she said

softly. "I was worried his crush would get retriggered if you were available. I mean, even if it was unrequited, you know, I thought maybe he'd just start thinking about you again and not about me anymore."

Oh dear. When Mona and I had talked in New York, she'd seemed perfectly secure in her relationship. But now I realized she'd been able to feel safe as long as I'd been wrapped up in another man.

"Oh, Mona," I said with a mixture of disbelief and sympathy. "It's so clear that Mark's only into you," I insisted.

I had seen the way that Mark looked at Mona, and I knew that his ditching her for me was an impossibility. He was in love with her. Perhaps I'd initially been an obstacle to this discovery of his, but that was ancient history.

"Well, anyway, it was terrible of me not to tell you," Mona said regretfully. "I'm sorry. And I'm really glad you're not with Aaron."

I was, too. And I felt like even more of a fool for having been with him in the first place.

The next morning, I turned in the dinner series outline to RG and immersed myself in work to avoid thinking about anything else. I spent the day tracking down a group of British scientists who'd recently discovered a protein that could be used to protect against neurological diseases. Though the protein didn't amount to a cure for Alzheimer's, Parkinson's, Huntington's, and others, it did offer a way to slow their destructive progress. By the end of the week, I'd located the scientists and persuaded them to present their findings at the first dinner of the series. And somewhere in the midst of all the international calls, I'd fallen a little in love with their accents. Long immune to my mother's Anglophilia, I'd suddenly come down with a mild case.

The scientists were coming and RG was pleased with the series proposal, so I finished off the week feeling proud of what I'd accomplished, which was the first positive feeling I'd had in weeks. I felt a glimmer of hope. Could this mean I might finally be moving on and ready to cheer up? By the following morning, I'd decided to make a trip to Mr. Lee's to further encourage the healing. It occurred to me to try out another pet store, but I needed some sort of continuity in my life given all the recent turmoil. Even if it was the certainty of feeling like I was getting ripped off.

"We have missed you!" Mr. Lee exclaimed. "What do you need? A Japanese fighting fish? There are some truly beautiful ones just in!"

Yep. I'd bet there were.

"I just want to look around for a bit," I answered noncommittally.

"Of course. Take your time, take your time," he replied.

He busied himself behind the counter, but I felt him watching every move I made. I spent some time looking at the snakes and wondering why people ever had them as pets. I mean, fish weren't cuddly, but snakes were just ridiculous. I couldn't understand the justification for buying them, unless the people that owned them simply enjoyed watching them devour frozen mice and rats and frogs for the fun of it. After a while, wouldn't that stop being exciting? Then one was just left with an enormous, bored python. That didn't seem like a good situation.

I already had python issues, having read about one in Florida that had escaped from its cage and entered the city's sewer system. It had been discovered coming out of the toilet by some poor unsuspecting woman trying to brush her teeth. I shuddered just recalling the account. What was worse, this hadn't been the first article I'd read about such an occurrence. It was around the ninth or tenth, which suggested that pythons slithering out of plumbing was a relatively common event. Accordingly, I couldn't sit on a toilet seat without looking into the bowl first. And even when everything seemed in order, I couldn't shake the feeling that I was incredibly vulnerable sitting in that particular spot. Considering how often I needed to use the toilet (not any more than the average person, but the point was it was a regular occurrence), I spent too much of my time stressing about pythons.

I walked over and examined the Japanese fighting fish.

"I think I'll take that one." I pointed decisively to a medium-sized fish with an orange fleck, with whom I'd felt an immediate bond upon eye contact. "Are they still three dollars apiece?"

Mr. Lee held up his index finger and thumb in a "little bit more" gesture.

I shrugged. The actual price of the fish, though constantly escalating in Mr. Lee's dominion, wasn't where the expenses racked up. It was the bowl and the pebbles and the food and the exotic seaweed and the little underwater castles that he convinced you that you needed. And though I already had all of those things, I found myself wondering if they were contaminated after another fish had died, and so tended to buy new, slightly varied sets. Mr. Lee held out my new charge to me in a plastic bag. Was all this tax deductible? I had a new dependent, after all.

I returned to my apartment an hour later, laden with a complete set of new products for my latest pet. Liza called as I was carefully monitoring the water temperature and preparing the delicate transfer of my new guy into his palatial estate.

"I went with the orange pebbles this time to match his little fleck," I informed her. "Plus, there's a treasure chest for him to hide in. No castle this time. I think the castle was a bit overwhelming."

"That's great," Liza replied in a tone that indicated she hadn't called to hear about my fishbowl decorating ideas.

She'd been very attentive since the Aaron showdown, but I could tell she was newly preoccupied with something. Which was fine with me, because getting back to our normal conversations made me feel better than anything else.

"What's up with you?" I asked obligingly, though I really did want her input on good names for my new tenant.

I was debating between Dr. Cincinnati, Clockwork, and other names I hadn't yet thought of. It was all right. There was still plenty of time before the christening, which generally happened in a ceremony a week after the purchasing of the fish. That week lag was important for the naming process, because this time allowed for their personalities to come out, or in the case of Shackleton, for the power to go out, transforming his bowl into a frozen wasteland.

"Well, funny you should ask," Liza replied.

She was now using a voice that suggested I sit down and brace myself for what she was about to reveal. I assumed it had to do with the football player she'd recently been dating. His name was Scooter and he was a third-string running back for the Redskins. He was chiseled and sure of himself and talked a lot about the theme restaurant he was launching with some teammates. He was apparently trying to get the Redskinettes, or Redskinistas, or whatever the cheerleaders were called, to sign on as waitresses. He didn't strike me as Liza's soul mate, but I made a decision not to be critical since I clearly needed all my energy to make sure I didn't choose a lying, cheating disaster of a boyfriend for myself. Let those who hadn't discovered their intended's betrayal via aggressive voicemail code breaking cast the first stone. I was shutting up.

"What's going on?" I asked, steeling myself for shock.

"Well, you know I'm a fan of your theory about sleeping with someone as a screening process to make sure they don't have any perversions that could really be a bummer later on," she began. "Because it makes sense—you want to know what you're up against before you get too emotionally invested. But have you ever had it work? I mean, where it turns out they do? How do you gauge how serious it is and whether you should bail or not?"

That particular theory had been developed after my one and only time of sleeping with someone on the first date. That one person had been Aaron, so the theory had clearly been fatally flawed from the get-go, though I hadn't known it at the time. I knew that Liza often slept with people way before I ever would, and I didn't want to point this out or seem judgmental, so I didn't feel that I could really answer her questions.

"What exactly happened?" I asked instead.

"He keeps a playbook," Liza explained in a tone of resignation. "He likes to sketch out the sex and go over it before we have it. Then during it, he sometimes calls penalties."

"Oh, Liza."

"I *know*," she answered.

"Do you at least get to wear pads?" I asked.

"This isn't funny," she scolded.

I thought it sort of was.

"What sorts of penalties does he call? Pass interference?"

Liza ignored this.

"Recently, he's started mentioning his video camera," she said morosely. "I'm worried he wants to tape us and review the plays later."

"You've gotta break up with him." I stated the obvious.

"I know," she replied. "I just needed to talk about it first."

She sounded resolved as we got off the phone, and I had to admit I was pleased that she was going to be around more. Although I guessed this probably meant I wasn't going to meet the divorced linebacker with whom she'd been planning to set me up. I imagined I'd survive.

I spent the rest of the day making the apartment as cheerful as possible and willing the fish to acclimate. I'd just put in *The Little Mermaid* soundtrack when Zelda called.

"Just calling to check in. I've been a little worried about you down here," she said.

I hadn't returned any of her messages since New Year's, which was very unlike me.

"I'm sorry I've been so out of touch. It turns out you were right about Aaron. I should've kept my eyes open. I shouldn't have trusted him. I should've listened to you."

There was a pause on Zelda's end of the line.

"If you'd done that, you wouldn't have learned for yourself," she said kindly. "But I'm sorry he hurt you. I wish I could hurt him back."

Could she? Was there some sort of renegade telemarketer revenge squad? I offered her Aaron's numbers just in case. She copied them down to humor me, told me to feel better, and promised to check in with me soon.

In the following weeks, as the Chinese New Year approached and my mood continued to improve, I contemplated potential resolutions. I generally enjoyed making them on this alternative schedule, because it allowed me extra time for research. As I watched the resolve of those who had adhered to the more conventional New Year's timetable crumble and deteriorate with every passing week, I gained a better understanding of the kind of resolutions one could realistically build to last. My studies indicated it was best to avoid fitness-regimen or teach-yourself-a-new-language–based ones, as these were generally the first to collapse.

Given my dismal feelings about romance, I was leaning towards making all my resolutions work-related. My only concern was the impact on Dr. Cincinnati, since by shunning amorous pursuits, I was willingly depriving him of a strong male role model. I resolved to mitigate this situation by lapsing into a deep voice every once in a while as I made the rounds of my apartment.

My decision to devote myself even more intensely to my job happened to coincide perfectly with RG's plans for a new bill. This new bill was intended to capitalize on the attention garnered by the dinner series, which thanks to the British researchers and their fantastic accents, had started with a resounding success. The bill would increase funding to the National Institutes of Health specifically for neurological disease research because RG believed that well-timed legislative and financial support, combined with the recent scientific breakthroughs, could bring about cures for Parkinson's, Alzheimer's, and Huntington's faster than many thought possible. I agreed with him, and I set about drafting the bill with a refreshingly renewed sense of energy and purpose.

And towards the end of January, Liza finally convinced me to foray back into the social scene. After much cajoling, she'd finally persuaded me to accompany her to Scooter's restaurant opening. She'd described it as "the hottest party of the year," assuring me that half the city was invited, and claiming it was the perfect setting for my comeback. I'd tried to back out at the last minute claiming an allergy attack, but she'd brought me Benadryl and shoved me into a cab.

As we waited to check our coats in the crowded foyer, I looked around gingerly. There really were a lot of people here.

"It's nice that Scooter still invited you after you guys broke up," I remarked.

"Uh-huh," Liza said brightly.

Wait a minute, I knew that tone.

"You did break up, didn't you?" I asked suspiciously.

Liza wouldn't look at me. Oh Lord.

"I tried to," she replied. "But he started crying and begging me to give him another chance and then he swore he'd change, and . . . well . . . maybe he will. I mean, it's really just the sex stuff I have a problem with," she justified. "Anyway, I should probably run say hi to him, but then I'm devoting my full attention to you. We're gonna have fun tonight. I want to see you happy again."

I smiled and shook my head as she flitted off.

"Be right back!" she assured me over her shoulder.

As I checked our coats, Charlie Lawton walked in. I had never really properly thanked him for saving me from the mutinous line at the airport newsstand by providing that crucial seventy-five cents. Also, for the first time, he really struck me as sort of cute. In our previous interactions, I'd either been too embarrassed or flustered or angry to really focus on this fact. And though I'd always been more of an Aquaman than a Superman kind of girl, which I supposed translated to Arthur Curry over Clark Kent, I could certainly appreciate the other aesthetic. I wasn't a superhero snob or anything.

"Charlie?" I inquired.

He looked up and smiled at me.

"Hi," he said.

Yes, he was definitely cute. I could see that now. Oh no, was that my neck rash starting? I willed the Benadryl to suppress any evidence of a sexual thrill. And actually, now that Charlie and I had made eye contact, all I could think about was the horrible, unfair article that he'd written about me. I shouldn't have called out to him. I couldn't be nice to him. I felt my smile disappear.

"Yeah, uh, thanks for helping me out at the airport," I said quickly. "Okay, gotta go."

"Wait a second," he said in a steady voice that stopped my turn.

I met his gaze again, despite myself.

"I need to explain something to you, though I realize you might not believe me," he continued. "The article about you that had my name on it was not the article that I wrote. My editors added that part about abusing office finances. They wanted something with a mean edge. I'm sorry I couldn't prevent it. I just wanted you to know."

I watched his mouth as he talked, because his lips had a unique curve to them. I took in every word that came out and I instantly believed him. There was something about his manner that seemed calmly honest—like he hoped people could see that he was telling the truth but he wasn't going to kick and scream to make them.

"Okay," I replied.

"I tried to tell you before, but you wouldn't have anything to do with me. And then at the airport, I had to race to catch my plane. Anyway, do we understand each other now?" he asked as he stuck out his hand.

"Yes," I answered sheepishly as I put my hand in his,

remembering too late that it was still sticky from a double-sided tape incident that afternoon.

He didn't visibly react to the stickiness. And his skin felt very warm. I didn't want him to release mine, but it became obvious that I was holding on too long. Feeling flustered, I let go and stared down at the ground. Why hadn't I returned his calls? Why hadn't I let him talk that night in Georgetown, instead of just screaming at him? Or at the Capitol Lounge after the filibuster ended? All this could have been cleared up long ago. I wondered if it would have changed anything.

"Sorry I'm late," a voice that was not Charlie's said.

I looked up at a woman I'd never seen before. Which meant that she definitely wasn't late to meet me. I watched Charlie slide his eyes away from my face towards her.

"Hi," he said, as she stood on her tiptoes to kiss him on the lips.

She looked at me inquisitively.

"Samantha, this is Veronica Dodd. Veronica, Samantha Joyce."

Charlie made the introductions with an impassive look. I smiled hello in a strained way, which I knew made me look like portions of my face had been paralyzed (and not in any sort of smoothing, cosmetic fashion), and said something about needing to check my BlackBerry.

I had just taken it out and was pretending to read an

important message while silently hoping that Charlie and Veronica would move along when Liza reappeared.

"What are you doing? No BlackBerrying allowed tonight," she scolded.

"Yeah, that's what gets you into trouble, isn't it?" Veronica remarked with a sly smile.

Charlie looked at her sharply, but she continued gazing at me. Was she trying to be funny? That was clearly a reference to the whole e-mail debacle. Had she been dating Charlie during that time? Did it matter? I didn't like her.

"What do you mean?" Liza asked in a challenging voice.

I knew I could count on Liza to have my back.

"Oh, I'm sorry. I didn't mean to joke about a sensitive topic," Veronica said unconvincingly. "I work with Charlie at the *Post*. I'm Veronica," she said as she stuck out her hand towards Liza.

"Liza," Liza replied. "And you're Charlie Lawton?" she asked.

Charlie nodded as he shook her hand, looking a bit embarrassed. It was almost as though he knew Liza had hung a voodoo doll of him from her ceiling fan. I planned to fill her in on Charlie's explanation about his editors very soon.

"So, are you working on any more ridiculously unfair articles?" Liza asked.

Not soon enough.

"Hey, no, it turns out that was sort of a misunderstanding," I interrupted, tugging on Liza's sleeve. "Charlie's editors added that. He just told me."

Liza gave Charlie a critical look.

"And you couldn't stop them, huh?" she asked skeptically.

"I tried," Charlie said sincerely.

Liza looked at him a moment longer before nodding.

"And what do you do?" Veronica asked Liza. "Besides jump to assumptions and insult people?"

"Would anyone like a drink?" I asked loudly.

"Bubbly water," Veronica ordered, not taking her eyes off Liza.

Huh. I hadn't expected to actually be taken up on the offer by her. But okay.

"I'll get that," Charlie said quickly.

I glanced inquisitively at Liza. Was it safe to leave her alone with Veronica? Probably not for Veronica.

"Would you like the regular?" I asked her.

Liza nodded. Charlie and I made our way to the bar.

"Are we wimps for fleeing the fight?" I asked him.

"Yep," he smiled.

Oh well, they could take care of themselves. And I was glad to have a little more time talking to Charlie now that he wasn't my nemesis.

"So, what's the regular?" he asked.

"Vanilla vodka and tonic with a splash of orange juice," I answered.

"Really? I've never heard of that," he replied.

"I know. I invented it. It's actually supposed to be vanilla vodka and a secret ingredient, but places like this never have the secret ingredient, so I substitute tonic instead," I elaborated. "It's not as good, but it does the trick."

"What's the secret ingredient?" he asked in an interested voice.

"I'd tell you, but I'd have to get you drunk first," I answered.

Charlie smiled.

"So, you're an inventor," he remarked.

I nodded, feeling proud. I was glad to have my accomplishment be appropriately recognized. Ever since reading a biography of Benjamin Franklin in fourth grade, I'd periodically attempted to invent things, with minimal success. Besides the tasty drink, my only other lasting achievement had been a hand-powered fan that simultaneously squirted water to cool one off. I'd been stunned to find this exact contraption sold at baseball games in the last few years. On the one hand, I was glad that this brilliant invention was being enjoyed by the masses. On the other, I felt robbed of my millions. I knew I should have taken out a patent.

We'd arrived at the bar. I gave the bartender my instructions and then Charlie ordered the bubbly water.

"And another one of her drink," he added.

I beamed. My creation was taking off.

"You know, speaking of inventions, today was the seventy-first anniversary of the invention of the Philly cheesesteak," I offered.

I normally kept these facts to myself, but I all of a sudden felt like sharing. Charlie looked intrigued.

"Well, that calls for a celebration then," he replied.

I smiled. Not many people understood that.

"Took care of that at lunch," I answered, patting my tummy. "Technically, cheese wasn't added until the 1940s. I cheated a little bit and had cheese on mine," I confessed.

It felt good to come clean.

"I won't tell anyone," Charlie assured me in a lowered voice.

"I'd appreciate that," I smiled at him.

We collected our drinks and left a tip. Charlie turned to me before we left the safe orbit of the bar.

"I'm sorry if Veronica offended you earlier. She can be a bit brusque, but that's just the reporter in her. She's really extremely smart," he said.

In my analysis, he'd started off that comment well, but really tanked at the end. It was nice to have him acknowledge that his girlfriend had been somewhat rude, but he didn't have to go and ruin the moment by praising her. I smiled tightly.

"No problem," I said.

"Not that that's any excuse," he concluded.

I felt myself soften. As we made our way slowly

back to Liza and Veronica, Charlie gave me a sidelong glance.

"Listen, I was wondering if sometime you might want to—what's wrong?"

My face had undoubtedly conveyed the horror I felt seize my body. I couldn't answer him. I could only stare towards the door, to where Aaron and Darlene had just appeared. Seeing Aaron was bad enough, and something I'd been seriously dreading. But seeing him with Darlene? That wasn't supposed to be happening. We'd dumped him together. Hadn't we? I watched as Aaron helped Darlene out of her stylish little coat. He leaned down to kiss her tenderly on the neck. She smiled at him and held her hand against his cheek. They hadn't seen me yet—they were too busy gazing lovingly into each other's eyes. I felt stunned and sickened and utterly immobile. Oh God, what if they looked up and I was just gaping at them? Why couldn't I move? My stomach turned over.

I felt Charlie's hand on my elbow.

"Right this way," he said softly as he guided me in the other direction, back towards our corner and out of sight. "Are you all right?" he asked gently.

Aaron and Darlene had gotten back together? No, no, no, no, I felt myself shaking my head.

"Samantha?"

I stopped shaking my head and let Charlie's eyes come into focus. He looked concerned.

"Oh yeah, I'm fine. I'm great," I said too loudly as I sucked down my drink, placed it on the table, and started in on Liza's.

I needed to get a hold of myself. And I needed to get out of there.

"Are you sure you're okay?"

Even when Charlie was being kind, as he certainly was now, he managed to have a sort of detached, observant way about him. I found myself both implicitly trusting him and fearing his judgment. He definitely seemed to be studying me.

"I'm sorry, I can't imagine what you think of me," I said, letting waves of self-consciousness wash over me.

I felt like bursting into tears. Charlie put his hand on my shoulder.

"I just think you're a little confused," he replied.

I felt taken aback. I hadn't expected him to answer. It had been rhetorical insecurity, better left floating out there. But now I had confirmation of my fears that he was judging me, on top of the shock of seeing Aaron with Darlene. Who did Charlie think he was? I didn't need to be talked down to.

"Oh, really," I said archly.

I was about to say more about how I thought he was a little condescending, and maybe a little confused himself to be dating a shrew like Veronica, but Liza suddenly appeared.

"Hey, wow, did you see the time?" she said in a very officious voice. "We've really got to go. 'Bye, guys." She turned to wave at Veronica and nodded to Charlie as she led me away.

I didn't even bother waving. Liza steered me towards the side of the restaurant, looking straight ahead. I knew what she was trying to do.

"I've already seen them," I informed her.

"Oh crap," she replied. "I was hoping to get you out of here quickly and bizarrely under false pretenses, and then break the news gently." She took a breath. "Well, do you want to face them? I've certainly got some things I'd like to say," she added threateningly.

I had to admit I didn't really feel up to it. She must have been able to see it in my face.

"Side door," she said definitively.

So much for my comeback.

February dawned both gray and sunny, which made me feel uneasy. I couldn't shake the feeling that I was entering a month I couldn't trust. And I felt particularly vulnerable after having been burned so badly by January, when I'd fought my way out of my dark haze, dusted myself off, and dared to think the worst was over, only to have been viciously snapped back into the depths. Would February be as cruel?

My only solace was that it had slightly fewer days to torture me. Though I distracted myself with work, the latest political news only thrust me further into my bad mood. Bramen had won the Iowa caucuses as expected and hadn't used the occasion to embrace a newfound humility.

"This is a victory for all of America," he'd shouted from a stage in Des Moines. "America's champion is on a roll!"

I was pretty sure "America's champion" wasn't generally a self-bestowed title. Had Aaron been responsible for that phrase? It was shameless, so there was a good chance he had. And had he tried it out on Darlene the way he'd tested lines on me? Ugh.

The following week, Wye had stunned everyone by winning the New Hampshire primary, but Bramen had quickly brushed off the loss by explaining that his campaign wasn't meant to appeal to a "small, homogenous group of folks who garnered too much influence over the system due to outdated rules." I was still somewhat of a novice in following presidential campaigns, but even I was pretty sure that badmouthing an entire state was not a smart idea.

But, annoyingly, it didn't seem to hurt him. The third of the month brought a spate of primaries, of which Bramen won the majority. There were at least ten more primaries in February and then thirteen in a single day on March second. Most of the people in the know asserted that the nominee would emerge on that day less than a month away, and most of them agreed that the nominee would be Bramen. I considered this extremely depressing news. Short of a miracle, it seemed as though Bramen was soon to be anointed.

On the other side, Brancy had swept the primary contests thus far, but neither Frand nor Pile seemed ready to concede defeat. Both hinged their comebacks on their performances in the South, where Pile was allegedly engaged in a full-fledged underground smear campaign against Brancy. If successful, Pile's dirty tactics could provide him with an upset.

As I skimmed through the news sites on a rainy morning, I tried not to focus on the dismal prospect of living in a country led by President Bramen, or, God forbid, another Pile. I felt physically nauseous at the thought.

I reached for the Tums and watched Mona pass by my desk, reading a folder. She seemed more dressed up than normal. I studied her closely.

"Mona," I said curiously, "what's that on your finger?"

"Oh, this." She blushed, reluctantly indicating a brand-new engagement ring. "Yeah, Mark proposed," she said sheepishly.

They'd only been dating two months! Were engagements allowed at that point?

"Congratulations," I managed to say through my surprise.

At least Mona could now be positive that Mark didn't harbor any residual crush on me. He'd proposed to her while I'd been lonely and available just down the hall. I doubted she'd need further proof of his devotion.

"Yeah, we moved kind of fast," she laughed. "Though

when you say 'I love you' on the first date, it sort of speeds everything up."

There were couples that actually did such things without disastrous repercussions? This was fascinating. I felt like Jane Goodall, studying a species so similar to myself and at the same time so undeniably foreign.

"Wow," was all I could say.

I'd heard Jane Goodall before on television and I knew that she was infinitely more eloquent.

"Have you all set a date yet?" I asked.

According to their timeline, it should be in the next six weeks or so.

"We were thinking about doing it in August during the recess," she replied. "That way, we won't have to miss too much work or anything."

In my opinion, a wedding and honeymoon were perfect excuses to miss work. Whenever I'd fantasized about my betrothal to Steve Martin, I'd always spent a bit of time thinking about where we'd go right afterwards and how much work I could get away with skipping. Work was certainly important to me, but building a solid foundation for the rest of Steve's and my life together seemed worthy of a substantial time investment. After all, our love was what would carry us through the tough times.

"And the wedding will probably be pretty small," Mona added.

Was that some sort of heads-up that I shouldn't expect an invitation?

"Small is nice," I said carefully.

I couldn't believe I wasn't going to be invited to their wedding. But fine, who needed to go to Chicago in August anyway? I could get heatstroke somewhere else just as easily. I smiled deceptively at Mona and made a show of getting back to my work.

When I wasn't working, I stayed home. The restaurant opening had been horrible enough to scare me away from any sort of social scene for a while. Liza reluctantly accepted my imposed isolation. She was spending a lot of her time with Scooter, who had apparently made tremendous strides with the help of therapy. He was calling far fewer penalties during sex. And almost all of them were minor.

Left to our own devices, Dr. Cincinnati and I started listening to Blind Blake almost every night before falling asleep. I found myself wishing I owned some kind of instrument. I was living the blues; why not try and play them? If embracing my pain could reveal some previously unknown and extremely hip talent, then maybe the suffering was worth it. Maybe.

On an impulse, I picked up a shiny but used harmonica at a pawnshop. After disinfecting it for three days to be sure it was as free of germs as chemically possible, I downloaded some "how to" instructions from the Internet, poured myself a glass of wine, and set about my work. I was terrible. I tried to convince myself that anyone would sound as bad when they first started, but I saw right through me. I decided to accept the unfortunate fact that it took more than being depressed to make it as a blues musician and explore some other talents.

It turned out I was quite proficient at picking up Chinese takeout. It was on my way back from yet another successful mission that I spotted Charlie and Veronica ahead of me on the sidewalk. They were stopped outside a store window and Veronica was pointing out something in the display. Charlie was looking attentively. He had his arms wrapped around her and she was holding a rose he must have given her. It all made for a typically romantic scene. I froze. Once they moved along, I made my way to the window Veronica had been pointing to. It was a stationery store with a window display featuring several different kinds of wedding invitations. Fear gripped my heart. Good God, were Veronica and Charlie getting married? That was a terrible idea.

My reaction surprised me. Why did I care whether they got married or not anyway? It wasn't any of my business. I really didn't know either of them, I told myself as I tried to unfurrow my brow.

But it was just all wrong. Veronica was awful and though I didn't know Charlie well, I'd really enjoyed talking to him at the restaurant opening. At least up until we'd spotted Aaron and Darlene. And then Charlie had condescendingly diagnosed me as "confused." Come to think of it, maybe he was arrogant and snide after all. I couldn't be sure.

Back at my apartment, I ate my moo shu chicken and mused about relationships. At the moment, it seemed that everyone besides me was in one. And so many of them were in the wrong ones. In my opinion, Veronica wasn't right for Charlie, Scooter wasn't right for Liza, and Bramen wasn't right for America. And I didn't even want to get started on Aaron and Darlene. The fact that all these relationships seemed to be thriving despite their essential wrongness left me feeling helpless and outnumbered. But I comforted myself with the idea that at least things couldn't get any worse.

The next day, they did.

During an interview that I watched from the office, in what must have been a calculated effort to appear more centrist, Bramen came out strongly against RG's bill for increased funding to NIH. The bill that I had drafted—the bill that had been steadily gaining support and was being touted as likely to become law. I watched in appalled amazement as he trashed the pending legislation.

Most of the pundits were saying that Bramen had the nomination sealed up and needed to start focusing on the general election by appealing to a wider base and combating the image many had of him as a political waffler beholden to his party's special interests. Bramen had apparently taken this advice to heart. I could tell from his expression that he thought he was distinguishing himself in a bold and startling way.

"At some point, those in my party need to stop spending Americans' hard-earned dollars like they don't have anyone to account to," Bramen thundered. "I'd like to find a cure for these terrible diseases as much as the next person, but we need to be smart and disciplined in our approach. We can't keep taxing and spending without a proven strategy."

The interviewer seemed as surprised as I was.

"Yet Senator Bramen, you cosponsored a new prescription drug benefit package with Senator Gary that's going to cost the taxpayers some money. Do you now regret your participation in that measure?" the CNN reporter asked.

"Of course not," Bramen scoffed. "There's an enormous difference between Senator Gary's NIH bill, which is nothing but a frivolous budgetary add-on, and my drug benefit package, which is going to provide much-needed relief to millions of Americans."

"Wasn't it Senator Gary who *initially* authored the drug benefit package?" the reporter asked.

"You're damn right it was!" I shouted at the TV screen.

Neither Bramen nor the reporter seemed to hear me. Bramen waived his hand dismissively, as if batting the question aside.

"Senator Gary floated a half-baked idea that he needed a lot of help with," he answered. "To say that he came up with the package is like saying Nestlé came up with the chocolate chip cookie. That recipe's been around for a long time. I'm the one that really got things cooking."

Mark looked as though he'd been expecting me when I arrived at his desk.

"I know, I saw it," he said before I could launch into my tirade.

"It was the most horrifying extended baking metaphor I've ever heard," I said through gritted teeth. "Has someone let RG know?"

"He saw it, too," Mark answered.

"What did he say about it?" I asked curiously.

"He's pissed off," Mark answered.

Good. But he'd been pissed off in the past and opted not to retaliate. Though I usually loved the fact that RG devoted himself to a bigger-picture view of the world and strove to stay above the fray, I longed for revenge. I was sick of taking the high road and getting beaten at every pass. Mark's phone started ringing.

"And here they come," he sighed with an air of resolve as he picked up his phone. "Mark Herbert," he said into the receiver.

That sounded so professional. I made a note to start answering my own phone in a similar fashion. Mona joined me as Mark fielded press calls.

"Unbelievable," she declared, shaking her head. "I just saw the replay of it on CNN. The Drudge Report already has a headline about Bramen dissing RG."

"I can't fathom why he would do such a thing," I replied.

Which was true. I knew Bramen was a jackass, but this sort of behavior seemed downright irrational. There were plenty of frivolous bills on the Hill to come out against. Why pick a meaningful one that was actually going to help people? Did he have something against RG in particular? These new on-the-record comments on top of the months of "unnamed source" criticisms suggested that he did. But I'd always heard that he was an equal opportunity asshole.

"He's a jerk to everyone," Mona agreed. "But he's been particularly threatened by RG ever since they got elected to Congress the same year. RG hasn't been as openly ambitious, but he's been better respected by everyone who works with them, and that really bugs Bramen."

Interesting. I had assumed that Bramen simply looked down on RG out of arrogance—it hadn't occurred to me that his hostility could have been born of jealousy.

I pondered this as I made my way back to my desk, where Janet immediately buzzed me.

"He'd like to see you," she said crisply into my ear.

"Now?" I asked incredulously.

"Now."

I raced to RG's office. He was sitting quietly at his desk in a thoughtful pose when I walked in.

"Hello, Samantha," he said.

"Hello, sir," I replied.

He paused for a moment before settling his features into a serious expression. A veneer of resolve swept from his forehead down to his chin. I'd seen this expression before. RG had made a significant decision.

"You saw Bramen?" he asked.

I nodded.

"It was unbelievable, sir. He didn't even—"

RG held his hand up. I fell silent, feeling a bit chastised. My face must have fallen a bit, because RG's features softened in response.

"I know," he answered more kindly. "I've just received a call from James Satchel," he continued.

Satchel was a senator from California and the head of RG's health care committee. The one he'd just convinced to hear testimony on the need for increased funding for Parkinson's, Huntington's, and Alzheimer's.

"James thinks that the committee's schedule is too full at the moment to be able to devote enough time as needed to the hearings. He's pulling the plug on them for the time being," he finished.

I gasped.

"What?"

We'd been slated to begin the hearings that week. The bill had already been generating tons of buzz and pledges of support.

"Clearly, Satchel feels pressured to be supportive of Bramen," RG continued.

Satchel had endorsed Bramen early on and become the West Coast cochair of his campaign. I'd read that the two of them had belonged to the same eating club at Princeton. But still, he was the chairman of a key committee. And he'd told RG how important he thought the legislation was. Apparently just not as important as collecting political chits in an election year.

"But . . ." I protested.

"There's no 'but,' Sammy. The bill is dead," RG said calmly. "The reality is that Bramen is completely in bed with the insurance industry. The particular companies he's tied to have never been all that eager for more research into neurodegenerative diseases unless there's a clear home run payoff. They'd rather have the money go elsewhere. They wanted our bill dead and Bramen killed it for them. It's a corrupt situation. End of story."

There wasn't bitterness in his voice so much as a sense of finality. I didn't know how to respond.

"But—" I stammered.

"Like I said, there is no 'but,'" RG interrupted. "That's simply the way it is. However, there is an 'and.' Bramen's dirty business destroyed our bill. *And* I've had enough of him."

That was the ray of hope I'd been searching for. I felt like my clothes might have even brightened in response.

"I just wanted to let you know, since you've done a lot of great work on this. We're not giving up on it. We're just delayed," he said.

I could almost hear the rallying music swelling all around us.

"Yes, sir," I answered.

I could tell that I was about to be dismissed.

"What are you going to do about Bramen, sir?" I heard myself ask.

"I'll be endorsing Max Wye at an event in Cleveland in the next week. You should keep that to yourself for the moment, please."

It was a succinct, powerful, invigorating response. That was brilliant! I knew that most people considered Bramen a shoo-in, but I believed in RG's instincts. Plus, the Ohio primary was coming up on March second, along with contests in a slew of other states. If anyone could deliver Ohio for someone, RG could. He'd been heavily lobbied for his endorsement by the other campaigns for quite some time now. So with a little luck, RG could be joining a winning bandwagon. And exacting sweet revenge in the process.

"That's great news, sir," I responded.

"I've liked Wye from the beginning. I was staying away from the contest out of respect for my colleagues involved in the process, but I don't feel that John Bramen deserves my respect anymore. I just need to explain myself to Conrad and Rexford and then get on with it."

"Can I help with anything, sir?" I asked.

"Yes. I'd like to have a health care aspect to the endorsement event. See what you can cook up."

Gladly. I returned to my desk, feeling as though a weight had been lifted. It was true that things hadn't been going well in my personal life, but who cared. I'd rather have no relationship than be stuck in a wrong one. And my professional life was providing plenty of excitement. I was fighting a good fight, and doing my part to help change things for the better.

Apparently I just needed to choose my battles. I doubted I could break up Charlie and Veronica, or Liza and Scooter. And though I'd thought I'd broken up Aaron and Darlene, it clearly hadn't stuck. Maybe I'd have more success helping to break up Bramen and America. It was a long shot, I knew, but I felt it was worth it. Bramen and his team didn't deserve to be front-running away with the nomination, so I was ready and willing to trip them up however we could. The stakes were high, but the grayness was receding and my vision was clear. In the reflection of my computer screen, I saw the beginnings of a smile spread across my face.

# Breathe in Deep, It's All Fresh Air

THE NEXT FEW days were filled with a sense of secret purpose. I became mildly alarmed at how much I took to the idea of revenge. I didn't want to be so titillated by it—I'd always hoped I'd be motivated by something purer and more positive, but I couldn't deny the excitement that getting back at someone provoked in me. Was I a bad person at my core? I decided to volunteer for some community service work to atone.

On Friday morning, I accompanied RG to Cleveland and drove with him over to the private airport, where we met Max Wye's incoming plane. Though I'd seen plenty of Wye on television, I'd never actually viewed him in person and he was shorter than I'd expected him to be. As he walked towards us on the tarmac, both of us looked up to RG, who stuck out his hand as soon as Wye was within arm's distance.

"Governor," RG said in a friendly voice reserved only for those he respected.

He had other friendly voices for people he didn't know or particularly admire, but this specific friendly voice I'd come to recognize during my time with him and take note of the person to whom he addressed it. I'd already been inclined to think highly of Governor Wye. Now I was determined to do so.

"Good to see you, Senator," Max Wye said.

They shook hands.

"This is Samantha Joyce, my health care guru," RG said as he indicated my presence.

RG was clearly being somewhat facetious, but that was the first time I'd ever been called a guru, in jest or not. What did being a guru entail? Should I be wearing robes of some sort?

"It's a pleasure to meet you, Samantha," Governor Wye was saying to me as he shook my hand. "I've been a fan of your boss's health care positions for a long time, so I guess you could call me one of your followers."

I smiled and fruitlessly battled my tongue-tied state. Wye seemed to accept the fact that I wasn't going to make any discernible human noise in response to his comment. He and RG moved on, climbing into the waiting car.

"Nice to meet you," I said to the closing door.

I was pretty sure I'd said it too softly to be heard, even if I'd managed to time it a little bit better.

For the endorsement event, I'd helped arrange for Wye and RG to tour a local hospital that had been impressively proactive in initiating clinical trials for the treatment of neurodegenerative diseases. The hospital administrators had also been extremely supportive of RG's prescription drug benefit package, so we enjoyed a friendly relationship with them. I climbed into the staff van behind Wye and RG's car and smiled at all the unfamiliar faces. Wye's team looked busy and important. I used the opportunity to check in with Kara, who'd taken time off from her thesis to help staff the event.

To: Kara Linden [klinden@csuohio.edu]
From: Samantha Joyce [srjoyce@gary.senate.gov]
Subject: On our way
Text: Everything good there?

I sent the message before realizing that Kara didn't have a BlackBerry. Curses, I was going to have to go the old-fashioned route and make a cell phone call. I appreciated the silent privacy of the BlackBerries—something I'd really begun to take for granted. I felt self-conscious as I dialed her number.

"Hey, Sammy," she answered.

She didn't sound that stressed. Just busy.

"Hey, we're on our way. Is everything good there?"

"Yep, although Wye's advance team is messing with my mojo," she complained good-naturedly.

I turned down the volume of my cell phone as I surreptitiously looked around. No one else in the van had heard that, had they?

"Oh, really? What sort of stuff?" I asked vaguely.

"Advance" teams went ahead of candidates' entourages to set up events and make sure everything went smoothly. They were supposed to make things easier.

"You know, just double-checking everything," Kara answered. "Ordering the hospital folks around. They're very gung-ho and professional, but they're not exactly charming the pants off people. I'm doing as much damage control as possible. And don't worry, everything's going to be fine," she assured me.

"I'm not worried," I said, a little too quickly. "Do you want me to call you when we're close?"

"Oh, we've got plenty of people on that," she said, with a laugh. "Tim here—the lead advance guy—keeps calling someone to ask if they're 'bravo.' Any idea what that means?"

"I think people say that when they're ten minutes away," I said, uncertainly. "Or maybe five. I think."

I wasn't exactly sure. Didn't people say "alpha," too? Right at that moment, the woman behind me barked into her cell phone.

"Roger, Tim, we're bravo to your location."

"Did you hear that?" I whispered into the phone.

"Yep," Kara answered. "Whatever it means, we'll see you soon."

"Great."

I was a little jealous of Team Wye's mastery of the fancy code words. They certainly weren't that necessary—saying "we're bravo to your location" took just as much time as saying "we're five minutes out." Actually, it took even longer. A full three syllables longer. It reminded me of a comedian's routine about hospital lingo that I'd heard a few years ago. The comic was making fun of the term "GSW" as an abbreviation for "gun shot wound." He pointed out that, due to the multi-syllable pronunciation of "W," the abbreviation took longer to say than the term it was abbreviating. I saw a similar futility in the whole "bravo" system. But it still sounded cool, which probably made up for its inefficiency.

Sure enough, we were arriving at the hospital by the time I'd worked through my thoughts about the bravo/GSW connection. I saw Kara waiting by the door, next to a very tall, young guy with stooped shoulders and an earpiece. Tim, perhaps? He certainly appeared aggressively involved. I wondered if the earpiece even worked or if it was just for show. And could I have one maybe? They looked fun.

We all jumped out of the van as soon as it stopped. My fellow passengers ignored me for the most part, buzzing into gear and creating a general air of importance around the car containing Wye and RG. I made my way to Kara and gave her a quick, unprofessional hug.

"It's so good to see you," I said sincerely.

She smiled back.

"You, too."

We turned to watch as the car doors opened. As Wye and RG stepped out, a small gaggle of press surged forward. Shouted questions added to the feeling of hectic electricity.

"Senator Gary, will you be endorsing Governor Wye today?" a reporter shouted louder than the others.

RG and Wye smiled and waved and walked straight into the building. I still hadn't gotten used to the necessary practice of just completely ignoring people's yelled inquiries, but apparently it was an accepted form of politically sanctioned rudeness.

While RG and Wye began their tour of the facility, Kara and I slipped down to the cafeteria to make sure everything was ready for the press conference to be held there at the conclusion of their visit. Zack was helping himself to some donuts at the back of the room. Kara and I directed our attention to the front, where Wye's advance team was busily rearranging the chairs. Kara rolled her eyes.

"They've been very concerned about the seating since early this morning," she explained. "Tim at one point insisted on a different sort of chair for Wye. I couldn't figure out the reason, until I saw it and noticed it was a few inches taller than the others. I don't know if Wye has a complex about his height, but his staff sure does."

Really? Did they need earpieces for that kind of work?

"He's not even that short," I protested.

Kara shrugged.

"That's just the tip of the iceberg. I'll spare you some of their other requests."

Hmm, that complicated my plans to be unrepentantly pro-Wye. Did he exhibit prima donna-ish tendencies? That was sort of a bummer.

"I'm sorry you've had to deal with all that," I said.

"I'm not," she replied. "It's a fun learning experience. And it makes me appreciate RG all the more."

That's for sure. RG wasn't always a joy to work with, but his character flaws had little to do with superficial things. He was serious about everything, including when he was being a serious pain, but even in those moments it was clear that his focus was on his mission rather than himself. I realized how rare this was the more I was exposed to other politicians.

My cell phone rang just as I spotted Zack accidentally splurting chocolate cream onto his tie.

"Hello?" I answered, though I'd meant to say "Sammy Joyce" in a very professional tone. I kept forgetting to try that out. Maybe next time.

It was Janet.

"Samantha, I have Senator Bramen returning RG's call. RG asked me earlier to patch him through to your cell phone. He said you'd be with him."

*Ack!*

"Hold on one second," I shouted as I sprinted for the elevator.

There was a crowd around it. I kept running to the stairwell and took the three flights two steps at a time. My lungs were burning. I had just burst into the hallway and spotted RG and Wye exiting a patient's room with the group of administrators when Bramen came on the line.

"Robert?" he asked.

I briefly thought about attempting to mimic RG's voice before thankfully choosing another option.

"I'm sorry, I'll have Senator Gary for you in just one second," I said as I gasped for air.

How professional did my panting sound? I signaled wildly for RG as I approached and covered the phone's mouthpiece with my hand.

"Excuse me, sir?"

Both RG and Wye looked up at me. One couldn't go throwing around "sirs" when there was more than one dignitary present.

"I have an important call for you, Senator," I more specifically addressed my words to RG.

He excused himself and followed me quickly to an empty room nearby.

"It's Bramen," I whispered melodramatically.

RG nodded and took the phone.

"Hello, John, thanks for getting back to me," he said evenly. "I wanted to let you know that I've made a decision to endorse Governor Wye."

I held my breath during the ensuing pause. I wondered what was going through Bramen's head. And whether Aaron was with him. Was he thinking about me?

"Well, I'm sorry you feel that way," RG said calmly. "But if my endorsement is that inconsequential, then there's no need for you to be upset about not getting it."

I felt myself flush with anger at what Bramen must have said to provoke such a response. I really hated him. And everyone who worked for him.

"Good-bye, John," RG said as he clicked out of the call.

And good riddance. RG shook his head once and looked straight at me.

"It's time for the press conference," he said definitively as he handed me back my cell phone. He also handed me his BlackBerry, which was the only proof that he'd been at all rattled by the conversation. Though I would have been curious to scroll through it, I cleared my throat instead.

"I think this is actually yours, sir," I nobly pointed out.

"Oh, right," he said absentmindedly. "Thanks."

We rejoined Wye and the others and made our way down to the cafeteria. As we entered the room, I saw Kara tap Tim on the shoulder. He put a hand to his earpiece and held up a "wait a minute" finger to her. Was he getting the word of our arrival? He could have just looked up for that information. Kara rolled her eyes at me.

Luckily, the event went smoothly. The hospital administrators beamed as RG praised them for their tremendous efforts and accomplishments. And RG's endorsement of Wye was forceful, passionate, and graciously received. He described how impressed he'd been watching Wye harness an unprecedented level of grassroots support.

"I've seen a lot of politicians during the course of my career," RG intoned. "But very few leaders. Max Wye is a leader in the best sense of the word—one who backs up his words with real action. This is not an endorsement I've entered into lightly. I am absolutely convinced that Governor Wye will be the next president of this nation, and that he will bring about important and wonderful change. I'm proud to help him in this effort and urge all Ohioans to join our team."

The crowd behind the ring of press burst into applause. I felt a warm sense of pride. I was accustomed to RG doing a good job on his feet, but there was something different about his getting personally involved with this campaign. I felt something stirring in the air around us—some possibilities that I hadn't previously entertained. In that moment, amidst that warmth, I felt like we could be on the cusp of something truly new. And that was exciting.

Wye spoke briefly and then he and RG spent a few minutes fielding inquiries from the press until Tim yelled "last question" from the sidelines. Would the journalists really go along with that? Who made up these rules?

"Governor Wye, if you were in the Senate, would you have voted for Senator Gary's prescription drug benefit package?"

I was surprised that someone would ask such a softball question. Though, having been hit in the face with a softball when I was younger, I had firsthand knowledge of the misnomer quality of that expression. It didn't stop me from using the phrase, it just meant that I always tacked on that addendum, making it sort of a drawn-out process. I could probably make things easier and quicker for myself if I just stuck with adjectives like "easy" or "straightforward."

Governor Wye took the opportunity to praise RG's efforts on the prescription drug benefit bill and reiterate his strong endorsement of it.

"And let me also say," Wye was continuing, "that I think it's a tremendous shame that John Bramen spoke out against Senator Gary's proposed NIH funding bill. It's a fine bill that would help support the kinds of efforts the impressive folks here at this hospital are involved in. It's a compassionate bill, and a pragmatic one, and I intend to sign it into law should I be entrusted with the presidency."

I was beaming by the time Wye finished his sentence. It was very generous of him to give that sort of high-profile exposure to the bill that had died a sad death by chairman neglect just a few days previously. I was happy that Wye had shed light on the situation, and had called Bramen out on his actions.

On that note, the press conference ended and we headed back to the airport. I felt exhausted but satisfied. And I was looking forward to getting back to D.C. to collapse on my bed, but RG and Wye had apparently made other plans during the ride.

"I've decided to join Governor Wye's swing through Ohio this weekend," RG informed me as we exited the vehicles. "Are you free to come along?"

I contemplated the question. I certainly didn't have any plans I needed to break. My only real obligations were to Dr. Cincinnati, and I could always get Liza to work her fish-sitting magic. Joining the Wye posse seemed exciting. Plus, did I really even have a choice here?

"Of course," I answered.

"Okay, good," RG replied matter-of-factly. "Joe's checking to make sure it's all kosher. We're scheduled to take off in ten minutes."

Well, that wasn't a whole lot of time. Would there be any issues with us flying on Wye's campaign dime when I was technically paid to work strictly on Senate business? I imagined Joe Noon would investigate that quickly and try to find a way to okay it. He was a resourceful chief of staff.

Sure enough, we were soon folded into the Wye hive and flying towards Toledo. While RG and Wye sat in a private cabin at the front of the plane, I tried to make connections with some of the staffers sitting near me in the rear, but they were apparently far too busy to be open to my friendship feelers. I resorted as usual to hiding in my BlackBerry.

"Those things'll make you go blind if you don't watch it," a voice above me said.

I looked up from my hunched, nose-to-the-screen position to see an attractive, older man half smiling at me like he was deciding whether or not to invest in a conversation. He was probably in his late thirties or early forties and had strikingly intelligent eyes. I didn't even notice their color; they glowed more with cleverness than a particular hue.

"Oh, I'll develop crippling arthritis in my thumbs long before that happens," I replied.

He let his half smile stretch into a three-quarter one as he slid into the seat across from me. He stuck his hand out.

"I'm Bob Espin," he said.

So this was Bob Espin. Former whiz kid political consultant turned slightly older whiz kid uber-consultant. He was a founding partner of K Street Group, one of the most successful consulting firms in D.C. Spearam had been one of his clients before her meltdown, at which point he'd been hired by the Wye campaign, where he'd wasted no time turning things around. From everything that I'd read, Bob Espin deserved much of the credit for orchestrating Wye's remarkable surge. So I certainly knew of his impressive reputation, but had never actually laid eyes on him. Although I had inadvertently e-mailed him, as he'd been on the "AD List" that had received my disastrous note to Aaron regarding cameras and a possible sexual reunion. During that horrible episode, Bob Espin had been the only one to write a response that had made me feel anything other than utterly mortified. His had been the one suggesting I use digital instead of eight-millimeter film to fully do justice to the whipped cream.

"Sammy Joyce," I identified myself as I shook his hand.

"I know who you are," he replied.

Great. I was hoping he wouldn't remember the name.

"Apparently, Senator Gary really relies on you for his health care work."

Oh. Well, that was nice. I felt myself blushing. Good Lord, was that my neck rash?

"And I read about your innovative ideas regarding dessert products," he continued.

I smiled, even though I was embarrassed. I didn't get the feeling that he was trying to make me feel uncomfortable, and his tone was on the charming side of inappropriate.

"Let's not speak of that," I said lightly.

Bob nodded.

"So, you're on board for a couple of days?" he asked.

"Yeah, I guess so," I replied, as I covered my neck with one of my hands.

I pretended I was slowly scratching a vague itch, allowing myself to keep my hand in the blocking position for quite a while. Why couldn't I will the neck rash away? Couldn't I just decide that I wasn't attracted to Bob Espin? He was certainly too old for me. I surreptitiously checked for a wedding ring. There wasn't one. So either he was one of those guys who didn't wear his, or he really was single. Although he could obviously have a girlfriend. He must have a girlfriend. He was too handsome and smart not to. None of these thoughts was calming my rash.

"It was sort of a last-minute development," I explained. "I actually thought we were headed back to D.C."

"Well, we'll have to make sure you're not disappointed by the change in plans," he said, as he turned the full force of his smile upon me.

I kept my mouth shut to prevent me from saying anything stupid or age inappropriate. I didn't have any experience flirting with an older man. I was immediately attracted to Bob, but didn't he consider me something of a baby? I straightened my back. Liza had told me posture had a lot to do with a look of sophistication.

Bob stood up just as a flight attendant made his way towards us.

"Ms. Joyce? Senator Gary is asking for you," the flight attendant told me.

"I'm headed that way myself," Bob said.

I got up quickly and followed him towards the front of the plane. Inside the small private cabin off to the right, RG and Wye were deep in conversation. They looked up and RG indicated that I should sit in a nearby chair.

"Hello again," Wye said to me.

"Hello, sir," I answered.

"The governor and I were just discussing the filibuster buster," RG explained.

"I followed the coverage, of course," Wye interrupted. "But your boss has been telling me the real story. You did some quick thinking coming up with that strategy."

I felt everyone staring at me, but was particularly conscious of Bob's gaze.

"You were responsible for Sanford B. Zines?" Bob asked quietly. "That was genius."

I was flustered to see a hint of raw admiration in his eyes.

"Thanks," I mumbled shyly.

"No one knew that Samantha came up with it, because Bramen took all the credit," RG continued. "But if she hadn't thought of it, that bill wouldn't have made it."

"Very impressive," Wye agreed.

What was going on here? I appreciated the praise session initiated by ridiculously powerful people, but I didn't understand its purpose, and I felt like I might faint from awkwardness. Was it possible that they'd only wanted me to join them in the cabin as a show-and-tell aspect of the filibuster story? It seemed that way.

"It was really lucky that it worked," I replied.

Could I leave now? On the one hand, it would be bold to depart before I'd been properly dismissed. On the other, this wasn't a royal court we were talking about, and I didn't really understand why I'd been called there in the first place.

"Well, I guess I should leave you all to your business," I said as I stood up.

"Before you go, Samantha, can you clear something up for us?" Governor Wye asked.

Yep, it turned out I should have waited for that dismissal. I sat back down.

"Yes, sir?"

"Your boss here has been trying to convince me that the bill you all fought for didn't go far enough," Wye began. "He insists that we have to deal with the reality that Canada offers prescription drugs at a considerable discount. I maintain that the good-faith prescription drug benefit package you all added to Medicare gets the job done and is all this country can handle at the moment. But your boss assures me that you have plenty of information that could persuade me that I'm wrong."

I looked at RG.

"Tell him some of the statistics," he urged me.

And that's when I realized that maybe I did play a crucial role for RG. He knew his policy positions better than most on the Hill, but he relied on people like me to act as a vault for all the tiny details. He often blew people away with his knack for specifics and deep understanding of so many different topics, but when it came to some particular health care issue, I knew more. That was only because I spent all of my time studying it whereas he mastered issues across the board, but it was still a shocking revelation.

I cleared my throat. I honestly didn't really know where to begin—there was so much information on the topic crammed into my brain. I decided to just dive right in and hope I didn't hit my head on the board.

"Well, forgive me for telling you things you might already know, but here it goes. Because of Canada's price controls, medicine can be bought there at about half the price that the same drugs go for in the United States," I began.

Everyone's expression indicated that I wasn't telling them anything new. I forged ahead.

"The current laws in the United States prevent anybody except the manufacturer from importing prescription drugs. However, law enforcement has long turned a blind eye to Americans returning from Canada with supplies of the prescription drugs that they've procured there for half the price they would pay in the U.S. And in the last few years, several independent operators have opened up prescription drug shops, both on the Internet and in malls and towns across America, that do mail-order business with Canada. A senior can go to one of these shops with a prescription and have it faxed or e-mailed to a Canadian pharmacy that then ships in their drugs. These operations have been both wildly popular and profitable."

"I've heard the fifty-percent-cheaper statistic a few times now," Governor Wye interrupted me. "But what does that realistically translate to for an average senior?"

"Well, obviously it varies on a case-by-case basis," I replied. "But most of the people I've talked to who suffer regular old-age ailments and need long-term maintenance drugs save around four thousand dollars a year by going the Canadian route. Though I've talked to many who have saved up to ten thousand."

"The man who came and testified before my committee last fall was a perfect example," RG interjected.

Good old Alfred Jackman. I imagined he was somewhere north of us at this very moment, no doubt seriously stoned.

"Mr. Jackman didn't have access to one of these mail-order operations. He actually took a bus to Canada to fulfill his prescriptions. For him and for most seniors, a savings of several thousand dollars is a significant boon," I continued. "Many of these folks had previously resorted to skipping dosages, selling their possessions to be able to afford their medicine, even asking to 'inherit' the leftover drugs of friends who had died. The Canadian option has been a godsend for a really ugly situation. So now that the Justice Department and the FDA are closing down these shops, seniors are becoming panicked."

"And the FDA's argument is that these drugs aren't being screened by them, so they can't guarantee their safety," Wye said.

"Right," I nodded. "Though there's nothing to suggest that the Canadian screening process isn't plenty stringent. But you get people like Don Ronkin on the radio shrieking about the government trying to poison people's grandparents, and everything gets muddled."

Wye nodded.

"So, what sort of policy position makes the most sense to you to solve this problem?" he asked.

He was addressing the question to me. I took a breath.

"I have to admit that I'm very envious of the effects of Canada's price controls. I think their health care situation is a lot better off than ours as a result. The prescription drug benefit that was passed this fall goes a long way towards helping seniors get their costs under control, but I believe that we must also push for an acceptance of these foreign imports. At least until we can fix the long-term problem of the skyrocketing prices of drugs in this country. The FDA could work with the Canadian pharmaceutical companies to institute a process that determines whether the drugs coming in are precisely what the pharmacies claim. I really don't think it would be that difficult if Congress turned its attention to the problem. The sticking point thus far has been that so many people leading the opposition to this idea have had their campaigns heavily funded by the pharmaceutical industry."

"Like John Bramen," RG added. "He only agreed to co-sponsor the bill we passed if we took out the importation proposal."

Wye nodded.

"But you say it's currently against the law to operate these storefront and Internet businesses that have cropped up, correct?" Wye asked.

"It is," I conceded. "But it's against a bad law, in my opinion. The existing regulations seem to be in direct conflict with both antitrust laws and principles of free trade. Shouldn't bad laws be changed if they are both in violation of good laws and detrimental to the well-being of millions of Americans?"

Governor Wye held my gaze for a moment.

"And the FDA and Justice Department are currently targeting only the suppliers, correct?" he asked.

"Yes, they haven't yet gone after the seniors buying the 'illegal' drugs. They're just trying to choke off their supply. The world's second-largest pharmaceutical company is already threatening to stop selling drugs to Canadian pharmacies that participate in mail-order arrangements with the United States. If they eliminate that option, seniors will continue making the arduous physical journey to Canada, but many of them live too far away or are too sick to make that a viable alternative. Surely, this country can come up with something better for its citizens."

I felt like I'd been talking for entirely too long. And my voice had taken on a sort of appealing, plaintive tone. I knew RG was already on my side on this issue, which was one of the reasons I loved working for him. But I understood the significant benefit of convincing Wye, as he had the platform to really make this an important issue during a national election cycle.

"Well, you make a very compelling argument," Wye smiled at me.

"No candidate in this campaign has been brave enough to take this on," RG added. "Everyone advocates baby steps, which are certainly the safest way to go, but not necessarily the most heroic. This issue needs a champion."

Wye turned to Bob Espin, who was reading a note that he'd just been handed by the flight attendant.

"What do you think?" Wye asked him.

Bob didn't seem to have to think about it at all. Perhaps he'd already had enough time to have his thoughts fully gathered.

"It'll create a needed buzz in the senior demographic, which will help us a lot in Florida and Arizona, and you won't have to give many details until after the election. People will come after you for it, of course, but there are enough sob stories out there about little old ladies choosing between food and medicine to make for some great commercials. It's bold, and people are responding well to anything bold. I think you should do it."

Huh, not the purest argument for action on the issue, but I supposed Bob wasn't being paid a ridiculous amount of money to pretend to be anything but crassly political.

"And of course I think it would be the best thing for the American people," he added, with a smile in my direction. "Now, if you'll excuse me, I've just got to take this call," he finished, indicating the note in his hand as he exited the cabin.

"Well, Senator," Wye turned to RG, "you're certainly lucky to have someone like Samantha working for you. You've made a persuasive case," he said to me. "I plan on giving it some very serious thought."

"Thank you, sir," I replied.

Before much more could be said, Bob strode back into the cabin and turned on the TV in the corner. CNN popped up on the screen.

"Apparently Bramen screwed up at his health care event this afternoon," Bob informed us.

We all focused on the TV, where a CNN talk show host was in the middle of addressing his guest panel.

"Last week, Senator Bramen offended the residents of New Hampshire. Today, he's managed to insult overweight people. What's going on? Is he giving it to us straight? Or is he simply stumbling?"

After the panel chimed in, CNN replayed the clip to fill in new viewers like us. It began with Bramen standing at a podium in the middle of a town hall. I instinctively scanned the crowd around him for Aaron, but didn't see him. Bramen cleared his throat as a woman in the audience asked a question about the FDA's plan to make calorie labels on food products more clear.

"More reading isn't going to get these people to lose weight," Bramen answered with what he seemed to consider a presidential scowl. "I'll be blunt, which I think is what this country needs. Those folks have got to stop stuffing their faces, get up off their fat asses, and work a little. Before we waste more government money coddling lazy people, we need to call on them to make a little bit of an effort."

My jaw dropped. Was this new bluntness supposed to make Bramen more appealing? I couldn't imagine it doing anything but backfiring.

Bob was chuckling.

"Thank you, John Bramen," he said.

RG was shaking his head. Wye looked decisive.

"Let's get a statement out when we land," he addressed Bob. "Condemning Bramen, asserting our respect for all Americans struggling with obesity and proclaiming the need for compassionate leadership, et cetera. We should move quickly on this."

Bob nodded, still laughing to himself. I blinked in amazement.

"Bramen's so *angry*," I remarked, not meaning to say it out loud.

RG looked at me.

"He's only going to get angrier," he said.

I believed him. I left the three of them to their work and made my way back to my seat for our landing, marveling at the new developments. As the pilots applied the brakes, I closed my eyes and pitched into my fastened seat belt. And even after we taxied to a full stop, I felt completely caught up in the forward motion.

# Buckle Down, Buckle Up

THE SENSATION OF speedy momentum only increased over the follow-ing weeks. Thanks to RG's considerable help and Bramen's continued unraveling, Governor Wye won Ohio in the March 2nd primary. Wye also took eight of the twelve other states, decisively usurping the front-runner role from Bramen, who appeared to have mortally wounded himself with his political missteps. I took tremendous personal joy in these developments, savoring the sweetness of revenge. I even considered sending a gloating e-mail to Aaron, but thought better of it. There was no need to go overboard.

Congressman Rexford and Senator Conrad dropped out of the race within a couple of days. Rexford announced that he was retiring from politics and was planning to start a political magazine. He declined to formally endorse anyone. Conrad gave a moving withdrawal speech and urged his supporters to throw their energy behind Governor Wye, whom he described as "a man who can make good things happen, and I don't have to tell you that we need some good things to happen in this country."

Bramen hung on for another two weeks, frantically scrambling to regain his lost momentum. Though I was thrilled at his misfortune, I was shocked at how quickly his stumbles seemed to have snowballed into unrecoverable disaster. His insensitive comments about overweight people had gotten considerable play, with crippling consequences. Bramen had clearly miscalculated just how obese and vengeful America really was. He hadn't helped his cause by both refusing to apologize and lashing out angrily at anyone who suggested he should.

And then the week before the March 2nd primaries, the *Washington Post* had run a brutal story written by Charlie Lawton that had dissected Bramen's extensive ties to the insurance industry more successfully than any article had done in the past. The timing couldn't have been worse for Bramen. The story had been published just before the AARP had planned to endorse him, and its charges had focused specifically on the conflict of interest between Bramen's industry connections and his pledges to provide quality affordable health care to older Americans. According to the article, Bramen had consistently sided with his wealthy industry friends to the detriment of hardworking, regular people.

The article had detailed dozens of examples, many of which also implicated a "Dr. Reynolds," whom I recognized as the evil Natalie's father—the very man I'd met on the street the day of Natalie's and my showdown over the bill. Dr. Reynolds was apparently extremely close to Bramen, having fund-raised the bulk of the senator's money over the years in exchange for legislative support for his special interest.

Charlie's article had also included a stunning paragraph illuminating Bramen's aggressive efforts to claim credit for the health care bill in the media:

Bramen often feeds spin directly to reporters, but also relies on loyal staff members to seek out journalists and offer "insider information" that reflects positively on him. This particular journalist was approached last fall by Aaron Driver, Senator Bramen's speechwriter, offering to "spill the beans on the ineptness of the Gary crew." The health care bill had just been passed and Mr. Driver called to iterate that "RG and his staff were dead weight that Bramen had to carry on his back. They're amateurs, and we had to spend a lot of time cleaning up their little messes." This journalist found no evidence to back up Mr. Driver's claims and so refused to include them. However, Mr. Driver did convince other publications to print his "information."

I'd sat in shock for a few minutes after finishing the paragraph. *Aaron* had been that unnamed source? That two-faced bastard! When that first quote had been published I'd assumed it had come from Natalie. And Aaron had encouraged that assumption, feigning outrage right alongside me. As similar quotes had popped up over the last few months, I'd continued to blame Natalie, but I now realized it had been Aaron all along. Those quotes had done real damage. Not just to me, but to RG. Romantic betrayal was horrible enough; he'd perpetrated political deception, as well? Aaron had better hope he never ran into me again.

Typically, Bramen did not react well to the charges made by the article. His crimes were bad enough, but Bramen's mishandling of their fallout just damaged him further. He was dying by his own sword, from political wounds inflicted out of clumsiness and anger. I considered it a surprising and important lesson about how quickly things could change in the world of politics. He'd led the pack for so many months, yet after just a few really bad weeks he was done for. It seemed so sudden. I suspected that karma might also be playing a role in Bramen at last receiving his comeuppance.

Bramen finally conceded in the middle of March after he lost Florida, Louisiana, Mississippi, and Illinois to the governor. I watched his withdrawal speech on CNN. Though the words he spoke were eloquent enough, he acted like a man robbed. He did endorse

Governor Wye, but implied that Wye would be strongest in concert with the skills Bramen himself already possessed in abundance. It was an odd method of campaigning for the vice presidential slot, but certainly a quintessentially Bramen-esque way to do so: by putting down the very man he was allegedly endorsing. And most of the pundits asserted that though Bramen was clearly stung, he would jump at the chance to be on the ticket in any fashion.

I took a deep breath as I switched off CNN. So that was that. RG's instincts had been correct. The Wye operation had successfully pulled off an extraordinary coup and Governor Wye was now officially the party nominee. I was happy and relieved with the way things had gone.

On the other side, Governor Cain Brancy had clinched the nomination quite handily. It hadn't ever really been in question, despite the establishment clout wielded by his rivals, the president's brother and the Senate majority leader. Once Brancy had been able to inextricably link them to the failed and immensely unpopular policies, tactics, and personality of the current administration, they hadn't stood a chance.

As for Borden Dent, though he'd never officially dropped out of the race, he had departed for Morocco for a movie shoot, which most people took to mean that he'd moved on.

Thus, it would be a seven-and-a-half-month contest between Wye and Brancy. Preliminary match-up polls placed them in a dead heat. Though people couldn't wait to get rid of the Pile gang, they recognized that Brancy was cut from a different cloth. In fact, Brancy had been gaining in popularity and seemed capable of bringing many of the disillusioned ranks back into his party's fold. Accordingly, he was shaping up to be a formidable opponent.

Throughout Capitol Hill, it felt as though we were off to the races. Everything attained a faster, more hectic clip and the weeks blurred by in the blink of an over-scheduled eye. Before I could fully adjust to the quickened pace, it was mid-May and the Hill was abuzz with gossip about potential vice presidential picks. Wye had touched off this gossip by indicating that he would be making a selection earlier than expected, as he was eager to get his team fully formed as soon as possible. Candidates generally waited until midsummer to choose their running mates, but Wye had already demonstrated his unconventionality, and it had thus far served him well.

I was more surprised than I should have been that RG's name was being heavily bandied about as the front-runner for the VP slot on the Wye ticket. After all, ever since RG's endorsement of Wye, the two of them had spent a fair amount of time with each other and had continued to hit it off. And yet, I hadn't really absorbed the consequences of their bonding. Might Wye really pick RG to be his running mate, out of all the possibilities? I, of course, considered RG to be the very best choice, but did Wye? I wondered along with the rest of the country, or at least along with the political junkie minority of the country.

News shows took to using a "Wye–Gary? Why Gary?" chyron when discussing the drawbacks and advantages of picking RG. I quickly grew tired of the wordplay. And along with the stress and excitement that RG's presence on the short list of VP candidates caused among those of us who worked for him, we also became familiar with the intimidating and intrusive process known as "vetting." Basically, Governor Wye's selection team delved into all things RG, determined to uncover any potentially damaging facts that would impact their decision whether or not to invite him onto the ticket. I felt strongly that they wouldn't find anything too unsavory—I had utter faith that RG had led a fairly exemplary life and career up to this point. However, on a Saturday afternoon in late May, things suddenly got very personal.

I was cleaning Dr. Cincinnati's bowl and listening to an old Johnny Cash album when my doorbell rang. Liza was away with Scooter for the weekend and despite a continued flirtation with Bob Espin, I certainly didn't have a boyfriend to expect, so I was surprised at the sound. I approached the door warily, my pepper spray cocked in my hand. My neighborhood was safe and it was the middle of a bright sunny day, but I'd seen one too many horror movies (against my will) to do anything except immediately concoct a dangerous and melodramatic scenario. So I was on high, heart-racing alert.

The two men at the door identified themselves as ex-Secret Service agents who worked for a security firm that had been hired by the Wye campaign to handle the vetting process. They asked if they could speak with me. Once they showed me their badges and I'd examined them for slightly too long (how easy was it to forge those things?), I let them in.

They settled into the couch across from me and smiled in a friendly way. I wasn't fooled.

"As you know, Senator Gary has pledged full cooperation during this vetting process and he assured us that you were an extremely trustworthy member of his staff," Agent Davis began.

He had? Well, that was nice. Should I ask them if he'd said anything else complimentary about me? Particularly about the latest environmental health impact bill I'd been researching? He'd been too busy lately for our regular meetings. Perhaps these guys were a good way to get some feedback.

Something about the way I could see their guns under their jackets made me think I'd better stay on subject and let them do most of the talking. I was certainly used to seeing security around the Capitol, and I'd had a fair amount of exposure to Secret Service agents, but none of it had been so up close and personal. I started sweating just from the uniqueness of it. And because I'd become uncomfortably aware of the messiness of my apartment. Would they include that in their file on me? If only they'd come a few hours later. I'd at least been scheduled to have the place cleaned by then. But could they tell I was someone who didn't always stick to her schedules just by the way I blinked my eyes? I quickly entered full-fledged paranoia about what these agents could or could not judge about me through their secret training.

"We'd just like to ask you a few questions about your personal life," Agent Davis continued.

It wasn't really a question, but I nodded just the same. And blinked pretty rapidly. I couldn't help it. Good Lord, was I developing some sort of tic? Now was definitely not the time.

"Great," I said brightly. "Fire away."

I immediately regretted the choice of phrase. My blinding smile faltered. Luckily, they were checking their notes.

"Is that your fish?" the other agent, Agent Ozols, asked me.

"Yes it is," I said, eager to prove my full cooperation. "His name is Dr. Cincinnati. He's a Japanese fighting fish."

Were there any other statistics I could include? I had meant to measure him to monitor his growth, but hadn't ever gotten around to it.

"Why did you name him Dr. Cincinnati?" Agent Ozols inquired.

"Oh, well, because I'm from Cincinnati. I mean, not actually, but nearby, and I went to school there. And I like fish and I work with health care legislation, and his little orange spot looks sort of like a stethoscope if you squint at it, and so . . . I don't really know, I just couldn't think of a better name."

The agent made some notes. I got the feeling I wasn't doing as well as I should be.

"Have you always owned fish?" Agent Davis interjected.

Was this a standard line of questioning?

"Um, I had a goldfish when I was little. He was named Goldie Goldhead—talk about a bad naming job. And then I've had, um, nine Japanese fighting fish before Dr. Cincinnati."

"In what period of time?"

Ugh, did we have to go into this? I wasn't proud of my fish murdering record. It didn't paint me in a positive light, though I swore I'd done everything humanly possible to keep them alive.

"In the last two years," I answered. "Actually, slightly less than that."

The agents looked intrigued.

"So, this is your tenth fish in less than two years?" Agent Davis inquired. "Have you gotten them all at the same store?"

"Yes, I have, though I've suspected for a while that the store sells bad fish. I just viewed it more as a challenge than a deterrent."

"So the same person has sold you all ten fish?" Agent Davis asked.

Was this my chance to bust Mr. Lee? Would they call

him in for questioning? Perhaps revenge was at hand! Though I was willing to bet the Secret Service had better things to do than intimidate crooked pet store owners.

"Yes, his name is Mr. Lee."

"And how long have you known Mr. Lee?" he asked.

"Just since I moved here. Almost two years."

"And have you ever discussed anything besides fish with Mr. Lee, during all your repeated visits to his store?"

What was going on here?

"Well, we talked about seaweed. And colored stones for the bowl. And little toy treasure chests and stuff."

"Uh-huh."

Agent Davis continued to make some notes, and then, to my surprise, Agent Ozols held up a picture of Mr. Lee.

"Is this the Mr. Lee you're speaking of?" he asked.

I nodded, confused. They really were quite thorough in their vetting process.

"And you've only known this man since you've lived in D.C. and began working for Senator Gary?"

I nodded.

"And you claim that you've only ever talked to him about fish?"

"Japanese fighting fish," I clarified. "And their accessories. And life expectancies."

"So, you would be surprised to learn that this man that you know as Mr. Lee is actually Sung Whang Koh, an agent of the North Korean regime?"

I doubted I could have looked more stunned if I'd been rehearsing for a month.

"Ye-yes," I stammered. "I'd be very surprised."

Mr. Lee? Get right out of town. No wonder he didn't know anything about fish. Oh my God, and they thought I had some sort of relationship with him beyond buying his tainted marine wares? No, no, no. I'd been suckered. I'd had my suspicions that he wasn't a genuine guy, but I had no idea he was a spy! This was shocking.

They were watching me closely. No doubt waiting for me to slip up.

"So, you would deny that you were using the excuse of buying multiple fish from Mr. Lee, a practice that required regular visits, to actually exchange government secrets with him?"

Wow, they thought *I* was a spy? Beneath the surprise and terror, I was flattered. It was almost as though I'd achieved a lifelong goal. Except that I wasn't a spy, and I did need to keep my non-spy job.

"I would definitely deny that," I said emphatically. "That's just not true. I had no idea about Mr. Lee."

Agent Davis made a note. I wished I could see what he was writing.

"And what about Kim Lee Joon?" Agent Ozols inquired, holding up another photograph.

This one was a woman. A woman I vaguely recognized. Next to her I could make out what looked to be a watermelon. That's who she was! The woman who ran the fruit stand near the pet shop. I'd occasionally bought pears and apples there on my way home, because it had seemed like a charming thing to do. I'd felt better about myself getting them there than at the supermarket. Clearly, I'd been a fool.

"She runs the fruit stand," I answered. "I've bought fruit from her. Is she a secret agent, too?" I asked nervously.

"Yes, she is," Agent Ozols confirmed. "So, you expect us to believe that you made regular visits to two separate North Korean agents completely coincidentally and on business that had nothing to do with government affairs?"

Yes? I knew it sounded far-fetched, in light of all this insane new information, but I was telling the truth.

"I swear I had no idea about them. I really just bought pets and fruit at those places. We never talked about anything else."

"It's possible they were cultivating a relationship with her, but hadn't approached her yet," Agent Davis said to Agent Ozols.

That seemed a weirdly unprofessional thing to say in front of me, but my heart leapt at the possibility that they were open to alternate explanations and might recognize that I was telling the truth. I had to stop myself from nodding vigorously in agreement with Agent Davis. I didn't want to antagonize them.

"It just seems like an awful lot of fish to go through." Agent Ozols was shaking his head at me.

Tell me about it. I was the one fighting the angel of death complex.

"I don't know how to convince you guys," I said, somewhat desperately. "All I can say is that I swear to you that I'm telling the truth."

Agent Davis watched me for a long moment.

"And did you ever discuss your visits with either agent to Senator Gary?" he asked.

"No," I answered with certainty.

I could be absolutely positive that I never brought up such trivial things with RG. After another fifteen minutes of questioning and double-checking, the agents thanked me for my time and went on their way.

I went straight to the kitchen and poured myself a "regular." As I was taking my first sip, my phone rang. It was Zelda, returning my message.

"Are *you* a secret agent of North Korea?" I asked, in a mildly accusatory voice.

"No," she answered. "But I would be if they paid enough. Is there a job opening?"

I appreciated the joking response, but immediately afterwards was seized by a fear that the Secret Service had tapped my phone. Would they think I was recruiting now? I got off quickly, promising Zelda I'd call her later. Then I turned up the volume on "Folsom Prison Blues" and drank my drink slowly, wondering what else I didn't really know about my life.

• • •

In the office on Monday morning, I got up the nerve to ask Janet to schedule some time for me with RG. I had to alert him about the vetting. And I probably needed to look into getting a lawyer. I was waiting to hear back from Janet and drinking my third cup of coffee while jittering my knee wildly under my desk when CNN turned yet again to the topic of whom Wye would pick to be his running mate. Sources from his camp indicated he was very close to a decision and the RG speculation had reached a fever pitch. Though I was obviously preoccupied with my potential espionage charges, I also felt an edgy sense of anticipation. As I watched, CNN broke into their own program to announce that, according to a source close to Governor Wye, he had just chosen RG to be his vice presidential nominee.

I slammed my mug back on my desk, spilling the coffee in the process, and jumped out of my chair. Was that true? Had I not sunk RG's chances with my accidental spy connections? And was he really, honestly on the ticket? I looked around for someone else to confirm. CNN hadn't always gotten everything right.

Mona came running down the hallway.

"Did you see?" she asked breathlessly.

I nodded.

"Is it true?" I inquired.

"Yes. Janet told me Governor Wye placed a call to RG about twenty minutes ago," she informed me.

Wow. I shouldn't have felt so stunned—I'd known he was on the short list for a couple of weeks now, but still, I hadn't ever let myself fully contemplate the possibility of his being chosen.

Within an hour, a staff meeting was called. RG had a thousand media requests and a plane to catch to Louisiana, where he and Wye were going to make the official announcement. But he took ten minutes to talk to all of us in his office. He looked very calm, but I could sense his excitement.

He thanked us for all our hard work, as well as for going along with the intensive vetting process. I looked down at the floor in shame. Did he know? He kept talking. He said that we were in for an important and thrilling adventure and he pledged to do his best to make us proud. And then we were dismissed.

I returned to my desk only to receive a BlackBerry from Janet calling me back into RG's office. I walked back with a feeling of intense dread. Surely, now was when I was going to get the axe. Mona, Mark, and Karen—a quiet environmental legislative aide who never talked to anyone—were already assembled. Joe Noon, RG's chief of staff, lurked in a nearby corner. Were they here to witness my firing? Or did they all also have inadvertent ties to the foreign underworld?

RG closed the door behind me.

"Thanks for coming back." He smiled at us, while Joe Noon observed from the back of the room. "I've asked all of you here because I would like you to consider making a transition to the campaign staff and relocating to headquarters in Louisiana through November. We obviously haven't had time to make a lot of hiring decisions, but if I can get you four in place, I'll feel ahead of the game."

I looked around at the others. They all looked happy, but none of them seemed amazed the way I was. Really? That's why he'd called us in?

"Sir, are you aware that the Secret Service thinks I may be some sort of North Korean spy?" I asked immediately.

Now Mona, Mark, and Karen did look astonished. I felt them staring at me. RG actually laughed.

"I heard about that, but you'll be happy to know you've been cleared," he informed me. "I just wouldn't recommend going back to that pet store if you can help it."

I exhaled in relief. Of course I'd been cleared. And RG wasn't mad. In fact, he seemed amused by the whole thing. Though I was mildly offended that he found the notion of my being a spy so utterly far-fetched. What, did he think I wasn't devious enough? I could have pulled it off. Maybe I'd fooled them all, sold state secrets for millions of dollars, and was planning to defect to Pyongyang at any moment.

I got my ego under control and focused on being grateful that I was no longer under suspicion. And I was being asked to join the campaign staff! This was definitely a promotion! Wasn't it?

The issue was clarified on the plane to Louisiana the following day when RG pulled me aside.

"I wanted to let you know that you won't be moving to Louisiana after all," he said.

I felt my heart plummet. Of course he'd reconsidered his decision. There were more competent people than me on whom to rely. I made an effort not to hang my head.

"I've made arrangements for you to travel full-time with the campaign instead," he said.

Wow. Really?

"Th-thank you, sir," I half stammered in reply. "I'll try my best to do a good job."

"I'm sure you will," he said with a small smile. "You did a great job helping me convince Wye to reconsider his health care positions a few months back. I need people around me who are capable of things like that as we go forward with this campaign."

He moved on to talk to somebody else before I had a chance to reply. An hour later, I reflected on his praise while watching from behind the outdoor stage as RG, Jenny, Jack, and Jeffrey joined Governor Wye and his wife and children before a roaring crowd of supporters and national media at the VP announcement event. I was both incredibly flattered and terrified by the promotion. I could practically feel the stakes raising around me. Please, please don't let me screw this up, I prayed to whatever gods were listening. I wondered what the chances were that I wouldn't.

I also wondered how the Garys managed to avoid

appearing like sweaty messes when it was ninety-five degrees and sunny. Governor Wye made a funny and heartfelt speech explaining why he'd chosen RG, and RG in turn talked simply but eloquently about how honored he was to be a part of this essential journey. Jack and Jeffrey stared wide-eyed out at the sea of colors and movement in front of them. They were almost two years old. Could they comprehend any of this? Could they feel the energy of it? I certainly could.

I'd been instructed to pack lightly, but for at least a week. I'd thrown in two pairs of dark pants, two skirts, six nice shirts, one jacket, and shoes that were more comfortable than stylish. Plus a deep red cocktail dress that I'd tossed in at the last second in a panic and that was now just taking up needed space. Now that we were officially being swept up in the Wye whirlwind, the campaign's unique universe was rapidly becoming our own. It was a universe of long motorcades and campaign planes and Secret Service and ever-growing entourages. I tried to notice all the crazy details of this strange new world, but I had enough trouble just keeping up with the frantic pace.

I envied the team of people around Wye, only because they already knew how to cope with this bizarre and hectic lifestyle. I wished there was some sort of manual I could quickly skim. But I was thrilled to be along for the ride, prepared or not.

Bob Espin blew by me, talking on his cell phone. I pretended not to be hurt. As I was checking my Black-

Berry to make sure I knew the schedule well enough to keep up with the next movement (not my term, but one that was regularly employed, to my juvenile amusement), I felt him back beside me. I looked up to see him covering the mouth of his phone.

"I owe you a drink later," he smiled at me.

"I hope you make it a good one," I replied.

He winked and then returned to his call and kept walking.

By nightfall, we had traveled to Ohio, California, and back to New Orleans in a long, exhausting day of officially announcing the ticket. As I wheeled my not-quite-compact-enough suitcase through the hotel lobby, I wondered how much time it would take me to adjust to this higher gear of existence. I was accustomed to long hours and deadlines and stress from my normal job on the Hill, but I could tell already that we had entered a whole other dimension of intensity. I understood that I was just one of a large team of people who were expected to operate excellently under tremendous pressure and with ridiculously little sleep, and that any mistakes made would have reverberations on a powerfully scrutinized national stage. This was enough to paralyze me with anxiety, but such paralysis wasn't an option. Above all, motion was the theme of our new existence. Standing still was basically just asking to be left behind.

I had just barely made it to the room I was to share with an unknown Wye staffer and had collapsed fully clothed on my bed, trying to get up the energy to request a 5:30 wake-up call, when the phone rang preemptively.

"Hello?" I answered curiously.

"Oh good, they gave me the right room. We're down in the bar. Come join us."

It was Bob's voice. I felt a little surge of excitement despite my utter exhaustion. Should I resist the invitation in a bid to preserve my health and sanity? Would he think I was a lightweight?

"I'll be down in a minute," I replied.

I glanced at myself in the elevator mirror a few moments later. I looked tired and rumpled. I did three quick jumping jacks to try and snap myself into another state, knocking my elbow hard against the emergency phone in the process. Hopefully it was dark in the bar and someone had some aspirin.

Bob smiled and stood up when he spotted me walking towards the corner table he was sharing with three other people, whom I recognized as I got closer. They were Gabe Ramper, Wye's campaign manager; Lana Martinez, Wye's communications director; and Walt Patton, Wye's spokesperson. The senior staff. I'd seen them on the plane and I'd been reading about them in The Note and the Hotline for the past few months, but we hadn't officially met. We introduced ourselves and Bob asked me what I wanted to drink.

What was good for a sore-elbowed, disheveled woman currently feeling out of her league? I settled on a margarita. As Bob flagged down the waitress, I wondered if there was a way to feel less intimidated. I hadn't realized when I'd accepted Bob's invitation that I'd be hanging out with the campaign's high command. Lana smiled at me.

"How are you holding up?" she asked.

"I'm too tired to tell," I answered honestly. "It's all incredibly exciting, though."

"Well, we're thrilled to have Gary on the ticket," Walt offered.

They were being nicer to me than I'd expected. Maybe it was because they knew Bob had invited me.

"Hey, are we doing another round of hiring after the announcement cycle?" Walt asked Gabe.

"Yep," he nodded.

I perked up with an idea.

"I have a recommendation if you're looking for advance staff," I blurted.

Gabe looked at me, a bit surprised.

"Okay. We always need more advance folks," he replied.

I imagined that was true. And they definitely needed better ones if Tim from the endorsement event was any indication.

"Kara Linden has done a lot of great work for Senator Gary," I said. "She helped set up the endorsement, and I know she'd be excellent for the campaign."

I couldn't imagine anyone better for setting up events

and ensuring that everything ran smoothly. Advance was perfect work for Kara, who was always one step ahead of everyone to begin with. And I knew that she would always have RG's best interests in mind, which was important.

"How do you spell her name?" Gabe asked as he typed it into his BlackBerry.

I told him, along with how to get in touch with her.

"Already taking over, huh?" Bob teased me.

It *was* a little bold of me. But I was happy to seize any opportunity to help fill out their team with smart, hardworking people who also just happened to be good friends of mine. Yet, had I gone too far? Was Gabe annoyed? Before I had a chance to revert to complete insecurity, Bob changed the topic away from politics and told a funny story about his first job taking orders for a florist. I sipped my margarita and enjoyed the sound of his voice.

Two hours later, he walked me to my room. I was considerably jollier by that point, though maintaining that happiness depended on avoiding any focus on the fact that I now had only four hours to sleep. Bob put his hand lightly on my shoulder as I checked my room number on my key card. Was I even going the right way?

"I'm glad you're on board." He smiled as he turned me towards him.

God, he was attractive. He pulled me to him. We'd been flirting sporadically for almost four months, and the kiss reflected the build-up. Perhaps he'd always been a good kisser, or perhaps he'd improved with his considerably more years of practice, but whatever the explanation, I felt I was in expert hands. My heart pounded faster as the kissing escalated quickly.

But all of a sudden, I remembered exactly where we were and who we were with. RG and Wye and their families were ensconced on a floor two levels up, which was where most of the Secret Service was as a result, but I suspected they roamed the other floors. Also, who knew if anyone had heard us and was peering out of their keyholes? And what would my roommate think if I didn't make it back that night? Not that Bob and I were doing anything wrong, but wasn't it a bit early to earn myself a reputation? I reluctantly pulled away.

"I should probably figure this out," I said, referring to my room key.

Bob smiled at me. He struck me as a man who was accustomed to moving fast—someone who had reasons to feel secure that he was always going to end up on top.

"Good night," he said, kissing me again.

I dizzily found my way to my room, caught up in a rush of happiness. What a fun turn of events. I touched my lips, remembering the feel of his. Could Bob Espin be the one for me? Judging from that kiss, it was a strong possibility. I felt myself grinning as I quietly opened the door and tiptoed in to avoid awakening whomever was asleep in one of the beds. The room was pitch black. I felt my way as best I could, praying that I chose the right bed to crawl into. Thankfully I did, and as I closed my eyes and let my brain swirl with the excitement and tequila and kissing of the day, I wished for it all to continue just like these first fresh hours of new, potential-pregnant adventure.

## A Brimmed-Over Cup

AFTER A WEEK filled with travel and scrambling and sleeplessness, I returned to D.C. for twenty-four hours for a "break." In the last six days, we'd been to Louisiana, Ohio, California, Arizona, New Mexico, Nevada, Minnesota, Alabama, and Arkansas. I felt ragged. Liza met me at my apartment, where I was deciding whether to do my laundry or just leave it for later and pack an entirely fresh set of clothes. I was too tired and hot to think straight. I'd turned off my air-conditioning before leaving for Louisiana the week before, and my apartment had soaked up the late-June heat and held onto it possessively. My trusty little AC sputtered to drive it away now, but I could practically hear the sweltering air molecules mocking its insufficient attempts.

"Are you okay?" Liza asked me as I fought back tears.

"It's just so hot in here," I complained.

I knew that my response was more about feeling

overwhelmed, and overheated in a figurative sense. I was genuinely excited about my new lifestyle on the road, but I reacted negatively to the sensation of being stretched too thin.

"It's going to be okay," she assured me. "Why don't we go someplace cool for an hour or two until your AC kicks in?"

I stared at her. Did she understand that the time unit of an hour or two was a precious and rare one? I had a lot to pack into these stolen moments. Maybe we were too different now to relate. She was living back in the old universe.

"Or, okay, let's just stay here," she continued, after reading my face. "I'll get you some ice water."

I did consent to sit down on the bed and drink the water for five minutes. It was during this time that Liza fixed me with a sorrowful gaze.

"I'm afraid I have a little bit of bad news," she said deliberately.

What? She and Scooter had broken up? I really didn't consider that a tragedy. I was pretty much just waiting for it to happen. Or could it be something about Aaron? I didn't really care about him anymore. I was with Bob now and working on a national campaign while Aaron was back here festering over Bramen's failed bid. I considered all of that good news.

"Dr. Cincinnati passed away this morning."

That was not good news. He'd died? But he'd been so healthy! I'd asked Liza to take care of him while I was gone and she'd moved him to her place so that she didn't have to keep on commuting to mine solely for fish care. Had he freaked out over his new surroundings? Did this mean Liza had killed him? I burst into tears.

"I'm sorry," Liza said impotently. "It was really very sudden. He seemed completely fine and happy and then the next morning he was just belly-up."

"Did you check to make sure he wasn't playing dead?" I asked.

She assured me that she had. Dr. Cincinnati was no Shackleton. In more ways than one, really. Though I'd grown attached to him, I'd never had the sort of bond I'd enjoyed with his predecessor. My emotional reaction to his demise was one part heartfelt, two parts complete exhaustion.

"I'm okay, really," I said through my sobbing. "I don't blame you."

Liza took my melodrama in stride. She dried my tears, helped me pack, and offered to go get me a new fish, this time from a more reputable establishment. I decided I needed to take some time off from pets for a while.

"Okay . . . well, is there anything we need to celebrate today?" she asked me in an attempt to cheer me up.

I followed her gaze to my calendar. My BlackBerry had already informed me that today was the twenty-seventh anniversary of the seventh time Roy C. Sullivan had been struck by lightning, according to an article I'd read on lightning strike survivors. Granted, the seven strikes had occurred over the course of thirty-five years, but that was still record-breaking for a single man. Who said lightning never struck twice? Certainly not Roy C. Sullivan.

Like all the anniversaries of the past week, I didn't feel that I had the time or energy to properly celebrate Roy's achievement. I tried to explain this to Liza.

"You're going to burn out if you're not careful," she said ominously.

I knew she was right. I needed to get it together. It was already the end of June. The convention was in six weeks, and then it would be a three-month sprint to Election Day. I knew it would fly by. I could handle this. I needed to be a part of it.

"I'll be okay," I said decisively.

We spent the rest of the day pulling me together. I even made myself go to bed ridiculously early to try to strengthen my sleep reservoir. I knew I'd be drawing on it soon enough.


The following day, on a bus barreling through Missouri with RG and Wye, Liza called me to check in.

"I'm going to flush Dr. Cincinnati now," she said solemnly.

She'd waited to do so in the event that I wanted to be a part of the ceremony. I hadn't been in a state to trek over to her place to do it the day before, so we'd agreed that I'd participate via cell phone.

"Do you have any last words for him?" she asked.

In fact I did. I had her repeat after me.

"*Namu amida butsu*," I said.

I had to repeat it three times before she pronounced it correctly. Or at least the way I had decided it needed to be pronounced in my mind. After the third time, I spotted Agent Roberts eyeing me from a few rows up. I imagined he and the rest of the Secret Service had been briefed on my North Korean spy connections by the vetting team. I put my hand over my cell phone.

"It's Japanese, not Korean," I assured him.

Was that any better in his eyes? I wondered about the strength of the Japanese government's spy system in the U.S. At least their country was more friendly towards us of late than the North Koreans.

"It's part of the funeral ceremony for my fish," I added.

It didn't seem as though I'd managed to appease his suspicions. He continued to watch me warily. I shrugged and returned to Liza.

"What does it mean?" she asked.

"It's a Japanese Buddhist prayer that I found on the Internet," I explained. "The site claimed that saying it with faith would lead to rebirth into a Western Paradise. I don't know if Dr. Cincinnati was Buddhist or Shinto or conventionally religious in any way, but I'm sure he'd appreciate the sentiment."

Liza agreed. She pressed play on "Octopus's Garden" per my special request, and flushed the toilet. I said my own silent good-bye. Then I got off the phone and returned to the land of living on a bus tour through middle America.

That afternoon, I got off the bus for an event in St. Louis and ran into Kara.

"I've been trying to get in touch with you," she exclaimed. "To thank you for getting me this job! It was perfect timing when they called—I'd just graduated and was trying to figure out how I could best help the campaign. I figured I'd just be a volunteer, but this advance gig is awesome!"

I beamed happily, thrilled that it had all worked out according to my plan. That so rarely happened.

"That's great," I said sincerely.

I was considerably less thrilled a moment later when Kara gently informed me that Aaron would be at the event, as he had recently joined Wye's speechwriting team. That was definitely *not* supposed to happen. Aaron was supposed to be gone from my life forever. And now he was just popping up again? Hired willingly by this campaign, after all he'd done? Wye's people must not be aware that Aaron had been the source of several quotes damaging to RG over the previous months. Surely they wouldn't have hired him had they known. Would they have? Why hadn't I been consulted? Ugh. This was awful and annoying.

"Forget him," Kara advised. "It's a big staff. He can be avoided."

I hoped she was right. I tried to calm down. RG and Wye were doing a lot of joint campaigning at present, but it was a safe bet that they would split up to cover more ground later on in the summer. Until they did, I'd just have to deal with Aaron being around, as irritating and unfair as that was. At least I had Bob on my side, for the moment at least. I wondered if Aaron was still with Darlene.

"Well, that just sucks," I concluded.

"I'm sorry," Kara said sympathetically. "Aaron's a jerk and he deserves to be punished. And rest assured that those of us in charge of things like staff accommodations will do our part to help make that happen," she added wickedly.

I smiled. It was good to have someone like Kara on my side. Her walkie-talkie crackled.

"I'll be right there," she answered into it.

She rolled her eyes at how official she seemed all of a sudden, before making her way through the crowd. Could it be long before she was sporting an earpiece? Even if she acquired the equipment, I knew she'd never truly become one of the Tims.

The event went well, and though my stomach dropped when I spotted Aaron, I managed to distract myself and maintain a healthy distance. He must have known I was around, and that avoiding any interaction was his best option. His presence added another level of high stress to campaign existence, but there wasn't anything I could do about it. No matter what it took, I was determined to ignore him and all the ways he had hurt me, and channel my energy into the cause that was bigger than all of us.

The following morning, as we rolled up to the courthouse of a small town with a population of about two thousand people, I felt my stomach seize with cramps. Bob was walking by me when the first wave hit. He slid into the seat beside me.

"Are you okay?" he asked, with a fair amount of concern. For him, at least.

I tried to appear alluring, but a grimace wasn't my best look.

"Something's wrong with my stomach," I reported.

"Why don't you stay on the bus for this stop?" he offered helpfully.

I nodded. I needed some quiet time to work on the health care portion of the convention platform anyway, I justified to myself.

"I'll see if I can find some Pepto or something," Bob said.

His BlackBerry buzzed. He kissed my hand and got back up.

"I'll check on you in a bit," he promised.

He was already scrolling to his message as he walked off. Though I really enjoyed being with him, I had resisted letting things go too far between us. I couldn't tell if he was intrigued or turned off by my attitude. I was def-initely attracted to him—I just wanted to feel safe before I let myself fully commit. And nothing about him or our current situation seemed stable in any way.

As everyone got off the bus, I closed my eyes and tried to relax my stomach into a meditative, non-cramping state. It didn't work. And I knew that despite my inten-tions, I was now in too much pain to make any progress on the convention platform. I looked out the window to try to distract myself from the feeling that I was being knifed from the inside. There was the courthouse with an enormous crowd in front of an assembled stage. On the other side of the street was a row of small storefronts. I spotted a LACEY FAMILY DRUGSTORE sign and struggled to my feet. I knew Bob had to be with Wye and RG as the event was taking place, and I needed some sort of re-lief as soon as possible, so I decided to take matters into my own hands.

I passed a gaggle of press on my way across the street. There was always a group of them who cased the perimeter of the crowd to try to get quotes from the "average citizens" attending the event. They liked to pepper their stories with local color and scavenged for details that would provide it. There was always plenty to go around.

A few of the journalists glanced in my direction with searching-for-a-story expressions. I was walking a bit unsteadily. I wondered if they thought I might be drunk at nine o'clock in the morning. That could make for an interesting tidbit. I was in too much discomfort to combat any mistaken impressions.

I clutched my stomach as I reached for the drugstore door. Before I made contact, it swung open to reveal Charlie Lawton with a can of soda in hand. Good Lord, what was going on here? Why was my life all of a sudden becoming so small at the same time it was swelling onto a national stage? Before I could muse this phenomenon, an exquisitely brutal cramp attacked and I felt myself sinking to the ground.

"Samantha!" I heard Charlie say, as he reached to catch me.

I must have blocked out a lot of the pain, because the next thing I knew I was on a bed in a tiny little hospital room, that, judging from the muted crowd roars, seemed to be about a half mile from the courthouse. Charlie was beside me, talking to a doctor who looked about sixty years old. He had a potbelly and a competent air. He seemed surprised to see us, but not unprepared. A nurse stuck me in the arm while I wasn't looking.

"Ouch!" I protested.

"Just something for the pain, hon," she said soothingly.

Charlie and the doctor turned towards me. The doctor looked relaxed. Charlie appeared worried. Whether it was about me or the story he was missing at the courthouse remained unclear.

"What's going on in there?" the doctor asked me, motioning towards my abdomen.

I described the sudden onset of crippling cramps and spasms as best I could. The doctor nodded.

"I need you to stand up for a second, sweetheart," he instructed me.

I knew what this was about. He was going to make me come down hard on my heels to observe the result. It was a standard check for appendicitis that I'd read about. But when my heels hit the floor the pain didn't worsen. I wasn't even sure it could get any worse.

"Hmm," the doctor mused. "Now, is there any chance you could be pregnant?"

No, there definitely wasn't, thank goodness. But this was getting a little personal, particularly with Charlie standing right there.

"Um, no," I answered softly. I glanced shyly at Charlie, who was staring at me with real concern in his bespectacled eyes.

The doctor appeared to be deep in thought.

"I'm gonna do an ultrasound to check for cysts or ulcers. I just need to go dig up the equipment."

I nodded. According to my extensive, hypochondria-induced research, this seemed like the appropriate course of action. The doctor left the room.

"Is there anyone that you want me to get in touch with?" Charlie asked.

I passed him my BlackBerry, too preoccupied with my misery to verbally note the irony of my handing over the device that had gotten me in trouble to the person who had written up that trouble.

"My parents are in there under 'Joyce.' If you could just let them know I'm in the hospital, but tell them I'll call them later," I struggled to say. "And I need to send the memo that's in the drafts section to campaign headquarters by ten AM. The address is Feldman at wye-gary dot—"

I stopped as I caught Charlie's expression. What was I thinking? He was a journalist assigned to cover the race. He was supposed to be impartial. He certainly couldn't legally do any campaign work.

"Forget about that last thing," I said. "Just my parents, please. And then you should get back to the buses," I added. "They'll be leaving in the next hour."

I knew the schedule. The tour was slated to hit five more towns before nightfall. Should I ask him to let Bob know about my condition? Or RG? It wasn't as though either one of them could stay behind.

"I'll get a message to Senator Gary," Charlie assured me.

I flinched in pain and gratitude.

"You're going to be okay," Charlie said, putting his hand on my forehead.

It was an intimate gesture for two relative strangers. And coming from him, it might have triggered my neck rash had I been myself. I appreciated his attempts at comforting me, but all I could focus on was the searing pain in my abdomen. I must have groaned, because Charlie was all of a sudden looking around for the nurse. I grabbed his hand before he could take it away. He stopped searching

the space behind him and turned back to me. As another wave of pain went crashing through me, I squeezed his fingers way too hard.

"You really will be fine," he said confidently.

I closed my eyes and concentrated on my breathing, making it as shallow as possible to avoid troubling my protesting body. Charlie left when the doctor reappeared and conducted the ultrasound, which didn't reveal anything out of the ordinary. The doctor looked thoughtful.

"I'm gonna give you something more for the pain that might knock you out for a little while," he informed me. "I need to double-check some things, but I've got a theory on what we're dealing with here."

I wanted to ask questions, but I didn't feel like I could talk anymore. I had to focus completely on bracing myself for the punishing spasms. The nurse came back in and gave me another shot. I closed my eyes and waited for it to kick in.


The next thing I knew it was the middle of the night. It took me a minute to fully wake up and remember where I was. My stomach still hurt, but not as horribly. And my throat felt parched. Would anyone hear me if I called out?

"Hello?" I whispered.

Someone stirred in a nearby chair.

"Sammy?" a familiar voice responded.

"Bob? Aaron?"

Who was that? I felt like I knew, but my brain was sluggish and slow to cooperate.

"It's Charlie," the voice said, from a closer vantage point.

Of course, Charlie Lawton. He had been by the drugstore. He'd taken me here.

"What do you need?" He stood above me.

He wasn't wearing his glasses and his hair looked a little rumpled. After he got me some water, he explained that my parents had been informed along with RG and the rest of the staff. The buses had moved on and everyone was spending the night in Jefferson City, but they all wanted updates on my progress.

"Why are you still here?" I asked, surprised.

I was glad that he was, but it didn't make any sense. He had no allegiance to me. And more importantly, he had a job to do elsewhere.

"I gave my word to your mother," he replied.

That explained it. My mother could pose a formidable force on the phone. But I didn't want to be responsible for Charlie jeopardizing his job.

"Well, you're not obligated to my mother anymore," I said. "You should go."

"I'd like to stay, if it's all the same to you," he replied.

"What are you telling the *Post*?" I challenged.

"That I'm working on a very compelling story. Which I am," he replied. "They have a more senior guy assigned to Wye who'll be covering all the joint appearances for the next three days anyway. But they don't have anyone working on an in-depth article about the influence Senator Gary is gaining over the direction of the governor's health care policies."

Was he trying to take advantage of me when I was still drugged? That didn't seem very honorable.

"I don't think I'm prepared to be your informant on that," I replied.

"That's fine, I have other sources," he answered. "I just need the time. And you're giving me that."

So then he wasn't really worried about me at all. Fine. If that's the way he wanted it. I was just deciding that I wouldn't talk to him for the rest of the night when I felt his cool hand on my forehead.

"Are you still in pain?" he asked. "Hold on a minute and I'll get the nurse."

I didn't want him to take his hand away, but I stayed quiet and let him leave.

The next morning, the doctor informed me I was suffering from irritable bowel syndrome, triggered by too much stress. I knew all about irritable bowel syndrome and had often prayed that I would never get it, largely because of the name. As if the condition wasn't bad enough, doctors had to add to the pain by calling it something embarrassing. It seemed unnecessarily cruel. I wished Charlie hadn't been in the room to hear the diagnosis.

"Unfortunately, there's no real cure for irritable bowel syndrome," the doctor continued. "You just have to reduce the stress in your life, since that's the main cause of irritable bowel syndrome. The thing about irritable bowel syndrome—"

"Can we please call it something else?" I interrupted irritably.

The doctor looked surprised. Charlie smiled.

"I mean, I've heard it referred to as IBS," I continued. "Which is much shorter."

It was true. It was an abbreviation that truly abbreviated.

"Okay," the doctor replied. "So you've got IBS and your colon is real agitated. I'd like to start you on an antispasmodic drug and keep you another night to make sure it does the trick. I can release you tomorrow as long as you promise to take it easy."

"Is it safe for her to be discharged so soon?" Charlie asked.

So soon? I would have spent two whole nights in the hospital. What, did Charlie just want some more time to work on his article in peace? Or was he possibly genuinely concerned?

The doctor assured him that it was safe. We spent the rest of that day and night in the same room, with me wandering in and out of restless sleep. Charlie kept me supplied with water and monitored my pain level, but mainly spent his time on his laptop in the corner chair by the window. For a second, I wondered how I looked, but dozed off again before I could make a move for a bathroom mirror. Through the earmuffs of a medicated dream, I heard the nurse and Charlie discussing how sleep was the best thing for me.

The following day unfolded in a similar vein, though with my waking hours gradually gaining on my sleeping ones. And thankfully, the antispasmodic began to work. So by 6:00 that evening, I'd been discharged and Charlie and I were speeding towards Kansas City in a rental car to meet up with the group. It was a five-hour drive, though the caravan of buses had taken a winding, circuitous route that had stretched it into two days. We took a more direct path, bypassing all the small towns as we whizzed down the highway, making up for lost time and ground to the tune of Led Zeppelin's greatest hits. Apparently, Charlie always traveled with a copy.

Two hours from Kansas City, I awoke from a fitful nap and watched the darkness pouring past the window. For the first time in what felt like the longest thirty-five hours of my life, I had an urge to check my BlackBerry and cell phone. I found my cell turned off in my bag.

"Do you still have my BlackBerry?" I asked Charlie.

He removed it from his jacket pocket and turned it over to me.

"It smells like oranges," he commented.

It did? I took a sniff. There *was* a slight tinge of

orange about the otherwise plasticy odor. This stumped me until I remembered that I'd stored an orange in my bag on the bus two days earlier. I imagined it had started to go bad by now.

I held my BlackBerry away from me and sniffed again. I couldn't make out anything. Charlie only could have noticed the orange scent if he'd held it right up close to his nose. Wasn't that a weird thing to do? Why would he have done it? Had he been wondering what I smelled like up close and given in to a little detective work? When he'd smelled the orange had he imagined my natural scent to be sweet and exotic—the aroma of a lady of the orange groves?

Or had he been trying to read my BlackBerry without his glasses on so he'd had to hold it very close to his face? I cast an accusatory glance in his direction, but he didn't seem to notice.

"Did you read any of my messages?" I asked suspiciously.

He *was* a reporter, after all. There were plenty of e-mails on there that would prove very interesting to a journalist covering the campaign.

"Do you really think I would do such a thing?" he asked.

He didn't look hurt so much as surprised. Which was enough to shame me into apologizing.

"Sorry, the drugs must be making me paranoid."

He smiled, which made me feel a lot better.

I buried myself in my BlackBerry for the next half hour. I had over thirty messages. Many of them were regarding my latest adventure. The four from Bob described the general progression that they took.

First off:

To: Samantha Joyce [srjoyce@wye-gary.com]
From: Bob Espin [bespin@kstreetgroup.com]
Subject: where r u?
Text: got the pepto. bus about to push off. r u close? i can stall them for a bit. talk to me.

Then:

To: Samantha Joyce [srjoyce@wye-gary.com]
From: Bob Espin [bespin@kstreetgroup.com]
Subject: re: where r u?
Text: can't stall anymore. r u ok?

About forty minutes later:

To: Samantha Joyce [srjoyce@wye-gary.com]
From: Bob Espin [bespin@kstreetgroup.com]
Subject: re: where r u?
Text: there's a rumor you're at the hospital?!?!?!! with a post reporter? what's happening? does that town even have a doctor? don't let them harvest your organs.

And then:

> To: Samantha Joyce [srjoyce@wye-gary.com]
> From: Bob Espin [bespin@kstreetgroup.com]
> Subject: raise your hand if you have irritable bowels
> Text: sorry to hear the news. let me know if you need to be rescued. write when you can. we'll be a'waitin'. —b.

The messages from Mark, Mona, and Kara were slightly more heartfelt, but followed a similar trajectory. It was funny reading them all at once. I felt as though I was enjoying a short story of my last two days—all laid out for me from a variety of viewpoints. And though I wished everyone hadn't been informed of my particular syndrome, it was nice to know they cared. There was one brief, sweet message from RG. And there was even one from Agent Roberts, asking if I needed any assistance rejoining the caravan. Maybe he was coming around on me. Or maybe it just made him nervous that I wasn't right under his nose where he could watch me.

I was eager to get back to the crew. It didn't occur to me to take any more time off than was absolutely necessary, no matter what the doctor said. Taking it easy just wasn't an option. I'd stay on my medication and try to stay as calm as possible, but I would work. There was too much work to be done not to.

"How are you feeling?" Charlie asked me.

"Good," I responded decisively. "Though I'm a little embarrassed about my complete inability to handle stress."

"I wouldn't look at it that way," he replied. "You've been thrown into extraordinary circumstances. You obviously internalize the stress, which isn't healthy, but neither is acting it out and yelling at everyone, which is the way so many other people on this campaign handle it. You're just too nice for that."

"And I've got the spastic colon to prove it," I answered.

Charlie smiled. I leaned back and watched him drive. He had an interesting manner about him even behind the wheel—he seemed completely in control but also a little too curious about the other vehicles on the road. He observed constantly, in an intelligent, absorbent way. I wondered what he was thinking.

"Do you like working for the paper?" I asked.

He paused for a few moments, which I liked. I never appreciated feeling like I was getting canned, practiced answers, even when I knew I had asked a question that the person probably had already responded to a million times. I enjoyed getting the sense that someone was sharing some original thoughts with me. Charlie provided that.

"I don't like it, but it's good for me," he answered. "I like finding stories, and researching them, and writing them up. I like getting to the bottom of things. But I suppose I had this idealistic notion that I'd be working for people whose only agenda was to break the truths of the world to their readers. I haven't found that to be the case. I know I was naïve. But the agendas get me down."

I took a minute to let everything he'd said fully resound with me.

"Would you prefer to be doing something else?" I asked.

"No," he answered. "I'd prefer to change what I'm already doing while continuing to do it. Does that make sense?"

It did make sense to me. And it provided proof that, like me, he was still committed to a basic idealism. I respected him for trying to make things better. And his words made me realize that our jobs weren't all that different after all.

Our conversation became more lighthearted in tone, but the subtext undercurrents remained deep. I really liked talking to Charlie. He was proving to be a fascinating mixture of relatable and intriguing, as the things he said managed to resonate and stimulate at the same time. I had gotten accustomed to feeling one way or the other with my conversational partners. I had grown used to compromising. It was nice to feel for once like I didn't have to settle for something less than I desired, even if it was only for a few hours, hurtling in a rented Ford Taurus down the dark highways of Missouri.

We pulled into the hotel around 11:00. Journalists

were staying on a different floor than the staff, so we parted ways in the elevator.

"Thanks again," I said sincerely, as the doors opened onto his level.

"Anytime," he smiled.

"Well, actually, this will hopefully just be a one-time breakdown," I said, indicating my stomach area.

He laughed. The doors closed on his "see you around," and I rode the rest of the way to my floor wishing that I'd had the time to say something in return.

Bob was waiting for me in my room. He'd arranged for me to have one all to myself, which was a lavish exception to the strict guidelines the campaign budget minders followed.

"You okay, Shorty?" he asked as he gently took me in his arms.

I'd objected to this nickname for me the first time Bob had used it because a) I wasn't short; and b) "Shorty" took no less time to say than "Sammy" (harkening back to the GSW/bravo to your location debate). Bob had noted my protests and then asked me if I'd listened to any rap or hip-hop music in the last five years. I shut up after that and decided that, to be cool, it was in my best interest to go along with the nickname. Maybe it gave me street cred. Regardless, I now sort of liked it. Bob could be very persuasive.

"Yeah, I'm good, thanks," I answered. "I'm glad to be back."

He lay down beside me on the bed and kissed me.

"We're glad to have you."

I closed my eyes and let him lie there. He ended up staying the night, just resting beside me. I didn't sleep as well as he did. I couldn't seem to manage it once I realized as I lay there that I wished I was still in the car with Charlie. Or in the hospital room with Charlie. Really, wherever Charlie was. I buried this thought when Bob took my hand in his sleep. I was dating Bob. I was happy to be dating Bob. I repeated this until I fell asleep and by dawn, I'd chalked the whole Charlie-yearning thing up to a post-trauma delusion and felt like I was back on track.

Which was a good place to be, because the track slowed down for no one. The bus tour continued across the country, parading through hundreds of towns and cities, past strip malls and pastures, by sign-wielding multitudes of people and desolate stretches of tar and asphalt. It swept on, caught up in its gathering momentum, in rain, heat, wind, and during an environmental event in St. Mary, Montana—near the melting mountain passes of Glacier National Park—there was even some hail. One bored and clever reporter used the opportunity to write up the event in terms of a "Hail Mary pass."

Even when the buses stopped, the motion never did. We split up from Wye, reunited, branched off again, and joined forces once more—in an always-choreographed-at-the-last-minute dance for the masses. RG traveled to California, Oregon, Washington, Idaho, Illinois, and

Florida in half a week. Clean clothes and bagless eyes and inner peace became relics of an era too far gone in the rearview mirror to even make out. In this case, the object was not closer than it appeared.

I paced myself alongside the rest—pretending that Aaron's frequent presence didn't bother me and operating in a heightened state of autopilot, determined to do my best without giving myself the breathing space necessary to accomplish the goal. There was no air of compromise, but it was implicit in the lifestyle. All we could do was continue the sprint, hoping against any reasonable hope that the finish line might get moved a little closer. Yet even in the midst of this, I was happy to discover that I'd managed to attain a better perspective on the craziness of the campaign. My hospital time off had forced me to take a needed step back and observe the larger picture. And as a result, I was able to feel less overwhelmed and more attuned to how all the fascinatingly frenzied parts fit into a more integrative whole. I thus became a better student of the experience.

RG had always been a workaholic, and now he had a mission worthy of his stamina. I still interacted with him on a daily basis and it seemed to me that he had transformed along with the process. He spoke more powerfully because the campaign's need for persuasive speaking infused him with a greater ability to deliver. He shook more hands because there were larger, more excited crowds than any he'd ever experienced before. He answered more questions, held more interviews, and offered more opinions—all because these things were asked of him. In these ways and others, he seemed to feast off the demands of this new existence, and somehow strengthen in the midst of chaos.

Jenny and the boys joined him as much as they could, but it was difficult for anyone to keep up with his velocity. I wondered from time to time about Jenny, as I watched her on stage with RG, or near the front of the bus—trying to listen to a briefing as she pleaded with Jack and Jeffrey to stop licking the fuzz off the seats. She seemed happy and supportive enough; but I wondered if she wished she could be more involved, or less. I wondered if she questioned the turn her life had suddenly taken, without time for too much discussion. Is this the path she would have chosen had she had more perfect information?

Governor Wye's staff continued to rule the greater roost, though they made a top-down effort to integrate us into the team. Notwithstanding this effort, there was a hovering superiority I sensed about some of the individual Wye staffers—as if they were unreasonably proud of the fact that they'd been a part of this journey for far longer and considered us an annoying group of neophyte interlopers. Granted, this was not the vibe from everyone, but a little dose of it went a long way. It was uncomfortably reminiscent of the Bramen dynamic, and it irked me that Aaron was once again involved.

Despite this unspoken tension between the staffs, Wye and RG appeared to click along as smoothly as they had at that first joint appearance in Ohio. When I watched the two of them together, I discerned a genuine partnership. Though I suspected that Wye went to great lengths to suppress natural competitive feelings and embrace the reality that RG was on his team to win for both of them, and for the greater cause.

The careful balance of their relationship became jeopardized by a series of midsummer articles revealing the extent of RG's influence on the tone and direction of the campaign. Rather than billed as a characteristic of a powerful partnership, it was suggested that this influence indicated that it was RG who was the real force behind the growing appeal of the ticket.

The spate of stories had been kicked off by Charlie's piece about how Wye had adopted all of RG's major health care policies and initiatives since the two of them had hooked up. It quoted one anonymous source as saying, "Health care issues haven't ever been his [Wye's] strong suit. He's happy to learn as much as possible from Gary and will definitely take his cues from him in terms of the platform." I had found this quote particularly shocking, since I had read it once before—in an e-mail sent to my BlackBerry from Susan Lambert, a health care policy advisor to Greg Saxert, senator from Wye's home state of Louisiana. Early on, after my very first plane cabin conversation with Wye, I had e-mailed her to ask about Wye's record and inclinations on health care. I'd worked with Susan before on various bills, and we'd stayed friendly. She'd been very forthcoming with information about Wye. I knew that her boss was jealous of the governor, but I also knew that Susan was very astute, and I trusted her assessments.

Had Susan sent that e-mail along to anyone else? Or had I been correct to suspect Charlie might have read my BlackBerry? Though Charlie was permanently assigned to cover RG, we had only interacted sporadically, as he always rode in the press bus and both of us were gaspingly busy. Plus, I'd seen him strolling hand in hand with Veronica outside a hotel in Carson City the week after our hospital adventure. I'd found that annoying. Though I'd successfully suppressed any recovering-from-IBS delusions that I'd harbored feelings for him, I'd still hoped he would have recognized by now that he deserved far better than her. The way she had leaned into him in such a conspiratorial and possessive way had sickened me.

The morning that Charlie's article appeared, I debated what to do. In one small way, the article was great for RG, as it accurately described the considerable influence he was wielding within the campaign on certain areas—namely health care and environmental and foreign policy. But in a larger way, it was unfortunate for him and the campaign as a whole, since it sowed possible dissension between RG and Wye, which was the last thing we needed.

On the surface, Wye treated the whole incident as a hilarious joke. In the hold room for an event in Milwaukee, where he and RG were talking and picking from a tray of raw vegetables, he teased RG loud enough for all the nearby staff to hear.

"I think I'll have a red pepper. But only if you like peppers, Robert. Do you approve of peppers? I'm waiting for your go-ahead."

The two of them guffawed. To a trained ear, their laughter sounded slightly strained, but it was a valiant effort. Bob and I had been talking when we'd stopped to overhear.

"We got trouble," he murmured, before entering the room to intervene.

I watched him go with a swell of pride at how good he was at his job. I knew we weren't the perfect match, but having Bob on the scene added an extra personal thrill to what was already a mind-boggling adventure. He was a big shot on the campaign, revered for his expertise and strategic brilliance. And he was with me. I didn't want to be superficial, but there was a part of me that found it all very exciting.

I listened for a moment as Bob made an easy joke and got them talking animatedly about another topic. And then I sought out Charlie. After negotiating the obstacle course of roped-off areas and clusters of Secret Service agents, I headed for the back to where the journalists often congregated. But before I could make it out the door, Aaron stepped in my path.

"Sammy," he said meaningfully, putting a strong hand on my arm.

I didn't recoil, but I certainly didn't melt. I willed myself to stay calm.

"Hello, Aaron," I said evenly. "What do you want?"

He smiled in a slightly injured way, apparently unaware that I now found him far more disingenuous than handsome.

"Well, I'd like us to be friends," he said. "I mean, we're going to run into each other a lot. And we're both grown-ups—"

"Are we?" I interrupted pointedly.

I thought about taking him to task for all the damaging "unnamed source" quotes that I now knew he was responsible for. I thought about yelling at him for all the ways he had betrayed me. But I decided not to. I didn't want to give him the satisfaction of thinking I cared enough about him anymore to still be angry.

"Yeah, okay, Aaron, we're both grown-ups. And everything's fine. Feel better?"

"Actually, Sammy, I really have some things I'd like to—"

He was interrupted by his ringing phone. He threw me an apologetic glance as he fished it out of his pocket.

"Sorry, hold on just a sec. Aaron Driver," he said into the receiver.

A look of extreme annoyance washed over his face.

"No, I am *not* interested in hearing about your new

long-distance rates. For the hundredth time, *stop* calling this number!" he shouted as he slammed his phone shut.

I watched him try to regain his composure.

"Telemarketer?" I asked innocently.

"They won't stop calling!" Aaron replied. "I don't know how they got this number, but my voicemail has been completely filled for the last three weeks with stupid sales pitches. No one else can get through!"

"Wow, that's really terrible," I said, with extreme secret satisfaction.

I'd have to thank Zelda later.

"Sorry. I didn't mean to get so angry, but I just haven't gotten much sleep," Aaron explained, trying to excuse his previously peevish tone. "For some reason, I keep getting hotel rooms next to noisy generators or ice machines or construction or *something*."

And I had Kara to thank for that. My ladies were looking out for me.

"But anyway, enough about me," Aaron continued in a much smoother tone. "I just want you to know that I still care about you and I hope we can get along."

"Yeah, sure," I replied indifferently. "I know what you are now, so there won't be any more nasty surprises. I can count on you to lie and cheat and plant nasty quotes. And you can count on me to not have time for that anymore. I've got to run."

I left Aaron looking like he had more to say. I was happy that I hadn't let him get to me. As I pushed through the door into the bright sunshine outside, I looked around for Charlie and soon spotted him pacing while he talked on his cell phone. His pacing didn't appear anxiety-induced; it seemed meditative. I studied its hypnotizing rhythm until he got off the phone and turned in my direction. I strode towards him through the sunlight.

"Hey there," he said kindly.

He shaded his glasses from the sun. Had he always been that tall, or was his shadow creating some sort of illusion?

"How are you feeling?"

"Oh, fine," I answered dismissively. "Listen, did you get that quote in your article from a message in my BlackBerry?"

"No," he replied, without hesitation.

It wasn't too quick an answer, or too defensive of one—it was simple and direct. And I immediately believed him. It occurred to me that it was objectively insane to do so, but I couldn't help it. He just radiated something pure that I couldn't ignore.

"Okay," I said, in an accepting tone. "Do you mind telling me where you did get that quote then?"

Charlie looked at me for a moment.

"I wish I could," he said sincerely. "But I can't reveal my sources."

Yeah, I'd always heard things along those lines. But come on, not even to me? Not even to completely eliminate any suspicions that might be lingering somewhere in my subconscious? Please?

He looked pretty resolved.

"What about if I guessed it? Could you just nod yes or no?"

He smiled.

"I'm afraid not," he replied. "But I promise I didn't get it from your BlackBerry. I told you before that I didn't read it. But I do miss it and its citrusy smell. It's the closest thing I've had to fresh fruit in weeks."

I scanned him quickly for any telltale signs of scurvy. Lots of people didn't realize that it was still possible to contract that disease. I'd suspected myself of having come down with it four or five times in the past two years. But Charlie looked pretty healthy to me.

"All right," I continued. "I suppose I'm going to believe you, scurvy or no."

"I appreciate it," he replied.

I held his gaze for a moment longer, until my buzzing BlackBerry diverted my attention.

To: Samantha Joyce [srjoyce@wye-gary.com]
From: Bob Espin [bespin@kstreetgroup.com]
Subject: off to another hospital?
Text: are your bowels getting irritable again? i've uncovered a six-pack of milwaukee's best. report back immediately for rations. tonight we drink the beast.

I smiled and looked up to find Charlie watching me.

"Good message?" he asked.

I shrugged. "It'll do."

He continued looking at me.

"I better get back," I said, indicating the door to the backstage area behind me.

"All right. See you around," he replied.

Part of me wished that he would reach out his hand and touch my forehead again, but he didn't. As I walked away, I decided to eat a lot more oranges. Suddenly, I wanted to smell like them.

## Surviving Ping-Pong

THIRTY-SIX STATES AND four weeks after my hospital stay, the campaign arrived in Miami for the national convention. One major poll indicated that the Wye–Gary ticket was just barely ahead of the opposition, while another one claimed we were just barely behind. It seemed safe to assume that the election was still up for grabs.

Governor Brancy had chosen Senator Blake Wallock of South Dakota as his running mate. Wallock had served fifteen years in the Senate, and gave off the air of a grizzled and competent veteran. So far, he and Brancy seemed to be successfully presenting a brand-new face to their discredited party. The current administration was furious at their distancing and consequently stingy about any support, which suited Brancy and Wallock just fine. As I watched their ticket take off, I worried that the Pile team might do something horrendous in the upcoming months, if only in a rage against their growing irrelevance. The country didn't feel safe in their hands. But there wasn't time for such free-floating anxiety. There was only a future to rush towards, as quickly as it was slamming into us.

Our time at the convention was brief and breathless. We arrived a few hours before RG was to give his speech. I had spent the previous days reviewing the section of his address on health care initiatives for the "new America," triple-checking all the numbers and making sure the positions had been adequately and eloquently explained. Luckily RG knew how to balance the specifics with the overall message. If I'd been left with the speech section in a vacuum, I worried that I might emerge with a wonkish and boring piece. But working within his already-set parameters, I felt more confident about what I could contribute.

RG and I were reviewing my minimal changes in his hotel room, with Jenny listening and offering her suggestions, when Joe Noon entered.

"Wye's team wants a look at your final draft again before tonight," he reported. "They're putting the finishing touches on his speech and just want to make sure there's not too much overlap."

RG nodded.

"Fine, fine," he said.

He remained laser-focused on the task at hand.

"Is there a copy I can give them now?" Joe asked.

RG indicated one on the table.

"It's not final, but it's close," he specified.

I watched Joe pick up the copy and walk back over to the door. As he held the door open and turned back to say something else to RG, I spotted Aaron waiting in the hallway. Our eyes locked before I deliberately averted my gaze back to the marked-up pages in my lap.

Aaron and I had continued to run into each other, but I'd done my best to avoid much more direct interaction. Not long ago, I'd gotten off the elevator on the wrong floor and observed a volunteer named Laurie leaving his hotel room early in the morning. They hadn't seen me as they'd kissed good-bye. I'd stepped back into the elevator and prayed to the God of Rapidly-Closing Doors to help me out. Thankfully, he had.

I'd also seen Aaron with Darlene smoking in the courtyard of a hotel in Cedar Rapids, Iowa, from the window of my room. And I felt sure there were others. I was occasionally tempted to check his voicemail messages out of curiosity, but managed to resist these urges. I knew that I didn't really care. Enough time had passed. I just remained surprised that I had so completely misjudged him. Even now, the sight of him made me grimace and shake my head.

Joe Noon left and RG and I returned to the task at hand. He didn't go for all of my proposed revisions, but he seemed pleased with my work. I could tell he was nervous for his speech by the way he kept listing things off on his fingers. That was a move he reserved for his more anxious preparations. Jenny gave him a shoulder massage as she made a phrase-change suggestion in the closing paragraph. I knew that Bob was coming in to review the speech and make last-minute suggestions, so I began gathering my things together. Should I say anything encouraging to RG? Would I see him again before his speech? I couldn't be sure.

"Good luck, sir, I know you're going to be inspiring," I said.

He looked at me, but didn't smile. Jenny did, which I appreciated.

"Thanks," he replied. "You've been doing a great job."

That was enough to keep me going. I made my way to the door.

"Oh, and Samantha," he said.

I turned with a questioning look. Was there more to go over?

"Yes, sir?"

"Good move dumping that speechwriter guy. He didn't deserve you."

He immediately looked back down at his papers at the same time that Bob opened the door, so I didn't have a chance to respond. Bob squeezed my hand surreptitiously as he passed and I found myself in the hallway, contemplating the scope of RG's observational powers. Aaron and I had broken up over eight months ago, and even when Aaron and I had been dating, RG had never given a hint that he paid any attention to my personal life. And yet on one of the most important days of his political career, when he was intensely focused on the

speech he was supposed to give in prime time to tens of millions of Americans, he'd noticed that I'd glanced at Aaron and felt uncomfortable. And he'd done something about it. At this moment, I felt like I might possibly devote the rest of my life to working for him.

Later that evening, in a holding room backstage, I sat with Mark and Mona as we watched RG deliver his convention speech. We followed along using Xeroxed copies of the text. I had to keep reminding myself to breathe. Over the previous few months, I'd grown accustomed to watching RG speak off the cuff to more informal audiences waving personalized signs, and it was odd to see the organized, uniform convention crowd clapping in coordination. But despite the inevitably scripted feeling of the event, I could sense that RG was connecting with the audience, both within the enormous room and beyond. As we heard his words resonate throughout the convention hall while they were simultaneously broadcast from the television before us, I imagined all the people throughout the country who were listening at this very moment. And I felt a powerful surge of pride. We had all come so far.

RG finished strong, as usual. I released a little bit of my nervousness as I watched the balloons and confetti coming down on RG, Jenny, and the boys, who were waving energetically to the cheering crowd.

The next evening I found myself backstage again, waiting for Governor Wye to deliver his speech accepting the party's nomination. I kept my distance from the room where Aaron was feeding last-minute changes to the convention staffers manning the TelePrompTers. RG and Jenny were in a holding room nearby, waiting to watch the speech and then join the Wyes on stage. Kara ran by with a friendly wave. She was doing advance for some delegates' events, before taking off that evening to prep our upcoming swing through South Carolina. She and I had managed to grab a few minutes here and there to catch up once a week or so, and stayed in steady BlackBerry contact. She'd finally joined the BlackBerry team when she'd signed onto the campaign. I found that her presence, both physical and in cyberspace, helped me feel more centered and in control.

Governor Wye stuck his head out of his holding room and yelled for a diet soda. He looked at me when he shouted the request, but I made no move to accommodate it. My response surprised me a little bit, but that just wasn't my job. Wye disappeared back in the room as various aides scurried towards the soda stashes. Would I have leapt into action had it been RG demanding the soda? I doubted RG would have gone about it that way.

Bob emerged from the room a few minutes later, looking a little stressed. He winked when he saw me and hurried down the hallway. I didn't get the feeling that anything was wrong, just that the prespeech tension had ratcheted past a comfort point.

Soon after, Fiona Wye introduced her husband and kissed him as he took the podium. I watched from a van-

tage point where I could see the back of Wye in person
and the front of him on an enormous TV screen in the
convention hall. The crowd took ten minutes to quiet
down enough for him to speak, which was a ridiculously
long time. As he began his address, I heard commotion
in the control room. I watched Wye's face on the TV
screen. He looked momentarily alarmed before regain-
ing his composure. What was going on? I glanced at his
back as he started using his hands to gesticulate during
his opening lines. And then I saw it. The TelePrompTers
were blank. They were supposed to be transparent, but
have words scrolling down them that only Wye could
see. The monitor directly across from him was dark, as
well. He didn't have his speech. And he was live on national television.

I ran over to the control room, where Aaron was
screaming at the staffers who were frantically punch-
ing things into their keyboards. No one seemed to
know what the problem could be. No one seemed capable of fixing it. Had they just blown a fuse? Wasn't
there a back-up generator or something? The timing
seemed too terribly perfect for it to be an accident, but
then again, I'd seen big things go wrong at the worst
times before.

I felt powerless and in the way, so I moved back to the
TV monitor to see how Wye was coping with the situation. He had a hard copy of his speech on the podium,
thank goodness, and he seemed to either know a lot of it

by heart or be successfully making things up as he went along. The crowd was responding well to his words, and didn't seem to notice that anything had gone awry.

He spoke this way for fifty-two minutes. The abused staffers in the control room never managed to get his speech back on track. As Wye was concluding, Aaron stepped up next to me.

"That was a disaster," he said bitterly.

I looked at him in surprise. In my opinion, Wye had actually done a great job. I said as much to Aaron, in as dismissive a tone as possible.

"Why do you say that anyway?" I added.

Though I wanted to just completely blow him off, I was intrigued.

"Did you read the speech he was supposed to give?" he asked. "It was amazing. He forgot some of the most brilliant parts."

I felt like gagging. I could tell from Aaron's tone that "the most brilliant parts" referred to passages he himself had written. His opinion of himself was sickening. I couldn't bite my tongue.

"You mean the stuff you worked on?" I asked.

He seemed relieved that someone could understand.

"I *slaved* over that thing. It was amazing," he declared.

I shook my head in disgust.

"You should at least pretend to make an effort to get over yourself," I advised.

He looked at me in astonishment, before his face tightened into a retaliatory mask.

"You're one to talk. How's Bob Espin in bed?" he hissed. "Worth the prestige and salary bumps?"

I walked away to prevent myself from using my pepper spray on him. And I suddenly realized how completely exhausted I was. From the campaign, from dealing with Aaron, from stressing about not letting myself get too stressed. I didn't want to end up back in the hospital. I needed a rest. So while everyone around me was starting to buzz off to various parties, I found a shuttle to take me back to the hotel.

Liza called me along the way to tell me how great everything had looked on TV.

"Are you sniffling?" I asked.

I'd heard crying in her voice.

"Scooter and I broke up," she confirmed. "But I'm okay."

"What happened?" I inquired.

"He was sleeping with the pastry chef at his restaurant," she sobbed.

I'd met that pastry chef. He was six foot five and his name was François, which had struck me as both clichéd and somewhat treacherous to pronounce. Ouch. That was rough.

"Oh Liza, I'm sorry."

"Thanks," she sniffled.

"At least it wasn't Sandra," I offered after a pause.

Sandra was the trampy seating hostess that Liza had been anxious about.

"Yeah, I guess," she agreed.

I did feel bad for Liza. She and Scooter had lasted quite a while, for her at least. I decided to send her a cookie basket as soon as we got off the phone. Until then, I distracted her with my tales from behind the scenes. She swore she couldn't tell that anything had been wrong with Wye's speech, which was good. And she flew into a rage over Aaron's behavior.

"Give me his number," she commanded.

I declined. Zelda was already torturing him enough.

"He's pathetic," Liza pronounced, spitting out the words.

That was true. And it was depressing that I'd ever had anything to do with him. He was truly horrible. But I decided not to think about it anymore. My shuttle was pulling up to the hotel.

"Are you going to be okay?" I asked.

"Yeah." She sighed. "At least the Red Sox are playing well. I really think this might be their year to win it."

"Uh-huh."

"Call me tomorrow?"

I promised that I would.


After the convention, we flew with Wye and his crew to New York, where we bused through a couple of upstate towns. At our first stop in Champlain, on the border between New York and Canada, I was startled to spot Alfred Jackman in front of the stage. He was all dressed up in a suit and tie, marveling at the crowd around him and playing with the rope that had been strung up as a flimsy barrier. Wye and RG were still in their hold, so I had a little bit of time. I made my way over to him.

"Samantha!" he exclaimed, with a delighted twinkle in his eye.

I gave him a hug and surreptitiously checked his pupils. They seemed fairly normal-sized.

"What are you doing here?" I asked him.

We were a long way from Ohio.

"Oh, I moved to Canada!" he proclaimed. "Just across the border," he clarified, indicating somewhere behind him.

"What?" I replied in surprise. "Really?"

"Oh yes," he answered. "It makes everything so much easier. I save a bundle on all the drugs I need. The Lipitor, the Nexium, the ganj—"

"Yeah, okay," I interrupted him.

Were there any reporters listening? There always were.

"So that's great!" I continued, eager to change the subject. "Did you just cross over for this event?"

"Uh-huh." He nodded happily. "I was hoping I'd get to see you again! And I got dressed up so I'd be sure to fit in this time."

That really was very sweet. And he seemed sober, as far as I could tell. I smiled at him. He seemed to have come alone. Did anyone ever look after him?

"Are you comfortable standing?" I asked him, with some concern. "I could get a chair for you or something."

He patted my hand.

"You don't worry about me. But let me know if I can do anything to help. I can tell people firsthand what good folks you and your boss are, you know."

Oh, I knew. And that's what I was afraid of. I knew he didn't mean it as a threat, but it felt a little like one. I was happy to see him, but I prayed he'd keep mainly to himself, far away from the cameras. He was entirely too open for comfort. Maybe I should just stay with him to manage the situation.

We exchanged contact information and I promised to send him a signed bumper sticker. And then we both watched as RG and Wye bounded onto the stage to the blaring tune of their latest campaign song. Alfred Jackman's face lit up and he cheered wildly along with the rest of the crowd. As I watched his wizened head bopping along to the beat, I felt my own spirits lift. Alfred Jackman was trouble, but the kind of trouble that brought a smile to my face.

Forty-five minutes later, I climbed back onto the campaign bus, feeling happy and relieved to have escaped without incident. I spent the rest of the day fighting off motion sickness and who knew what other kind of maladies as I reviewed Brancy's latest statements on health care and tried to pick apart his policy in time for the upcoming debate. The established formula for such a process was to attach real-world consequences to his plan proposals. As in, "under Brancy's misguided plan, an uninsured family of four living on minimum wage would pay twice as much for emergency care as a family making over a hundred thousand dollars a year." And it would be even better if the uninsured family of four were named. Until the trend changed, the name of the game was individual examples and personal testimonials. I had always considered it a cheap and cheesy process, until I had actually spent time talking to uninsured families of four facing tough times. Now I thought of these people as I did my part to help provide them with better chances.

Early evening, we pulled in to Madison Square Garden for a massive fund-raiser. The affair was star-studded, but tragically, Steve Martin-less. I wasn't needed at the event and retired to my hotel room early, where I called my parents for the first time in two weeks.

"You're alive!" my dad exclaimed.

My mom picked up the extension.

"We've been looking for you everywhere, but we haven't seen you on C-SPAN," she reported.

"Yeah, the press isn't too focused on me," I responded. "They tend to waste all their energy on the presidential ticket I'm working for."

"Do they know you were in the hospital? That's a compelling human interest story about the sacrifices campaign staff members make," my mom suggested seriously. "Political campaigns need to be humanized if we're ever going to get young people invested in them."

My mom taught a course at her college about young America's disillusionment with politics.

"How are you feeling?" my dad asked.

"Pretty good," I responded honestly.

"What's your gut feeling about the race?" my mom inquired, before adding that maybe she should have phrased that differently.

My gut still felt a bit delicate. But I knew what she meant. Did I think Wye and RG were going to win? My immediate impulse was to say yes. But did I? I thought we deserved to win. I thought there was a good chance. But I really didn't know.

"I'm not sure—it's still so close," I said. "But I really hope we can pull it off."

I hoped it with everything inside me.

"What have you guys been up to?" I continued. "Is there anything new?"

"We decided to start getting the Internet after all," my mom said in response. "And Tivo. Without them, we were missing too much campaign coverage, and I was bloody well sick of feeling out of the loop. Now I feel like we can stay on top of everything."

"She likes reading all the blogs," my dad reported.

I did, too. And I secretly suspected that I myself would be a fantastic blogger, though I'd have to get past the ickiness of the name. Maybe I could call myself something else. After a few more minutes of talking, I got off the phone with my parents, promising to stay in better contact. I'd just lain down to get a few moments of precious rest when Bob showed up at my door.

"Can I join you?" he inquired.

I was surprised that he wasn't out at one of the parties. But also pleased. He looked very handsome despite the long day's work. Soon I was curled up in his lap as he kissed my neck and listened to the stories of my day. He laughed at my Aaron impersonation and agreed that he was a moron. And he massaged my hands as I talked. I could tell that Bob genuinely liked being around me, but I wondered if he was getting frustrated that our relationship wasn't more physical. I was certainly attracted to him—we just never seemed to be in the right place or time to figure out how to be together in a more serious way.

As if to illustrate my point, the minute things started heating up, we heard my roommate's key card in the door and pulled away. And then as we made our way to Bob's room to pick things back up, he received an urgent BlackBerry from Wye. I almost laughed at our plight. I was dating a thirty-nine-year-old and it was my most hampered relationship since high school. I wondered if he found it as amusing. At least he kept showing up.

We temporarily parted ways with Bob and the rest of the Wye caravan the following morning for our solo swing through South Carolina. RG was still thriving amidst the insane pace. The only real complication was that he was losing his voice, which led him to start compulsively eating cough drops. I began to worry about the digestive ramifications of this new development, but decided to keep my mouth shut. Luckily, Jenny joined us in Columbia for a drop-by at the state fair and took control of the situation.

As we pulled into the fairgrounds, my BlackBerry beeped to alert me that it was the seventeenth anniversary of the summer I memorized Dr. Seuss's *The Lorax*. And as we climbed out of the cars for RG to do a walkabout, "I am the Lorax, I speak for the trees" ran over and over through my head.

The fair was packed with farmers and tourists, all there to celebrate "South Carolina's thriving food and agriculture industry." As we weaved our way through the throngs of people, RG attracted various degrees of interest. Many people ran over, eager for a handshake or an autograph. Of these, only a few confused him with somebody else, "the guy who guest-starred on *Seinfeld*" being my favorite misidentification. Other people acted a little cooler—acknowledging RG with a wave or nod of the head that communicated they knew who he was but didn't feel he was any more important than the next guy was. This response generally indicated either a difference in political opinion or a healthy self-esteem. There were also those who pointed RG out but didn't initiate any sort of direct contact, as though he were a zoo animal to be observed and commented upon but not approached, because how could a creature of another species understand where they were coming from?

There was a subset of the zoo lookers—those who stared but had no idea what they were staring at. They knew RG was someone, and therefore gaped at him accordingly, but without any glimmer of real recognition in their eyes. And then there were the few who seemed not to notice at all—too busy or too uninterested to slow their pace or glance in RG's direction.

I sat absorbing the spectra of reaction as we walked in the skin-crisping sun through a labyrinth of produce stands and unsafe-looking rides. RG kept his easy smile and quick replies throughout, no matter what was thrown at him. And plenty was. An enormous middle-aged woman in a checkered jumpsuit asked him to kiss her pig for good luck. A seven-year-old boy ran up to show off his biceps. A scraggly stray dog tried to mate with his leg. An aging farmhand asked him his opinion of Britain's prime minister. A young mother praised his support of the Family Leave Act. A young father asked him to keep their baby's placenta as a keepsake. A cotton candy machine operator wanted to know if he and Wye got elected, would he like a cotton candy machine for the White House?

RG spoke to each person as if his or her question or request was the most important part of his day. It was a skill that impressed and baffled me. I felt sure I would never be able to approximate such serene tolerance. His endurance astounded me. It also helped me understand why he sometimes had such little patience around his staff—the reservoir got drained dry from interaction with constituents and colleagues. After all, no one could possibly have an utterly limitless supply.

We made our way past the Chubby Checker exhibit (Andrews, South Carolina, was evidently the childhood home of the famous musician and canonizer of "The Twist") and around the Giant Vegetables That Look Like Famous People stand (carefully sidestepping a huge carrot that uncannily resembled Rob Reiner), and back out to the waiting cars. On the whole, it constituted a very successful state fair visit. Lots of exposure, minimal bruising.

As we rolled towards the coast, Mark passed around some brownies that Mona had sent him that morning. While Mark had begun traveling on the bus with us, Mona was camped out at campaign headquarters in Louisiana, overseeing all of our crazy scheduling issues. Despite her heavy workload, she still managed to send Mark something every few days and they talked constantly. I tried to stay in regular touch, as well. Once RG became the VP pick, Mona and Mark had postponed their wedding date until after the election and were now planning a small holiday ceremony. I still hadn't gotten a bead on whether or not I was to be invited. I comforted myself with the aid of Mona's tasty baked goods, while I watched Jenny try to substitute RG's sugary lozenges with Chloraseptic spray.

I imagined that RG's elusive voice was the result of too much speech making, but I couldn't rule out the possibility of laryngitis or some other bronchial infection. Contagious conditions were a whole other issue when one spent seventeen hours a day either in the midst of large, unscreened crowds or in very small, closed spaces with the same group of people. One sickness could take us all down. I held my breath when I passed too close to RG, upped my vitamin intake, and monitored myself carefully.

At least my habit of carrying around bottles of hand sanitizer liquid had caught on and now everyone on the bus was doing it. Even the reporters had gotten in on the action. I felt proud to have so successfully spread a little bit of germ neurosis in such a short amount of time. And I felt sure that it was cutting down on the instances of disease.

I e-mailed Mona to let her know how delicious the brownies were. I pretended that this was just a kind gesture and not part of an ongoing lobbying effort for a wedding invitation. I was a nice person after all. The kind who one would want at their wedding, dammit. She wrote back quickly.

To: Samantha Joyce [srjoyce@wye-gary.com]
From: Mona Richmond
[mlrichmond@ wye-gary.com]
Subject: re: will you marry me instead?
Text: Hey Sammy, Glad the brownies were a hit. Guess who I ran into coming out of a B&B in

the French Quarter? Porter Dalton and Susan
Lambert! Scandalous, no? They were sooo
bummed to be spotted. Keep me posted on all
the bus tour fun I'm missing! Take care,
Mona

I'll say that was scandalous. I looked around for someone to immediately spread the gossip to. Alas, everyone looked busy. It was really their loss. Porter Dalton
was Governor Brancy's campaign manager and chief
political strategist. I didn't know much about him, except that he wielded a ton of influence in their campaign and that he was married with two kids. Susan
Lambert was Senator Greg Saxert's health care aide.
Saxert and Wye were both Louisiana politicians from
the same party and usually on the same team—the
team opposing Brancy and Porter Dalton.

Susan had been the one with whom I'd e-mailed
about Wye's health care positions, the very e-mail that
I'd suspected Charlie of illicitly reading from my Black-
Berry. If Susan was sleeping with Porter, I could bet he
was privy to her thoughts on her boss and Governor
Wye. Porter would be very interested in these, and
would surely use anything he could to the advantage of
the Brancy–Wallock ticket. Didn't Susan realize this?
Did she care? Maybe she was getting information in
return—who really knew?

Upon reflecting on the ramifications of this fascinating bit of information, I was relieved to have outside proof that Charlie Lawton had been telling the truth regarding his anonymous source in the article he'd written about RG's influence over Wye. Clearly, there were other ways for him to have gotten this information. Unfortunately, the Brancy team had immediately seized upon Charlie's article to make the case that Wye was an easily swayed and ineffective leader. They had deftly played up this theme. If Wye couldn't control his own ticket, they wanted people to ask, then how could he control the country?

At the following stop, I sought out Charlie as he climbed off the press bus.

"Hey there," he said easily.

His hair was getting a little long around his eyes, but I liked the way it dipped down near the black rim of his glasses. Was I standing close enough for him to smell the new citrus shampoo I'd bought?

"Hey." I smiled back. "Guess what I heard?"

He looked interested.

"My friend saw Porter Dalton and Susan Lambert at a motel in New Orleans together," I continued.

"Huh," he answered impassively.

His expression remained steady.

"Do you by any chance happen to know Susan Lambert?" I asked.

"Yeah, I do, actually," he answered. "She was in my class at NYU."

Aha! I refrained from visibly "aha-ing," and tried to match his nonchalant air.

"Oh, that's interesting," I offered blandly.

RG was heading towards the stage.

"I better get to the press area," Charlie said with a smile. "See ya around."

That mystery resolved, I watched Charlie make his way to the assembled pack of journalists and whip out his notebook. He watched the introduction of RG along with the rest of them. Except he turned around and glanced back at me once, and I hadn't yet averted my gaze. I hadn't meant to still be staring at him, I had just gotten in one of those observational trances. I looked quickly down at my BlackBerry and hurried away.

After a long day in the Carolinas, made even more stressful by the news of an approaching hurricane (which led me to spend a lot of time looking around and wondering how much of the terrain we were blazing through was on a collision course with destruction—did it sense it? Was it scared?), we piled onto the plane and flew to Madison, Wisconsin. There, we were greeted by a gigantic rally, complete with a designated protest area. Ronkin's weasel had continued to crop up in various places, and as the campaign picked up speed, he'd been joined by a host of other agitators, both costumed and not. By this point, I'd grown accustomed to their presence and took solace in the fact that their shouts were consistently drowned out by the much more supportive roar of the crowds.

We rejoined the Wye team the following day in California for another huge rally and fund-raiser. My body had long ago given up on trying to constantly adjust to the changing time zones. It seemed resigned to a medicated, caffeine-stimulated, zombie-like state of existence. I'd resorted to a diet of bland foods in an effort to appease my rebellious colon, but there was nothing I could eat or do to make up for the sleepless nights and stressful pace. I felt as though I was in circadian freefall. Many days, I woke up not even sure where I was. I'd stare out the hotel window, looking for clues. Were there any visible landmarks? Evidence of a northerly or southerly climate? More than once, I'd had to check the complimentary newspaper lying outside my door to inform myself of my location. The whole thing was very disconcerting.

I was pretty sure that it was San Francisco we were spending the night in before re-splitting from the Wye posse the following day and tromping back to the East Coast, then criss-crossing back three days after that. I apologized to my system while continuing to ply it with stimulants, as I had a fair number of briefings to assemble before I was allowed to get any sleep.

I was making my third trip to the soda machine and wondering if it just made more sense to buy a lot of them at once and store them in my room (and deciding that no, the exercise and change in scenery was good for me), when I ran into Charlie. He had a selection of sodas in his arms.

"Hey," I said warmly. "Are you on deadline, too?"

"Actually, I get a little break tonight. I'm transitioning over to the Wye pool tomorrow," he answered with a smile.

What? He was? Why was he happy about that?

"Is that like a promotion?" I inquired.

"I suppose." He shrugged. "I've liked covering Gary. But change is good, too. There are some different things I'd like to investigate."

I felt very unsettled. I tried to get it together.

"Okay, well, good luck," I said.

"Thanks," he said sincerely. "Any parting advice?"

I searched my brain. Don't leave? That probably wouldn't fly.

"Don't forget about us."

He smiled at me.

"Don't worry," he replied.

"Do you need help carrying those?" I heard a voice call from down the hall.

I turned around and saw Veronica peeking her head out of a hotel room. Charlie's hotel room? It appeared that way.

"Uh, I'm all set," Charlie answered.

He glanced at me a bit ruefully. I fumbled for my change.

"Well, I better get there before they run out of soda," I said brightly.

I hurried down the hall, feeling crappy and wondering if there was any chance he was watching me go.

The next morning, Bob stopped by while I was packing. I had wanted him to show up at some point during the previous night, but he hadn't. There was a rumor that Wye had been in a temper that he'd taken out on his senior staff into the wee hours.

"I had to stay up all night with Max," Bob confirmed regretfully.

It still rattled me when he referred to Wye as "Max," but that was the sort of relationship they had.

"Is there some sort of problem?" I asked.

"Nothing out of the ordinary," Bob answered. "All the numbers still look good. I think we're pulling ahead."

It was September. We needed to be pulling ahead if we were going to end up ahead. I zipped my bag and sat down on the bed facing him.

"How are *you*?" I asked.

He seemed a bit surprised by my sincere tone. He smiled at me in the way he did when he had no intention of being serious.

"I'd be better if you took your shirt off," he answered.

I ignored him.

"Any word from your ex-wife?" I inquired.

I had only recently found out about her. Apparently she reappeared to cause problems whenever she got wind of Bob dating someone new. I imagined this commitment to disruption had kept her pretty busy, as Bob seemed like the sort of person who'd had his share of girlfriends.

"She'd like for you to take your shirt off, too," he replied.

"Huh. I'm sensing an emerging consensus."

He nodded happily.

I started to pull my shirt over my head, then put on a show of stopping short at the sight of my watch.

"No time," I pronounced, smoothing my shirt back into place. "Maybe if you'd shown up a little earlier . . ."

Bob groaned. "Curse Max and his stupid presidential campaign," he complained.

I smiled.

"When do we cross paths again?" I asked.

I'd been too tired to look at the latest schedule.

"Ten days," he replied as he pulled me into his lap.

That seemed like a long time. Especially when I thought about Charlie. Bob kissed my neck, while I pretended my sadness was for him.

"Do you know you smell sort of like oranges?" he asked.

I pushed myself to my feet.

"I've got to go," I said in a hurry.

"No, wait, it's a good thing," he protested.

"No, I know. I'm sorry. I just don't want to miss the bus . . ." I answered.

I picked up my bags, kissed him good-bye, and hurried away. Then I rushed onto the campaign bus and into my work, distracting myself with the hundreds of tasks for the day.

# Can You Know All Along?

IN THE MIDDLE of September, Charlie Lawton broke a momentum-shattering story claiming that Governor Wye had plagiarized the oratory of an obscure Indian politician in his recent speeches on the campaign trail. He quoted passages from Tilak Kumar, a man known mainly in the southern part of India, followed by nearly identical excerpts from three of Wye's speeches. I read the article with my heart lodged firmly in my throat.

Ten years previously, Tilak Kumar had rallied the people in his region to better their circumstances with his eloquent thoughts on the relationship between inter-connected humanity and the need for commitment to public service. It appeared that Wye had been attempting to do the exact same thing in this country, unfortunately, with almost the exact same words.

Charlie included a statement from Wye that he was

"completely unaware of the similarity and it was a genuine mistake." But nothing more.

I finished the article and sunk my head in my hands. Oh God, what did this mean? Was this the end of our hopes? Had everything we'd worked so hard for just been thrown in our faces? I knew lesser scandals had killed campaigns in the past.

Before I could mourn for too long, my BlackBerry and cell phone started screaming for attention. Which was how things continued throughout the day. We all felt violently launched into full-fledged crisis mode. The fact that it was six weeks before the election added a heightened sense of panicked nausea. There might not be enough time to recover.

RG was clearly taken off guard, but did the best he could, given the shady and inconclusive circumstances. He refused to duck the press, but rather responded to their inquiries, constantly reiterating that Governor Wye was an honest and honorable man who wanted the truth to come out as much as everyone else did.

And the truth came out a little further the following day. Charlie Lawton landed another front-page story with a follow-up on the bombshell. He identified Aaron Driver as the main architect of the stump speech in question, and suggested that it was possible that Governor Wye was telling the truth when he claimed he had no knowledge of the plagiarism. The article asserted that it was "well known that Governor Wye has little interest in writing his own speeches. He has long relied on a constantly revolving stable of speechwriters to craft the communication of his message while he focuses on other things he deems more important."

In my opinion, this didn't paint Wye in the most fantastic light, but it at least suggested he might not be a plagiarist. And interestingly, that Aaron was. Aaron had already proven himself capable of unconscionable political deception when he'd planted those disparaging quotes the previous fall, but this latest stunt was shocking even for him. According to the article, "Aaron Driver refused to comment and has retained a lawyer."

The following day he was officially fired from the campaign and conclusively blamed by everyone who could get a quote in the article. Only Wye tempered the criticism, claiming to be "saddened" more than angered. By nightfall, the campaign had released a statement from Aaron accepting full responsibility and confirming that Wye knew nothing of "what Mr. Driver termed 'the borrowed phrases.'"

To complete Aaron's downfall, the *Post* published a quickly researched exposé of his extensive gambling debts. Apparently, he owed over seven hundred thousand dollars to casinos in Connecticut, New Jersey, Las Vegas, and New Orleans. An angry riverboat casino manager had contacted the *Post* when he'd read the plagiarism stories, and its journalists had rapidly uncovered widespread evidence of what appeared to be a gambling addiction. According to the casino employees interviewed for the article, Aaron had a habit of going on overnight binges fueled by alcohol and "a fair amount of cocaine," as reported by one very observant and very stupid pit boss. Willingly admitting to the media that there was cocaine use in one's establishment didn't strike me as the most intelligent move.

Though everyone was startled by the developments, I felt I had both more of a right and less of an excuse to be truly stunned. When I really thought about it, I knew that had someone asked me if Aaron was capable of these actions, I would have said yes. After all, he was a gambler at heart. He had gambled that Darlene and I wouldn't find out about each other, he had gambled that he could get hired by the Wye campaign even after trashing RG in the press, and he had gambled that he could "borrow" someone else's words and get away with it. He gambled in every area of his life, so it made sense that he would gamble just as rashly with his money. He was addicted to shortcuts, no matter what the risk. And even when I'd been infatuated with him, I'd occasionally experienced a nagging fear that he was hiding some sort of criminal behavior. I could remember one time in particular I'd been convinced he was going to tell me he'd done something terrible. He'd told me he loved me instead. Which, in retrospect, was a crime in and of itself.

So in many ways, it made sense to me that he had turned out to be guilty of more than just infidelity and political backstabbing, for he was a deceiver of massive proportions. Yet, on the other hand, it surprised me that someone as ambitious as Aaron would behave so recklessly. I knew he had grand designs for his future—had his hot-shot success given him a delusion of invincibility? Had he come to think he was blessed with spectacular, limitless luck?

Though I believed that Aaron deserved all that he was getting, I began to feel a tiny bit guilty—as though by hating Aaron and wishing evil upon him, I had managed to actually wreak something truly horrible. He was the one who had made all the mistakes, but it was strange that the worst ones had caught up with him all at once. Did the timing have to do with my mental voodoo practices? Was I much more powerful than I'd previously imagined? I certainly still loathed him, but I also felt sorry for him. Was he possibly headed to jail? Or just ignominy?

In the following days, the campaign valiantly attempted to limp back into a sprint. There was no question it was significantly wounded. Not surprisingly, the Brancy–Wallock operation was making the most of the recent disclosures and their attacks, along with the truth, were taking a toll. Before the story broke, we'd been ahead by five points. Now we were down by four.

Though I was sick about the repercussions, I didn't blame Charlie for the story. I wondered how he'd broken it, and whether he'd thought of me as he'd written it, and how it felt to be the creator of such a maelstrom. I wished I could ask him these things. But even when we reunited with the Wye caravan, it became clear that the members of the press were not to be sought out. And particularly not Charlie Lawton. He'd certainly made a name for himself.

Bob no longer had any time to make stripping requests, as he was in full damage control mode, moving Wye right through the controversy and onto the offensive. With Bob's guidance, Wye did his best to shake off the tarnish of the charges and explain how the mistake had happened—how he'd never intentionally stolen another's words. And yet, people were loath to hear him parse a multitiered explanation. They were worried they had been betrayed—that the new voice onto which they had dared to latch their hopes had sounded too good to be true.

More days passed. As the scandal refused to subside and the numbers continued to slide, we all began to feel trapped in a situation out of which we couldn't escape. But we couldn't afford to be stalled, we couldn't handle being broken down! There just wasn't time! I felt a collective sense of panic and frustration growing. But there didn't seem to be much I could do to combat it.

Trudging down the stairwell of a hotel in Seattle, I came upon RG on his way back from the gym. It was 5:00 AM in early October and things still looked bleak. I gazed morosely at him.

"What's going to happen?" I asked plaintively. "Can we recover?"

He looked back at me with an expression of energetic resolve.

"We can try," he said decisively.

And try he did. When no one was sure whether they could trust Wye or not, RG stepped in to restore the faith. He threw himself into an even more relentless pace, and at event after event, he articulated a clear and persuasive message that directly addressed people's crisis of confidence. He proclaimed passionately that Wye's only mistake had been to hire a person of questionable integrity. Of course no red flags had been raised over passages extolling the virtues of empowerment and civic duty, for those were the very things Wye believed in. Of course he didn't object to sections of his speech about the need for a common understanding and transcendence of one another's differences, because that was what his campaign was all about. His only crime was trying to inspire the American people to shape the sort of future they deserved. And this clearly made him a fantastic leader.

I listened to RG and fervently prayed to all my various gods that the people would agree with him. Enough of them seemed to hear my prayers. As RG took his case to the airwaves and the highways, the numbers slowly crept upwards. By mid-October, we were in a statistical dead heat.

The debates in the final month were savage and personal. Watching Brancy and Wye tear into each other made me worry that too many people would be turned off simply by the tone. I found myself cringing and wanting to look away, which couldn't be a good thing.

Yet even with the vitriol, I considered Wye immensely more compelling. I wondered if I was too biased to have a realistic reaction, or if other people would be inclined to feel the same way. I did a little informal polling from my shared hotel room in Minneapolis.

"You're spot on," my mom insisted. "Wye's policies are more progressive and he's selling them well. Brancy's different from Pile, but not different enough. People are brassed off with those daft old ideas."

I found my mother's astute review reassuring. And a little British.

"I like Wye's tie a lot better," Liza reported. "And he's pretty tan."

Leave it to her to analyze the fashion angle. Though I certainly wasn't discounting it. Tons of people made their decisions according to slightly insane criteria, in my opinion. Bob had told me a hundred times that appearances mattered more than substance. I never wanted to believe him, but still, it made me feel better to think that we might have both on our side.

"And of course I agree with his positions," Liza added. "But he just looks more interesting."

I concurred. Wye's trademark forward-leaning stance continued to convey a feeling of overwhelming energy and onward momentum. Brancy, in contrast, appeared carefully controlled and calculatingly relaxed—like a person who counted his chews before swallowing. One of my college friends had insisted on doing this; she had masticated every food morsel she'd consumed exactly twenty-five times. I had written term papers in the time it took for her to get through a healthy meal.

"I think Wye's proposal for a tax credit for parents trying to pay for their kids' college education sounds good," Zelda informed me when I checked on her opinion. "It just seems like he cares more for real. I'd rather hang out with him, you know? I don't know what I'd say to that other guy."

I respected Zelda's opinion on all things marketing, so her analysis gave me hope.

"I'm going to make sure everyone here votes," she assured me. "Keep up the good work. And let me know if you need any more revenge help. The girls really got into harassing that Aaron jackass. It gave a different sort of meaning to our days. So just say the word—we're up for more anytime."

I thanked her and told her I would keep it in mind. And would have asked her to slip some pro-Wye–Gary lines into her regular phone marketing pitches if I hadn't been aware that doing so would constitute a federal offense. She'd certainly done enough for me already. I just hoped the campaign's telemarketers were making as persuasive a case for the ticket as Zelda was able to for reduced long-distance rates.

I watched a few minutes of the networks' post-debate coverage. As usual, they had corralled a group of undecided voters to watch the debate under their supervision and provide them with their immediate impressions.

These human guinea pigs even got to turn a dial as they watched to register in the moment whether they were reacting positively or negatively to what was being said.

And yet despite all this high-tech coddling, the members of the group, whom the network anchors kept referring to as "undecideds," didn't seem to feel much pressure to make up their minds. Most of them proclaimed that they still just didn't know for sure. What was wrong with them? Had they been living under rocks? It wasn't as though Brancy and Wye were even remotely similar. I found the undecideds' inability to make up their minds incredibly annoying. And I suspected that their prolonged indecision was just a ploy for further attention, since they were such a wanted demographic. In my opinion, they were wearing out their welcome.

I recognized that my impatience was a reaction to the high level of stress and uncertainty that I'd been living and breathing during the last few weeks. I'd been taking my medicine and trying to stay calm, but I felt fully saturated with all kinds of toxins. And though I was perpetually exhausted, I found that I couldn't sleep well, even given the rare opportunity to rack up some hours. There was just too much to worry about, too much to try and get done, too much that was entirely out of my control.

In the final week of the campaign, I accompanied Jenny Gary to Pennsylvania, where she made a speech to a women's group about the importance of the upcoming election. She'd asked me to go along, because she wanted to make a special plea to those women concerned about the health care issues that would be greatly impacted in the next four years. I was happy to provide the information she needed to make her case, as well as to offer any moral support for the effort.

Jenny had grown more comfortable in front of crowds and her easy warmth came across when she spoke. She had plenty of joke material, thanks to the insanity of chasing after two-year-old twins amidst a national presidential campaign, and the packed auditorium responded well to her.

On the plane ride back to reconnect with RG and the others in Illinois, we sat beside each other.

"Do you think it went all right?" Jenny asked calmly.

I really did. I thought it went great. I told her as much.

"Good," she said decisively, and closed her eyes.

I studied her face as she rested. Was she as worried as I was? Did she think we were going to win? Bob had forwarded me the latest numbers, which had us ahead by one point, with a margin of error of plus or minus four points. That certainly didn't put me at ease. Jenny opened her eyes to see me staring at her. To my surprise, she took my hand.

"Oh, sweetie, you look so traumatized!" she exclaimed.

I did? I hadn't meant to show it. I opened my mouth to explain that there was nothing to worry about, and was horrified to find that I couldn't speak. Good Lord, were my eyes welling up with tears? My emotions were revolting against my control. This was mutiny!

I struggled to stop the tears from falling, to no avail.

"Sammy, it's going to be okay. No matter what happens," Jenny was saying kindly to me.

I couldn't believe I was putting her in the position of reassuring me. What kind of staffer was I? This was pathetic.

"Thanks," I gasped. "I'm sorry about this. I'm fine," I added unconvincingly.

I managed to calm down and regain control of myself soon enough.

"I guess I just want things to work out so badly," I tried to explain. "There's just too much at stake."

Jenny smiled at me.

"That's why Robert has such a soft spot for you," she said soothingly. "You really do care so much. And that's wonderful. I believe we're going to win, because I think most people agree with Max and Robert about the really basic things. So let's keep believing. Let's save the sadness for another week."

I nodded in agreement. She held on to my hand for the rest of our descent, and I felt comforted for the first time in a long tortured while.

Election Day awoke to different cadences across the country. In Ohio, where I watched RG and Jenny cast their votes, it was greeted with cool sunshine pulsing through the swirl of falling leaves. I checked the Weather Channel to get a sense of the other rhythms. Early, lashing snow in Minnesota; thumping, hurricane-jilted rain in Virginia; lilting haze in southern California. In each place, I visualized voters tromping to the polls. What were they wearing, both out of style and necessity? I followed them along in my mind's eye, careful not to break the meditation until they had cast their vote for Wye and RG.

For most of the day, I felt as though I was hovering somewhere around my body, but nowhere close to actually being in it. This strange, detached, timeless sensation carried me through what would otherwise have undoubtedly seemed like endlessly dragging, clawing minutes.

RG visited "get out the vote" organizations across Ohio, Massachu-setts, New York, and Pennsylvania before we landed in Louisiana by late afternoon. We made our way to a large hotel in downtown New Orleans that the entire Wye–Gary operation had commandeered for the evening.

By 6:00 PM, there was little to do except wait for the results. RG and Jenny were holed up with the boys and other family members in a large suite at the end of the hall. Wye and his family were on the floor directly above us. The staff was scattered in a dozen rooms on both floors. I found myself in front of a television in a room packed with twenty people, Kara, Mark, and Mona among them.

By 7:00 PM, we were doing well, but not phenomenally, with thirty percent of the precincts reporting. Whenever a state was called, there were either raucous cheers or deathly silence. I realized that the only thing I'd eaten all day was a tin of Altoids.

At 8:25, a rush of results descended and CNN called the election for Wye and RG. The room erupted around me, but I sat in shock, as time slowed to a trickle. I vaguely heard a champagne cork popping, felt a blast of cool November air as someone opened a window to scream out, caught a glimpse of a roaring, surging New Orleans crowd celebrating wildly on TV. I hovered above and around and within this, wondering at the surreal otherworldliness of it all. I finally forced myself to focus on the newscasters, who were saying that with eighty percent of precincts reporting, we'd surged ahead by ten points and had clinched nearly a third more electoral votes. As the truth rose around me, I felt like I had suddenly zoomed back into my body, and that I was getting used to how it felt again. Had I always used these eyes to see? My muscles and senses and skin felt different and fresh. And I knew that I was new.

At the victory party on the massive stage that had been erected outside the hotel, I celebrated with everyone else and made frantically ecstatic phone calls to Liza and my parents. None of them were too long; I had no desire to distract from the present before me.

I wildly cheered as Wye addressed the crowd on behalf of himself and RG. I wondered if there was a chance I might burst. That was the only sobering thought.

A few hours later, Kara and I were splitting a bottle of champagne off to the side of what had been turned into a dance floor. The room was still packed with people— the new president- and vice president-elects, senators, governors, members of Congress, and regular old citizens and campaign staffers all celebrating together. Mona and Mark danced happily by us.

"When are you going to RSVP to our wedding?" Mona shouted merrily to me.

What's this now?

"I didn't know I was invited," I replied in surprise.

"Have you checked your mail in the last three months?" Mark inquired.

Interesting. You'd think I might have. Liza had been collecting it, but I hadn't even given it a thought. Things like mail and being in one place for more than a few hours and general normalcy hadn't been a part of my recent life.

"I'll be there!" I beamed at the two of them.

They grinned and danced away. I turned back to Kara and smiled as she refilled my champagne. I felt a wave of warmth towards her.

"You have to come back to D.C.," I insisted.

I needed help adjusting to this new reality. I needed my own personal advance woman.

"Oh, I am." She smiled. "Do you need a roommate?"

Did I? I did if I got a new place. A new, fun, non-lonely place!

"What are your thoughts on Japanese fighting fish?" I inquired.

Kara's phone rang with a call from her boyfriend and she excused herself for a second.

"Tell him D.C. always needs good actors!" I yelled, as she walked away.

She smiled back at me. I felt a hand on my shoulder. Oh, please let it be Charlie.

It was Bob.

"Hey, Shorty. Congratulations," he said as he leaned in to kiss me.

He smelled like victory. I kissed him back. As I pulled away, I looked past him into the crowd. And I did spot Charlie—my first sighting in weeks! He looked like he'd stopped midstride, and his gaze was trained on Bob and me.

I tried to wriggle some distance away from Bob. I wished I could wriggle back in time and not return his kiss. I couldn't read Charlie's expression, as usual. Bob could tell something was wrong.

"What's up?" Bob asked.

I looked back at him. I really, honestly, didn't know. His intelligent eyes searched my face.

"A group of us got access to the roof deck on top of this place," he said slowly. "We're taking up champagne."

I stared at him, trying to sort through my thoughts. His eyes registered something at last.

"You're not coming, are you?" he asked.

I held his gaze for a moment and then slowly shook my head. He nodded.

"I'll see you around, Shorty." He smiled sadly at me.

And then he walked off into the crowd. I didn't stop to wonder what had gone wrong. Bob was fun and thrilling, but he wasn't for me. Not when someone else was. I started immediately towards Charlie, but he had vanished. Where? How could I find him? I had to talk to him. I thought I might possibly die if I didn't.

I ran out the doors onto the stage that I had gazed up to just hours before. It was deserted now, though strewn with spent streamers and confetti. I felt a sudden sadness—a remorse that seemed out of place but nevertheless real. My shoulders sagged for a moment as I looked around. The podium and microphone were still set up. Who was in charge of taking that down? Was the mike still on? I walked over and tapped it with my finger. It was on, all right. What did I have to say?

"Will this be on or off the record?" a voice behind me asked.

Thank you, thank you, thank you, I closed my eyes and whispered, before turning around to face Charlie. He had two drinks in his hand. He was holding one out towards me.

"I got you a regular," he said.

I took a sip. "How did you guess the secret ingredient?" I asked, surprised.

Charlie shrugged. "I have my sources."

I smiled at him. "You know how I was kissing Bob a few minutes ago? That's over. It never really began actually. I mean, I'm not with him. I'm available," I blurted, with characteristic smoothness.

Liza would be cringing.

"I mean, not that there's anything between you and me. And, of course, I know you have a girlfriend, and—"

"We broke up, actually," Charlie interrupted.

Oh?

"Why?" I asked, even though I didn't really care, as long as it was true.

"I didn't see her as part of the life I wanted to have," he said simply.

"Oh, well that's great. I mean, I'm sorry," I floundered. "I know breakups can be hard. I actually broke up by means of a diorama in third grade and even that was—"

He interrupted me again, but this time with a kiss. Then he straightened and looked me in the eyes.

"Do you want to kiss me?" he asked directly.

"Yes," I answered happily, as I gently removed his glasses.

We kissed for a long, enfolding while. I felt my new skin tingling wildly. And when we pulled away, he pointed to my arm—the same one that he had bruised with his belt buckle over a year before.

"Are you okay? I think you have some sort of rash," he said.

I looked down in surprise. He was right. I had a beautifully raging rash, not just on my neck, but completely covering both arms and legs. I hugged him joyfully.

"That's an excellent sign," I said.

"If you say so," he replied, before kissing me some more.


Hours and hours later, in our very own hotel room, I watched Charlie peacefully sleeping and struggled to contain my joy. I was happy to stay in the moment with him, to revel in feelings I'd truly never experienced before, but I was also relieved that I could envision a meaningful future together. I felt a sense of calm elation as I reflected on the knowledge that Charlie and I were after the same things in life. I knew it was rare to have found someone who also sincerely wanted to make things better—someone who was willing to battle the worst in politics to make room for the best. Charlie would do so from the pages of the *Post* and beyond. I would do so within an administration committed to change. We were going to make a fantastic team. I stared down lovingly at him and lightly touched his face. I didn't want to wake him up, but I almost couldn't wait to kiss him again. I focused instead on trying to still my racing heart, to no avail. So many good things had happened at once that I was way too energized to rest.

I decided to share my happiness with all the people who had suffered and celebrated alongside me on this crazy journey. I took out my BlackBerry and created a mass e-mail—something I had never anticipated willingly doing again. But things were different now. I felt at home.

I included my parents, my grandparents, my cousins, and my elementary, high school, college, and postgrad friends. I added RG and Jenny and the entire Senate and campaign staffs. I even included the people at NIH, all of the advocacy groups, much of the unions' membership, Sanford B. Zines, and Alfred Jackman. I would have included Ralph and Steve Martin if I had known their e-mail addresses. And to all of them, I wrote a heartfelt message:

To: Sammy's Friends
From: Samantha Joyce [srjoyce@wye-gary.com]
Subject: Thank you
Text: For the most incredible year of my life, and for helping this wonderful cause to succeed. We did it!!! I have never been so happy, I have never felt so proud. And excuse me for being a little corny, but I've never been so sure of my mission in life. Tonight has convinced me that for now and forever, I must continue to do everything in

my power to serve the greater pubic good. And now, I'll be doing it in the White House!!!
xoxoxoxo, Sammy

I snuggled happily next to Charlie and was finally, thankfully drifting off to sleep when my BlackBerry buzzed on the table beside me. I turned over and checked it.

To: Samantha Joyce [srjoyce@wye-gary.com]
From: Robert Gary [rgary@gary.senate.gov]
Subject: re: Thank you
Text: I think you meant "public good." Either way, all the best. See you tomorrow.—RG